AVENGER
CHRIS ALLEN

vinci
BOOKS

By Chris Allen

Black Ops Intrepid

Defender
Hunter
Avenger
Helldiver

For my boys, Morgan and Rhett, for whom I write every word

Vinci Books

vinci-books.com

Published by Vinci Books Ltd in 2025

1

Copyright © Chris Allen 2024

The author has asserted their moral right to be identified as the author of this work in accordance with the Copyright, Designs and Patents Act 1988. This work is a work of fiction. Names, characters, places and incidents are the product of the author's imagination or are used fictitiously. Any resemblance to actual persons, living or dead, places and incidents is entirely coincidental.

All rights reserved. No part of this publication may be copied, reproduced, distributed, stored in any retrieval system, or transmitted in any form or by any means, including photocopying, recording, or other electronic or mechanical methods, nor used as a source for any form of machine learning including AI datasets, without the prior written permission of the publisher.

The publisher and the author have made every effort to obtain permissions for any third party material used in this book and to comply with copyright law. Any queries in this respect should be brought to the attention of the publisher and any omissions will be corrected in future editions.

A CIP catalogue record for this book is available from the British Library.

Paperback ISBN: 9781036703431

Printed and bound in Great Britain by Clays Ltd, Elcograf S.p.A.

The Sword of Interpol

When extremists plunged the world into dark decades of war and nations mobilized for vengeance, the shadow of remorseless terror and unrestrained violence called for a new generation of crime fighter.

The UN Security Council turned to INTERPOL - the International Criminal Police Organisation – to raise a new division of elite men and women, hand-picked from across the globe.

Skilled, fearless and unrelenting - part police officer, part soldier, part spy - they would be international in every way, ordained to fight fire with fire, no matter how dreadful the crime nor how treacherous the adversary.

So it was that INTREPID - the Intelligence, Recovery, Protection and Infiltration Division – came to be.

Human trafficking is a vicious chain that binds victims to criminals. We must break this chain with the force of human solidarity.

—United Nations Secretary-General Ban Ki-moon
*High-level Meeting on the Appraisal of the Global Plan of Action to Combat Trafficking in Persons
New York, May 13 2013*

Chapter One

MANGOCHI, REPUBLIC OF MALAWI

The retreating rumble of the DC-3's engines was all that remained after the momentary explosion of noise upon exit. Military aircraft, old and new, weren't renowned for their creature comforts and inside, the old Dakota was nothing more than an excruciating din with less than enough room to swing a cat, underpinned by the smell of aviation fuel – leaping into the darkness and leaving all that behind was liberating. Outside it was quiet, there was plenty of space and, above all, fresh air. Alex Morgan sucked in a deep lungful and then another, forcing his chest to rebel against the tightly fastened straps of the parachute harness. He allowed himself a moment to enjoy the adrenalin rush, feeling the fresh blast of cold night air pushing against his face and body as he stabilized his position.

Morgan, an agent of Interpol's deep-cover Intelligence, Recovery, Protection and Infiltration Division – otherwise known as Intrepid – pulled the ripcord of the MC-4 Ram Air Free-Fall parachute and felt the familiar tug as the canopy erupted, unfurling above him. He looked up into the center of the blossoming rectangular canopy as the cells filled with air. He reached for the steering toggles and took control, checking his bearings against the memorized reference points he could see on the ground. There was hardly any wind tonight and the full moon lit the landscape for miles in a serene silver-gray hue. There were the cluster of lights to the south-west of Lake Malawi that was Mangochi and the mouth of the Shire River, then the looming shadows of the hills of the Namizimu Forest Reserve to the north, and there, directly beneath him, was the latticework of tracks and dry creek beds that led to a small enclave of buildings due east of Kwilembe.

Morgan was relieved. The parachute – and the plane for that matter – had been scrounged. He'd needed a means of insertion at short notice; a way to cover some serious miles and get on the ground quickly, and, as a former officer of Britain's elite Parachute Regiment, Morgan knew only too well how best to achieve that. Besides, he was expected to improvise. The effectiveness and success of Intrepid's clandestine operations around the world relied on agents operating, as far as possible, as lone wolves. That was what Intrepid's chief, and veteran of Special Operations, General Davenport expected of them, which meant finding simple solutions to otherwise complex problems.

In this case, a call to a trusted friend and former Parachute Regiment comrade eventually connected Morgan with a retired Portuguese Air Force pilot who, according to Morgan's contact, wouldn't ask awkward questions if the money was right. After the PAF, Captain Henrique Barboza had settled in Maputo with his Mozambican wife and now flew wealthy tourists to nature reserves all over south-eastern Africa in a reconditioned war-surplus DC-3 Dakota. Barboza had agreed to assist in any way he could on the basis that Morgan's enterprise was fundamentally righteous and, more importantly, Barboza himself would be paid upfront and in cash. He threw the parachute in for free because he'd apparently won it in a card game and had no use for it. Morgan knew the plane worked, but parachutes had a nasty habit of not letting you know they didn't until it was too late to ask for another. But Morgan liked Barboza. The man was a brigand at heart, which appealed to Morgan's healthy respect for living just outside the rules. He put that down to his own piratical heritage which, according to family lore, made him a direct descendant of Sir Henry Morgan, the infamous Welsh buccaneer. They had reached an agreement, shaken hands and the deal was done. Simple.

Morgan was supporting a joint human, drugs and arms trafficking operation involving various African police forces, Interpol and, covertly, Intrepid. Codenamed Operation Usalama, it was the first time Morgan had been back to Africa in almost three years. He'd been deployed to the fledgling Republic of Malfajiri, West Africa, on his inaugural mission as an Intrepid agent, tracking down gunrunners and evacuating ex-pats, including children, from the middle of a civil war. That time, he'd almost lost his life. Worse still, the brutal torture and murder of his close friend, MI6 agent Sean Collins – whose body had been dismembered, burned and thrown like garbage into the grounds of the British Embassy in the Malfajiri capital Cullentown – had been the catalyst for it all.

This time, Morgan's target was another fugitive from international justice wanted by Interpol for drugs and arms trafficking, and more recently for extending his interests to include trafficking in human beings. Fusani Chomba had eluded the authorities for years but under the umbrella of Operation Usalama the cooperative efforts of the Eastern and Southern African Police Chiefs Regional Cooperation Organizations, EAPCCO and SARPCCO, finally uncovered his location. Chomba had found a safe haven in Malawi near a small village called Kwilembe, eighteen miles north-east of Mangochi and only sixteen miles from the Mozambique border. The intelligence on his refuge indicated that it was deliberately located within a populated area and heavily guarded. Storming it without the high possibility of unnecessary civilian casualties was beyond the immediate skills or resources of local police. With some subtle guidance from Interpol, the involvement of the Malawi military was not deemed necessary. Instead the task of apprehending him found its way on to General Davenport's desk and now, for the fourth or fifth time in his life, Alex Morgan was in Africa.

Morgan prepared for landing. He'd jumped at only four thousand feet, so he wasn't encumbered by unnecessary high-altitude gear – there hadn't been time for anything like that. This job was rough and ready. It had to be. They'd been tracking Fusani Chomba for ages and now they had to get him out.

As so often happened during the final hundred feet or so of a night jump, the landmarks that had been so well lit by the moon disappeared and the ground became nothing more than an endless black void. Estimating the remaining seconds to impact, Morgan pulled down halfway on the toggles to check the parachute's speed and braced. If he pulled down too hard and misjudged his rate of descent he could stall the canopy, which could bring him down like a ton of bricks, or even backward. Moments later, he landed hard among a copse of acacia bushes about a mile from the small cluster of buildings near Kwilembe, where Chomba's house was located. Jumping in at a safe distance from the target reduced the chances of being detected and allowed him to stash the parachute, prepare his gear and approach the location covertly. Morgan felt the landing more than usual and cringed as his knees protested against the collision. He stumbled, his legs tangled in a low huddle of acacia, and fell flat on his back. After sitting for a moment to take stock, he stumbled to his feet, hid the gear around the base of the acacias, and painfully extracted half-a-dozen two-inch thorns from his shins and calf muscles.

Morgan was traveling light, dressed in Helikon SFU combat gear, and armed with only a Sig Sauer P226 and an M4A1 fitted with a suppressor. It took him half an hour to cover the mile to Chomba's location. He made straight for the northern end of the village, paralleling the one and only road through it, scouring the shadows for a vehicle or any sign of disturbance, and working methodically round the back of the settlement. He kept at a low crouch, moving from cover to cover past the ramshackle houses to his right and the open, wild bush to his left, the M4 gripped tightly in his hands, ready to fire. The entire scene was a blur of black and gray, with minuscule flickers of orange light just visible through the occasional flimsy rag of a curtain. It was almost impossible to see, but still Morgan searched, keeping himself to the shadows on the edge of the dwellings.

There were animals and humans to be avoided as he closed in but he eventually reached a poorly constructed six-foot-high whitewashed stone wall that was the reference point he'd been told to look for: the rear boundary of Chomba's house, situated at the end of a long dirt road. It was the only dwelling in the area with such a high wall and, thankfully for Morgan, it backed on to open bushland rather than another property.

He checked the battered TAG Heuer watch he'd worn

on his left wrist for well over fifteen years. It was two minutes to 1am. He was bang on schedule. Right now, Captain Barboza would have the Dakota circling high above, preparing to land. Morgan had two hours to grab Chomba and get him to Mongochi airstrip, so that meant commandeering a car. Barboza would be on the ground from 2am, so if Morgan managed to get there earlier, all the better. Once aboard they'd head straight for Tanzania and Morgan would hand Chomba over to Interpol Dar es Salaam. Sounded straightforward, but nothing ever was in this business. Although, so far, everything had been going a little too easily …

The hairs on the back of Morgan's neck bristled.

He'd heard something, or sensed it. He couldn't be sure. Instinctively, he leaped into the shadows at the nearest corner of the wall. Some stones had fallen out of the wall and he squeezed the toe of his boot into the gap, checked that it would take his weight without crumbling and then stepped up, grabbing for the top. Careful not to make a sound, he got a hand over and held on tight, ready to launch himself into the yard. He remained still for a moment, listening, then raised his head high enough to look over and into the yard. He took his time, scanning slowly, right to left and left to right, searching for any signs of activity. All was quiet. There was nothing stirring in the yard and the house was in total darkness.

"So, where are all these guards then?" he whispered to himself. Something wasn't right here.

Morgan raised himself up until his waist was level with the top of the wall. He reached over, placing his right hand as far as possible down the other side while keeping a firm grasp on the top with his left. Then he flipped his body over and lowered himself quietly into the yard.

Remaining hidden in the shadows, Morgan used the moonlight to assess the house and possible access points. It was a modest, single-story, brick rectangle with square windows, a long porch and a corrugated-iron roof. It was remarkable only for its similarity to the many others like it in the area. Smart. Chomba obviously didn't want to draw attention to himself by living ostentatiously in some grand mansion, which told Morgan the man was keen to maintain his freedom. Between Morgan and the rear of the house was an open expanse of yard. It was about an eighth of an acre, with patches of uneven scrub sprouting from the dirt. A semicircle of milk crates that probably doubled as chairs sat in an expectant huddle near the porch. All in all, the yard was empty but for a lone mopane tree that grew tall and close to the house. Staying put in his dark corner, Morgan turned to the areas the moonlight couldn't penetrate, searching for any sign of a problem, but saw nothing.

He stepped forward, keeping his right flank hard against the shadows of the northern wall. The M4 was slung across his chest and the P226 holstered. Morgan brought his hands up to the pistol grip and stock of the M4, reflexively testing the tension in the sling. It wouldn't do for it to snag if he needed to bring the weapon up to fire. Estimating that thirty feet along the wall would get him as close to the house as possible without being seen from it, Morgan continued, treading carefully, his breathing steady, controlled. He soon reached the end of the shadows. His next move was to cross the yard. It was open, moonlit and exposed, but there was no other choice. Taking a deep breath, he rushed from the wall, leaving the cover of darkness, heading for the mopane tree.

The blow smashed him across the chest, pushing the M4 into his rib cage heavily. It was inflicted by a branch, gnarled and heavy, wielded by someone big enough to put serious force behind it. Morgan stumbled backward, the air forced from his lungs. Stars exploded across his vision as he fell, striking his head on the ground, hard. Morgan was dazed but conscious enough to know that the strike was reactionary, albeit forceful enough to put him on his ass. He sensed the assailant standing over him, raising the branch high, preparing to deliver the death blow on the center of his exposed skull. He had to get back up. With a grunt, the man brought the branch down with the force of an axe used to splinter kindling. Morgan rapidly locked his forearms in a tight cross over his face. The branch smashed into his arms and pain shot ferociously through his entire body. It was just the opportunity he needed.

Using the assailant's forward momentum to his advantage, Morgan grabbed the branch at the second of impact. His legs exploded upward, both feet connecting perfectly with the other man's torso. The move catapulted his attacker up and over Morgan, throwing him into a winded heap flat on his back. As the man tried to regain his breath, Morgan was already back on his feet. The guy sat up, pushing off with his hands to try to stand again just as Morgan leaped to the side and planted a heavily booted kick to the side of the man's head. The guy fell on to his side then pushed up again. He was tough.

But Morgan was on the offensive. He scooped up the discarded branch from the ground and swung it as hard as he could at the guy's face. It was perfectly placed. Morgan felt the jaw crack. The guy fell back to the ground again with a dull thud. Morgan stood over him, still holding the branch, waiting for any further signs of resistance. There were none. He felt for a pulse. It was faint but there; he'd pull through eventually but would need help. General

Davenport's words came back to him: *"Don't go leaving a trail of corpses across Africa. Just get Chomba and get out." Easier said than done, sir*, he thought, but at least he'd managed to achieve the brief on this occasion. Morgan took a second to examine his attacker. The guy was tall and thin, nothing like the physical description of Chomba, who was said to be short and solidly built. So, not Chomba. That was good.

Breathing heavily, Morgan dropped the branch, withdrew back into the shadow of the mopane tree and took stock. Apart from a few grunts and groans, there'd been no noise during the altercation, which had taken just seconds. All was silent again. Jesus, he really didn't see that one coming. How could he have missed it? Morgan spent some extra time watching and listening but there was nothing else happening and, so far, no follow-up goons to take him on or even any lights coming on – inside or out. Just silence. Maybe he'd surprised his opponent, which suggested that the guy was supposed to be on sentry duty but had fallen asleep and then heard or saw Morgan approaching. He must have grabbed for his gun, couldn't find it in the dark, and so reached for the closest weapon.

Morgan felt around carefully at the base of the tree where the man would have been sleeping. It didn't take long before he found what he was looking for. He knew by the feel of it that it was an FN FAL, a *Fabrique Nationale* 7.62 millimeter light automatic rifle. Or SLR, self-loading rifle, as they used to call them back home. Old school. There was no way he was going to carry around the FN. He didn't need it; it was long and cumbersome, and getting rid of it quietly would waste time. So, it would stay where it was but not in a condition for anyone to use it against him. Morgan quietly removed the magazine and pulled back the cocking handle, ejecting the round that was already in the breech.

Then he eased the cocking handle forward again as quickly as he dared so it wouldn't jam, opened the weapon and extracted the rat's-tail breech block, which he threw, along with the magazine, over the wall.

Morgan moved cautiously through the shadows to the porch, which ran along the entire rear of the house. He stepped up on to it and walked quickly to the back door. He grabbed the knob and turned. It was unlocked, for the sentry no doubt. He took a deep breath and slowly pushed the door inward with his left hand, careful not to allow any unexpected squeals from the hinges to warn anyone that he was in town. His right hand was grasped firmly around the pistol grip of the M4 with his forefinger resting on the trigger. The place was in full darkness with only a few slivers of moonlight reaching the interior so it was difficult to see anything, but he soon realized he was in a kitchen by the lingering smells of the night's meal. He crept on through the kitchen, stopping and listening and allowing his eyes to adjust to the darkness. What was that sound? He paused, mouth open and eyes closed, listening. It stopped. Nothing but silence. He moved deeper inside and repeated the process – stopping, listening, vision adjusting, breathing controlled. There it was again. It sounded like 1980s synthesizer music, fast paced, and accompanied by voices and explosions, getting louder and building in intensity. A wry smile broke across Morgan's face as he recognized what he was hearing. No way. He continued for another five paces until he was well inside the house.

His vision had adjusted fully now and he saw through the darkness as well as an average person would see outside at dusk. It was the central living area, sparsely furnished, with nothing more than a long sofa against the wall under the front window to his left, a couple of arm chairs and side tables, and a coffee table, which was low and square; the usual stuff. At the far end of the room was a snooker table and beyond that a door that led into a bedroom. It was the only door on that side of the room and beyond it was the source of the noise he could hear. Through the door, Morgan saw a white light flickering, illuminating the room an eerie gray, occasionally interspersed with flashes of color and darkness in equal measure. It paused, then began again, in the same peaks and troughs of monotonous repetition. He crept on through the empty living area, stepping carefully over the refuse of what looked to be a party – empty beer and wine bottles, bowls, plates, glasses and some clothes. The place stank of marijuana, booze and sex. Each step brought him closer to the bedroom. As he reached the door he could clearly see the room's layout, complete with occupants.

There was a huge bed in the center, basic bedside tables, and a chipped, rickety-looking wardrobe. Morgan approached cautiously but despite all the noise there was no apparent activity. He stepped over the threshold and everything went dead quiet. Christ! His hands tightened around the M4 and he drew the barrel upward ready to fire with the butt pulled firmly back into his shoulder. There was still no movement. Two extra paces into the room told him all he needed to know. A TV screen about half the size of the wall it was bolted to had been left on and filled the room with light. On the screen the menu page of a DVD was going through its looped sequence of spliced highlights. You've got to be kidding, thought Morgan. It was one of his favorites from childhood, a B-grade sci-fi cult classic called *Trancers*, featuring time-traveling cop Jack Deth. The silent moments came and went as the sequence reached its climax and looped to begin again. Morgan grinned. Of all the places. But it was the bed that held his attention.

A man, overweight, not tall, was sprawled naked on the edge of it and bundled beside him were two young women, also naked. A third woman lay sprawled in a heap on the floor between the bed and the screen. She must have fallen off at some stage and got comfortable there. Fortunately, they were all asleep, and judging by the chorus of snores, deeply so. Great! How the fuck was he going to extract Chomba from among the tangle of his brides without causing a ruckus?

"Sometimes, Mr Morgan, you're left with no alternative but a direct assault!" The wise words of the regimental sergeant major from Morgan's days as a young officer cadet came to mind. *Fair enough then, sar' major. Direct it is.*

Morgan took his cell phone from a pocket and moved in close to the edge of the bed. He stood for a while studying the sleeping man's face carefully via the light of the screen, comparing it to images stored on the phone. Yep, he was satisfied. Definitely Chomba. He leaned in close and sniffed. The man stank of too much alcohol and too many joints. His breath was rancid.

Morgan eased the M4 back down to his side, still slung, and extracted the Sig Sauer P226 from the leg holster on his right leg, placing it down on the bedside table. Then he looked around and found a discarded sarong that appeared to belong to one of the girls. He grabbed it and draped it over his own shoulder and back. Given what he was about to do, he didn't fancy the idea of having Chomba's recently engaged tackle dragging all over him and he couldn't very well deliver him naked into the custody of Interpol Dar es Salaam once they reached Tanzania. He took Chomba by the hand, slipped the man's legs over the edge of the bed and dragged him up into a sitting position. Chomba was fat, practically comatose and a dead weight, and lifting him was not easy. Morgan got down as low as he could beside the bed and toppled Chomba awkwardly forward until he fell across Morgan's left shoulder and on to the sarong, in a classic fireman's lift. Morgan stood up and hefted his captive into position. Then he retrieved the P226 from the table, gave Jack Deth and his compadres on the screen a nod of thanks for providing the background noise, and walked out of the room.

No one even stirred.

Chapter Two

MONG KOK DISTRICT, KOWLOON, HONG KONG

"Mei-Zhen, quickly!" cried Chi, beckoning her frantically, his voice shrill above the din of machinery. "Quickly!"

"What is it?" she replied, running to her young colleague. Mei-Zhen instinctively crouched beneath the window that looked over the factory floor. The main area contained ten rows of long tables, each with twenty sewing machines on them. The operators kept their heads down, working eighteen-hour days, seven days a week. On the outskirts of the factory, behind a series of large garage-style roller doors, were the heavy machinery and electronics areas. Productivity was paramount in all three workspaces but safety was negligible. In the heavy machinery areas, almost every piece of equipment had been modified to remove safety shields to reduce delays in the manufacturing process. Some workers had lost their fingers or, worse, hands or eyes, but workers were easily replaced.

"What are we looking at?" asked the young woman.

"There. Oh my God!" Chi exclaimed, directing her attention to the nearest corner of the sewing-machine area.

Two men in black suits were beating one of the sewing-room supervisors with rattan canes. Everyone else ignored the violence, terrified, obediently continuing with their work in order to avoid the same treatment.

"They're working their way across the floor, picking people at random. That's the fifth person I've seen them beating! They're coming this way!"

"Please, calm down, Chi," said Mei-Zhen, firmly. "We mustn't let them see us. Please."

Her words did little to calm him. He was only fifteen and employed as the office assistant, which meant that he did the photocopying, ran errands and fetched coffee and cigarettes. These two new arrivals had carried out arbitrary beatings over the past couple of days but so far the office staff had been spared. They were not sure their luck would hold and Chi was terrified and inconsolable. He let out an involuntary scream. Mei-Zhen clutched him to her tightly, trying to quieten him, but it was too late. The two men in black were heading toward the staircase. Somehow they'd been noticed, or the scream had been heard on the factory floor, despite the deafening sound of the machinery.

Mei-Zhen Tan heard their heavy footfalls strike the metal stairs. When they kicked the door open she was standing defiantly in front of Chi, ready for them to do their worst.

Chapter Three

THE CENOTAPH, WHITEHALL, LONDON

To the casual observer they were just two people, clearly senior officials – they had that look about them – making their way purposefully but unhurriedly along Whitehall from the Cenotaph, following the close of the Remembrance Day service.

Her Majesty Queen Elizabeth and other members of the Royal Family had already left, concluding the official observances and heralding the departure process for hundreds of military and government officials, representatives from other nations, and the thousands of citizens, mostly ex-servicemen and -women, who had gathered, as they did every year at the eleventh hour of the eleventh day of the eleventh month, to pay their respects to those who had made the ultimate sacrifice in war. Between Big Ben and Nelson's Column, Whitehall was a mosaic of multinational uniforms, winter overcoats, umbrellas, and, of course, the red poppies of Flanders Field.

The man was well over six feet tall, distinguished looking, with his gray hair and beard, and dressed in a charcoal, knee-length overcoat, complemented by a black scarf and leather gloves. Navy blue pin-stripe trousers were visible below the hem of the coat, falling perfectly upon black brogues polished to a high sheen. He had an old-world regal appearance about him, similar to Prince Michael of Kent, and favored his right knee when he walked, giving him a barely discernible limp.

The woman to his left was not as tall but still close enough to six foot in her low heels. She was younger than him, probably by at least ten years. She had pale skin made paler by the slash of red lipstick she wore, in striking contrast to her dark eyes and jet-black hair, taken back in a French pleat beneath her plain felt hat. She wore a close-fitted black overcoat, belted tight at the waist, accentuating the swell of her breasts.

These two were well known to each other. Their body language said as much as they walked along the sodden pavement back toward Westminster, weaving their way through the throng of other officials and attendees, occasionally stopping to chat with young veterans, some in uniform and others in suits, who stood waiting respectfully for the dignitaries to depart.

The more astute observer would have noticed that the pair were not walking alone, although they were being given some privacy. Behind them, maintaining a professional distance but within acceptable reaction parameters, were two men, thirty-something, fit, solidly built, and serious faced. Bodyguards.

The trained observer would note that the two men were there to protect the woman. Their attention was clearly more geared toward her exposed left side and in front of her, searching for any sign of threat. A third member of the protection team was walking ahead of the woman. There didn't appear to be any special protection measures in place for the man, although appearances could be deceiving.

She was Dame Violet Ashcroft-James, DCMG, chief of Britain's Secret Intelligence Service, or "C" as the chief is traditionally known. He was Major General Reginald "Nobby" Davenport, CBE, DSO, MC, chief of the Intelligence, Recovery, Protection and Infiltration Division of Interpol, otherwise known as Intrepid.

"It breaks my heart to see so many young men in wheelchairs, Nobby," said Ashcroft-James. "So many amputees too. The trauma of what they've been through is written all over their faces. Hard to believe we're still sending our young off to war. Will we never learn?"

"Sadly, I don't believe we ever will, Vee," General Davenport replied with a sigh. "War is in our blood. Has been for millennia and will be for many more, I'm afraid. And who are we to talk? We both make life or death decisions every day, do we not?"

They walked on in silence for a little until she moved even closer to him and slid her arm under his.

"I remember when you used to go away," she began in a low voice. "All those years ago."

"Almost thirty," he replied, looking at their linked arms thoughtfully.

"Oh, don't be so horrible! Surely it can't be that many?"

"Give or take," he said, smiling.

"My God. What was the reason the first time – after you had to leave London and return to Aldershot with the Parachute Regiment? Northern Ireland, I suppose … Does that sound about right?"

"Yes, I was with 3PARA then," he said. "We were called in for an emergency tour and stayed for six months."

"Then you joined the SAS and I didn't see you or even

hear anything for months at a time; constantly in and out of Northern Ireland and God knows where else. That was the most terrible part of it ... the not knowing. And then, just when I thought I'd have you back for a while, it was the first Gulf War. Desert Storm."

Davenport breathed in deeply and took his time over replying. "Why all the ancient history, Vee?" he asked. "It was all so long ago."

"Seeing all these servicemen, I suppose, and being among them with you. It's just brought it all back to me. What it felt like whenever you went away. Never knowing where you were or what you were up to. Do you ever wonder what it might have been like if ..."

"If?"

"If we'd made it. Stayed together, I mean."

"Bloody hell," he said. "You really are reminiscing now, aren't you?"

"I'm serious," she said. "Do you?"

"I suppose it's crossed my mind from time to time, but it was all so long ago. You've been happily married for many years. And I've had my share of disasters since." He laughed. "But I've been happy, too. I don't believe in regret. Life's too short. We all make decisions, good or bad, and then we must live with them."

She remained silent, walking along with him, still arm in arm, huddled against the bite of the cold wind that bowled them along. They continued so until they eventually turned right on to Great George Street. After a time, Davenport broke the silence.

"Is everything alright, Violet?" he asked. "You don't seem yourself today."

"I'm fine, Nobby, really," she said. "It's just that we seem to be having so many of these memorial occasions of late;

one can't help but reflect on one's own life. When I'm surrounded by all these young men and women in their uniforms, doing whatever is asked of them and, in many cases, never being the same again, my thoughts inevitably return to you. To war and separation. Now our lives have moved on. We're both so immersed in our own contributions to the security effort that sometimes I forget what drew me to it in the first place, don't you?"

"My dear—" he began in a gentler tone.

"No, Nobby, it's OK. I didn't mean to embarrass you, believe me. Silly of me. I'll be all right." She stopped walking as a gleaming black Jaguar XJ pulled up discreetly against the curb nearby. The bodyguard who had been walking ahead of them took up position beside the car. Still maintaining surveillance of the surrounding area, he opened the rear door in readiness for Ashcroft-James to get inside. An identical car pulled in behind the first. "May I offer you a lift?" she said.

"No, thank you, Vee," replied Davenport. "The walk will do me good. Why don't we catch up soon for lunch? It's been a while."

"That would be lovely," she said, somewhat distracted. "I'm about to head off to France for a short trip, meetings and so on, but I'll get my assistant to call Mrs Jolley and we'll put something in the diary. OK?"

"Sounds perfect," he replied. "Do take care of yourself. And don't get up to any mischief over there."

They hugged, Davenport kissed her on the cheek and Ashcroft-James climbed into the back of the car. She waited until the door was shut before she reached into the folds of her overcoat for her phone. She smiled at Davenport as the car pulled away, taking a hard right past the Palace of Westminster and heading for Vauxhall Cross. She speed-dialed a number.

"It's me," she said. "I've been chatting with him all morning. Tried a variety of angles, but couldn't get a bloody thing out of him. Impossible to say whether he has any current interest or not." A pause while she listened. "No, I wouldn't discount it. But he isn't giving anything away."

Chapter Four

KOWLOON, HONG KONG

Alex Morgan stared through the billowing steam straight into the pair of cold eyes that met his, challenging him with an interrogator's calculating precision. The stark brilliance of the downlighting cut through the haze, intensifying the angular structure and hardened features of the face, giving it a cold, impersonal quality.

There was damage and triumph in equal measure in the eyes as they stared back at him, flaunting an encyclopedic knowledge of his darkest moments and secrets: the lies, deception and betrayals that were an inherent part of his line of business. The job. How much of him was now just the job? What was left of the man he was before the soldier and, ultimately, the agent?

Feeling self-conscious, Morgan looked away from the eyes, shifting his attention to a more detailed examination of the face, searching for some point of reference that would return him to familiar territory. The once occasional laughter lines around the green eyes were fast becoming a permanent feature; there was a tight cluster of three short scars on the left-hand side, a long, slightly crooked nose – the result of a dodgy repair – and flecks of gray were taking up residence amid the dark hair at the temples; all classic signs of the subtle, unavoidable changes that under intense scrutiny make something once very familiar suddenly unfamiliar. Morgan's study inevitably returned to the eyes. There was no escaping them. They remained ruthlessly fixed, staring him down. It was the eyes that told the real story, the truth. They were tired and aged beyond their years, with none of the optimism or energy of youth. They'd seen too much.

Annoyed and struggling to fight off his melancholic mood, Morgan glanced away from the mirror and plunged his shaving brush into the piping hot water of the half-filled basin. An involuntary shudder rippled through him and, dropping the brush, he grasped the basin with both hands, steadying himself. *No, not again. Not now.* His heart began to pound and his scalp began to claw at his skull, pulling his skin taut across his face. He closed his eyes, not wanting to face them mocking him from the mirror. He hung on tight to the basin. In a few moments the spasm had passed. With a trembling hand, he retrieved the brush from the hot water, squeezed away the excess, and then swirled it determinedly around and around in the wooden bowl of scented soap until he'd achieved just the right consistency.

Not good, he thought. *Not good at all.* This was happening far too often. He couldn't afford for it to happen while he was working. He just had to get through this mission which, after all, should be straightforward babysitting, and then he'd tell the general he had to take leave, whether the old man liked it or not. His chin and cheeks white with lather, Morgan began to scrape away the stubble.

An hour and a half earlier, he had flown into Hong

Kong from Tanzania. Thankfully, the rest of his mission to extract Chomba from Malawi had gone smoothly. Morgan had manhandled him out of the house and in a matter of minutes had him tightly secured and face down in the back an old Land Rover he'd located out front. It had been a tense thirty-minute drive to Mangochi Airport to meet Barboza. The two of them had hauled Chomba on to the DC-3, strapped him into a seat and were away.

But now with Operation Usalama finally behind him, Morgan was dog tired, fed up and in desperate need of a break. With ten years of protracted military combat operations under his belt and four more of seemingly endless back-to-back operations as an Intrepid agent, he was in the grip of mission fatigue and these episodes of self-doubt were happening more frequently, each one more intense than the last.

Intrepid, known unofficially as the 'Sword of Interpol', became fully operational in September 2006. The Secretary General of the United Nations had proposed its creation in the aftermath of 9/11 and the UN Security Council had turned to Interpol – the International Criminal Police Organization – to raise a new division of unique young men and women, handpicked from across the globe, to take on the worst of humankind. In a break from the official Interpol charter, these agents would not be facilitators of cooperation between the law-enforcement agencies of member nations, they would be enforcers of international law – part soldier, part policeman and part spy, empowered in every way to, as the Secretary General declared, "fight fire with fire." For official purposes, the ambiguously designated IPS Division of Interpol's Terrorism sub-directorate was based in Lyon, France. However, the actual operational headquarters were located in London and accessed via an unremarkable door off Broadway behind a labyrinth of latest generation biometric security measures, not far from St James's Park tube station.

Morgan, a decorated veteran of East Timor, Iraq, and Afghanistan, had risen to the rank of major in the Parachute Regiment before being recruited to Intrepid in 2010. In one of his increasingly frequent bouts of cynicism, Morgan mused that he'd been deployed so often during the past two years he could scarcely remember where the hell the covert entrance to the London headquarters was. His numerous attempts to take leave had all been indefinitely shelved. Just prior to his departure from Tanzania, his orders changed and he was redirected to Hong Kong, to assist fellow agent Dave Sutherland in providing 'top cover', an allusion to the way in which jet fighters give overhead fire support to ground troops: they were providing backup for another agent. All Morgan knew so far was that she was ex-Interpol and new to Intrepid. He wasn't enamored of the idea of sacrificing his precious leave to babysit someone green. He hoped she knew what she was doing.

The sat-phone on the edge of the basin buzzed. Morgan sighed and checked the time: 8.30am.

He read the message. As expected, it was from Sutherland.

Welcome to HK, bud. Hope you're ready. Your room in 30.

ACK, Morgan typed, and hit send. *Here we go again*, he thought.

He finished shaving, dropped his towel and stepped under an already steaming shower. He allowed the hot water to sting his skin. It was a ritual of sorts, not that he ever thought of it like that; a few moments of peace and solitude to purge the turmoil and uncertainty that had become his life.

Just got to hold it together a little longer. A day or two more and you're done.

Chapter Five

KOWLOON, HONG KONG

Elizabeth Reigns folded away the sofa bed, neatly replacing the cushions. Responding to the kettle's whistle, she walked stiffly across to the kitchenette of her small, sparsely furnished, one-roomed apartment, complete with en suite bathroom the size of the average refrigerator. She lifted the kettle from the single portable gas burner, which she'd bought because the hot plate didn't work, and turned off the gas. She took a cup from the wooden drying rack on the sink, dropped in a bag of green tea and poured water on top of it. Then she took the tea and sat down at the vinyl-covered card table by the window, looking out on a solid brick wall that was within touching distance if she raised the grimy window. As she lifted the cup to her lips she realized that her hands were shaking. She immediately put the cup down on the table, placed her hands on her thighs, closed her eyes and began a well-practiced meditation regime her mother had taught her many years before.

Reigns, a newly recruited Intrepid agent operating under the cover name Mei-Zhen Tan, was Chinese American; her father was from Los Angeles and her mother from Shanghai. She'd been born and raised in the USA and, on her mother's insistence, spoke Mandarin and Cantonese fluently, which was exactly why she'd been chosen for this operation. In fact, she'd never before been to Hong Kong, and was a complete unknown in this part of the world. Reigns had been instructed to take a job as the office manager's assistant and book-keeper with a designer apparel, mobile-phone parts and engine-component manufacturing operation in the Mong Kok district of Kowloon. The business was a 'black' factory owned by Triad crime boss Wu Ming, running a significant manufacturing operation with a large workforce of illegal immigrants, and she had been covertly infiltrated to investigate it.

She had taken the shabby apartment on the basis that it was close enough to the factory that her travel time was kept to reasonable limits, but out of the way enough to discourage unwanted attention from her fellow workers. The twenty minute bus ride to the factory gave Reigns the chance to prepare herself mentally for each and every day spent working in that hellish place. The events of yesterday afternoon had increased her sense of vulnerability exponentially.

After five minutes, Reigns concluded her meditation. She took up the tea again, albeit now lukewarm, and thought through her plan for the day. She had only an hour before her scheduled meeting at the Mong Kok Ladies' Market. Today of all days she had to make it, but she knew she had to show her face in the office first. If she didn't, her absence would be noticed. It would be cutting things fine but she had no other choice.

Reigns finished her tea and checked her watch. It was time. She stood up slowly, feeling the coarse fabric of her clothes catch against the welts and scabs left on her flesh by the beating she'd been given the night before when she had protected the young office boy, Chi. She strode purposefully across the room, ignoring the pain, and pulled the chair out from under the doorknob where she had wedged it. It was a crude security measure but effective enough in causing delay and buying her time to react. Standing still for a moment at the door, she drew in a deep breath, held it for a few moments and let it escape slowly. Then she opened the door and stepped out, ready to take on whatever the day had in store for her.

Chapter Six

POLICE HEADQUARTERS KOWLOON WEST, HONG KONG

Inspector Victor Lam of the Hong Kong Police Force's Organized Crime and Triad Bureau, the OCTB, saw a familiar figure approaching him and was instantly filled with dread. The man was Chief Superintendent Chan Man-kin – Fat Freddy Chan – and he was the last person Lam wanted to run into right now, but it looked as though he had no choice. He nervously stepped up the intensity of his search for a fugitive packet of menthol cigarettes, hoping he might manage to avoid being seen by Chan and somehow escape before being cornered. However, in a matter of seconds, Chan had managed to plough his way through the maze of narrow gaps and cul-de-sacs between the desks of the OCTB, and appear in the doorway of Lam's shoebox-sized, windowless corner office.

"Where are you running off to now, Lam? Another of your special errands? If I didn't know better, I'd say that you were trying to avoid me."

Chief Superintendent Chan bore no resemblance to the fit young man who had been a classmate of Lam's when they were both recruits at the police academy back in the early 1980s. Now Chan was grossly overweight and the buttons of his uniform tunic strained under the pressure. His face was oily and heavily pockmarked. A large brown mole the size of a coat button protruded from his right cheek. It had long strands of wiry hair growing from it. He clung desperately to the merest few strands remaining on his otherwise bald head, which he combed over almost from the tip of his right ear. The thick lenses of his spectacles magnified two predatory brown eyes.

"I'm working, Chan, as you can see," Lam replied, feigning indifference. He put on his suit jacket while still searching for the packet of cigarettes, worried about the time. "You do remember what that is, don't you?"

"Work? Not really," came the shameless reply. "I'm chief superintendent now, if you hadn't noticed. I have other people to do that for me."

"I don't have time for your chit-chat, chief superintendent."

"Of course you don't. Still the crusader. The cop who doesn't need help. Doesn't need friends. Am I right?"

"You've got it wrong. As usual. I pick my team according to the task at hand. I get results that way," Lam replied. *Damn!* Now was not the time for this. "Was there something?"

Chan turned and waved toward the OCTB office, bristling with plainclothes detectives and uniformed officers going about their business.

"You handpick your team based on the task, do you? Interesting. So, are you saying you don't trust your colleagues?" he said, loud enough for those nearby to hear. "These fine, upstanding men and women of the Hong Kong Police!"

No, but I don't trust you. That's what Lam wanted to say but knew he couldn't. Instead he allowed his silence to answer for him.

"You're a fool. You've always been one," Chan continued in a conversational tone. "Ever since the academy. Incorruptible. And what do you have to show for it? You're still just a lowly inspector, nothing more. You are tolerated only because of a freak success early in your career. Now you are nothing but an annoyance to the hierarchy. And what of your private life? Divorced. Estranged from your children. You're too stupid to realize that when this job has finally chewed you up and spat you out, no one will even remember your name. So, tell me, Lam, isn't it about time you started thinking about retirement? Bowing out gracefully now? Finally making some friends? I can help you with that."

"I don't need friends like your friends," Lam said, meaning it.

"I think you need them more than you realize. And sooner rather than later."

"I'm not interested. Now, if you don't mind, I'm working." He checked his watch discreetly. He had to make the rendezvous on time. If he was late, his contact would abandon the meeting and he couldn't let that happen. "So, why don't you step aside and let me get on with my job?"

"What exactly are you doing this morning? You seem anxious to get going. Perhaps I could come with you?"

"I'm meeting an informant so I'm going alone. I don't need you and I don't need your friends." Lam gave up on finding his cigarettes and moved toward the door. Chan did not move.

"You should watch your step." This response, issued from behind clenched teeth, was delivered with an air of menace that Lam had never seen in this man, and he had known him for many years. "There are more people than you realize taking an interest in what you are doing. Your personal obsession with influential people in this city has not gone unnoticed and I would suggest that you avoid stepping on any more toes ... including mine. Or you may find yourself retiring earlier than you had anticipated."

Lam remained silent, bowing his head, reluctantly respectful. He was unsettled by what he perceived as the new level of threat in Chan's voice. Still, he needed to stand his ground. He couldn't afford to show fear. "These influential people you're talking about, the ones I'm apparently obsessed with – they are criminals, you know that, don't you?"

Chan slithered the final few steps until he was completely inside Lam's office and blocking the doorway. He leaned closer to the desk and, from under the pile of paperwork, retrieved the pack of cigarettes Lam had been searching for. He flipped it open, extracted a cigarette, placed it between his teeth, lit up then threw the packet back at Lam, who just managed to catch it.

"You know, I came here to help you, Lam," said his superior, fat tongue awkwardly forming the words as the cigarette bounced on his dry brown lips. "I offered you the hand of friendship and the opportunity to retire with dignity. But you've made it clear that you do not want my help. So I will warn you instead." He reached behind and shut the door with a click. "I don't care if you live or die. In fact, you are worth more to me dead, but to kill you myself would be foolish. So, I am telling you to end this secret operation you are running – immediately. Your crusade has come to an end. If you do not, there will be consequences."

"But I—" Lam caught himself mid-sentence as Chan

added, "You should have been more careful when you agreed to help ... Interpol."

Lam's blood ran cold. How could Chan know that? Only the assistant commissioner was aware that Lam was assisting an Interpol operation, and even he didn't know the details. That was the arrangement with Interpol. In fact, they had specifically demanded Lam's discretion with regard to his superiors. The assistant commissioner was a good man, a man Lam had known and trusted for many years. It couldn't have come from him, of that Lam was certain. Chan could be bluffing, although Lam didn't believe he was. Not this time anyway.

All Lam could say in reply was, "I don't know what you're talking about."

"Have it your way," said Chan. "Walk away from this operation now or you'll be dead before I have my lunch and I won't give you another thought." He remained silent for a few seconds, fixing those deadly brown eyes upon Lam. Then a cruel, knowing grin split his features. "You and your little girlfriend should have been more discreet. Isn't she a bit young for you? I'm giving you until midday. Let's see if you can pull her out in time."

With that, he opened the door and walked slowly across the expanse of the open-plan office. When he reached the foyer he pressed the elevator button and turned back to face Lam, tapping a finger to his wristwatch. Then he disappeared into the elevator.

Chapter Seven

KOWLOON SHANGRI-LA HOTEL, HONG KONG

Five minutes early, at 8.55am, Dave Sutherland tapped on the connecting door to Morgan's deluxe harbor-view room and strolled in.

Commander David Sutherland, former US Navy SEAL and recipient of the Navy Cross for extraordinary heroism, earned during combat operations in Iraq, was about Morgan's height – around six feet tall – tanned and powerfully built. He had piercing gray-blue eyes, his head was shaved to the scalp and he wore a bulky diver's watch on his left wrist. As he entered, Morgan looked across the room, still in the process of buttoning a lightweight collared shirt over a concealable Kevlar vest. A navy blue sports coat was draped across the back of a chair and the tools of his trade were laid out on the table: P226 Sig Sauer, spare magazines, holster, magazine pouches, and an ASP baton; all ready for action now that he'd completed his customary weapons and equipment check. His preparation was taking longer than usual – another attack of tremors had struck him just before Sutherland entered the room.

"Still not ready?" Sutherland quipped, opening his brown leather bomber jacket to reveal his own holstered Sig Sauer, spare magazines and ASP baton. "I guess the old pros are always showing the young pups how it's done! You take about the same amount of time to get ready as most women I know."

"Old is right. Forty next birthday, yeah? You'll be in a walking frame before you know it," replied Morgan, relieved that his comrade didn't seem to have noticed anything unusual in his appearance or behavior. "Anyway, how would you know how long it takes a woman to get ready for anything? What woman, besides your mum, would have any time for you?"

"Screw you. How was Africa?"

"The usual – hot." Morgan finished buttoning the shirt and flicked his head to a pot of coffee that had just arrived via room service. "So, how are things here, Dave?"

"We'll get to that." Sutherland threw a small, tightly rolled bundle onto the table beside Morgan's gear, walked over, poured them both coffee and handed a cup to Morgan. "Wear that under your jacket until we get to the car; there's a black ski-mask in the pocket. If everything goes pear-shaped and we need to do anything outside the vehicle, then at least we'll only get shot at by the bad guys. I've got one for Reigns, too."

"Is that supposed to make me feel better?" asked Morgan, unrolling the bundle. It was a lightweight, black, zip-front vest of the type common to most law-enforcement agencies, only this one had POLICE written in English and Chinese in large yellow letters across the back and a small HK Police Force crest on the left breast. "So, tell me about Reigns. She's some Interpol analyst, right, or am I missing something?"

"She *was* an analyst but that's not the half of it. She's a graduate of Johns Hopkins University – international studies, specializing in human trafficking. After college she joined the United Nations Inter-Agency Project on Human Trafficking, deployed to all of their key centers out here – China, Cambodia, Thailand, Vietnam; you name it. After that she was with the Rapid Response Unit for the Office of the High Commissioner for Human Rights. From OHCHR she got snapped up by Interpol and worked as a criminal analyst in the Washington office. All that time she's been involved with Johns Hopkins in a thing called the Protection Project – it's not-for-profit, human rights, that kind of stuff. She's no dummy and, so far, she's doing well on this job."

Sutherland was obviously impressed by her. Morgan wasn't convinced.

"She sounds like an academic, not an operator," he said. "One of those typical UN types – deploy to the Third World, earn a packet, but never set foot outside your fucking air conditioning. How did the boss find her?"

"He attended a human rights conference that this Protection Project was hosting. Reigns made a presentation and impressed the hell out of him. Before you know it, here she is – our latest recruit in the field on her first solo job."

"Sounds like tokenism if you ask me. The old man's getting soft and we end up babysitting," Morgan replied sourly. After some final adjustments to his tactical equipment, he picked up his coffee cup and dropped into a chair within the room's large bay window. Victoria Harbour and the Hong Kong skyline stretched out behind him, with the CMA CGM *Jules Verne*, one of the largest container ships in the world, in view.

"Jesus! What's got into you, bud? Sounds like you've got an issue with this girl and you haven't even met her yet."

"Don't worry about me, Dave," Morgan replied, annoyed. He drank some coffee. "I just want to get through this one and take some down time. That's all. The sooner it's done the better."

"OK, well, trust me when I tell you, you've got nothing to worry about with Reigns. She's good."

"If you say so. When do we start moving?"

"We could get a call any minute. You all set?"

"I'm all set," replied Morgan, sensing unease in Sutherland's tone.

"How much do you know?"

"Not much," Morgan replied truthfully. "I received a mission summary from headquarters and read it inflight, but it was just the headline stuff."

At this point, all Morgan knew was that he and Sutherland were on standby to extract Reigns, potentially under hostile circumstances if things went south. Morgan and Sutherland had been dispatched together on similar missions before. They were a good team and General Davenport used them as his primary extraction team, as and when required. So, other than it being hazardous, Morgan knew next to nothing about Reigns' operation here, or who they might be up against if they had to get her out in a hurry.

"We're currently in the middle of phase one of a major operation. This bit is all about finding a guy named Wu Ming. He's a big-time crime figure in this part of Asia – drugs, weapons, prostitution, protection, you name it. The guy is a master at establishing legitimate businesses as smokescreens for his illegal activities while remaining a ghost. He's been getting away with it for years."

"Why haven't HKPD done anything before now?"

"They've been trying but he's too well connected. One

of those guys who everyone knows is neck deep in bad shit, but somehow never gets his hands dirty in public. They haven't been able to pin anything on him. He's believed to be heavily into the slave trade, although HKPD couldn't prove it. But that all changed when his name suddenly came up in a global human trafficking investigation being coordinated by the UN and Interpol which, as you know, includes your last job, Operation Usalama.

"Basically, the Hong Kong cops were working with Interpol on some recent leads into a trafficking ring operating throughout Asia, and out of nowhere they had a breakthrough. Until recently, Wu Ming had only been suspected of playing a role in moving migrant labor in and out of Hong Kong, but then a former Kowloon business associate of his moved to the US and ended up charged with migrant smuggling violations by US Immigration and Customs Enforcement, for illegally employing a foreign national in domestic duties. When ICE traced the background of the victim, a Filipino, it turned out she had originally entered the forced-labor cycle as a prostitute in a brothel known to be run by—"

"Wu Ming?" said Morgan.

"Correct. And that's what brought him to the attention of the international authorities, and eventually us."

"Sounds like getting Al Capone for tax evasion," Morgan said. "The line of least resistance."

"Something like that, but whatever works, right?" replied Sutherland. "The chance to establish a link between a major organized crime figure in Asia and the movement of migrants around the world for the purposes of exploitation was sufficient to get all the agencies talking to each other. Before the general sent me out here with Reigns, he told me that he wants to direct the entire operation, from bottom to top. Like I said, this Wu Ming lead is the strongest anyone's got into what is believed to be a global cartel, so we're going for it. Our objective is to find Wu Ming, confirm his identity, and follow the trail from him to the next link in the chain, who, apparently, is the ultimate target."

"Do we have any idea who that is?" asked Morgan.

"I gather the general has his sights on someone big, a woman known as the Night Witch. She's in the system but only under her alias. You know, one of those Blue Notices with a silhouette instead of a photo."

"Night Witch?" Morgan scoffed. "Very fucking helpful."

Interpol Notices were urgent alerts published by the General Secretariat and dispatched to the law-enforcement networks of member nations. They covered a wide range of issues and were color-coded to alert authorities instantly to the specific basis of the alert. A Blue Notice was issued to authorize the collection of additional information about a person's identity, location or activities in relation to a crime.

"The chief's had a rocket up his ass about human trafficking ever since his meeting with the UN Secretary General a couple of months back, and he's had the Intel geeks working round the clock to come up with an actual identity for this Night Witch. Once they're done it'll be no surprise if you, me or Reigns get handed the UN Security Council Special Notice "For Intrepid Action," containing the name of the general's new favorite candidate for rendition. Meanwhile, while the geeks are tapping away at their keyboards, the primary focus here on the ground is to substantively prove that Wu Ming is connected to the people traffickers, ideally the Night Witch. Once that's done then phase two will begin and things will get serious."

"You'll follow the trail from him to this Witch?"

"Exactly."

"And how does Reigns fit into all this?"

"So far as the police department here is concerned, Reigns works for Interpol and has been sent to Hong Kong to liaise with a guy named Inspector Victor Lam regarding a trafficking investigation. That's all we've given them. Lam is acknowledged as HKPD's foremost expert on these Triad guys and is therefore the perfect choice to assist her."

"What do we know about him, and how did she get him to cooperate without telling his superiors what we're really doing here?"

"Like I said, she's good. She's been cultivating him as a potential asset for some time, long before she was sent here, building up rapport and trust, using her previous Interpol role as cover. She had to convince him to work for us covertly, running the operation as if it was one of his own while keeping the operational details secret from HKPD. He took some convincing. He's a solid guy, a by-the-book kinda cop, but she's a pretty tenacious woman. The short version is that he arranged for her to get a job with one of Wu Ming's supposedly legitimate front companies – a factory here in Kowloon, specializing in fake designer clothes, light manufacturing, that kind of thing. They needed a bookkeeper. The timing was perfect – they had a tip-off about the vacancy from one of Lam's informants."

"Let's just hope all this effort leads somewhere," Morgan said, feeling he was stuck on a never-ending rollercoaster. Despite his general sense of mission fatigue, he was eager to get moving; he didn't handle sitting around waiting very well at all. "How has this thing been running while Reigns has been on the inside?"

"Lam holds covert meets with her – pre-scheduled before she was infiltrated. I stay well clear of the play, but occasionally check in with him by phone in lots of veiled speech to get the latest info she has passed on ... ambiguous chat about my 'niece,' 'Grandfather' ... you know the drill. She's been inside for over a month, and until yesterday there's been nothing to report. I was starting to think we were wasting our time here but the general was adamant we should stay the course for at least three months before re-evaluating. Things have just changed."

"Changed, how?"

"Last night, Reigns activated her early-warning signal. We couldn't send her in with one of our Gucci sat-phones with all the bells and whistles, so we came up with a standard, very simple digital distress flare – a seven-digit code: two-eight-three-six-four-three-seven, which on a keypad corresponds to the word 'Avenger' – that she could tap out on the standard, albeit slightly enhanced, commercial cell phone she's carrying. The code comes direct to me and, of course, the comms geeks back at headquarters in London."

"Meaning 'Standby, something's happened, and you may need to get me the fuck out of here?'" Morgan said.

"Pretty much," replied Sutherland. "She'll probably need to extract within the next twenty-four hours. Now, she sent the code late last night, around eight pm. And if I know her, she sat on that decision for as long as she could before she decided to send it. That in turn prompted the general to pull you in from Tanzania. Hence, the late notice. I'm not expecting to hear anything from her again unless she actually needs to be extracted. Meanwhile, she has a scheduled meet with Inspector Lam at the Mong Kok Ladies' Market this morning. It's about twenty minutes' drive from here, depending on traffic. If she shows as arranged at nine-thirty then all's well. If not, Lam will contact me, and you and I will get our asses in the car, get into that goddamn sweatshop she's been working in, find her and get her the hell outta there. Until then, we sit tight and wait."

"OK," Morgan said, hoping they'd get the "all's well" option rather than the alternative. He didn't know how much fight he still had left in him.

Sutherland's cell phone buzzed. He checked the number. "It's Lam," he said to Morgan, then answered: "Go ahead." Sutherland's eyes remained fixed on Morgan as he listened.

Morgan's fists clenched and his right leg began to tap involuntarily as he watched Sutherland's expression change from attentive to concerned. So, not the "all's well" option then. Wordlessly, as Sutherland continued to listen, the two Intrepid agents left the room, heading for the hotel car park.

Chapter Eight

MONG KOK LADIES' MARKET, KOWLOON, HONG KONG

Inspector Victor Lam sat chain smoking and drinking too much coffee. To any passerby, he was just an average middle-aged man, thin and unremarkable, with a thatch of gray-black hair, wearing a cheap dark blue suit, shiny from overuse and smelling of old tobacco. He sat balanced precariously on a rickety metal chair, shoulders hunched, outwardly unconcerned by anything going on in the vicinity. His appearance belied his mental state. He noticed everything.

Lam's eyes, hidden behind unfashionable sunglasses, were feverishly studying the scene before him. He'd been in the game long enough to know that there was never a time for complacency and his unexpected run-in with Chan that morning had unsettled him. Lam had seen too many friends and colleagues lose their lives as a result of a momentary lapse of attention and he wasn't about to join them. Underestimating Chan and the power and reach of his associates would be a fool's mistake. In circles inhabited by crooks and cops – and crooked cops like Chan – life was cheap. Killing was nothing more than a thrill for the apprentices of the criminal class in the Kowloon underworld and, for someone like Chan, arranging for some street kid to put a knife in Lam's back would be no more significant than stubbing out the cigarette he'd helped himself to earlier. While Lam was in no hurry to die, the thing that had caused him the most anxiety about their encounter that morning was Chan's reference to 'his little girlfriend'. So, although to all outward appearance he was calm, Lam was at the very limit of his composure. The phrase 'dead by lunch' kept playing over and over in his mind.

Fat Freddy Chan, a chief superintendent of police. Christ! What a joke – a dangerous joke.

Lam waited anxiously for the girl to appear. Their operation was blown, that was clear, and it was time to pull her out – but what if she didn't show? What if Chan and his associates had already got to her? No, he wouldn't contemplate it. That kind of thinking was bad for morale. Lam reassured himself that making the call to the Interpol contact and telling him about his run-in with Chan, emphasizing his superior's exact words, had been the right thing to do. It wasn't panic, it was a legitimate action because, despite his sloppy appearance and general uselessness as a police officer, Chan's connection to the underworld made him dangerous. The Interpol man seemed to agree. His orders were clear – sit tight, Interpol officers were en route.

Now all Lam could do was wait and pray that the girl arrived at the rendezvous on time and unharmed.

With the disdain and cynicism that only a seasoned cop can muster, Lam took a moment to peruse his fellow citizens, crammed together in a corner of the market. He watched the various stall keepers and wondered what it would be like to only be concerned with selling souvenirs, or clothes, or fish. There was a young man painstakingly positioning dozens of pieces of imitation jewelry and fake designer watches across a table that looked like it was about to collapse under the weight of it all. He used the same care one would expect if they were the real thing. Beyond him, Lam saw a woman, older than the young man, fussing dutifully over colorfully embroidered ladies' slippers, while another was coaxing some European tourists into buying a set of Chinese opera masks. Yet all these things were on the periphery of what he noticed.

His observation cut through the minutiae of normal people's lives, past the tedium of overspending tourists who waddled through the tight confines of the markets, struggling under the weight of their purchases. Lam saw straight through it all, to the secret drug deals, the standover men, the muggers and the thieves. They were all there in plain sight, right out in the open, alongside the tourists and stall keepers; local petty criminals honing their craft, together with the Triad try-outs striving to establish themselves in the junior hierarchy. Now, more than ever, he felt their number and proximity as if they were closing in around him. Were they? Fear flared in the pit of his stomach.

Fuck, what a life, he mused, lamenting for a moment the path he'd chosen all those years ago. He stubbed out his cigarette and immediately lit another. Lam was a career cop – his background and upbringing made him a street cop. Born and raised in Hong Kong, he'd fought his way up from the streets of West Kowloon to the police academy and had been on the force for nearly thirty years. His rank was hard won, earning promotion through sergeant to inspector by actually solving crimes and locking up crooks. There were only two guys still left on the force from his class at the academy. One was Chan and the other was Assistant

Commissioner Kwong. Meanwhile, Lam had been passed over for superintendent more times than he could remember. But that was the way he liked it. He was no careerist, never destined for the senior ranks. His place was here, on the street, being a real policeman. He couldn't allow himself to be scared off by the likes of Fat Freddy Chan.

He caught sight of a clock amid the clamor and activity and rechecked his watch, praying that she'd be approaching any second now. If she was late, even by less than a minute, he'd have to presume the rendezvous had been compromised and abandon it. Today it was scheduled for 9.30am and, despite Chan's unexpected visit, Lam had managed to get there ahead of time. He liked to be in place early so she could be sure that he'd be there, waiting for her.

Chapter Nine

Dave Sutherland pushed the Range Rover hard along Princess Margaret Road, north toward Mong Kok.

"Fuck!" he yelled. "She's been sold out and we don't even know if she's still alive."

"And Lam was clear that the threat from this Chan guy was credible?"

"A superintendent of police threatening that your contact will be dead by lunchtime's pretty fucking credible, man."

"And we can't call her?"

"No, it would break protocol. All we can do is get as close as we can to the factory in Mong Kok and hope that she makes the meet with Lam in—" Sutherland checked his watch, "—thirteen minutes. If she doesn't, then we're going in."

Both men had discarded their jackets and were wearing the HKPD-issue police vests. They were hurtling at breakneck pace down the highway, weaving in and out of the three lanes crammed with vehicles, past advertising billboards covering high-density developments, and through the sweeping bend around King's Park as they prepared to exit. They raced beneath a pedestrian overpass; a banner that read *If You Drink, Don't Drive* in English and Chinese was lashed to the railings. On the left Morgan saw a Caltex and a Shell petrol station positioned end-to-end just ahead of a big blue sign that indicated they were fast approaching a sharp left turn to Ho Man Tin, a half-left toward Mong Kok or else straight ahead along Route 1 to Sha Tin. Double-decker buses just like those back in London were everywhere, and as they reached another bend in the road, Sutherland pulled into the far left-hand lane for Mong Kok, pushing the car into high revs.

"I don't like it," he said. "This Chan guy is a new development. The fact that he even knows about Reigns is bad news."

"And how the fuck do they know about Lam's connection to us – to Interpol, I mean?" Morgan mused. "How far now?"

"A couple more miles. Fuck it!" Sutherland thumped the steering wheel. "We can't lose her."

"We won't, Dave," Morgan replied. "Just stop driving like a grandma and get us there."

As they headed onto an off-ramp, the speed limit suddenly dropped to fifty kilometers per hour, with warnings painted on the tarmac to SLOW DOWN, but Sutherland ignored it all, planting his foot down firmly and sideswiping a taxi along the right shoulder. The Range Rover surged off the narrow ramp at 65 mph. The move nearly cost them a collision with a bus but Sutherland skillfully redeemed himself and was on track to regain some ground when an old woman, struggling along behind a walking frame with bulky shopping bags strapped to it, wandered out on to the pedestrian crossing at Nairn House, oblivious to the fast-approaching, two-and-a-half-ton Range Rover with a maniacal Texan at the wheel.

Sutherland was left with no choice; he stood on the brakes and grit his teeth. Morgan's eyes fixed on the old woman and his hands tightened hard against the plush interior of the vehicle, leaving permanent impressions in the leather trim of the armrests. The gap between them and the woman diminished terrifyingly fast, every yard of road disappearing beneath the car quicker than the last. Morgan's field of view was consumed only by the old woman's face, which she had now turned to them, petrified. She was standing dead still in the center of their lane. The anti-lock braking technology of the vehicle worked perfectly but it was a tense few seconds before Sutherland's pull to the left saw them flash past, missing her by only a couple of feet.

Sutherland recovered the vehicle, stamped on the gas and spun the wheel hard left onto Argyle Street. They raced beneath the overpass and through the busy intersection of Argyle and Waterloo, continuing straight down the narrow double lanes of Argyle before they merged into four again as they headed toward the markets.

"We just crossed Sai Yee Street," Morgan called out. "Time now is zero-nine-two-five."

"Roger that," Sutherland replied. "This traffic is no goddamn help."

"You're making good time, Dave. Let's focus on the possibility that she's alive and well at the meet with Lam, and we won't even be needed."

"You trying to convince me or yourself?"

"Me."

They ploughed through the congestion, weaving in and

out between cars, trucks and buses. A string of restaurants, followed by a 7/11 and then a Panasonic billboard flashed past on their right before Sutherland spotted the left turn he was looking for directly ahead.

"Hang on!"

Morgan extracted the black ski-mask from his pocket and prepared to pull it on.

Then, as the Range Rover screamed off the main road and down a narrow single-lane side street, the shrill peal of Sutherland's phone told them a text had been received. Morgan grabbed it.

"It's a message from Lam."

Chapter Ten

He saw her.

Lam made sure he was leaning forward in his seat. It was one of their agreed signals and meant "OK, but proceed with caution." If he'd been leaning back it would mean that everything was definitely not OK and she should immediately abort the meeting. He knew she'd now be searching for the second sign: his coffee cup positioned on the left-hand corner of the table, pointing directly toward her direction of approach, although it would be difficult to see, given the constant motion around them. Thankfully a break in the crowd allowed him a clear view of her and she of him. Her bag was slung over her left shoulder, meaning "all clear." His face turned to her for a micro-second, and while the cup and bag were sufficient acknowledgment to assure each other that they were clear and their meeting could proceed, he was troubled by the expression on her face. It was the first time he'd seen her look like this. Normally brimming with confidence, this morning she was scared.

Lam watched intently as she crossed the last few yards to his table. She was tall and fair-skinned, with long black hair pulled into a braid, her body lean and fit beneath tight black pants and Mandarin collar jacket. This morning her deep brown eyes were shaded behind fake Prada sunglasses. That was unusual. But she had made it and she was alive.

He quickly tapped out a text to Interpol: *She's here. All OK. Standby.*

They were now over a month into the operation and Lam was confident that Mei-Zhen Tan knew all she needed to know about this place, including all the alternative routes between here and the illegal factory she had infiltrated. At a glance, she could orient herself north-south and, importantly, she had memorized the random assortment of cafes and stalls they had preselected as their primary and secondary meeting points. The market had been chosen because it was close to her workplace and it was busy. It also fitted her cover as a newcomer to Hong Kong; irregular visits to a favorite new market were to be expected should somebody be taking an interest in her movements about the city.

"Good morning," she said quietly, as she sat down opposite him.

"Good morning," Lam replied, and gestured to the green tea he'd bought for her. "Are you all right? You seem …"

Mei-Zhen Tan removed her sunglasses and Lam saw fresh bruising around her right eye and cheek.

"My God!" he hissed under his breath, careful not to draw attention. His fists clenched upon the table. "Who did this to you?"

"It's OK," she began, calmly replacing her glasses. "I

was punished for getting in someone's way. It could've been worse."

"It's not OK. I understood that the objective of getting you a job in that place was to enable you to get your eyes on their financial records, so that we – I mean, you and Interpol – could try to establish a connection to the principal operators." He looked around quickly to ensure they weren't being overheard. "Specifically Wu Ming. That's the only reason I agreed to this."

"I can take care of myself," she said. "But I can tell you, things aren't good in that place right now."

"Things have changed out here, too, Mei-Zhen," he said, frustrated. "Something happened to me this morning and I must tell you about it before we go any further. When I've told you, I know you'll agree we have no choice but to pull you out and establish 'round-the-clock surveillance on the factory instead."

She took a deep breath. "I'm not ready to pull out, Victor."

"Please, Mei-Zhen. Let me tell you this first."

"Go ahead, but it better be convincing."

"The operation is blown," he began, not pulling any punches. Lam took her through his confrontation with Chan back at the station. She remained silent throughout, listening intently as they maintained a systematic yet discreet surveillance of the area. When he'd finished, she asked about Chan, obviously looking for background on him and the credibility of his threats. Lam revealed he'd held concerns about his superior's loyalties for many years. He concluded by telling her that he had just spoken with the Interpol contact, the American, with whom he had been required to communicate over the past month.

"What did you tell him?" she asked, obviously troubled. "Does he know about this Chan person yet?"

"Of course."

"Damn it!"

"I contacted him specifically because of Chan. Have I done something wrong? The American is your contact, the one that you connected me with."

"What did he say?"

"He told me to stay put and that he would make contact with me here."

"He's on the way here? Did he say anything else ... anything about me?"

"Well, no. We don't go into detail on the phone. Have they tried to contact you?"

She shook her head. "That would be against protocol. No, he'll wait to hear from me."

Lam swallowed, thinking that he had made some monumental mistake, despite the fact that he had been following Interpol's instructions. Then he blurted out, "Wait. When I saw you just now I sent him a message that you were OK and to standby."

"And have you heard back from him?"

Lam grappled his phone from the table. He saw the message displayed on the screen and turned it around for her to see.

ACK. Standing by. Local.

She relaxed slightly, but was still clearly troubled, glancing around, searching in every direction.

"Listen, Victor, I'm not pulling out. Not yet, anyway. We're close, really close."

"Have you not heard a word I've said? Chan told me we'll be dead by lunchtime if we don't shut this down. They know about you. Haven't you risked enough already? Going back in there—"

"How many years have you been hunting these guys?" she asked. "And what about all of the effort that's gone into getting us this far? You can't seriously think I'm about to pull out now."

He glanced down and remained quiet. She leaned closer to him across the table.

"Listen, you're a good man and nailing these guys is personal for you. Believe me, I get it." The warmth in her tone reassured him. "You need to have faith, Victor. There's backup now. You're not on your own anymore, but that's as much as I can say. I'll leave it to my colleague to fill you in."

"OK, OK," he responded, rubbing his face with his hands. "Will you people ever let me in on whatever or whoever it is you're really after?"

"When the time is right," she said. "Just understand that this is one piece of a much bigger pie."

A quick, unexpected movement caught Lam's attention and he narrowed his eyes as he tried hard to determine who it was. A split second of anxiety gripped him when he realized it was someone he knew.

Chapter Eleven

The sound of fingernails drumming impatiently against the rough wooden surface of the table was the only sound to be heard in the smoke-filled room. The three heavily armed men positioned around the walls remained absolutely silent.

Wu Ming sat at one end of the table with his back to the large window overlooking the factory floor. The black silk jacket he wore strained at the seams. His perfectly round head was completely bald and his lined skin was the color of copper. His eyes were tar-black slits with no visible sign of the whites at all. He was still well muscled for a man of his age although a paunch had developed over the years. The big hands resting on the table, one drumming its surface, the other holding a cigarette, were like rocks waiting to be hurled at someone. Everything about him exuded cruelty.

The door at the far end of the room opened and a man wearing the uniform of a Hong Kong Police Force chief superintendent entered. Two younger men in black suits, white shirts and black ties followed him in. They remained at the back of the room, either side of the door. The policeman took up the seat he was directed to, immediately to the right of Wu Ming.

"I'm sorry I am late," Chief Superintendent Chan Man-kin said awkwardly. He was used to wielding authority but not in this company. "I'm afraid it was unavoidable."

"You have some news for me, Freddy?" Wu Ming answered, disdainfully. "Is there a problem?"

"Yes, it concerns Inspector Victor Lam. You recall that name?"

"Of course. I shot him years ago. Sadly, he did not die. So, he's an inspector now. What of it?"

"It has come to my attention that he is collaborating with Interpol." Chan risked a direct glance at Wu to reinforce the significance of the information, but received no reaction. "I believe he has recently managed to infiltrate this very factory with an undercover policewoman, possibly herself an agent of Interpol."

Wu Ming remained outwardly unmoved although the drumming on the table abruptly stopped. "And how do you know this?" he asked.

"I have a reliable source who works in the office of the assistant commissioner responsible for this district. My source tells me that Lam is reporting to the assistant commissioner personally on this. No other areas of the department are involved."

"Who is the assistant commissioner?"

"Kwong," Chan replied.

Wu Ming appeared to deliberate for a moment, considering the name.

"What about this policewoman, who is she?"

"I don't have a name but I have a photograph. One of my officers just took it. Very pretty," Chan said lasciviously.

He removed a cell phone from the pocket of his shirt, tapped the screen to open the gallery, and handed it across. "Do you know her?"

Wu Ming did nothing more than pass a cursory glance over the image. His visits to his factories were so rare he didn't have the first clue what any of the staff looked like. Instead, one of the men behind him stepped forward, looked at the picture and mumbled something in Wu's ear. He summoned one of the black suits standing by the door. The man instantly appeared at his master's side and also looked at the image. He nodded and inclined his head in the direction of the factory office. Wu took in a long breath through his nostrils and slowly released it. He nodded to the black suit, dismissing him. The man returned to his position by the door.

"What are you doing about Inspector Lam, Freddy?"

"I have two officers following him as we speak. They believe Lam is being investigated for corruption," Chan answered. "He went to the Mong Kok market to meet this girl. They are both there now."

Wu Ming stood up and walked slowly across to the shelves that overflowed with the materials and tools needed to keep the apparel manufacturing side of the business operating. "I need to go and receive the little Russian bitch. I want her to keep thinking she's actually in control. In the meantime, you bring Lam to me here, immediately," he said, poking idly through the paraphernalia on the shelves until he extracted a large pair of scissors, a screwdriver and a hammer. He weighed this in his hand then, addressing the man in the suit, added, "The moment the girl returns, you bring her in here and question her while I think what to do with her. I want to know how much she knows and what she has passed on to her superiors."

The men in the black suits nodded obediently and disappeared in silence. Wu Ming turned to the rest of the room, gesticulating with the hammer.

"Get out there, find whoever it was who hired her and drag them in here right now!"

Chapter Twelve

Still without knowing who he'd seen, Lam's mind was screaming at him. It was definitely someone familiar; someone whose details were stored deep within his subconscious. Who was it? A cop? His mind trawled through the possibilities, trying to recreate a composite image from the blur he had seen. He stared over Mei-Zhen's right shoulder into the crowd, searching for the face. He could sense her tensing in response to his sudden preoccupation. She was preparing to disappear when he raised his hand just an inch above the table.

"No. It's OK," he rasped. "Don't move."

"What was that?" she asked. "You looked like someone just walked over your grave."

"Maybe they did," he replied without humor, still searching.

"Are we good?" She took a deep, controlled breath.

He nodded although he was still unsettled. There was just too much activity. Too many faces. Who had he seen?

Lam was conflicted. Despite Chan's threats to their lives,

the uncertainty surrounding the operation's viability and his instinct telling him he should convince Mei-Zhen not to go back in, he was also a cop impatient for progress; probably more so than her. He couldn't stomach the idea of the operation being derailed, especially now. Chan's warning to him was proof that they were on to something.

Lam had spent most of his career working these cases, identifying the emerging players, their weaknesses and patterns of operation. He had been pushing shit uphill for years, but now he knew them all – the big names in the region. The involvement of the Triads in human trafficking was his particular specialty and it had made him very unpopular in certain circles. The forced labor trade was an accepted part of life in this part of the world and the operators who kept it running were well connected. But he was determined to continue; so determined, in fact, that he had kept the details of Interpol's infiltration of the factory from his immediate superiors, convincing them that he was merely assisting an intelligence analyst in a mid-level investigation. Only Assistant Commissioner Kwong knew the real story and even that had been sanitized. Maybe Chan was right. Maybe Lam was nothing more than an annoyance to the hierarchy and they saw this Interpol connection as a final 'make or break' – with emphasis on the 'break'.

Mei-Zhen had spent a month working at the factory and, despite her best efforts, had found nothing that, from an evidentiary perspective, could link Wu Ming unequivocally to its operation or the transnational human trafficking consortium to which he was suspected of belonging. The fact that the factory ran exclusively on the back of forced labor was an issue that, to date, had been overlooked by the powers that be – Wu Ming was too well connected. But if there was even the slightest hope of cracking the consortium, or even just Wu Ming's part in it, Lam felt that they had to try, no matter what the personal risk to them both. If they made it through then maybe he would finally retire and leave Hong Kong for good.

"So, if you are hell-bent on going back in there, tell me why," he found himself asking her. "Tell me what has changed."

"Things there were going along without incident; all routine, nothing noteworthy. But there's been a significant buildup of activity over the past week, and out of nowhere two new arrivals showed up. Mid-level management types in identical black suits, obviously nothing to do with the factory stuff."

"Enforcers, coming in ahead of someone important?"

"That's exactly what I thought ... like a recon team. They arrived without notice, even the factory managers were caught off guard, and within no time these new guys started getting rough – with everybody." She gestured to her bruised face. "If you get in their way, even just walking past ... well, enough said."

Lam drank his coffee and lit another cigarette; he knew not to offer her one. Instead, he remained silent as she continued.

"Late yesterday one of the factory supervisors was beaten within an inch of his life because something wasn't done right. I don't know what. It all happened downstairs and I couldn't see from my desk in the office, but I heard the commotion as it erupted. One of my colleagues called me over and I managed to get a look. Downstairs, the two new arrivals were standing over the supervisor. He was cowering on the floor with blood all over his face and shirt. The entire factory, over a hundred people, just kept working, blind with fear. Then the new guys left him lying there and paid us a visit upstairs."

"So, what then?" Lam asked, as his attention was once again distracted. Was he being paranoid, or was there something really obvious going on here that he was missing? The sense that they were close to success, close to something big, was overwhelming. His professional mind and ego were telling him to stay put and let the operation continue to run, but his gut, his body's self-preservation mechanism, was telling him otherwise. He began scouring faces in the crowd. "Sorry, please go on."

"OK, now you've got me worried. Let's get this done ASAP in case we have to vamoose. The beating seemed to be nothing more than a demonstration. Letting everyone know who's boss ahead of someone even bigger arriving. Sure enough, yesterday a man arrived with a full entourage of lackeys and bodyguards." Mei-Zhen pulled out her cell phone and sent an image to his. It arrived on Lam's cell with a ping. "I managed to snap this late yesterday. It's only a partial, I know, but … it's him, right?"

"Wu Ming!"

"There's no mistaking him. I can't remember how many hours I spent looking at pictures of him before I came out here to Hong Kong. Everyone in the place was terrified when he walked in. They all knew who he was, that's for sure."

"It's him," Lam whispered, barely able to believe it. "He's much heavier than when I last saw him but there's no mistaking those black eyes of his. You ran a hell of a risk taking this photo."

"I had to. Anyway, you have it now. You told me once that you'd seen him up close," she said. "Care to expand?"

"It's definitely him," said Lam. A flood of memories hit

him. "It was 1988," he began, eyes still fixed on the screen. "Back then, Wu Ming was just an emerging player in the Hong Kong crime scene, a gangland enforcer who controlled certain corners of Kowloon through violence and cruelty. At the time, I was a newly promoted sergeant, recently appointed to Organized Crime. I was part of a joint operation with Narcotics to bust a drug ring operating within the Walled City. You ever heard of it?"

"Of course," she replied. "But I thought you guys never ventured into that place?"

"Some of us did," Lam said, remembering. "One day I chased Wu and another man, Lai, into the Walled City. It was all dead ends and alleyways, and so dark ... there was water everywhere. I chased him and chased him until we ended up in a stand-off that turned into a gunfight. They shot at me and I shot back. I killed Lai and got three bullets in my guts from Wu. He disappeared and I was left for dead. A local man dragged me clear and left me out in the open on the edge of the city, where I could be found by my squad."

"I had no idea," she said. "No wonder this is personal for you."

"You know, I've spent twenty-five years pursuing Wu Ming and I've never managed to track him down until now. Thanks to you."

"Well, don't pop the champagne just yet. I have more."

"What? Tell me."

"Something big's about to go down there. It's not just about Mr Wu being in town. I know there's something else."

Lam remained absolutely quiet, waiting for her to begin.

"The beatings continued last night and there'd been more this morning before I arrived. Extra muscle arrived last night, too, after Wu Ming and his crew. They looked

European. Russian, maybe. Real bad guys. All gym junkies in suits that were way too small for them, and all with buzz haircuts and gang tattoos on their hands and necks."

"How many?"

"Half-a-dozen or so. They marched in like stormtroopers and cleared us all out, even the two enforcers in the black suits made themselves scarce around these guys. Someone important was about to arrive and they didn't want any of the riff-raff to see."

"Someone more important than Wu Ming?"

"Yeah, and when she arrived everything changed."

"She?"

"She," Mei-Zhen confirmed. "And she *is* the main show."

"Can you ID her?"

"Not yet. Like I said, they cleared us all out, but I heard the commotion and her voice for just a few seconds. She was issuing orders to someone as they walked in and she definitely sounded Russian."

"If you didn't see her, how can you be sure she's the one in charge?" Lam asked.

"Because when she spoke, everyone else was instantly silent. She didn't have to raise her voice and, even though I only heard her for a few seconds, she had authority over all of them. She sounded almost sultry. Eastern European. Have you ever heard of someone like that operating here in Hong Kong?"

Lam shook his head. Even the thought of an Eastern European woman operating on Triad turf was almost impossible to comprehend. "So we still don't know what she looks like?" he said.

"That's the whole reason I have to go back in. She's due

in this morning. Last night was just a recce. Today they have a meeting upstairs. There could even be others coming."

"Mei-Zhen, at this point in my life, and after so many years committed to bringing these people down, I'm prepared to do just about anything. You and your people obviously know more than I do, and it's paying off. But do you really think you should go back in?"

"I can take care of myself."

Lam believed her.

"Anyway, if what you say about this Chan person is correct, he hasn't dropped the hammer on us – yet. He's giving you the chance to shut it down before he rats on you. That means we should have at least until lunchtime to ID this woman. Remember, as far as they're concerned, I'm just an out-of-town half-blood who needs the money and speaks the language. Besides, now that the queen bee has arrived, they want me around as errand girl. This meeting is happening soon and I have to get back for it. We can't afford to miss the opportunity." She glanced at her watch. "I gotta go."

"OK." He still had doubts, but he knew that she was right. "I'll settle up and leave in two minutes, and Mei-Zhen …" He looked at her earnestly. "Please be careful."

She stood up, smiled and walked away, disappearing into the throng of locals and tourists. Lam watched her for as long as he could, keeping an eye out for any untoward interest. Satisfied, he rummaged through his trouser pocket, extracted some change and dropped it on the table. Then he lit a fresh cigarette and strolled casually away.

Victor Lam took the opposite direction from Mei-Zhen, heading north along Tung Choi Street toward Mong Kok railway station. He wanted to buy her some time before reporting back to the Interpol contact. He kept his wits about him, constantly checking to see if he was being followed, but once he was about quarter of a mile away he felt confident he was clear. He immersed himself in the crowded streets, his thoughts awash with images of Wu Ming and what Mei-Zhen may be heading into. He still couldn't get his mind off the face that he'd seen through the crowds at the market and was frustrated that he couldn't recall where he'd seen the man before. And had it been just one man, or could it have been two?

Something wasn't right. Now that he was away from the meeting and thinking more clearly, Lam realized that sending Mei-Zhen back in had been a mistake. He was regretting not calling the man from Interpol first before agreeing that she would go back in. His gut was telling him the time had come to summon backup, and if he needed things to happen quickly then he had to call on the support of the only man he trusted. He extracted his cell phone from a pocket. He didn't want to make the call but felt he had no choice.

"Kowloon West District," the call was answered in Cantonese.

"Put me through to Assistant Commissioner Kwong," he replied. "This is Inspector Lam from the OCTD." He took a deep breath as he waited to be connected.

"Lam?"

"Sir, I'm sorry to trouble you," he began. He didn't know how much he could say on an open line.

"Yes?"

"I'm in Mong Kok. I've just had a meeting with an informant at the markets. I'm concerned that my operation has been compromised—"

The squeal of tires diverted him from his conversation back to the street. His head turned in the direction of the car but his reaction was too slow and as the car's wheels locked into a sudden skid, Lam saw rather than felt it hit him. The impact had been perfectly calculated to stun and injure rather than to kill, and Lam was thrown to the ground. His left side took the brunt of the impact with the pavement, followed by his head. Dazed and bleeding, he rolled painfully onto his back, his legs still beneath the car. His cell phone clattered against the iron shutter of a store front.

Two men in identical black suits worn with white shirts and black ties, appeared above him. A gun was drawn and pointed at his head.

Chapter Thirteen

Following a different route from the one she had used on her way to meet Lam, Elizabeth Reigns worked her way through the crowded streets and alleyways of Mong Kok. Careful to discourage unwanted company, she followed the usual counter-surveillance drills back to the factory, all the while outwardly maintaining the persona of Mei-Zhen Tan. Adhering to the tradecraft fundamentals that Intrepid's Tom Rodgers and his assistant Sophie Tavernier had taken her through back in England was instinctive to Reigns now. After six weeks in-country and over a month of that working within the illegal factory as Mei-Zhen, tradecraft had become her default, her lifeline. Such was her mindset that recollections of her training sessions with Rodgers and Tavernier down in The Pit, Intrepid's secret close-quarters combat training center, deep beneath the streets of Westminster, now seemed no more than an obscure dream to her. She was no longer a candidate under assessment; she had risen to the status of agent-nominee, and success on this, her first operation, would see conferred on her that greatest of honors: becoming an agent of Intrepid. Of course, no one outside the agency could ever know that.

Elizabeth Reigns could scarcely believe how much her life had changed since that chance meeting with General Davenport during her presentation to the Protection Project expert panel a little over a year ago. Now here she was, on the other side of the world, where lessons learned in training were essential to her survival. She was neck deep in the cold reality of an agent's life.

Ten minutes after leaving Lam at the market, Reigns turned down the narrow lane, tightly packed with crates and trash, that led to the rear entrance to the factory. The familiar stench of rotting vegetables and fish hit her, catching at the back of her throat. She fought the impulse to gag, took a final look into the street and, satisfied, stepped up to the door. From the outside it looked like so many others in the vicinity, wooden and painted no particular color, only this door was reinforced with steel and had a viewing portal. She tapped twice, knowing her identity was being verified by CCTV at three different angles. After a few seconds of waiting for her image to be confirmed and checks to ensure that she was alone, the slide was pulled back with a metallic clang and a pair of shaded brown eyes – belonging to an armed guard – conducted the primitive but nonetheless effective final step in the access-control process. Then the portal closed and the door creaked open just enough for her to enter.

Inside, the entrance hall was no more than four feet square. It was whitewashed, grubby, and reeked of body odor. The guard, an automatic on his belt and a shotgun stashed behind him, sat on a stool directly behind the door, in the corner formed by the left and back walls. There was no wall to the right side. The dirty whitewash continued up a steep wooden stairway to the second-floor landing. The door on the landing opened into a small anteroom containing two more armed guards. Also covered by CCTV, this room was fortified much like an old jail cell, with heavy metal bars on the walls and ceiling and a reinforced metal floor. This was the secure airlock to the factory floor, designed to keep unwanted visitors out and factory workers in. To Reigns it seemed almost prehistoric, with not even swipe or keypad access, and the CCTV was early 1990s. As for the guards, they were local hired help: no training but paid enough to be loyal, which meant reckless and dangerous. There were three other such rooms within the factory. These performed the same purpose, controlling access to key areas, including the factory floor and worker accommodation.

Bypassing this level, Reigns continued, ascending further to the third floor, the office level where she worked. On this landing there was another steel-reinforced door. She stopped in front of it and knocked twice. While waiting for it to open, she looked down the two flights of stairs and realized that the armed guard at the entrance was staring up, scrutinizing her. It didn't usually take this long to get inside. The warning to Lam came back to her – '*dead by lunch*'. She took a sharp, involuntary breath and knocked again.

The door opened slowly, too slowly. Inside were three men instead of the usual two. Their expressions were impassive, their proximity intimidating. Reluctantly, she stepped over the threshold and walked tentatively to the rear door that connected with the office area where she worked. The door behind her slammed shut. Then the additional man, the third one, opened the next door for her but today, rather than simply being allowed to walk through on her own, the third man followed close on her heels and closed the door behind them.

She quickened her pace to distance herself from him and strode purposefully along a short corridor to the entrance to the office. When she reached the door, she turned the knob. Locked. She tried it again, rattling it loudly within the confined space. Definitely locked.

Fear filled her head and heart. She looked back at the third man, her escort, standing dispassionately a few feet from her. He jerked his head, indicating that she should proceed instead to the door further along, at the end of the corridor. It was one she had never been through before – she'd never been allowed to. On the rare occasions she'd tried, it had always been locked.

Reigns' mind raced. What lay behind that door? Did they know about her? What the fuck were her options?

As the man shepherded her toward the door, Reigns knew that all she had to fall back on was her training – she had no weapons of any kind. Her only experience was what had been learned down in The Pit on the fighting mats and on the range with Tom Rodgers. Flashes of their combat survival sessions came back to her. Step by step, scene by scene, it all returned: muscle memory and the science of it, determination and controlled aggression. Her survival instincts and hand-to-hand combat skills had been developed and honed by one of the best in the world. Rodgers had trained and tested her over and over, and she had prevailed. With that thought, she allowed fear to disperse to make room for the adrenalin that was building, returning the confidence and faith Reigns had in herself and her abilities.

They reached the door and she opened it.

Chapter Fourteen

"What time you got?" asked Sutherland.

"Ten-thirty," Morgan replied. "What are we doing for your birthday? You having a party?"

"Why the hell would I want to celebrate turning forty?"

"Because you should," replied Morgan. "Any birthday's worth celebrating in this business, especially forty."

"I'll be back in the States on the day. You're welcome to come over if you're not deployed. I think a bunch of guys from the teams want to get together at McP's for a few beers. Drown my sorrows for getting old! Otherwise, I guess we could do something in London when we get back from this one." He added, "You're right, man, every birthday is a goddamn milestone in this business."

Morgan remained silent, contemplating that disturbing reality. He knew only too well the temptation to overthink one's own mortality, and while there was plenty of time to do that when not on an operation – usually well into the last couple of scotches of the night – there was no such luxury while deployed. He had to forget he was a borderline burn-out and focus.

"I don't know if this is the right time to tell you," Sutherland began. "I'm thinking about leaving the firm."

"Seriously?" Morgan asked. "Come on, Dave. You can't let a bit of birthday misery get to you like this."

"I'm dead serious, bud. I've already flagged it with the general. He agreed we'd discuss it when I get back from this one."

"Jesus," said Morgan. "What will you do?"

"Naval Special Warfare Command has offered me a desk job training SEALS, or I might retire and do something completely different."

"What – you going to consult on movies or something?" Morgan joked. They'd both previously contemplated the idea.

"Hey, don't knock it! I'll be just like George Clooney in *Three Kings*. Can't you see me on the red carpet?"

"Jesus, get a grip. If you look like Clooney, then I look like Henry Cavill."

"Asshole!" Sutherland said. They both laughed. "Anyway, truth is, we all have a shelf life, man. There comes a time when you have to get out ahead of your expiration date."

The two of them fell silent. Sutherland had been Morgan's friend and operational partner for almost four years. Not so long in the scheme of things, but as Intrepid agents, their bond had been forged under the most dangerous circumstances and, as far as Morgan was concerned, those four years were the equivalent of about twenty for normal people. Recruited direct from the SEALS, Sutherland had been with Intrepid since its inception in 2006 and Morgan knew that General Davenport held Sutherland in the highest regard. As did Morgan.

Due to the intensity of the work there were only ever ten operational field agents at any one time. The expected tenure of an attachment to Intrepid was usually no more than five years, although the rule didn't apply if General Davenport deemed an agent exceptional. And after almost eight years, Sutherland was the only one of the original ten still on the books. One had been killed and two others had retired wounded, while the remaining six had returned to their parent organizations around the world.

Morgan felt that these facts had been bearing down on Sutherland for some time, like he'd been trying to outrun a lit fuse but was slowing and the gap was gradually closing. Morgan needed to get his friend's mind – and his own – back on the mission. And while Morgan didn't relish the thought of having to break in a new partner, they'd have to leave this talk about retirement for some other time. Meanwhile, he owed it to Sutherland to be on top of his game. Fatigue or not, he couldn't let his friend down.

"I don't like this, Dave," he said. "Sitting around out here; two foreigners in a flash Range Rover. We need to keep moving."

"You're right, bud," Sutherland replied, easing the vehicle into gear and pulling into the traffic. "I was hoping Lam might call in and give us the all clear. Their meet should have ended half an hour ago."

"How close can you get us to the factory? Just in case."

"I can get pretty close but there's nowhere to pull in over there, we'll have to keep mobile and circle the joint without being right under their noses."

"Let's do that," said Morgan. "This sitting-around-waiting shit is starting to bug me."

Without another word, Dave Sutherland moved the Range Rover skillfully through the narrow roads and lanes, driving randomly in ever-widening circles, away from the markets and toward the factory.

"Hang on a second," said Morgan. "Is it just me or are there suddenly too many HKPD patrol cars around here?"

Chapter Fifteen

Elizabeth Reigns fought hard to control her emotions. This was something the training was designed to prepare you for, mentally and physically, but you never really knew how you'd react until it actually happened.

The door opened into a large room, about thirty feet by thirty. It looked like a storage-cum-hangout room for the factory supervisors. Along three walls, metal shelves were stacked head high with boxed spools of thread, rolls of fabric, packets of zips, buttons, pins, needles and scissors scattered in every spare bit of space, even spilling from the lower shelves onto the floor. The room was lit by a dirty, chain-hung fluorescent tube and a large window on the far right wall that overlooked the workshop below. Beneath the window was a wooden table with an assortment of mismatched chairs scattered untidily around it. The table was strewn with newspapers, porn, ashtrays and unfinished coffee. It stank of sweat and cigarette smoke. To her left, Reigns saw a wooden chair lying on its side in a pool of blood, with a pair of men's shoes and four lengths of rope.

There were signs of something large having been dragged from the center of the mess and taken out through the door in the opposite corner. A hammer, covered in blood, lay on the floor nearby.

Ten feet from her, directly beneath the fluorescent tube in the center of the room, Inspector Victor Lam lay in a crumpled heap on the floor. He was on his side, wrists and ankles bound, clenched hands covering his face and knees pulled up tight to protect his abdomen as two men kicked the shit out of him. Reigns got the impression that this was just the softening up process, 'the appetizer', as Rodgers would have called it.

The two middle-management enforcers were nearly identical: Chinese, late twenties, about five-eight, with slicked-back hair. When she'd first seen them, in their black suits, black shoes, white shirts and thin ties, Reigns had thought it must have been some bizarre homage to Tarantino's *Reservoir Dogs*. She tagged the first one as Mr Black and the second Mr Blue. Somehow, the private joke gave her confidence amid the stark terror she was trying to fight back. Mr Black was more solidly built than Mr Blue and he was the one who had beaten her when she had tried to protect Chi. They stopped what they were doing when they registered her arrival. Leaving the badly smashed-up Lam in the fetal position, groaning and spitting blood, they turned to face her. A pair of starving street dogs preparing to pounce on a cat.

"The pretty secretary is back," said Mr Black slyly, swaggering up to her and bouncing on his toes, trying to achieve a height advantage over Reigns' five-ten. It wasn't working. "How are you, little flower?"

Before she could speak, the back of his left hand smashed her hard across the right cheek, the very spot he had targeted the day before. Reigns stumbled under the force of the impact, the already bruised flesh and bone absorbing it all. Her eyes filled with tears but she remained upright. Dazed and unsteady, she lifted a shaking hand but was slapped again with equal force. She let out a cry of anger and brought both hands up to her face, tears streaming. Mr Black struck a third time, this time from the other side. Reigns allowed herself to crumple to her knees. It was what he was looking for – to subdue her and bring her well beneath his own eyeline, asserting his power.

She looked up, awaiting another assault. Instead, Mr Black sneered, snatched her handbag, which had fallen to the floor, and retrieved her phone. He waved it in front of her face like a trophy and, without looking, clicked his fingers. Mr Blue responded by placing a cell phone – obviously taken from Lam – into Mr Black's hand.

"Now, let's connect the dots," he said. For a few moments he thumbed the keypads of both phones until a look of triumph appeared on his face. He pressed his thumb down on one and, inevitably, the other rang. "And so we have it – book-keeper by day and friend of the police by night."

He lifted Lam's phone in one clenched fist and prepared to strike her again when a muffled voice from the floor caught his attention.

"She is my niece, you bastards," groaned Lam. "Let her go. I told you, she has nothing to do with any of this."

Mr Blue responded by kicking and stomping on the inspector. Mr Black watched the assault with the casual indifference of a man waiting for an empty chair in a barber shop.

"That's not what we have heard, Police Inspector Lam," he said, waving one finger at him. Mr Blue kept kicking.

"We have a mutual friend who told us that this bitch is not your niece. No, she is your plant. A policewoman from Interpol!"

"Ridiculous," Lam managed breathlessly. "You've got it wrong."

"Maybe, but we're not taking any chances. Not with the Witch arriving—" he checked his watch, "—in less than ten minutes."

"Witch?" mumbled Lam. "What does a witch have to do with us?"

"Nothing," replied Mr Black. "Although she'll probably enjoy watching you both die. I believe she likes to watch. But don't worry. Your old friend Wu Ming is waiting to see you, and your pretty little *niece* is going to be given to the Witch as a gift."

"Let us go!" Reigns cried out as loud as she could, taking the opportunity to straighten up and fill her lungs. She felt blood coursing through her body again, preparing. She took a mental snapshot of the room, tagging Mr Black and Mr Blue directly in front of her and the third man, the guard, behind her.

"No, we won't be letting you go, pretty secretary," Mr Black replied. "That would not make the boss man very happy. He's promised you to the Witch and that's what's going to happen. Now, by the look of it, there's one other number in here that you've contacted recently." He thumbed through her phone. "Unusual for a young woman, wouldn't you say, inspector? So sad, your niece doesn't have many friends."

Regaining her composure, Reigns could see that Mr Black was calling the other most recently used number on her phone – Dave Sutherland's.

It was now or never.

Reigns brought her attack mode online. The thought of Dave Sutherland receiving a call from her, strictly against protocol, was all she needed to reinforce the harsh reality of her new profession. She was an Intrepid agent, obliged to consider herself the last line of defense in protecting the rights of the weak and vulnerable, any time and anywhere in the world, no matter what the cost. Well, that time had come.

Theatrically, Mr Black placed her phone on speaker and held it high above his head so they could all hear it. The phone rang twice before it connected. The hollow crackle of open airwaves filled the room. A surly grin of conquest was smeared across Mr Black's face, mirrored on that of his obedient dog, Mr Blue. They waited and waited. The call had been answered yet there was nothing but silence at the other end. Reigns watched Mr Black intently. She saw his self-assurance fade as he listened, mesmerized by the quiet. He was expecting the caller to ask for her, only it didn't happen. Silence filled the room. Mr Blue stopped kicking Lam.

Reigns knew exactly what this was. The call to Sutherland from her cell phone was off schedule. At the other end of the line, Sutherland too was waiting, listening.

Annoyed, Mr Black looked straight at the phone and said, with all the menace he could muster, "Who the fuck is this? Answer!"

With Mr Black's attention on the phone, Reigns called out with everything she had their pre-arranged crisis word: "AVENGER!"

Mr Black and Mr Blue looked blankly at her, stunned by the randomness of her cry. In that moment, she sprang into action. She snapped into a fighting stance, finely tuned muscle memory positioning her: right foot slightly back, knees bent, legs shoulder width apart. Her hands came straight up to her face balled into fists, right hand to the side, left hand leading. The extent of her fear and submission had mostly been an act and now months of dedicated training and drilled precision took control. Mr Black stared, utterly perplexed, realizing too late what was about to happen.

With the power of a hydraulic press generating from her back and shoulders, Reigns executed an explosive right cross, connecting with the point of Mr Black's jaw. She felt the elation of a perfectly placed hit and immediately followed with a textbook combination: left foot jab to his chest and right foot round kick to the side of his head. Her muscular right leg unfurled with a crack like whiplash, driving Mr Black from his feet and across the floor. She spun and dropped into a push-up position, facing back the way she had entered, staring straight at the knees of the third man. He had drawn a weapon, an automatic, from the waistband of his trousers and was attempting to fire as she vanished beneath his line of sight.

Using his confusion to her advantage, she pushed off with her hands and twisted on to her back, scything her long legs around in a semicircle to sweep the guard's legs out from under him. The man fell in a heap on the floor, his weapon clattering from his hand. Reigns continued her attack, scissoring his head and neck with her calves before locking him in tight between her knees. As he grappled to pull himself free she struck fiercely at the side of his head with two unrestrained blows that took him to the verge of unconsciousness. Releasing him, she grabbed his gun, leaped to her feet and finished him off with a kick to the head. Reigns' decimation of Mr Black and the guard had taken just seconds.

In a flash she was facing down Mr Blue with the guard's gun in her hand. Mr Blue, smiling nervously but unsure, had Lam by the hair and the muzzle of an automatic against his temple. Mr Blue began to issue a threat, but without hesitation, Elizabeth Reigns fired twice into the center of his body. The rounds hit his chest and he slumped across Inspector Lam. To her left, Mr Black was recovering, a gun in his hand. Coldly, efficiently, Reigns turned to him with the weapon locked steady in both hands and fired again.

Both rounds hit Mr Black in the face.

Chapter Sixteen

Sutherland forced the Range Rover through mountains of alleyway trash like a snowplow. The big vehicle managed to get through it, almost to the end of the narrow alley, but before they hit the wall, Sutherland turned sharply to the left, using the leading side bumper to breach the entrance to the factory, splintering the door.

Morgan, already out, hurled himself across the bonnet. Shooting the first guard, caught between the wall and the vehicle, he slid through the fractured door and powered up the stairs with Sutherland hot on his heels. The two agents were a few steps short of the first landing when the door opened and a hand appeared holding an automatic, firing blindly down the stairway. Sutherland braced himself against the rail and unleashed a barrage of rounds at the hand and into the confined space behind it. Under his covering fire, Morgan took the last few steps and shouldered his way into the room, firing at the two men inside. Sutherland joined him.

"Two down," Morgan said, after verifying both guards were dead.

Sutherland moved quickly past and was ready to burst through the next door when they heard gunfire from the floor above. "Upstairs!" he yelled.

In the time it took them to head for the stairs, the door to the third-floor secure airlock burst open and a battered and bruised Elizabeth Reigns appeared, supporting a staggering Inspector Lam with one arm. She had an automatic in her right hand and was dragging the policeman clear of the room.

Sutherland momentarily lifted his ski-mask so that Reigns could see who he was. "You called for home delivery?" he said, with a broad smile.

"Thank God!" she exclaimed when she saw them. "There are more coming, guys, lots more. We've got to get out of here!"

"Cover me," Morgan yelled to Sutherland. Reaching Reigns, he said, "I'll take him now. You get down to the Range Rover and drive."

Without another word, Sutherland raced up the stairs and covered the door. Morgan grabbed Lam and slung him over his shoulder in a fireman's lift, and Reigns sprinted down the stairs. The sounds of yelling and heavy footfalls above told them they had run out of time. It sounded like half-a-dozen men, if not more, were about to come barreling out of the third-floor airlock.

Reigns reached the downstairs entrance in a few bounds. Morgan watched as she checked that there weren't any unexpected gunmen waiting for them outside, then clambered over the bonnet, jumped behind the wheel and reversed clear of the doorway. He was a few paces behind, Lam still across his shoulders. As he reached the street, he wrenched open the rear passenger door, threw Lam unceremoniously inside and slammed the door shut. Gunfire erupted in the stairway.

"Get going!" he said to Reigns. "Get out of the alley and wait! If you're compromised, leave us."

The engine howled as she stamped her foot to the floor and the Range Rover lurched toward the main road. In the background police sirens were wailing, getting louder. Morgan hurled himself back inside the factory. Braced against the wall, he let off almost an entire magazine over the top of Sutherland's head, who was just a few steps short of the bottom and firing back up the stairs.

"Come on, Dave!" Morgan yelled over the waves of rounds now being fired at them. Wood splintered from the walls as ricochets bounced everywhere in the narrow funnel of the stairway.

"Fuck!" Sutherland cried as he jumped the last two steps. "Fuck! Fuck!"

Morgan grabbed him and threw him outside. "Are you hit?" he said as they ran.

Sutherland reached behind his shoulder. His bloodied hand told them both he was.

With years of training and experience under their belts, the two agents instinctively fell into a break-contact drill – one man firing while the other moved, alternating as each leapfrogged past the other until clear of the firefight.

"How bad is it?" Morgan yelled, running past Sutherland, who was behind a skip, firing back at the door.

"It's OK. Just a fucking ricochet! It's nothing."

"Still want to retire?" Morgan slid in behind a pile of wooden crates, most of which had been pulverized when a retreating Reigns ran over them. Looking back, he saw their pursuers had reached the bottom of the stairs and were spilling out of the building, taking cover wherever they could across the dead end of the alleyway. Rounds were coming at the Intrepid agents from everywhere. Morgan and Sutherland were returning fire but they didn't have anywhere near enough ammo for this to go on much longer.

"Dave, you go first," Morgan yelled, changing magazines. "I'll cover you till you're clear of the alley. When you're set, call me back."

"Roger," Sutherland replied. "Stand by to give 'em everything you've got, man!" With that, he was sprinting past Morgan, zigzagging and jumping over debris as he went. Morgan was firing as fast and as furiously as he could to cover his friend's withdrawal.

"OK, Al," he heard his partner cry. "Stay left. Run straight back to me and get around the corner!"

Morgan sprinted parallel to the endless stream of ammunition from Sutherland's Sig, while behind him the rate of fire from their pursuers was ramping up, cracking and popping in his ears as he hurtled headlong for safety. The police sirens were nearby. They must have been closing in, searching for this alley among the hundreds of others. Morgan had no idea who had called them in but he hoped they'd arrive in time.

Chapter Seventeen

"Let me speak to them," said Lam from the back seat when he heard the sirens. "They need to know what has happened."

"We can't wait, Victor," Reigns replied. "As soon as my guys are clear, we're getting out of here!"

Reigns saw three HKPD squad cars racing down the street and caught sight of both Intrepid agents racing from the end of the alley in her rear-view mirror. They were wearing police vests and she remembered something Sutherland had told her. Fumbling beneath the driver's seat, she retrieved one of the same black, zip-front vests with POLICE emblazoned across the back and the HK Police crest on the front. Pulling it on, Reigns jumped from the driver's seat, waving the squad cars toward her, then faced back to the alleyway, covering her colleagues.

"Come on! Come on!" she yelled.

"We're good," Sutherland replied. "Get back in!"

The two agents, firing and moving the last few yards, covered each other every step of the way. Reigns was behind the wheel as the first rounds started to reach the Range Rover. Somehow, the bleeding and broken Inspector Lam managed to fold the back seats down flat. He reached through to the button on the dashboard that activated the rear tailgate and pressed it. All Morgan and Sutherland had to do was leap in.

"Great work, Victor!" said Reigns.

Sutherland got to the vehicle first and dived in backward as the rear door was opening, still firing to cover Morgan. When he finally leaped in beside Sutherland, Reigns put her foot down and launched the vehicle forward with a screech of tires. The rear door was wide open but they were both inside, so Sutherland reached out to close it.

"Fuck! I reckon that's about as close as I ever want to—"

It was as far as he got. His body was extended wide across the opening and the last wave of rounds from their pursuers struck Sutherland across the chest, neck and abdomen.

Chapter Eighteen

"What's the closest fucking emergency room from here?" Morgan yelled over the screaming engine noise and constant blaring of horns.

"QE ... Queen Elizabeth Hospital," Lam replied, struggling to speak or even breathe due to his own smashed ribs and concussion. He turned to Reigns. "Near King's Park."

"Get us there," cried Morgan. "Break out the trauma kit for me," he said to Lam. "It'll be under your feet. And take this. Call the hospital. Tell 'em we're coming in. Then call your boss and explain what went down. We need full HKPD support at the hospital until we can get our people involved."

Morgan tossed his phone to Lam and grabbed the trauma kit that was handed over in return. It was a small sports bag containing Israeli-made hemorrhage-control compression bandages, tourniquets, blood-clotting agents and morphine, along with other emergency items like clips, clamps, scissors and sutures. Sutherland lay cradled in Morgan's lap. Blood was everywhere. It was gushing from his neck and oozed from the wounds beneath his trousers and vest. He was still and quiet, eyes open, but he was struggling, spitting blood.

Morgan had a hand clasped down hard over the neck wound, trying desperately to apply pressure, but the blood kept coming. With his teeth and spare hand he began tearing open a bandage pack. *Fuck!* Was he shaking? No. No, he had this. He was OK. Sutherland needed him to be OK. There was no time for anything fancy, and using the anti-clot or morphine would only complicate matters for the medics at the other end. All he could do was try to stem the flow of the bleeding and keep his friend alive until they handed him over to the experts. Morgan grappled with the first bandage, wrapping it as best he could around Sutherland's neck. Then he set to work, getting him out of the vest. It was difficult – Reigns was driving as fast as she could to the hospital but the constant stop-start of the traffic and swaying of the car made everything ten times harder. Just as Morgan was getting the vest off, Sutherland starting coughing hard; blood and spit sprayed from his mouth and his eyes started rolling back. Morgan didn't say a word. He knew Reigns was going as fast as was humanly possible – yelling at her to step on it wouldn't make any difference.

Morgan saw the main damage was on Sutherland's left side. He'd been struck exactly where the Velcro fastened along the vulnerable flank area of the vest. He guessed by the amount of blood down that side that the left lung had been badly damaged, most likely collapsed. He turned his friend on to that side, allowing gravity to do what it could to keep the blood from affecting the hopefully intact right lung. Then he checked Sutherland's airway and breathing and set to work as best he could, sealing the wound and applying yet another bandage. *It's taking too long*, he thought. *It's taking too fucking long.*

Morgan went in search of other damage. "Fuck! This is impossible," he hissed under his breath. The amount of blood combined with the confined space of the rear compartment and the constant irregular motion of the vehicle as Reigns raced across Kowloon to the hospital were frustrating all his attempts to save his friend's life. In the midst of it all, he realized that Sutherland's eyes were fixed on him, silently imploring him to succeed. Morgan smiled down at him.

"Don't go getting all miserable on me, Dave," he said quietly. "I'm just making everything look worse than it is, so you can tell everyone how much of a cluster I was next time we're at the Red Lion."

The slightest flicker of a smile came from Sutherland's eyes. It wasn't much but it was enough.

"Stay with me, mate," said Morgan. "And don't go getting any ideas while I do this next bit."

Undoing Sutherland's belt and pulling down his trousers, Morgan found two more wounds, one in the lower gut and one at the top of the left thigh. Reaching beneath Sutherland, he located an exit wound in the lower back but couldn't find one in the leg. The best he could do was grab the few bandages left in the kit, tear them open with his teeth and keep padding the entry and exit wounds.

"How long?" he called to Reigns.

"Less than a mile."

Sutherland's eyes closed.

Chapter Nineteen

"I'm sorry, Victor. I know this goes against the grain for you as a police officer but this is the way it has to be for us. Dave knows that."

"I understand," Lam replied, struggling to speak. "I'll take care of him now. You must take care of yourself, too, Mei-Zhen, and your colleague."

Reigns smiled and squeezed his hand. Lam's face was battered and bleeding, and he was straining to breathe against the pain of his broken ribs. Still, he was a fighter and she knew he would hold out until the medics arrived. They were on their way. Above all, she knew he would take care of Sutherland. Reigns reached around under Lam's arm and helped Morgan prop him up against the wall outside the emergency reception area of the hospital. Then, as quickly as they dared, they carefully lifted Sutherland from the back of the Range Rover and laid him down next to Lam. Sutherland was a dead weight. He didn't look good. He was covered in blood and bandages, his eyes hadn't opened and he was completely unresponsive. Everything had happened so fast, Reigns wasn't even sure if he actually had a pulse. Morgan was adamant that he did, so she wasn't about to question it; this wasn't the time. Sutherland and Lam were where they needed to be and she knew the medics would only be minutes or even seconds away. Reigns and Morgan had to disappear.

"We've got to go," she said urgently in his ear. "We can't be here."

Morgan looked up. He was by Sutherland's side, issuing final instructions to Lam and clearly conflicted by the prospect of leaving his badly wounded friend behind. Reluctantly, he acquiesced. He wished Lam well and, turning back to Sutherland, said, "See you soon, mate."

Reigns was already at the wheel with the engine revving. Morgan jumped in beside her and the Range Rover vanished from view.

"OK," he said. "Back to the hotel, grab our things and straight to the airport."

"Airport? Why the airport? We have work to do here."

"There's work to be done but not by you and not by me," he replied. He was reloading magazines and making sure the Sigs, his and Sutherland's, were functional and fully loaded. "You're compromised and I have to get you out and back to London as soon as I can. So, yeah, we're heading to the airport. Hotel first."

Without another word, Reigns tore through the gears, racing the vehicle around the twists, turns and ramps of the hospital grounds, speeding beneath the Gascoigne Road overpass and on to the narrow double lanes of Jordan Road.

"Here, keep that handy," Morgan said, stowing Sutherland's Sig, muzzle down, in the cup holder beside the gearshift along with a spare magazine. "We're not out of the woods yet."

"Really? You think they'll come after us?"

"I wouldn't rule it out," he said. "They'll be pretty pissed that you've escaped and I'd say they'll be keen to get you back by any means possible. For as long as we're on their turf they'll have a shot. So, the sooner we get you the fuck out of Hong Kong, the better."

The mounting wail of police sirens in stereo threatened to drown out their conversation. Morgan turned and Reigns checked the mirrors. They saw two HKPD BMW motorcycles with lights flashing approaching fast along Chatham Road from the south-west as they neared the interchange leading to Princess Margaret Road. The lead cop was waving them down.

"Fuck it!" Morgan exclaimed, thumping the dashboard. "We don't need this."

"What do we do now?" Reigns asked. "We should stop, right?"

"Yeah, we should," he agreed, checking the navigation screen on the dash. "Head to that side road up ahead, it leads into Hong Kong Polytechnic. That way we can't get blocked in."

Reigns eased off the speed and drew the Range Rover expertly across the lanes of traffic and into the side road. Morgan took the Sig from the cup holder and handed it to her. She took it in her left hand, resting it in her lap well out of sight. Morgan positioned his loosely beneath the folds of his jacket. Behind them the cop eased off too and as the Range Rover pulled to a stop he coasted up alongside Reigns' window and raised his helmet visor. His colleague pulled in behind them. Reigns kept the vehicle in gear with the clutch depressed, handbrake engaged and the engine idling steadily.

"Is everything all right, officer?" she asked.

"Yes, ma'am," the officer replied. "We have orders from Assistant Commissioner Kwong to escort you wherever you need to go."

"That really won't be necessary, officer," said Morgan firmly. "But thank you and please thank the assistant commissioner."

"I'm sorry, sir, but I have my orders. Now, if you'll—"

The first rounds caught them all off guard.

As the heavy burst peppered the side of the Range Rover and the police officer speaking to her, Reigns had no choice. She released the clutch, pushed the accelerator flat to the floor and disengaged the handbrake in one fluid motion, pushing the revs instantly to red. The vehicle roared away from a standing start just as the second officer began to engage the as-yet-unseen source of the incoming gunfire. Morgan instinctively clambered between the front seats to the back section of the Range Rover. When his Sig Sauer P226 exploded into action behind her, Reigns knew that Morgan had acquired the target.

"It's a black Alfa Romeo sedan!" he yelled. "Can you see it?"

"Got it!" Reigns replied. In the driver's side wing mirror she could make out a guy hanging from the Alfa, awkwardly clutching what looked like a Chinese-made QBZ-97 assault rifle. They were closing fast. The guy was changing mags and about to re-engage. Morgan was blasting away as best he could but the Sig was no match for sustained fire from an assault rifle.

"We need cover," he said. "Get us out of here!"

Reigns tore the wheel to the left, heading down the side

road toward the Polytechnic. The Alfa followed. A second later she realized it had been a mistake.

"Jesus!" she cried. "Gate! The road's blocked." Thinking fast, Reigns sized up her options. Morgan was still firing but it wouldn't be long before they were blocked, totally outgunned, and others arrived to support the Alfa. It was directly behind them, closing fast and twenty feet from their rear bumper while the Range Rover was bearing down upon the heavy metal gates blocking access to the Polytechnic. With a quick final glance at the mirrors, Reigns made her decision.

"Brace yourself. Now!"

Morgan grabbed on to anything he could find.

She stamped on the brakes and the Range Rover responded, coming to a sudden but controlled dead stop in the center of the road. The driver of the Alfa Romeo had no time to counter the move and the sedan slammed into the rear of them. Morgan was thrown hard against the back of Reigns' seat and groaned as the wind was forced from his lungs. She wasted no time. At the moment of collision, she threw the big car into a tight U-turn, tires squealing, and opened up the exposed flank of the unsuspecting stalled Alfa to a broadside. Morgan, tumbling around in the back, was thrown against the passenger-side rear door but dived back behind Reigns, opening up with everything he had on the driver of the Alfa.

Reigns stole a look over her shoulder. The Alfa Romeo wasn't moving.

"Did you get him?" she asked.

"Yep," said Morgan. "Let's get clear, ditch this fucking car and find a taxi."

Chapter Twenty

RESTAURANT LE DIANE, HÔTEL FOUQUET'S BARRIÈRE, PARIS, FRANCE

"OK then, I guess we've discussed this particular course of action through to its natural conclusion." The man's accent was pure Boston, Ivy League, most likely Harvard. "Can I take it that you're both happy to leave the next phase of the negotiations to me?"

The superb luncheon was finally coming to a close. As the conversation began to wrap up, the last of the dessert plates and wine glasses disappeared and invisible staff began to serve coffee.

"I think so," the second man replied. His accent was Swiss. "If we allow her to progress her current arrangements with the Chinese then it would certainly save us a great deal of trouble. And if you can encourage her to meet your people in Los Angeles that would be timely, to say the least. What do you think, my dear?"

"I think that to date we've allowed things to progress at an appropriate pace," the woman answered. Her accent was very British, Oxbridge educated. "We know that she has a strong grasp of the business, she can handle difficult partners, cross-border transactions and movements, and is clearly not averse to maintaining strict control measures on her people and operations. We know she's good. We're confident in the numbers and we've substantiated most, if not all, of the background. So, yes, I agree. I think it's time we moved things along, and if you have a team in LA then they should meet her there. It's time to tie things up, and the sooner the better."

"What about your friend, the general?" the American asked. "Is he showing any interest in this? It would be helpful to know."

"Unfortunately, I can't comment with any certainty. Normally he's reasonably open to sharing information. Of late, not quite so."

To a casual observer, the elegantly attired trio sitting by a window with a view over the Champs-Élysées looked just like any other high-end gathering discussing business over lunch. The first man, the American who had offered to lead the merger negotiations with their potential new business partner, was about fifty-five with closely cropped blond hair. He was dressed impeccably in a pale gray suit with a fine check, a white shirt with narrow purple stripes and a dark green tie ornamented with subtle splashes of purple, to complement the shirt. To his right, the other man, the other side of sixty and completely bald, was more conservatively dressed than his colleague, in a navy blue three-piece suit and pale blue shirt worn with a burgundy tie. Both of them shone with health and vitality, assiduously trim with no sign of the midlife paunch or sagging jowls too often associated with highly successful men in the grip of middle age, for whom indulgence was a daily privilege. Both clearly enjoyed the success that had come to them and went to great lengths to prolong their ability to savor it.

The woman was extraordinary. She was striking to look at, with fair skin, full lips, soft brown eyes and thick, shoulder-length, raven hair, which she occasionally tucked behind her left ear, conveying an air of playful seductiveness. Her full figure was cloaked in a fitted black leather jacket, black blouse and skirt, with knee-high black leather boots. Her minimalist approach to jewelry enhanced her contemporary elegance. She was fifty-two, but looked forty.

These three were part of a larger group of twelve, consisting of a chair and eleven members. The dozen referred to themselves collectively as The Board and presided over a multinational, multi-billion-dollar enterprise. But unlike other boards, run in accordance with charters and laws and governed by stock exchanges and government watchdogs, this board was silent, operating below the radar, the power behind the publicly listed corporation. Ultimately answering only to itself, it pulled strings, influenced and manipulated situations, individuals, governments. Its very existence and the identities of its membership were more closely guarded than the most sensitive of any country's top secrets. Retirement was mandatory at sixty-five and the retiring member invited a new member to join. New members were appointed after an extensive vetting and selection process lasting, in most cases, years, and a final, unanimous vote. Membership was international and kept strictly to the very top-shelf corporate and government executives of CEO and director-general level. The board operated in the shadows of global commerce and yet, with the official corporation as its instrument, was a major influence on most markets. No names were ever used when in each other's company. This was the rule by which they lived and they never broke it, no matter how seemingly innocuous the occasion or circumstance. Many years before, board members had decided upon a suitable motif by which it would identify itself, one that would reflect its beyond-the-law modus operandi. So it was that the stylized, blood-red profile and headdress of a Native American chief became the official emblem of the enterprise, The Renegade Group of Companies.

The board members quietly concluding their meeting at Restaurant Le Diane were the three responsible for strategic assessments and recommendations.

"Very well, it's settled then," said the American. "I'll have my people meet with her first and will report back to you both once I've reviewed their findings. Then, if we intend to proceed, I'll extend my stay in LA to meet with her personally."

Chapter Twenty-One

INTREPID HQ, BROADWAY, LONDON

"Miss Haddad is here, sir," said Mrs Jolley from the door. "Shall I send her in?"

"Yes, please." General Davenport's tone was grave.

Mrs Jolley, his loyal and trusted personal assistant of many years, withdrew quietly with a nod to the general's Special Projects Officer.

Returning the nod, Mila Haddad entered the general's office. A graduate of the American University of Beirut and the University of Toronto, with degrees in Arabic Languages and Criminology, Haddad had been, in Davenport's words, "rescued" from her role as a research assistant to a judge of the International Criminal Court in The Hague in order to keep the general on his toes. As far as Davenport was concerned, she was absolutely essential to Intrepid's ongoing success and, vitally, its evolution.

"Good morning, sir," she said.

"Good morning, my dear," replied Davenport, stepping out from behind his desk. His mood was decidedly somber despite the warmth of the greeting. "Would you mind joining me over here, please? I'm sick of the bloody desk already."

Davenport was dressed in his trademark charcoal, today a wide-pinstripe three-piece suit, which hung perfectly upon his tall frame. With his thinning hair brushed straight back and immaculately trimmed gray beard, he had a ducal appearance. The general invited her to join him at the circular mahogany coffee table surrounded by leather-covered chairs where he preferred to hold his more personal discussions. "Tea?"

"Please." She sat down.

The oak-paneled walls of the office were adorned with awards, photographs and mementos from Davenport's career. Well-worn berets from his days with the Special Air Service, Parachute Regiment and United Nations hung on a coat stand in a corner by the door. A framed image of the Falkland Islands and a photograph taken with Queen Elizabeth, at his investiture as a Commander of the Order of the British Empire, were among the highlights. This was his inner sanctum, the War Room as he called it. It was the epicenter of all Intrepid operations.

As Davenport's Special Projects Officer – and quasi-Chief of Staff until a permanent chief was appointed – it was Haddad's job to brief him on the most recent developments in Hong Kong, even though on a personal level she was still struggling to accept what had happened overnight. It seemed unbelievable. Davenport poured her green tea and eased the cup and saucer across the fine old mahogany table before topping up his own coffee.

"Very well, let's get started."

"Of course, sir." Pushing a curl of hair away from her eyes, Haddad placed an iPad on her lap, to refer to as she spoke. Gathering her thoughts, she began.

"At approximately zero three hundred hours this morning our time, ten hundred hours in Hong Kong, three of our agents – Morgan, Sutherland and Reigns – were involved in an armed engagement during an operation in the Mong Kok district of Kowloon. During the exchange Commander Sutherland sustained multiple gunshot wounds, specifically to the neck, chest, abdomen and leg. All three agents successfully disengaged. However, given the extent of Commander Sutherland's injuries, they were left with no choice but to go directly to the emergency trauma wing of Queen Elizabeth Hospital in Kowloon. Major Morgan administered immediate treatment en route to the hospital. Agent-nominee Reigns drove.

"Accompanying them in the vehicle was a fourth person —" Haddad consulted the iPad, "—Inspector Victor Lam of the Hong Kong Police Force. Inspector Lam was Agent Reigns' contact and has been assisting throughout her infiltration mission. I understand he was run down by a motor vehicle and abducted immediately following a scheduled rendezvous with Reigns, and then subjected to repeated physical abuse. Agent Reigns was in the process of recovering him when Agents Sutherland and Morgan arrived to assist. According to Major Morgan, who spoke briefly with Inspector Lam, Agent Reigns acquitted herself admirably and was responsible for neutralizing two men and subduing a third, resulting in the successful recovery of Lam."

"Very well," said Davenport, adding gravely, "What's the situation at the hospital?"

"An assistant commissioner by the name of Kwong – commander of the HKPD Kowloon West district – has made the necessary arrangements with hospital administrators. Meanwhile, following protocol, so as not to be compromised, Major Morgan and Ms Reigns were forced to leave

Commander Sutherland in the care of Inspector Lam and the HKPD at the hospital."

"Drop and run. Bloody hell. Even though we're prepared for it, it doesn't make it any easier. Morgan would not have enjoyed that at all," said the general. He fell silent for a few moments. Haddad watched him; he seemed conflicted. "Any more news on Commander Sutherland?"

"Nothing, I'm afraid," she said. "He's still in surgery. There were significant complications associated with the chest wound. A bullet hit a rib and tumbled, causing major damage to his left lung. It was completely collapsed by the time they arrived at the hospital. I attempted to get an update before I came in but the hospital isn't prepared to comment until they've heard directly from the surgeons."

General Davenport listened intently to everything she was saying, taking in each detail. "What about Interpol and the US Embassy, are they on board yet?"

"Yes, sir," she replied. "Interpol Beijing sent a liaison officer, who is at the hospital now, and a senior official from the US State Department is onsite and has arranged for a US Marine to be stationed inside the room with Commander Sutherland once he is out of surgery. There's currently a Marine outside the operating theatre. That coverage will remain in place when he's moved to Intensive Care. We've also arranged for one of our administrative recovery teams to deploy to Kowloon. They're on their way now to take care of Commander Sutherland. If he makes it, they'll arrange for him to be transported back to the United States as soon as he's well enough and he'll convalesce there. If not, then they'll recover his body and return it to his family. They'll also wrap things up with Interpol and the Hong Kong Police and will deal with things like the hotel, the vehicle and so on."

"What about Morgan and Reigns?" Davenport asked. Concern for all his agents, particularly Sutherland, was etched upon his face. "Where are they?"

"Retrieving their gear from the hotel, the Shangri La Kowloon, then they'll head to the airport. Fortunately, the Gulfstream that brought Major Morgan in from Tanzania last night is still on station in Hong Kong. It's refueled and good to go. They'll be back in London by midnight."

"Very well. Make sure they're accommodated for the night and we'll convene in COBRA tomorrow at ten am."

"It's all arranged, sir. Ms Reigns has her apartment behind the Royal Festival Hall over on the South Bank and Major Morgan stays at the Rembrandt in Knightsbridge when he's in the city. So, we've taken care of it already."

"Thank you. Excellent work. Please keep me appraised as the day progresses. I want to know the moment there is any change in Commander Sutherland's condition."

"Of course, sir."

Chapter Twenty-Two

QUEEN ELIZABETH HOSPITAL, KOWLOON, HONG KONG

Jung-Woo "Andy" Chow took great pride in his work. He had been at QE in the Repair and Maintenance division for almost fifteen years. He began his time at the hospital as a cleaner and general duties assistant but over the years he'd moved into the repair side of things. Today he'd spent most of his shift repairing a broken smoke-extractor fan in the hospital's furnace area; one of the least pleasant areas of the entire hospital, given what had to be incinerated down there. He didn't enjoy the task and as he finished showering and dressing in his own clothes ready to go home, he felt that the smell would cling to him for days.

It was 11.30pm as he walked out of the maintenance staff's entrance at the back of the hospital. The crisp freshness of the night air made him catch his breath then instantly fill his lungs, inhaling clear oxygen and blowing away the staleness of the day. Andy enjoyed the routine relief he felt on leaving the hospital at the end of every shift. For him it was a job, not a vocation. He didn't have a vocation other than looking after his family and, for a man who had begun life on the wrong side of the tracks, the job at QE had been his salvation. He had thanked God every day for the past decade and a half that it had come his way.

Andy walked along the outer edge of the vehicle ramp and across the car park toward the bus stop on Wylie Road. It was well lit around the hospital but inevitably got a lot darker the further away he walked. That didn't bother him. The grounds were familiar, as were the people around after the late shift. When he reached the stop he stood patiently waiting. The bus would be along soon.

It was then that he noticed a car parked about fifty feet down the road. The lights were off but he saw the blaze of a cigarette from within. At the moment he noticed the car and the cigarette, he heard the engine start and watched the vehicle approach him, moving slowly and very close to the curb. He was unsure what to make of it but remained calm, watching as it came closer and closer. Eventually the car eased to a stop directly in front of him. It was a dark, late-model sedan. He couldn't be sure exactly what kind. He didn't take any interest in cars these days.

The driver's door opened and a man dressed in a dark suit stepped out. The man was big, much bigger than Andy. His strong build and demeanor were intimidating. He didn't look at or acknowledge Andy in any way. Instead, he walked around the front of the car, past Andy, and opened the rear passenger door, indicating that he was expected to get in. Stunned by the situation, Andy didn't move. Never in the many years he had worked in the hospital had anything so extraordinary happened to him. He kept looking from the driver to the back of the car, uncertainty clouding his face.

There was another blaze of light followed by a puff of smoke from the far side of the rear seat. A deep, no-

nonsense voice commanded in Cantonese, "Get in. I don't have all night."

At this point the driver stepped forward and ushered Andy into the vehicle. The door slammed shut before he had managed to shuffle properly on to the seat. The driver returned to the front and the car took off, slowly at first, heading north along Wylie then gained speed on the approach to Princess Margaret Road.

"There must be some mistake," Andy began, looking at the dark, solidly built figure on the seat beside him. "You must have me confused with somebody else."

"It appears to be you who is making the mistake, Jung-Woo Chow. Do you not remember me? Has it been that long?"

"I'm sorry," he replied, shaking. "I'm just a maintenance worker at the hospital. I'm afraid I don't know you."

"Handy Andy," the voice said jovially. "Handy Andy. Is your memory coming back to you now? Surely you haven't forgotten the man who gave you your name."

Andy's blood ran cold at the sound of that voice. The demons of his past were reaching out to him.

"Mr Wu," he whispered. "Where are you taking me?"

"Home, Andy. Where else?" came the calm, almost paternal reply. "I'm taking you home. But don't worry. All we need to do is talk, then I will drop you at your door and disappear once again."

"What do you want to talk about? I don't understand. I haven't been involved in anything since—"

"Since I got you that job at the hospital. You remember that, yes?"

"Of course."

"And do you remember why it was necessary for me to get you that job?"

After a long silence, Andy reluctantly answered, "Yes."

"Yes. See, it's good, you already have your memory back. It will make our talk much easier if you remember."

Andy remained silent.

"Now, Handy Andy, these past fifteen years – they would have been so different if you had spent them all rotting in Shek Pik Prison. Don't you agree?"

"Yes."

"But, of course, you weren't rotting in Shek Pik, were you? No. Instead you married a beautiful girl. You had children. You got a job that paid well. Everybody left you alone and, all this time, nobody knew you were a cop killer. Nobody except me."

Andy looked out of the window, ashamed of his past.

"You would never have survived maximum security, Andy. With your pretty face, you would have been the favorite of the inmates and the wardens. You probably would have lasted two, maybe three years. Everybody's bitch." Wu laughed to himself. "Funny, don't you think, how all that evidence just disappeared?"

Andy felt the blood drain from his face. His hands were sweating against his polyester trousers. He couldn't bring himself even to speak.

"It would be a pity if your wife and children disappeared, too, just like all that evidence, now, wouldn't it?"

Andy turned sharply to face the dark silhouette of a perfectly round bald head and powerful shoulders. He knew there was no point in retaliating with some pointless threat about the consequences of harming his family. They were just words after all; words that he could not possibly match with actions. The threat to his family placed Andy instantly under the power of this man.

"Yes, there's that spark of violence I remember so well

from your younger days. That's good, very good. Let's keep that vengeful fire burning," said Wu Ming. "I treated you as my brother then and for all the years since. I left you alone and made sure others left you alone, too. But all that time you have been in my debt, and now you have your chance to clear the slate."

Andy's eyes blazed with hatred and frustration but he held his tongue.

"What do you want me to do?"

"Your job allows you access to anywhere in that hospital, correct?"

"Yes," he answered.

"Excellent. You will do this one thing for me. When it's done, you'll never hear from me again. The slate will be clean. If you don't, then you'll wish you had gone to prison all those years ago."

Chapter Twenty-Three

INTREPID GULFSTREAM G650, SOMEWHERE OVER
CHINA

"Better?" asked Morgan.

"Much. I needed that," Reigns replied. She was dressed in jeans and a loose-fitting sweater, towel drying her hair. "I felt like shit."

"It's amazing how much better you feel after a shower."

They were in a Gulfstream G650 ultra-high-speed jet, one of an exclusive fleet specifically modified for Intrepid by Gulfstream's Special Missions Program Office. Outside, the aircraft looked like any other privately owned jet: white, with non-descript markings and insignia. Inside was a different story. The forward section immediately behind the cockpit was the flight-crew cabin and galley. The mid-section was divided into an enhanced first-class standard seating area for six, including a table and briefing area with state-of-the-art digital communications and video facilities. Beyond that, the rear section was divided into two private staterooms, a secure weapons storage area, restrooms and, at the very rear, a small but adequately appointed incarceration space.

Having retrieved the last of the evening meal clutter, the flight attendant had withdrawn to the crew quarters and now the two agents were alone at the table.

Morgan had poured drinks for them. His was Sullivans Cove whisky. He handed Reigns a Bacardi and ice. She dropped into the seat opposite his, draped the towel over her shoulders and gratefully accepted it. Morgan noticed a slight tremor in his hand. He withdrew it quickly, hoping she hadn't noticed.

"It's what you wanted, right?" he asked.

She took a long sip. "Yeah, it's perfect," she said, openly studying him. "Thanks."

"My pleasure. So, are you OK? Hell of a day."

"I'm doing fine," Reigns said. "What about you? Been a hell of a day for you, too."

"Me? Don't worry about me," he replied, too quickly, immediately doubting how convincing he'd sounded.

"You're thinking about Dave," said Reigns. It wasn't a question.

He nodded, staring into the Scotch. Sutherland had been shot to bits and all Morgan could do was dump him outside the hospital emergency room in a pile of ragged bandages and an ocean of blood. He couldn't think about it. He had to believe his friend would pull through.

"Just wondering if there's anything I missed. You know, anything that could have been avoided."

"I was there, too, remember. We were all in the thick of it. There weren't many options with all those bullets buzzing around." Her voice was calm and her words measured. "We had to get Lam out of there and once we were in that car we were sitting ducks, but we had no other choice. If we'd tried to fight it out in the alley or escape on foot we would all have been cut down in minutes. Those guys own those streets and everyone on them."

"I know, I know," said Morgan, rattled by her composure. He felt the complete opposite and found himself suddenly resenting her for it. "He should have kept his fucking head down."

"Dave was trying to protect us by closing that rear door."

"Don't you think I know that?" He stood up and paced the gangway. "He knows the score. Anyway, the medics must have patched him up by now."

After a couple of minutes of silence he returned to the table and took a long drink, barely able to suppress the pain and frustration he felt. His hands betrayed him again, so he pushed the glass away. It slid across the table. Reigns stopped it. Morgan slumped back in his seat and stared up at the ceiling.

"You know, when I was just a girl," she began carefully, "my mom taught me how to calm myself when I was upset or angry about something. I still do it. I think you should try it."

"I'm fine, Reigns," he said. "I'm nowhere near fucking angry yet."

"Humor me," she said. He didn't move or reply, only glared across at her, trying to work her out.

Reigns stood up, took a step around the edge of the table so that she was by his side, and pointed one long, slender finger at him.

"Listen, Morgan, if I have to beat the shit out of you until you relax, I will," she said. "So, we're doing this, whether you like it or not."

There was a brief pause before he laughed. Reigns did too. It was impossible not to.

"OK, OK. Jesus! You win," he said. "What do I do? You're not going to swing a crystal on a chain, say 'look into my eyes,' or any tree-hugging shit like that, are you?"

"Don't be an idiot. Get up and let's go sit in the comfy chairs. This table makes me feel like I'm back in college."

Reigns took him by the hand and led him to the lounge seats away from the table. She sat him down.

"Sit back. Rest your head. That's it, get comfortable. Hands on top of your thighs. Eyes closed."

Morgan obeyed. Reigns reclined his seat and then sat facing him. He could feel how close she was.

"OK, all set?"

He nodded.

"Good. You're finally doing as you're told. Now, focus only on my voice and your breathing."

"What if I start heavy breathing?"

"Shut up. I'll tell you when you can start heavy breathing." She gave him a smile he wasn't expecting. "Take a slow, deep breath. I said, slow. Focus, Morgan."

"I can't focus now." He grinned, eyes still closed.

"We can focus on other stuff later, if you're a good boy. Now, try again. Take it right down into the very base of your lungs and fill your chest as much as you can. Good. Hold it. That's right. Now, slowly release the air through your nostrils. Slowly, until absolutely all of it is out. Good. Now, again. Breathe deep. Fill your lungs …"

Morgan had no idea how long it took but he succumbed completely to her, mesmerized by the soothing control of her voice as she gently guided him down into a deep, meditative state. His subconscious streamed images of Elizabeth Reigns. Her smile. Her hair. Her eyes. When she eventually began to lead him back out of it, he remained as he was, sunk into the seat, eyes closed, limbs and body heavy and immobile. He felt as though he was still on the edge of a dream.

"Once we're done with this job, let's fly back and check on Dave," he heard himself say, but his voice was hoarse and disconnected, like it belonged to someone else.

"That's a great idea," she replied, her own voice little more than a whisper. "Where will they take him to recover?"

"Back to the SEALS. Coronado. Navy hospital. He'll be safe there. Plenty of people he knows ..."

Morgan's thoughts drifted again into a disjointed stream of Sutherland, Wu Ming, Africa, and, in the center of it all, Reigns. He could see her, just as she was before she'd headed off to the shower, sitting across the table from him, providing her input to the operational report Morgan was tapping out on the laptop. He remembered how close she'd been, leaning across, adding her unique perspective on what had gone down. After all they'd been through, her energy and resolve were captivating.

Morgan's previous fixation on taking a leave of absence to rest and recuperate had vanished. He couldn't even think about that now. No sooner had he resolved that issue than Reigns appeared again. His mind toyed with the intimacy he'd felt with her, being under the spell of her meditation, her gentle tone of voice and the calm she had so easily introduced to his thoughts and feelings. It was the first time he'd been alone with his thoughts since arriving in Hong Kong that morning. Now he was airborne again and en route to London, preparing for whatever the general had in store for him – for them – next. Flashes of his mission to apprehend Chomba in Malawi returned to him and he considered the parallels to the covert infiltration he'd carried out solo in Corfu a year earlier, apprehending the fugitive Serbian war criminal Milivoj Šerifović. Then there was the Wolf. Then Drago. A showdown. Gunfire. Charly – Reigns!

Morgan woke with a start.

"Jesus, did I just fall asleep?"

"Yep, you did," she said. She smiled at him from her seat, legs crossed, resting too.

"How long?"

"About half an hour, I guess."

"Bloody hell. Sorry." He sat up and rubbed his face.

"Don't be sorry. We haven't stopped all day until now. What is it that Tom Rodgers says about the body shutting down after an operation? The euphoria of cheating …"

"… the inevitability of death. Yeah, I remember."

"You feel better?"

"I do actually," he said. "Whatever you did, it helped. I appreciate it."

Morgan stood, stretched, walked into the galley and poured himself a second scotch. Reigns joined him. She rattled the ice cubes in her empty glass and handed it to him.

"So, did you get the report done?" she asked.

"Yeah, I sent it off while you were taking your shower. As well as today's stuff, I had to include my report on Africa. That's where I was before I arrived in Hong Kong. I just hope I covered everything." He refilled both their drinks, handed hers back to her and they returned to their seats.

"I wonder if there'll be any correlation between the African end and the work you've been doing here – you know, the networks."

"It's very probable," she said. "So, what happens now? I mean, with Dave."

"HK cops and Interpol will look after him until our people arrive from headquarters to sort out the details."

"And what about us? I mean, what usually happens once you get back from an operation like this?"

"Usually, you'd take a break, but I suspect that's not what the boss has in mind for us. By the time we're back in London, the Intel team will already have worked through the info we've just sent them about today, particularly your observations from the factory. We'll be back by midnight, London time. Then we'll get our heads down until we regroup at headquarters in the morning."

Morgan paused for a moment, looking at her.

"What?" she said.

"Nothing, only what the hell made you sign up for this? It's been bugging me."

"What does that mean? Why should it bug you?"

"Well, you don't exactly come from a typical background to be working for this outfit. You'll forgive me for saying this but up until this morning, you haven't really been the type – or have you?"

"Is there a type?" she challenged, and sat forward in her seat.

"I suppose not," he replied. She was right, of course, but still he wanted to understand her. "So, humor me. Let's face it, you've never been a shooter. Apart from the résumé spiel, which I already know, what drew you into all this?"

"You really want to know?"

"Of course I do. I know you can handle yourself, you proved that today." For a moment he could see that she thought he was deliberately baiting her. He wasn't. "Seriously, I'm curious. It's in my nature."

"Well, if we're cutting to the chase, I'm here because my father was in the South Tower of the World Trade Center when it came down. God, it's almost twelve years ago to the day. He worked for Euro Brokers and their floor was above the second impact, United 175. He went to work that day just like any other. I was just a kid. He kissed me on top of my head like he did every other morning, walked out the door and I never saw him again. He was with a group that were trying to get up to the roof, hoping they'd be rescued from there. They didn't make it. My mother never recovered from it. They were so much in love. Her grief was so intense that cancer took her within two years."

"Jesus. I'm sorry," Morgan said quietly. "I had no idea."

"When the general approached me and I learned about Intrepid, it made a lot of sense to join. I want to make the world better, you know. In any way I can."

She leaned back in her seat. They fell silent for a long time, quietly comfortable again in each other's company. Morgan felt a strange familiarity with her and felt guilty for pushing her to dredge up the past and revisit the loss of her father. He enjoyed her company, but she'd been through enough for one day.

"I'll always be indebted to you and Dave for getting me out of there. God knows what would have happened if you two hadn't arrived when you did," she told him.

"Don't mention it. It's just what we do, and it's what you do, too. You're one of us now, remember? Besides, from what I saw, you had it under control. We were just there for back up, and you'll be there for us next time the crunch comes."

"Thanks, but still," she said. "It was amazing. I only hope—"

"Don't say it," Morgan told her earnestly. "Whatever happens, happens. We've just got to go with it in this job. Dave knows that. If we were like normal people we'd be back there with him right now, but we're not normal, not any more. Normal things don't exist for people like us. If it was me on that hospital bed, he'd be exactly the same."

"My new reality, huh?" Reigns got up and paced for a while, stretching and arching her spine with her hands in the small of her back.

"I'm afraid so. Trust me, if we'd been anywhere else earlier tonight, we would have found a good bar, got on it and forgotten all about our day, but that wasn't an option for us in Hong Kong. Your face is known to those people, so we had to get you out of there." He looked up at her, ready to make another point, when something occurred to him. "Bloody hell! How tall *are* you, Reigns?"

"Five-ten," she answered with just a hint of light-hearted challenge in her voice. "Why, does that bug you, too?"

"Not at all," he answered. "Just don't stand too close to me if you're in heels."

Reigns picked up her Bacardi, her long fingers curling around the glass. She paced the center of the cabin. Morgan watched her and knew she was reliving the events of the day, mulling them over, searching for answers of her own. But unlike Morgan's earlier frustration, she was energized by the challenge. This job, this life, was all new to Reigns. It was exhilarating to watch her.

"Wu Ming was down there with his bodyguards. Showing off his entrepreneurial flair – his factory," she said. "Asshole. Bald head, black eyes, Chinese-style suit. And the European body builders were down there too, with their buzz cuts and tight suits. When I saw them, a couple of them were already running toward the stairs leading to the room I was in. They'd heard the shots but had to cross the factory floor, through the sewing tables and stools. That slowed them down and gave me the chance to get out with Victor."

She took another sip of rum.

"I could see her," she said, voice slightly slurred by exhaustion and the calming pull of the drink. "She was tall, taller than me, towering over all of them. She's white and built like an athlete, fit and strong. High cheekbones, Eastern European type, you know. Short blonde hair, really short, like an eighties cut, lots on top but not much around the sides ... which makes sense when you think about the buzz cuts on her bodyguards. Her hair was almost white-blonde, like peroxide. That's her. That's the Witch."

"You mentioned the Witch in your report, but how can you be so sure?" he asked. "I thought all we had was a Blue Notice without an identity?"

"Because I know in my gut it's her. Identifying herself as the Night Witch will have some significance to her, somewhere in her history. A family connection maybe; someone she loved or respected. Assuming that identity gives her strength; a persona nothing like her own to hide behind."

Morgan listened in silence as Reigns moved slowly about the cabin, exploring her thoughts in much more detail than she had outlined within the report. He could see that although she was consumed by her assessment of the Night Witch, she was tired. Eventually she returned to her seat, curling up like a cat and laying her head against the palm of her hand, long black hair dropping like a curtain behind it. She just sat there, looking at him. Studying him. Morgan fought the temptation to go over and comfort her. She was, after all, an agent just like him. She needed to deal with the violent chaos of her first confrontation in her own way. It was a rite of passage and today she'd earned hers, tenfold. All Morgan could do was be there, observe, and if she wanted to talk, listen. For now he was happy sitting across from her, enjoying her proximity and the calm he felt when he was close to her.

"The moonlight across the top of the clouds looks pretty incredible. Spectacular, in fact," he said, looking outside, wanting to say something unrelated to their traumatic day. "Don't you think?"

With feline poise, Reigns unfurled herself from the luxurious depths of her seat, took a pace forward and leaned over, resting her hands on Morgan's knees so she could gaze from the same window.

"It's definitely spectacular," she said, turning to him. "You know, Morgan, despite everything that's happened today, you and I haven't been properly introduced or even said hello to each other. Isn't that a bit weird?"

"Come to think of it, it is pretty weird," he said, looking up at her. He offered his hand. "We should remedy that immediately. Alex Morgan. I'm very pleased to meet you."

"Elizabeth Reigns," she replied, her hand warm as she took his, smiling. "I'm very pleased to finally meet you, Alex Morgan. You can call me Beth."

"And you can call me Alex Morgan. I like the way you say it."

They remained quiet against the gentle hum of the Gulfstream's pressurized cabin, their faces close, holding each other's gaze for just a second too long. Morgan could smell the apple fragrance of the shampoo she'd used. He could feel her body arching toward him, her breath warm against his face, when suddenly she released his hand.

"Whoa! Are we having a moment?" she asked ingenuously. "Because I think we are."

"I think it was very close to being a moment," he replied. "But then you called it and ruined everything."

She hit him hard in the arm and they both laughed, a little awkwardly. But she didn't step away. Morgan was drawn to her raw, unabashed confidence. The elation of surviving death and violence was a powerful stimulant. They had prevailed and a primal reward had been earned. He wanted her and he knew she wanted him. The need was urgent.

"Screw you, Morgan," she said, teasing him. "You're not getting off that lightly."

She sighed deeply and ran a hand through his hair and across his face, her eyes never leaving his. Morgan's hands found her waist and he held her, enjoying the feel of her, remembering the thrill he'd experienced seeing her in action, imagining her taut, finely tuned body naked.

"We could get in serious trouble if anyone finds out about this," he said.

"Yeah, I guess we could," she said. And began kissing his face, slowly, softly. "So maybe we shouldn't, right?"

"Yeah, we definitely shouldn't."

Morgan allowed his hands to find their way beneath her sweater. His fingers caressed the soft velvet valley in the small of her back. Reigns leaned into him, arms resting on his chest and her body curving instinctively toward his. They kissed like that, Morgan holding her, Reigns resting upon him, for minutes. It began fervently with the energy and abandon of two people not in control of their own bodies, but then something changed, something that shocked them both, although neither of them thought about stopping. Their fervor fought a deep sensual connection that made them pause.

Reigns stood up. Taking Morgan's hand, she drew him from the chair to his feet. Then she stepped in close, reached her arms around behind his back and rested her head upon his shoulder. Morgan wrapped one arm around her waist and with the other began to gently stroke her hair.

"I'm not asking for anything more than tonight, Alex." She sighed deeply and he felt her breath warm the skin beneath his T-shirt. Then she lifted her face to look at him. "But right now I need this and I know you do too. So, if we're not going to do this, then let's not go and do it back in my cabin. Fuck the consequences."

Chapter Twenty-Four

QUEEN ELIZABETH HOSPITAL, KOWLOON, HONG KONG

Jung-Woo 'Andy' Chow was back on shift at the hospital.

Earlier in the evening he had walked in through the staff entrance at the back of the hospital to commence the night shift, just as he had done every working day for the last fifteen years. He'd smiled and said hello to colleagues in the Repair and Maintenance division, stowed his bag carefully within his locker in the staff changing room and dressed in his overalls. He met his supervisor, who handed him his task sheet for the night, then collected his gear from the equipment cage. Then he set off from the Facilities Management area and headed across to D block.

Chow took the service elevator to the seventh floor and pushed the maintenance trolley out in front of him as he exited. It was quiet up here, just as he'd known it would be. It was the time between the end of visiting hours and the shift change, when the night shift staff and the graveyard shift were all on the floor doing their respective handovers. He had to be done by then. There'd be too many people around if he left it till late.

"Hi, Andy," called someone from the nurses' station.

Andy gave her a friendly, slightly awkward wave and kept his eyes on his trolley.

"What are you up to tonight?" she asked.

"Toilets!" he replied.

"Good times," she answered just as a phone rang. She gave him a friendly wave and took the call.

Andy made a show of heading to the men's toilet. After knocking on the door to check that it was vacant he walked in, placing a "Closed for Maintenance" sign outside as he did so. Inside, he leaned against the basin and rubbed his eyes. His jaw and fists were clenched tight. How could he go through with this? He thumped his fists against his forehead repeatedly. How could Wu Ming expect him to do such a thing after all these years? Andy was taut with confusion, pacing back and forth across the small room, challenging himself angrily in the mirror, splashing water on his face.

He hadn't slept at all the previous night and his tossing and turning and generally unsettled behavior had worried his wife no end. It was totally out of character for him to be concerned about anything. On numerous occasions throughout most of the morning and into the afternoon she had pressed him to tell her what was wrong, but he couldn't tell her. How could he? Where would he start? In all these years she had learned nothing of his past. She still thought that he had been just a simple delivery boy before they met, which was mostly true. Although who he made deliveries for and what the deliveries were was a secret he would take to the grave. At least, he had hoped to take it to the grave. After all these years he'd never for a moment expected to revisit that part of his life, but it had caught up with him again. All he could do was make it go away, and the only way to do that was to carry out what Wu Ming had asked of him and wipe away his debt. Andy was a simple man. He didn't think about the cop he'd killed. He'd blocked most of that incident out of his mind. His only concern now was not losing the life he had made for himself ever since that day. Whatever happened, he could never go to jail.

After five minutes he straightened up, gripped the trolley and walked out, collecting the sign on the way.

He walked in the opposite direction from the nurses' station. He knew which room he was headed to and he knew what to expect when he saw it. Nervously, he turned a corner at the end of the corridor and made his way, with the wheels of the trolley squeaking along in unison, toward room number six. As he reached the corner and looked down the length of the corridor, he could see what he'd been told to expect at the far end.

A United States Marine was standing beside the door to room number six. He was young, about twenty-five, in uniform dress: white cap, light brown short-sleeved shirt with medal ribbons, dark blue trousers with a wide red stripe down the outside leg, and black boots polished to a mirrored sheen. Andy couldn't see it from where he was standing but he knew there would be a holstered sidearm on the Marine's right hip. The moment he moved fully into the corridor and the squeaking trolley wheels announced his arrival, the Marine's gaze turned to him. Andy kept moving; he remembered enough about the old days not to do anything out of the ordinary. Still, he felt an overwhelming sense of anxiety coming on. His blood was racing through his body, under pressure from a raging heartbeat.

He heard the Marine say, "Do you know this guy, Doc?" followed by a familiar voice answering, "Oh, sure. That's just little Andy Chow. He's worked here longer than I have." Andy looked up. He never spoke to the doctors, but he was as familiar to the man as he was to most of the staff at the hospital. After fifteen years of routinely working in every building in the place he was now part of the furniture. Just little Andy Chow.

Then – disaster – the Marine waved him over. Andy walked slowly toward him. He managed to assume his most humble expression, head slightly bowed, shoulders hunched, shuffling along with his squeaking wheels aimed straight at the Marine.

"I'm sorry, sir," said the Marine politely. "But I gotta check your gear. Would that be OK?"

Andy knew it wasn't a request. He nodded cooperatively, said, "Sure, sure," as agreeably as he could manage, and stood back a couple of paces.

The Marine stepped forward and with great precision and economy of effort gave Andy a thorough pat down and then searched the trolley, beginning with the tool box, followed by the cleaning products and toilet rolls.

"I gotta make sure you don't have any weapons of mass destruction in here, you know what I mean?" the Marine joked good-naturedly. "Looks like you're all good, sir."

"Thank you," said Andy, smiling.

"Oh, just a minute," said the Marine. "One last thing."

Andy froze as the Marine extracted a short metal baton from a deep pocket in his trousers. With an expert flick, the Marine extended the baton. Andy's heart almost stopped as the man then leaned forward and thrust it into the water of the mop bucket on the end of the trolley. He jabbed the baton into the bucket a number of times, hearing nothing but a series of dull metallic clunks as the tip of the weapon foraged for anything untoward. Nothing.

The Marine smiled. Grabbing a rag from the trolley, he wiped the baton dry and then, dropping to one knee, slammed the tip hard into the floor. The weapon collapsed back into its handle just as it was designed to do and was returned to the pocket without further fuss.

"Thanks again, sir," said the young Marine. "You're good to go."

Andy's heart began to beat again. He had to regain his composure. He was in danger of shaking visibly. He said, "Thank you," to the Marine and stepped away. There was a women's toilet about ten yards along on the left-hand side of the corridor. He walked purposefully but unhurriedly to it, knocked on the door, waited patiently for a few seconds, opened it, placed his 'Closed' sign in the corridor, followed his trolley inside and quietly slid the bolt across.

It took him another five full minutes to regain his composure, but he used the time productively. He drew up the sleeves of his overalls all the way above the elbow, and plunged his hands into the very bottom of the metal mop bucket on the trolley. He rummaged around inside the bucket, beneath the fresh soapy water, until he was able to extract the flat, circular metal box that had been given to him and which he'd fitted snugly into the base of the bucket. He pulled the round box out completely and rested it on the basin. He wiped his hands and the box with paper towel until everything was absolutely dry.

Then, slowly and methodically, he twisted open the box's lid and took out the Smith & Wesson .357 Magnum Model 360 with the two-inch barrel.

Chapter Twenty-Five

CONFERENCE AND OPERATIONS BRIEFING ROOM, INTREPID HQ, BROADWAY, LONDON

"Good morning, sir," Mila Haddad called from the briefing podium at the front of the room as General Davenport walked in. Alex Morgan and Elizabeth Reigns sat at the far end of the table closest to the podium. They stood up as their chief entered the room. It was 10am sharp.

"Good morning." Davenport approached Morgan and Reigns and said, "Good to see you both back and in one piece. I'll see you both separately after this to discuss the details of your respective assignments."

"Thank you, sir," they replied in unison, each shaking the general's hand in turn.

"Good news about Dave, sir," Morgan said. "Mila just filled us in."

"It is indeed. According to the chief surgeon at the Queen Elizabeth Hospital, he's responded well to the surgery. Very encouraging."

"He's as strong as an ox," said Morgan. "If anyone could survive that, it's him."

"I agree, and what he needs now is to rest and recover

while we get on with the job of tracking these people down."

Morgan nodded. Any thoughts he'd had about mission fatigue or taking leave had been shelved. With his friend lying in Intensive Care on the other side of the world, Morgan knew there was no better place for him to be than back in the field, tracking down the bastards who'd shot Dave, and the sooner the better.

The Conference and Operations Briefing Room – COBRA – was located within the very heart of the secret Intrepid Headquarters building in Westminster. It was a large, modern, windowless space, arranged in a fashion that was standard for such facilities, with a video conference-capable central screen surrounded by an array of smaller screens, with additional monitors positioned high along both flanking walls. In front of the main screen, dual briefing podia faced a long central table, supplemented by a dozen black leather swivel chairs. Ceiling-mounted sensors designed to detect the latest surveillance technology prevented unauthorized communication to or from the room. Access to COBRA was via two secure airlocks: one in the southern wall at the rear, which was usually reserved for VIPs and where Davenport had entered; the other via the western wall, which led directly into the Operations Room.

General Davenport took a seat at the top of the table, closest to where Haddad was standing at the briefing podium. Directly opposite sat Morgan. Reigns had moved around the table to sit beside him.

When they were all settled, Davenport dropped his spectacles on to the table and leaned back in his chair.

"OK, Ms Haddad, let's get started."

"Thank you, sir. I'll summarize where we currently

stand as at the cessation of operations in Hong Kong and then I'll hand over to Elizabeth."

"Very well," said Davenport. "Proceed."

Haddad rested one hand upon the podium and tapped a few commands into an iPad with the other. As a series of images and graphics began to stream across the screens around the room, she began her briefing.

"It will come as no surprise to you that the Hong Kong Triad boss Wu Ming has gone to ground. There was no trace of him at the factory when the HKPD arrived and it appears likely that he was tipped off by this man." A new image replaced the grainy, black-and-white police-file images of Wu Ming.

"This is Chief Superintendent Chan Man-kin. He is currently in the custody of the commander of HKPD's Kowloon West District, Assistant Commissioner Kwong." Another image change. "Kwong is a highly respected law-enforcement official and has a solid reputation within Interpol circles. He is providing every resource to assist us and has offered the opportunity for us – well, officially for Interpol – to sit in on the interrogation of Chief Superintendent Chan. To that end we dispatched one of our Intel people from Beijing across to Hong Kong last night. They're eight hours ahead of us so I expect the interrogation is underway as we speak. I'll update you the moment we receive any information resulting from that.

"One thing is clear: a meeting occurred between Wu Ming and a European woman, yet to be formally identified but currently known by the alias 'Night Witch,' who we believe to be a major new global player in the human trafficking arena. It is evident that Wu was keen to impress the European during the visit to his factory, which suggests a business collaboration between them – possibly a merger, or even a takeover of his operations in the Asia-Pacific region. Given that the global profit made from the exploitation of human beings in forced labor situations is estimated to be in the order of thirty billion dollars US annually, and that the Asia-Pacific area accounts for thirty percent of that amount, the potential combining of these two operations is considered to be a significant development.

"Our original interest in the Night Witch was as a result of previous intelligence regarding an unidentified European woman emerging as a person of interest in Asia, Latin America and the Caribbean. Our decision to infiltrate Agent Reigns into the factory in Kowloon was prompted by a recent US Immigration and Customs Enforcement investigation into Wu Ming. We saw an opportunity to work with ICE and hopefully identify a connection between him and the European. I'll now hand over to Elizabeth."

Reigns stood up from her seat and walked confidently around to the podium. Morgan caught a hint of her perfume, *Si* by Giorgio Armani, and despite his focus on the operation, for a moment his concentration wavered. She'd barely looked at him since she'd entered the room.

He hadn't seen her since they'd parted company at Heathrow in the early hours of the morning. Two separate cars had been sent to collect them and there wasn't much of a chance to chat once the jet had taxied to a halt in its private hangar. As she was collecting her thoughts and taking control of the audio-visual technology, Morgan found himself admiring her. Her taste in clothes was impeccable. She was dressed in a navy three-piece pinstripe suit, with an off-white blouse worn open at the neck. Her long hair was down. He remembered it tumbling forward last night and brushing across his face, and her magnificent, sculpted body above him, illuminated by the glow of the dimmed lamp in her cabin. Before she began to speak, she bundled up her hair casually in one hand and drew it over her right shoulder.

"Good morning," began Reigns, addressing them all. She made no eye contact with Morgan. "Current estimates indicate that over twenty million people globally are victims of forced labor, including those trafficked for sexual exploitation purposes. Women and girls account for seventy-five percent of all trafficked victims. Almost sixty percent of victims are trafficked for sexual exploitation while the remaining forty percent will find themselves in forced labor situations. About half of all trafficked victims are moved across borders within their geographic regions, while the remaining numbers are an even split between straight domestic or internal trafficking, and inter-regional trafficking – meaning that they are moved beyond their own geographic location. Common destinations are the Middle East and Western Europe. East Asia tends to be the primary transnational origin point for most victims, which coincidentally pointed us in the direction of Wu Ming."

A series of slides appeared around them – global maps identifying agencies by name and location, statistical information on human trafficking, lists of international law-enforcement operations, images of victims, and mug shots of individuals arrested or wanted for trafficking offences. It was both a compelling and an ominous backdrop to the days and weeks ahead. The scale of the problem and gravity of its impact upon victims was profound. The arrest of Chomba in Malawi and the extraction of Reigns from Hong Kong had been Morgan's first exposure to the world of human trafficking and the more he learned about it, the more he found himself wanting to take on the main players.

"Some time ago, in collaboration with a number of

Interpol's National Central Bureaux, Europol and various other law-enforcement and intelligence agencies around the world, we identified a new figure emerging on the European scene. All we had to go on was anecdotal material buried within hundreds of hours of recorded statements taken by European police agencies during interviews with victims of human trafficking. What made this person so interesting was that there was no intelligence available that would enable us to categorically identify them, nor any actual evidence to link them to a crime. We just knew there was someone new operating in the space and that their influence was becoming significant, at least at grass-roots level. Normally there would be some kind of criminal history or profile available as the majority of traffickers tend to be men operating within their own countries of origin. They usually move into trafficking from other criminal activity because it is so lucrative.

"However, when women become involved they tend to operate at the facilitator or middle-management levels rather than the upper echelons, and are mostly involved in the trafficking of girls for sexual exploitation. Which, as we pieced together various threads of information, led us to the conclusion that this new player was in fact female, young – most likely late twenties to early thirties tops, of Eastern European extraction – possibly Ukrainian. Her age and nationality would suggest sexual exploitation as the most likely way she entered the criminal arena. Other than a lot of theories and speculation, she's been a ghost, a complete enigma to authorities. All we had was a very vague physical description of her as young, attractive and, apparently, quite tall.

"This led us to issue an Interpol Blue Notice in order to gather as much information as possible regarding her identity, location and criminal activity. Then in 2012, a situation in El Salvador resulted in the issue of a Red Notice for a Salvadorian national, a male by the name of Gaspard Mateo Ponciano, accused of running a sex-trafficking operation throughout Central America. Questioning by local authorities didn't manage to get too much from Ponciano himself. However, in statements taken from his victims – young girls lured into sexual servitude on the promise of domestic work – information emerged about a tall, beautiful European woman known only by the alias 'Witch' or 'Night Witch,' predominantly the latter. None of the victims had direct contact with her and only a couple actually saw her from a distance. Mostly they'd heard Ponciano referring to the Night Witch."

"There's some incredible history behind this Night Witch reference," Davenport said. "Have you looked into that?"

"Yes, sir," said Morgan, wading in. Reigns looked at him. "They were a squadron of female pilots of the Soviet Night Bomber Regiment during the Second World War, and the most highly decorated female unit in the Soviet Air Force. The Nazis called them *Nachthexen*, the Night Witches."

"Precisely," said Davenport. "That's the only other reference I've ever heard of to a Night Witch."

"I had to Google it," Morgan confessed.

They all laughed and Reigns finally smiled at him.

"So, apart from Major Morgan's groundbreaking intelligence-gathering capabilities, have you managed to establish any connection there, Miss Reigns?"

"There's a definite Eastern European connection, sir. Nothing concrete yet, but we're continuing to explore it and have compiled a list of every woman recorded as a serving member of the Soviet Night Bomber Regiment. Once we have an actual name for our Night Witch, we'll check to see if there are any further connections," Reigns replied.

"While I was embedded within Wu Ming's factory in Hong Kong I overheard the term 'witch' being used by members of Wu Ming's crew while discussing the imminent arrival of their high-profile visitor – the woman I subsequently observed on the factory floor, flanked by her bodyguards. My observation married with what we already knew about the appearance of the Witch. She's tall – in fact extremely so – white, Eastern European features, athletic physique, with very short blonde hair, almost white-blonde. My seeing her at first hand and confirming this description has enabled us to refine our search through the database. In the meantime, while analysis continues, we've had an encouraging new development, which I received news of just prior to coming in here."

Morgan watched Reigns with an intensity that surprised him. Despite their profession, despite what she'd been required to do in Hong Kong, and despite the fact that she was, like him, an agent, trained to kill and survive under the worst conditions imaginable, there was a softness to her that he could not get out of his mind. Her effect on him had been such that he'd scarcely thought of anything else since arriving at Heathrow. *Jesus! You're getting fucking soft, Morgan. Snap out of it and listen.*

"Overnight our Intel team has been scouring every known source to identify the Europeans I described. Through Interpol Beijing's sub-bureau in Hong Kong, we've been working closely with HKPD and authorities at Hong Kong International Airport, and one of our analysts stumbled upon an anomaly over a certain batch of passports."

"How so?" asked Davenport.

"Well, to start with we were looking for people traveling into and out of Hong Kong under EU passports and of course there were literally thousands to review. However, overnight one of our analysts decided to take a different approach and started looking for European names traveling under non-European passports. She eventually found these guys." Reigns tapped another series of commands into the iPad and the screens flickered as new images appeared. They were the scanned front pages of passports and showed one young woman and half-a-dozen men. "In terms of their ages and general physical descriptions, all resemble the people I observed at the factory, all have European names, but they are all traveling on Belizean passports."

"Didn't I read an Interpol report recently about a passport racket operating out of the Belizean immigration department?" said Morgan. "A number of senior officials were charged or at least under investigation over it."

"Correct," Reigns replied. "Did you Google that as well, Morgan?"

"Hey, don't knock open source," he replied.

"So, over the past ten years, hundreds of blank passports have been stolen and ended up on the black market, but more recently there has been evidence that a group of officials were actually facilitating the issue of passports to non-Belizean citizens who didn't meet the official criteria for holding one."

"And you reckon that's how these guys got hold of their new identities?" Morgan asked.

"It certainly looks that way," said Reigns. "I'd say they've changed their names but kept them European so as not to raise suspicion. Plenty of Europeans have relocated permanently to the Caribbean over the years, but most of them have done it legally. Holding a Belizean passport not only gives these people new identities and a new nationality, it also drastically simplifies their travel through the borders of the fifteen other member states of the Caribbean Community."

"Gives 'em plenty of options if they have to scatter unexpectedly," Morgan noted.

"Where are these people now, Elizabeth?" asked Davenport. "Do we know?"

"According to our most recent information, they dispersed in pairs when they left Hong Kong. Two flew out to Taipei – the girl with one of the men. The name on her passport is Ştefania Yovenko. Two flew to Manila and the last pair to Bangkok. But all indications are that the Witch and her flock are now converging on home."

"Which is where exactly?" Davenport asked.

"Belize."

Chapter Twenty-Six

CONFERENCE AND OPERATIONS BRIEFING ROOM, INTREPID HQ, BROADWAY, LONDON

"We were working as private contractors on that Grenville case for the British Government." Tom Rodgers, Intrepid's close-quarter combat chief instructor, had joined them. Turning to Morgan and Reigns he said, "Grenville was a British millionaire who'd gone missing while holidaying in Florida. He came from old money, good family, in line for a knighthood ... that kind of stuff. Only thing was, he went a bit off the rails after his divorce, chasing younger women, lots of 'em, and spending heaps of cash. It was a no-brainer he ended up targeted – wealthy, good-looking, not quite in his fifties. When he went missing in America, well, it was just the type of job for Peter Fleming to look into. Jobs 'requiring discretion,' as Pete used to say. He used to get a lot of off-the-books-type work, mainly in the US, because he'd moved there with his wife, Madeline, when he retired from the army. That's how I ended up working for him when I left the Bureau. It was all legit stuff but sensitive, you know; stuff that government folks couldn't show too much interest in without other people paying attention. So they'd get Pete to take care of it for them."

General Davenport, Morgan, Reigns and Haddad were all sitting around the table listening to Rodgers recount a long-past mission he'd worked on with Peter Fleming. Davenport and Fleming had served together as officers in the Special Air Service for many years. Davenport was best man at Fleming's marriage to Madeline Clancy and godfather to their daughter, Charlotte-Rose – Charly. In 2006, Peter Fleming had been killed in Central America while investigating Grenville's disappearance. Last year, an attempt had been made on the life of his widow, now the Presiding Judge of the International Criminal Court for the former Yugoslavia, and then Charly had been abducted; part of a grand scheme by a fugitive former Serbian general and indicted war criminal, who was attempting to subvert the course of international justice. Fortunately, those issues had since been resolved, but now Davenport smelled a connection between Reigns' trafficking operation and the murder of his old friend. Rodgers was the link.

"Tom, while she was in Hong Kong, Ms Reigns observed a woman, identity yet to be confirmed, at an illegal factory in Kowloon run by a senior Triad figure. It's the woman we're most interested in. To all intents and purposes she was welcomed there as a VIP. Ms Reigns heard one of the local enforcers refer to her as the Witch. So far, all we have is this reference and a physical description: young, tall, Eastern European. Now, some time ago, I recall you mentioning something about a young woman associated with the Grenville case. Possibly even something to do with the name Witch. What can you tell us about that?"

"Well, that was the whole thing. All of the information we received told us Grenville was with a young European girl. We tracked their movements from south-eastern USA all the way through Central America. The various border-protection agencies we spoke to all confirmed that he was traveling with a young woman and that her name was definitely kind of Russian." Rodgers furrowed his brow. "Dasha ... Devora ... Darja ... Darja! That's it. Darja. Darja Voloshyn. Jesus, I haven't thought about that for a long time. And, yeah, as far as we could work out, she was nicknamed the Witch, too. We never managed to find a picture of her, with or without Grenville. It was the strangest thing, like they had a constant shadow always in the background to make sure that if anyone did manage to snap a pic then it disappeared, pronto. And when we traced their steps through the various places they'd stayed or visited, no one except border control had the slightest recollection of her using the name Darja Voloshyn. There were a string of other names that staff recalled – I can't remember them now, it was a long list – but no Darja Voloshyn. So she'd been hiding her identity everywhere they went together, and for all we knew, probably kept it hidden from Grenville, too."

"I recall he ended up in Belize," said Davenport, with a swift glance around the table to emphasize this further connection. "Why there, of all places, do you suppose?"

"Pete could never make sense of it either," Rodgers said. "He couldn't imagine a guy with Grenville's money and connections ending up there – but I could."

"What do you mean? Had Peter missed something?"

"Well, you knew him better than I did, general. He never missed a trick," Rodgers answered. "But one thing about Pete – he was a real gentleman. Old school. I grew up in Detroit and we didn't have much call there for being gentlemanly. Pete found it difficult to accept that a guy like Grenville could be, well ..." Rodgers paused, looking uncomfortable.

"Come on, Tom," Davenport urged.

"Led around by his dick, general." He immediately turned to Reigns and Haddad. "Sorry. No other way to say it."

"I see," Davenport replied quietly. The others were all smiling. "I gather you felt otherwise?"

"For sure," Rodgers answered. "I told Pete as much, too. Grenville was doing whatever the new girlfriend wanted, and it looked to me like she intended for them to end up in Belize all along. I don't know why but it just seemed that way, the further along the trail we got. I mean, the places they were going ... the bars and restaurants they were frequenting in Florida and then in Mexico, Cancun, wherever they were – they weren't the sort of places you'd expect to find Grenville, but they were definitely the right places for a young Russian bride with a sugar daddy on her arm and no money worries."

"Russian bride. Are you sure about that?" asked Davenport.

"Nothing conclusive, only what the circumstantial evidence was suggesting to us at the time. Like I said, we couldn't find an image of them together and, apart from Voloshyn, we couldn't find any other name we could definitively assign to her; just a series of nicknames or pseudonyms and then that Witch thing ..."

"I know the two of us talked about this before, Tom," Davenport said, "but never with any real attention directed toward the girl and, more particularly, the Witch angle.

How did the tag originate? I knew Peter very well, and I know you, and I can't imagine either of you using a term like that unless there was an actual reason; something that sparked the reference in the first place."

"I guess we must have picked up what people were saying about the girl during our investigations. I remember we interviewed a guy who owned the bar at a place called the Paradise Palms Resort down there. Grenville and the girl used the bar a lot because they were staying at the resort. It's all coming back to me now. The guy's name was Vasquez. He limped real bad, and the bar was called Domingo's. I guess that was his name. He was the first one who really impressed upon us that she was, well, in his view anyway, a witch."

"How so?" asked Davenport.

"He said it was a feeling he got from just being around her," Rodgers said, clearly trying to make sense of it himself as he recalled the details. "I even remembered kidding around and asking if she put a hex on him or something, but the guy didn't laugh. He was freaked. He said that she was like a chameleon, could almost change her appearance right in front of you." Rodgers scoffed. "I mean, Pete and I put it down to a little too much tequila, but the guy was adamant. It was like a voodoo thing to him. He said if she came into the bar with Grenville and she was happy, then the whole place was happy. If she wasn't, then the mood was dark and there'd almost definitely be violence. And then she'd just sit there watching it all happen. He also said that they only ever saw her at night. If Grenville was in the bar during the day then he'd been on his own. She only surfaced when it was dark."

"Were you able to get a physical description of her?" asked Reigns.

"Yeah," answered Rodgers. "Tall, gorgeous and blonde ... you know, like half a million other European girls backpacking their way around the world, right? But her real name, the one she kept off the hotel registries as they traveled, was definitely, like I said, Voloshyn. Darja Voloshyn."

Chapter Twenty-Seven

INTENSIVE CARE UNIT, D BLOCK, QUEEN ELIZABETH HOSPITAL, KOWLOON, HONG KONG

Lam sat quietly at Commander David Sutherland's bedside, keeping silent vigil. The room was dimly lit except for the single fluorescent tube behind the bedhead and the gentle glow of a dozen life-saving machines going about their business. Their soft noises were a calming, almost hypnotic undercurrent.

Lam had been officially discharged from the hospital. After some clothes and personal effects had been collected from his flat and delivered to him by his daughter, he'd washed, dressed and thanked the hospital staff who had looked after him so well, including the two young uniformed officers who'd stood guard at the entrance to his room for the past twelve hours. Now, he was tired and his injuries were still causing him pain, but he wanted to check in on Sutherland; he had promised Mei-Zhen and her colleague that he would. Thankfully his daughter understood and had decided to wait for him down in the hospital's main reception area. He'd told her he wouldn't be long.

Victor Lam had had to be granted special dispensation

just to be inside Sutherland's room. Only the medical staff specifically responsible for the patient, and the US Marines allocated to his protection, were allowed within five feet of the door. But on the personal authority of Assistant Commissioner Kwong, Lam had been authorized to make a brief visit. After all, even in his own battered and weakened state, he had somehow managed to maintain enough pressure on Sutherland's most critical wounds to keep him alive until the medics had arrived.

Right now Sutherland was in an induced coma. He would remain that way until the surgeons agreed otherwise. The doctor on duty outside had told Lam that Sutherland had pulled through by the skin of his teeth but was now in a satisfactory and, above all, stable condition. His vital signs were considered to be well above average for a person who had just endured ten hours of drastic, life-saving surgery. Lam wasn't surprised. The man lying still on the bed beside him was one of the strongest, fittest-looking people Lam had ever seen. Behind the strips of white gauze and the tubes that ran into the nostrils and down the throat, the face was lean and hard and the jaw strong. The shoulders and arms above the textured white fabric of the hospital blanket were heavily muscled. Sutherland's silent, dormant power, coupled with an occasional twitch of the hand closest to Lam, gave the impression that the simple flick of a switch would restore the man to full consciousness. Lam knew now that there was much more to Mei-Zhen and her colleagues than he had previously imagined. They were specialists, that much was clear, but exactly who they belonged to, what country or agency, he had no idea. One thing he knew for sure, they were nothing like any of the Interpol people he'd ever come across.

Lam heard a voice, loud and authoritative, in the corridor: one of the Marines, calling out, "No! Don't shoot!" followed immediately by a single explosion that boomed unnaturally within the quiet sanctuary of the ICU recovery ward. A heavy-caliber gun fired at point blank range. A cacophony of panic-stricken screams for help immediately ensued, accompanied by the anxious clamor of terrified people running to safety. Lam instinctively leaped to his feet, unsteady at first, but then he was up and moving fast toward the noise. The door was thrust open as far as it would go, hitting its limits with a loud bang. A man, short and dressed in hospital overalls, raced in. His right arm was up and he was clutching a revolver. Lam's unexpected presence clearly took the gunman by surprise. For a moment they both stood frozen, staring at each other with just a couple of feet between them. Then the man in the overalls turned fast and brought the gun around to aim directly at the chest of the policeman. Lam was unarmed and too far away – he had to close the distance between them if he was to have any chance at all of survival. He did the only thing he could think of. Drawing in a deep breath, he launched himself upon the gunman with all the force his damaged body could rally.

The two men fell to the polished floor in a death struggle. Not a word was uttered by either of them, just an exchange of primal grunts and short, sharp breaths as each fought to conquer the other. Lam's strength was failing him already. The past twenty-four hours had taken their toll. His hands were wrapped around the weapon but he was grappling clumsily, fighting to keep the muzzle away from the center of his body and away from Sutherland's bed behind him. But the man in the overalls was strong and his assault was frenzied and Lam was growing weaker by the second. His hands were slipping from the gun. The small man obviously felt it and saw his chance. The weapon was torn from Lam's grasp and he instantly felt the muzzle being jammed hard into his gut.

"No!" he cried.

The muffled blast impacted like a heavyweight fighter's sucker punch into Lam's gut. His mouth fell open in shock and an involuntary gasp for air. He clutched protectively at the wound just as the warm treacle of blood spilled through his shirt and oozed over his hands. Victor Lam felt himself being pushed off the other man. He tumbled on to his back on the floor. His vision was tunneled, fixated on the image of the other man staggering to his feet then standing, raising that short, deadly arm in the direction of the bed. Directly at Sutherland.

Again, there was a thunderous boom from the gun, followed by another. Then there was light, coming in from behind Lam. He felt and heard a deafening succession of *crack-crack-crack* as a second pistol fired multiple rounds over the top of him. The gunman in the overalls was turning to the door. He let off another round and then nothing but *click, click, click*. He fell to the floor beside Lam.

Everything went dark.

Chapter Twenty-Eight

GENERAL DAVENPORT'S OFFICE, INTREPID HQ, BROADWAY, LONDON

"This information from Tom is a game changer," said Reigns.

She and Morgan were facing the general across his desk. Following the briefing in COBRA, Reigns had dragged a very reluctant Morgan "down to the dungeon" to observe the Intelligence Section. As a result of Rodgers's debrief on the Grenville case, Reigns had initiated an immediate search of Intrepid's database, which included access to almost every intelligence and law-enforcement network in the world. They were searching for one name in particular: Voloshyn. She told Morgan that the experience of seeing analysts at work, witnessing all the effort that went into providing him with information in the field, would be good for Morgan's "professional development." He had acquiesced because he enjoyed being around her. Three hours later they were back in Davenport's office.

"We got literally dozens of hits, including photographs, physical descriptions and a criminal history," said Reigns.

"Splendid. What information have you come up with?"

"Darja Voloshyn: born in 1980, Simferopol, Ukraine. Known to have used a number of aliases, including Dashenka Vitko, Dashechka Voytko, Dashunya Varga; clearly using her actual initials. According to an Interpol Red Notice issued on February fifteenth 2005, she was wanted by the Judicial Authorities of the Ukraine for aggravated robbery, misappropriation of property by means of abuse of authority, homicides committed in other specific circumstances in collaboration, and fraud – forgery of travels documents … the list goes on. She has a number of lesser charges to her name dating back to the late nineties when she was still in her teens – drugs, petty theft, that kind of thing – but there was also a charge of robbery with violence against a young male, which resulted in her being incarcerated in a juvenile justice facility for twelve months, all before her eighteenth birthday. However, despite the Red Notice, nobody has ever managed to track her down. In 2005, Voloshyn simply went off the grid."

"And a year later she was with Grenville when Peter Fleming was on his trail," Davenport observed. "But hang on, didn't you say that the name on the passport of the young woman who flew out of Hong Kong to Taipei was Yovenko?"

"That's correct, sir," replied Reigns. "It is inconsistent with Voloshyn's pre-2005 practice of basing aliases upon her own initials, but there's no reason why we should rule her out just for that."

"Tom and Peter's original report into Grenville's kidnapping and murder referenced complicity among local officials in Belize, and their apparent involvement in other criminal activities," said General Davenport. "I suppose, with the passport scam they had operating, it wouldn't be a problem to get a passport in any name."

"For sure, and on the flip side, until now there's also been nothing concrete to connect Voloshyn to the Night Witch. However, we ran a check on a list of members of the Russian 588th Night Bomber Regiment, the actual Night Witches, and we found a Major Dahlia Voloshyn, a highly decorated pilot with the regiment. She earned the title Hero of the Soviet Union, was awarded the Gold Star Medal, the Order of Lenin and three Orders of the Red Star. She was also Darja Voloshyn's great-grandmother."

"How very interesting," Davenport replied. "Clearly, the granddaughter has latched onto her grandmother's wartime gallantry, identified with it and clung to it; a childhood hero, mentor perhaps, and despite her eventual corruption of the ideal, an imagined version of herself."

"Most definitely," said Reigns. "And the parallels between Darja Voloshyn's criminal record and those crimes attributed to our Night Witch are substantial, particularly with regard to violent tendencies, including sexual violence against both men and women. And then we hit what appeared to be a dead end."

"Which was?"

"Darja Voloshyn was killed in a car accident in Poland in 2007."

"Damn! So where on earth does that leave us in terms of the Night Witch – back to square one?" said the general.

"Not exactly, sir," Morgan began. "The physical description of Voloshyn that we accessed from the Ukraine Ministry of Internal Affairs is interesting. She's listed as six foot tall, athletically built, some tattoos and with a prominent birthmark down the right-hand side of her face. Now, generally, that as good as matched the body of the girl pulled from the car by Polish police at the time of the accident. Their initial identification was based on the ID they found at the crash site – passport, driver's license, credit cards – all of which belonged to Darja Voloshyn. However, when the body was returned to her family in Ukraine, her mother was adamant that it was not her daughter's. For a start, there was no facial birthmark, which nobody seems to have checked against the photo ID she was carrying, and the tattoos were different. Fingerprinting eventually confirmed that the dead girl in the accident was not Voloshyn at all, but a missing Romanian girl named Oana Saguna, who bore a striking resemblance to Darja Voloshyn and, of particular interest, came from a very similar background: broken home, minor drug offences, fell into crime, and then vanished around the age of seventeen. She was drunk at the time of the accident, twice the legal limit."

"The profile is very typical of girls who are targeted by traffickers, sir," said Reigns. "They're young and vulnerable, and have usually run away from home to escape domestic violence, abuse, or even just to search for a better life. Predators are constantly on the look out for them."

"And you think, at some point, this young girl, Miss Saguna, came into the circles frequented by Voloshyn?" asked Davenport.

"You recall I mentioned earlier that when women become involved in trafficking they tend to operate at the middle-management level, and are mostly involved in the trafficking of girls for sexual exploitation? When I was an analyst with Interpol, I led the team responsible for compiling the Blue Notice that was issued in relation to the Night Witch. The profile we'd developed of the Night Witch was that she was most likely late twenties to early thirties tops, possibly Ukrainian, and a victim herself. All of which we know fits perfectly with the profile of Darja Voloshyn. So, yes, I believe Voloshyn knew Miss Saguna, personally or through her connections and, based on their physical similarities, saw an opportunity to make herself disappear."

Davenport nodded. "I see."

"Added to that, everything about the woman I saw in Hong Kong fits the psychological and physical profile we'd put together – her strong physique, authoritative voice, the statement hairstyle and outwardly confident demeanor – they're like an armor that conceals her actual personality. Deep down, at her core, she's been damaged, most likely when she was very young. And as she matured, she rebelled against whatever it was that damaged her – drugs, abuse, rape. It was clearly traumatic. So much so that when she eventually escaped, she reinvented herself in order to survive. So if we consider the age, physical descriptions, ethnic origins and so on, and we compare Voloshyn's criminal history to the Witch's reported appetite for violence, it's highly probable that the Night Witch and Darja Voloshyn are the same person.

"I think Grenville gave her a start as far as money was concerned – in fact, I'm sure she managed to coerce quite a healthy nest egg out of him before doing away with him. But then I think she underestimated the extent of the interest that followed his disappearance. It shocked her and she needed a way to distance herself from further unwanted attention. So she used her connections in Poland. They targeted Oana Saguna, filled her full of alcohol and drugs, and put her behind the wheel of that car. It was an accident arranged to make it look as though Voloshyn had been killed, nothing more than a botched attempt to bury her past and move on."

"At the expense of an innocent young girl's life," said Davenport. "What's our next move?"

"Our current thoughts are Belize," said Morgan. "We know from Tom's recollections that Voloshyn inveigled Grenville down to Belize back in oh-six, and both Grenville and Peter were killed down there. We also know that the crew Beth saw in Hong Kong all dispersed on Belizean passports. Now, as far as this job is concerned, Beth's been blown. So she'll remain here in London for now and follow any leads she can to find Voloshyn's latest identity. Meanwhile I'm going to get myself down to Belize via Guatemala as soon as possible. I'll aim to take a room at the Paradise Palms Resort — it was the last place Tom and Peter had a lead with that bar manager, Vasquez. It's still operating, so it seems the most appropriate place to begin."

"Very well," said Davenport. "Excellent work, both of you. Best you get started—"

The door to his office opened and Mila Haddad entered.

"I'm sorry to interrupt, sir, but you all need to see this."

Haddad crossed the room and, taking up a remote, turned on the large digital TV screen set upon the wall to the right of the general's desk. As the screen came to life, she looked straight at Morgan, her face full of concern.

He fixed his eyes on the screen. BBC World News was leading with a story coming out of Hong Kong.

"Wait, isn't that Queen Elizabeth Hospital in Kowloon?" Reigns asked, already knowing the answer. Morgan didn't respond.

"It appears that a member of the hospital staff opened fire within the Intensive Care ward, killing at least three people ..."

Mrs Jolley entered the room.

"Sir, I have Assistant Commissioner Kwong on the line for you from Hong Kong."

Chapter Twenty-Nine

BELIZE, CENTRAL AMERICA

The girl woke with a start and the shock of it made her catch her breath. The room was dark, almost black, but for a sliver of light beneath the door in the corner. The silence and cold were frightening. She had little recollection of where she was or how long she'd been there. Hours? Days? She couldn't remember. Had she taken something, or been given something? All she knew was that her head was throbbing, the left side of her face felt twice its usual size and her mouth was dry as sand, with a distinct taste of blood. She took a deep breath that made her head throb even more and tried to roll onto her back, but one of her wrists, the left one, wouldn't budge. She tried to pull it free but winced in pain as it stayed rigid and immovable.

Her mind's eye teased her with flashes of memory: a rustle in the mangroves, a sudden splash, a putrid stench, a snap, then falling, screaming, running. Panic set in as she pulled and pulled and pulled again, trying to free herself, but the rattle of handcuffs against a metal bed frame reminded her of where she was and what had happened, and all she achieved was taking another layer of skin from her already bleeding wrist. The pain made her stretch and her entire body unwound gratefully, her long, slender legs reaching as far as they could before she felt her toes wriggling beyond the end of the mattress. There were no sheets, blankets or pillows, and when the coarse fabric and stitching of the old mattress rasped against her skin she realized she was naked.

Her eyes filled with tears. She dropped her face back on to the mattress and began to sob.

There was a time, she remembered, when she'd been important, when she had moved in the much-feared circles of the *Zmajevi* and was the main girl of Drago, their *Šefa*, chief of the Dragons. Drago was much older than her, she didn't know exactly how much, and he was cruel, but at least he wasn't her depraved, alcoholic father. All she knew was that Drago's money, and the clothes and drugs he gave her, made her life with him bearable; back then, she was somebody. She was beautiful, envied even. She'd wielded power over men with her flawless skin, white like porcelain, and perfect platinum hair that fell dead straight all the way to her waist. And, of course, because she belonged to Drago. She could walk into any nightclub she wanted, wearing little more than lingerie, stilettos and a leather jacket, and crowds would part to make way for her.

But that was long ago. Drago had been arrested and now, without his protection, she was back to being a nobody, just another girl no one knew or wanted. Now her skin was red and sore from too many hours spent in the sun and living rough during her days on the run. Her lips were cracked and tasted of blood, and her feet were blistered and raw. Wondering if she'd make it to her nineteenth birthday, she sniffed back tears and sank her face deeper into the musty fabric of the mattress, pulling pointlessly against the cuffs.

The door crashed open. She recoiled into the fetal position, back against the wall at the head of the bed. The sudden burst of light forced her to avert her eyes until slowly, reluctantly, she turned back to face the shadowy outlines gathered around the bed. There were four of them looking down at her, maybe more – she couldn't be sure because all she could see were silhouettes; her eyes were still adjusting to the glare of the light from outside. However many there were, they were all taunting her in gutter-level Russian and Polish. She instantly remembered the man leading them: he was older than the others, bald and big, with the face of a boxer, all smashed and flat. There was a tattoo of three triangles on his left cheek and dozens of thick scars that looked like they'd been slashed into the skin of his tattooed forearms. She didn't know what any of it meant but it terrified her. Their proximity, their words, their eagerness; all of it. She knew what was about to happen. They were describing it to her in excruciating detail.

"Jovana?" A woman's voice carried into the room from somewhere outside. It was soft and soothing, calling for her. "Jovana?"

Oh my God! she thought. *I am saved.*

"Ah, Jovana. My sweet little girl." The comforting warmth of that voice broke through the clamor of the men, and their foul taunts fell silent.

Jovana's vision was clearer now and she looked up to see a woman, tall and beautiful, stepping up to the edge of the bed and then sitting down on it, very near to her.

"Are they not treating you well, my darling?"

Jovana shook her head nervously, not knowing what to say. She remained curled up and trembling at the head of the bed, eyes darting across the faces of the men still standing around her, leering at her hungrily.

"There, there," the woman said quietly. "I'm here now and everything is going to be all right. Godek, you and your beasts must stand back. Can't you see you're upsetting her? Hasn't she been through enough already? Somebody bring me a glass of water for her."

Godek and his men – all muscle-bound, in tightly fitting T-shirts and covered in tattoos and markings similar to their leader's – shuffled back obediently and leaned against the walls. One went off to another corner of the room. She heard the squeal of an old tap being turned and a rush of water. The man returned, handed the woman a glass, and rejoined the others.

Now it was just the two of them, two women – like a mother comforting her frightened daughter.

"Take this, darling," the woman said, her voice full of caring and compassion. "You'll be feeling better in no time."

Jovana took the pill she offered without a second thought and drank down the small tumbler of water gratefully.

"There, that's my dear girl."

The woman was wearing a short halterneck dress in a bright tropical print. She reached out and ran her slender fingers slowly along Jovana's bare calf, exploring it tenderly for minutes, then over her thigh and hip as far as her torso. Jovana's skin reacted to the gentle caress, coming to life under the touch of those soft fingers.

"You really should not have run away, my darling," the woman said, speaking to her as if she were a child, making everything alright again. "I have been so looking forward to meeting you. You see, I'm going to give your life back to you; all of the clothes and the money. You'd like that, wouldn't you, my darling?"

Jovana nodded weakly, gazing up into the woman's stunning gray-blue eyes.

The woman stood up. At a click of her fingers, Godek stepped forward. Twisting Jovana's fettered hand roughly, he fumbled with a key and unlocked the handcuffs. Jovana's right hand shot straight to her bloodied and bruised left wrist and she rubbed it, relieved beyond words to be released. Then she felt her body slowly beginning to relax, melting into the mattress, the tension and fear slipping away. She was free.

"Stand up now," the woman ordered. "Stand close to me so I can see you properly."

Still frightened, Jovana didn't move. Instead her eyes remained fixed on the woman, who was now standing over her. To Jovana, huddled against the bedhead with her arms wrapped protectively around her legs, the woman looked like an Amazon. Easily six feet tall with striking features, tanned skin and short white-blonde hair, she commanded the room. The men hadn't made a sound from the moment she'd entered. Jovana watched as the woman's hand reached out for her, long fingers splaying open impatiently, invoking her obedience.

"Now, girl. On your feet."

Jovana acquiesced, peeling herself away from the wall. She shuffled to the edge of the bed and allowed her bare feet to drop to the rough floor. She felt drowsy. The woman took her hand and guided her from the bed until she was standing up straight. Jovana's legs were unsteady, just inches from the woman, and she realized that she was almost as tall and not dissimilar to look at. Without any more soothing words to calm her fears, the woman proceeded to scrutinize every inch of Jovana's body and face, turning her around, lifting her arms, pulling her hair, examining her teeth and feeling her breasts, as though she was considering the purchase of an animal. Jovana's nakedness heightened her sense of exposure and vulnerability. She could feel the eyes of the men crawling all over her like ants on her skin as the woman continued the examination. She was feeling dizzy and bewildered, as though she was observing what was happening around her but not participating. Finally, she felt the woman's splayed fingers upon her face and she was pushed back on to the bed.

"She's perfect, Godek," the woman said to the leader. "Absolutely perfect. I want her cleaned up, well fed, rested and looking a million dollars by the end of the month. Understood?"

Godek grunted his acknowledgment. The woman was clearly in charge and Jovana's heart instantly filled with hope as she listened. Was this to be her savior after all?

"Thank you! Thank you!" Jovana mumbled from the bed, her speech slurred and almost incomprehensible. "I'll do anything you want. Just tell me."

"Yes, you will, my darling, starting right now," the woman replied without emotion. "And I expect you to make this worth my while. I get bored so very easily if I'm not enjoying myself. Someone get me a chair and a cigarette."

Uncertain what was happening, Jovana watched anxiously as a sumptuous, expensive-looking chair she hadn't noticed before was dragged from a corner and positioned in the center of the room, facing the bed. The woman sat down, draping one leg lazily over a heavily cushioned armrest and fixing her gaze directly upon Jovana. One of the men placed a cigarette between her full red lips and lit it. The others crowded around the bed, laughing and taunting Jovana, ogling her. Then they began removing their clothes.

"OK, I'm ready," said the woman, blowing out smoke and getting herself comfortable. She waved a hand and the men closed in around her. "Tonight and tonight only, she's all yours. You can do whatever you wish to her, so make the most of it. I want her to know exactly what's waiting for her the next time she even thinks about escaping."

Chapter Thirty

INTREPID HQ, BROADWAY, LONDON

"It appears that a hospital maintenance man was engaged to conduct the assassinations of both Lam and Commander Sutherland. There is some suggestion that he was seen earlier on the ward where Lam had been recovering but missed him as the inspector had already been discharged. Of course, we now know that Lam had remained in the hospital and was visiting David at the time of the assassinations. The gunman was provided with the perfect opportunity."

Tears were streaming from Mila Haddad's eyes, although she remained stoic and in control as she briefed them. Elizabeth Reigns, tears welling in her own eyes, was determined to hold it together. Beside her sat Alex Morgan. He was dead still but she could feel the rage boiling within him, like a mine-shaft packed to the gunnels with dynamite, silently waiting for someone to light the fuse. So far he'd barely said a word. He just sat in silence, concentrating on Davenport, not making eye contact with anyone else

"And Dave was just lying there," he said. "A sitting fucking duck."

"I know it's of little consolation," said Davenport. "But David was in an induced coma. He couldn't have been aware of anything."

"Not that anybody knows for sure," growled Morgan.

"Do we have any information on the gunman, sir?" Reigns asked, wanting to break that particular train of thought. "You said he was a maintenance worker. How does that fit with all this?"

"Nothing concrete yet. Kwong believes there will most likely be some kind of underworld connection, though he'd worked there for fifteen years and was well regarded by all who knew him. Nobody could have expected this of him, which, from the point of view of whoever orchestrated the killings, made him the perfect choice."

"We know who orchestrated it," said Morgan. "Wu Ming and this Night Witch creature. That's where we need to direct our attention."

"We've been compromised in Hong Kong, so for now we'll be leaving any direct attempts to locate Wu Ming to the Hong Kong Police. We'll monitor their progress via liaison officers embedded within Interpol. Meanwhile, our focus will remain on Central America."

"We're not going to do anything in Hong Kong? We should be going straight back in there and hunting these bastards down!" Morgan's tone was bordering on disrespectful.

Davenport bristled. "We'll do nothing of the sort. Locating Darja Voloshyn is our first priority."

"We need to be in Hong Kong now, while the trail is fresh. I understand we can't send Beth back in there but what about James Lee or Liu Yang?" Morgan argued.

"They're both great agents and have tons of experience throughout Asia."

Davenport's response was abrupt. "I'll not risk another agent by inserting them into a situation that's already compromised. Hong Kong is out. We will commit our resources to Central America, until I say otherwise." Morgan opened his mouth to speak again but Davenport cut him down. "That's the end of it."

An icy silence descended upon them. Morgan's knuckles were white upon the arms of his chair. Reigns thought he was about to kick the fine mahogany coffee table across the room. She could see Davenport appraising Morgan. The loss of Sutherland had hit him hardest, and the combined effects of mission fatigue and bereavement were palpable. Reigns knew Morgan's history and wondered whether or not there was an element of post-traumatic stress beginning to surface. Guys like Morgan and Sutherland had been at war for over a decade; it was not inconceivable that even men of their courage and experience would be affected by what they had seen and been through. They would be inhuman if they hadn't.

"Where to from here then?" he asked reluctantly.

"Our recovery team will take care of David and repatriate him back to his family in the United States. In the meantime, if there's anything we can do to ensure his loss was not in vain, it's to see this operation through to its conclusion. That means you head to Belize, as planned."

Morgan remained silent, his body rigid with tension. Reigns could almost hear his teeth grinding.

General Davenport stood up and, with great poise, turned to Reigns and Haddad. "Would you mind giving us a moment." It wasn't a request.

"Of course, sir."

Reigns tried to catch Morgan's eye but he wasn't looking. His jaw was clenched tight and the explosion she'd sensed before seemed imminent. "Alex, I'll wait outside," she told him.

When Reigns and Haddad had left the room, General Davenport strolled to the windows overlooking Broadway and St James's Park station. His hands were in his pockets and his shoulders were square and resolute. He remained quiet for a time.

Morgan took the opportunity to stand and compose himself too; he felt the shakes coming on again, the blood draining from his face, and a sinking feeling, like a piece of glacial ice had broken away and was plummeting down the center of his back. He strolled in the opposite direction, facing instead the shelves and frames that lined the walls of the War Room, trying to manage the breathing exercises Beth had taught him on the Gulfstream. His chief's personal history surrounded him and Morgan was immediately reminded of the many reasons why he had invested his unequivocal respect, loyalty and admiration in this man over the past three years. *Breathe deep, hold, release. Breathe deep, hold, release.*

"I need to know that you can handle this," Davenport said. "Because I'm not about to send you into the field if you can't."

"Yes, sir. I understand," replied Morgan, but he knew his demeanor must betray him.

"You're not sounding very convincing."

"You can't leave me out of this. I'll be fine once I get going. You know I'm no good sitting around on my hands.

I need to be moving, down there, taking these fuckers out."

Davenport turned away from the windows and walked slowly back across the room to face his agent.

"You don't have the monopoly on loss, Morgan." His tone was composed and adamant. "None of us does. In this organization, we have no option but to put ourselves beyond any personal feelings and, in this case, focus on our considerable responsibility to the millions of people around the world who, right at this moment, are the victims of these traffickers. I accept that the news of Sutherland's murder has hit you hardest of all, but I don't need a loose cannon on my team. These people are, to the best of our knowledge, the ones responsible for the death of my friend Peter Fleming, too. But you won't hear me issuing you with any 'shoot to kill and fuck the law' orders. We aren't the bloody CIA!

"If we're going to bring these people to justice then I need you to be focused, objective and, above all, able to act decisively when the time comes. I have every confidence that Elizabeth will confirm the identities and location of the Night Witch and her associates, sooner than you think. And when she does, you'll have your opportunity to take the fight to them."

Morgan remained silent.

"Avenge Sutherland's death, by all means," said Davenport. "And if you find yourself in circumstances where you have no choice but to kill, then that's a decision only you can make. However, if you leave this office with your head full of nothing but revenge, then you're a bloody fool. I've already lost one good agent taking these people on. Don't make it two."

Chapter Thirty-One

BELIZE, CENTRAL AMERICA

"Get up!" The harsh order woke her. It was spoken in Polish by the leader of the pack, the animal with the smashed face: Godek.

There were no windows in the room, so she was forced to squint again against the sudden surge of light from the doorway. Godek was standing at the open door, looking away, smoking and disinterested. There was no trace of concern or remorse for what they had done to her the previous night, just cold detachment as though he was letting an animal out of its cage to get some exercise.

"I haven't got all fucking day," he said, and flicked the butt of his cigarette at her.

When she moved, her entire body protested. She couldn't sit, the pain was excruciating, and her shaking arms were too weak to hold her upright. When she tried to stand she fell back against the bed and slumped to the floor. When she turned to gain a hold on the bed she saw the blood stains, her blood, on the mattress, but she was beyond crying. She'd done that for most of the morning until exhaustion, pain and fear plunged her once again into a deep sleep filled with dreams of fields, oceans and sunshine. Now awake and back in the harsh reality, her mind had managed to detach completely from who she really was, enabling her to function, at least perfunctorily. While on the surface she had physically acquiesced to the conditions of her captivity, mentally she had withdrawn all of the contours of her usual persona and closed them down. It was a survival mechanism, not something that she chose to do; she had been through so much already for one so young that her mind and body were now conditioned to default to this state.

"If I have to come in there, bitch, I'll drag you out by your fucking hair."

Jovana didn't respond. Instead, she pushed herself up onto the bed again and stood shakily for a few moments until the dizziness passed and she felt able to walk. Then she stumbled to the door.

Godek tossed an oversized T-shirt on the ground in front of her and stepped away. She could hear his footsteps on a concrete path outside. She picked up the T-shirt slowly, fearing she might collapse if she bent over too quickly, and pulled it over her naked body. It smelled like a dog had been sleeping on it.

When she went outside she saw that she had been in a small building no more than fifteen feet square, made of cement blocks with a flat, thatched roof and a door. The building was in the middle of mangroves that had all but overgrown it and she was instantly struck by the humidity, sounds and odors of her surroundings.

Godek led her in silence along a path bordered on both sides by a tall wire-mesh fence, meandering through the trees deeper and deeper into the mangroves. Almost in the very instant that she remembered something about that fence, Godek said, "You won't try to climb over that again. Domingo won't let you get away twice," and laughed to himself.

After a minute or so she noticed that everything was getting brighter and realized that they were reaching a clearing where the heavy foliage above them made way for sunlight. She thought she could hear the ocean.

The fenced path ended at a solid metal gate set in a wall. The whitewashed brickwork was at least ten feet high and disappeared in both directions. There was a wide cleared gap between it and the edge of the mangroves. Godek stood at the gate and banged on it three times. Jovana could hear the rustling of keys and a heavy bolt being pulled back with the squeal of rusted metal. The gate opened and a man appeared carrying a machine gun. He looked Mexican, she thought, brown and leathery, not very tall, with pitch-black hair and a straggly beard. His expression gave away nothing. No words were exchanged. He barely acknowledged Godek and didn't even look at her. Once they were through she heard the gate close behind them, the bolt sliding home and the keys being used the lock the padlock.

Beyond the wall there was vegetation, ferns mainly and some palms, thick and low and cut back from the path like they were maintained by a caretaker. They continued walking for only a short time before they reached a scene she could never have imagined in her wildest dreams.

At the end of the path the vegetation stopped suddenly, opening on to a courtyard the size of a football pitch. In the very center stood a pool, long and wide, with crystalline blue water, cream-colored tiles laid all around it and sunloungers dotted randomly along its edges. Tall palm trees swayed in a gentle breeze at the far end of the pool and ran in straight lines inside the walls of the compound. Beyond the pool, framed by the palm trees, stood a house. It was a palatial, multilevel villa, painted cream, with huge picture windows, sliding glass doors, and wrap-around verandahs on all levels.

The sounds of the ocean reached her as Godek continued walking around the pool to the house. Jovana followed him, reveling in the feeling of soft white sand beneath her bare feet. She drew the smell of the sea deeply into her chest and crunched her toes in the sand before they reached the poolside and stepped across the sun-warmed tiles.

They skirted the edge of the pool, eventually reaching a corner of the house. Godek descended a short set of stairs, following a narrow path to a basement door. Another windowless room? Another cell? More of the same treatment? Jovana stopped dead in her tracks, unwilling to proceed voluntarily into the darkness. The man, sensing her reticence, turned and glowered at her.

"Get down here," he barked.

When she stalled a moment too long he came back up the stairs, grabbed her by the arm and pulled her after him.

Jovana tripped, narrowly avoiding falling flat on her face. The man dragged her to an open door and threw her inside.

Chapter Thirty-Two

THE REMBRANDT HOTEL, LONDON

Alex Morgan sat crumpled within the comforting embrace of a sofa in a quiet corner of the lounge bar. He was halfway through a Carlsberg. He'd been to his room and changed from his suit to jeans, casual shirt and a very well-worn pair of R. M. Williams boots – his favorites from Australia. An equally well-worn houndstooth sports jacket was thrown across the arm of a chair next to him.

He was exhausted. Even to the casual observer, everything about him said so. The shock of Sutherland's death had stripped the last of his energy reserves and he was now barely capable of functioning beyond reclining and drinking, which, fortunately, was all he wanted to do – have a beer or two and remember his friend. If he could manage it, he might even wander over to the Bunch of Grapes on Brompton Road and settle in for a couple of pints, do some thinking and then hit the hay early. He just needed to be normal and do normal stuff like a normal human being, at least for one night; God only knew what the next few days or weeks would have in store for him. Right now he was burned out and needed recovery time while the admin team sorted out his flights to Belize and Reigns searched for a target.

Elizabeth Reigns ... He didn't see that coming. He'd known her for probably twenty-four hours, give or take, and since returning to England, even with Sutherland on a slab, he couldn't stop thinking about her. Jesus! Seeing her operating in the field, Morgan had known she was something special. He couldn't help but be impressed. But was he only impressed by her in the field, or was there more to it? What the hell had come over him? He had to shut down any thoughts about being attracted to her and realign his priorities.

Morgan took a long drink, stretched back lazily in the sofa and closed his eyes, running a quick diagnostic over his current state of mind. One thing he knew for sure, he couldn't get the images from the back of the Range Rover out of his mind. The blood everywhere; the back of the vehicle awash with the stuff, all over Morgan and all over Sutherland. He remembered trying to find the wounds and, as quickly as he found them, applying the bandages while yelling instructions to Victor Lam. Reigns driving frantically through the traffic. And in the midst of it all, Sutherland. Quiet. Stoic. Helpless. Flat on his back, coughing blood, and that distant "don't let me die" look in his eyes. It was familiar to Morgan. Too familiar: a look he'd seen in others clinging to life, soldiers, brothers, knowing you're their only hope. Knowing you won't let them down. Can't let them down!

"Hey, stranger. What're you doin', sitting here all on your lonesome?"

Morgan sat up suddenly, rubbing his eyes. When he

opened them they were moist and red. "Hey," he replied wearily. "Aren't you supposed to be working?"

Elizabeth Reigns dropped on to the sofa close beside him. She was still in her business suit, although somehow she'd managed to relax it. She was smiling at him but couldn't hide her concern. She pushed her hand gently through his thick, dark brown hair, brushing the fallen fringe back from his brow.

"I'm done for the day, and besides, I needed to check in on a friend," she said, her voice gentle and caring.

"How'd you know I'd be here?"

"Mila told me you always stay at The Rembrandt when you're in town and somehow I knew I'd find you in the bar. Is that beer? I thought you were a scotch man."

"Sometimes there's just nothing better on Earth than a nice cold beer. Anyway, tonight I'm on leave," Morgan said. He waved at the barman with his almost-empty glass. "So I'm going to have more than one."

"Well, you've earned it. Shame you can't take more time off. You should, you know."

"There's work to be done," he said. "You heard the boss."

"Still, you look pretty beat, Morgan. And I think everybody would agree you could do with some down time."

"What the fuck does that mean?"

Reigns placed her hand on his thigh. Her touch was instantly soothing to him and he felt his angry reaction slip away. She was telling him to calm down without telling him to calm down. It was effective.

"When we left the general's office, you were biting the head off anyone who came near you. I think everyone in the building heard the door slam as you left. Metaphorically speaking, of course."

"Was it that obvious?"

"Afraid so," she said. "Mrs Jolley described you to me as 'spirited and headstrong.' I won't tell you what Mila said."

"What? Pain in the ass?"

"Let's go with that."

They both laughed at Morgan's bad habit of wearing his heart on his sleeve. He knew himself well enough to accept it. He'd always been that way. Even as a kid. When something or someone pissed him off, everyone knew about it. And it used to get him into trouble, especially with his superiors in the army, although those issues diminished as he climbed the ranks himself. An old friend from the US 82nd Airborne once remarked that if Morgan had been an enlisted man instead of an officer, he probably would have spent most of his time in the brig.

The barman arrived.

"Drink?" Morgan asked her.

"Sure. Sauvignon blanc," Reigns replied.

"Sauvignon blanc, there's a nice one from Marlborough, New Zealand, on your wine list, and another Carlsberg, please." The barman nodded and withdrew.

The two fell silent. She held his gaze for a few extra seconds. Morgan caught the lingering pull of her fragrance and remembered how good she'd felt when he'd held her on the plane.

"You'll just have to put up with me a bit longer," he said. "At least while we get this Night Witch thing sorted out."

"I suppose I will," Reigns replied. "I'm sure I'll cope."

The drinks arrived.

"Well, here's to you," he said, raising his glass. "Welcome aboard, Reigns."

"Idiot," she said, smiling.

Morgan was glad of company, especially her company. He could easily have become morose otherwise. Like many soldiers, he had his superstitions about certain things and courting bad luck by stating the bleeding obvious was one of them. They all knew their business was dangerous. There was no need to dwell on it. Sutherland's preoccupation with his own shelf life had been a harbinger. Remembering it unsettled Morgan, but Reigns' unexpected arrival had instantly improved his mood.

"What's your take on this witch thing?" he asked.

"Which bit of it exactly?"

"The whole identity thing and how she's managed to stay under the radar all these years. I mean, there can't be that many young, attractive European women operating in that business. Right?"

"Actually, I think you've hit the nail on the head there. I believe there are a lot more young, attractive European women operating in that space than we think."

"Seriously?"

"I'm not ready to drop this on the general yet, so keep it to yourself, but I think we're dealing with a doppelgänger, or even a bunch of them."

"What, like, exact doubles?" he asked. "Isn't that a bit paranormal?"

"Sounds that way. But rather than magically conjuring up ghosts, or spirit doubles, or anything like that, I think our girl employs actual doubles of herself to allow her to be in multiple locations at one time. The accident in Poland triggered the idea for me. Especially given how similar Oana Saguna was to descriptions of the Witch. I believe she's also interested in the occult and likes to promote some kind of supernatural image. You heard Tom say that this barman you're going after in Belize saw her transform. Remember, he said if she was happy, the whole place was happy. If she wasn't ... then run for cover. She's created the illusion of being changeable, like a chameleon, and the strategy spooks simple folk and makes them believe she's something that she's not. In reality, she's simply employing one of the oldest tricks in the book." Reigns made a play with her hands to demonstrate. "She's distracting our attention with one hand, while doing the serious stuff over here with the other."

"So, she has a small army of fembots she's selected because they look like her, and sends them out to do her dirty work. Is that what you mean?"

"Exactly. The girls are most likely victims of her trafficking operations and she selects them from among all the others she has working for her and offers them an 'out.' Believe me, after the degradation, abuse and psychological trauma these girls experience in sexual servitude, anything would be better. And I mean anything."

"And I suppose these poor kids end up feeling some sort of gratitude toward the bitch for freeing them?"

"Most likely. She becomes their liberator. It's inevitable they'd form an attachment to her, as misguided as that is. They'd be prepared to do just about anything she asked of them."

"Captive bonding."

"Yep. Meanwhile she remains hidden somewhere well out of harm's way and only travels when absolutely necessary."

"Her very own trafficking ambassadors," Morgan said without humor. "Clever, if it wasn't so fucking treacherous. So what are your thoughts on Belize then? Turned up anything yet?"

"I still have to prove all this but I'm trying to focus on

the bits in between the details we have. Tom's theory about why Humphrey Grenville ended up in Belize and the apparent familiarity of the bar manager with Voloshyn suggest she liked the place. Add to that the fact that Peter Fleming was also killed down there, just as he and Tom felt they were getting close to uncovering something, and you start getting a real sense that we're on the right track."

"The Night Witch was protecting her territory?"

Reigns nodded. "Look, I could be wrong but it's definitely worth investigating. Meanwhile, the info about the sex trafficking ring operating out of El Salvador interests me, too."

"You mean that Ponciano character?"

"Yeah, we've already identified four separate cases of wealthy foreign men being lured to Central and South America, areas they normally wouldn't go, who then went missing. And, surprise, surprise – they all disappeared post 2006, after Voloshyn dropped off the grid and after the Grenville-Fleming case. In the new cases, we've found many similarities to the way she lured Grenville, only the targets weren't anywhere near as high profile as he was. I think she learned a lesson from taking on a relatively well-known public figure."

"She had a scam going to get money out of all these guys?"

"Looks that way, especially in the early days when she was getting herself set up – operating capital and so forth. Extortion under the threat of violence is a pretty standard way to earn a dollar in that part of the world. I think she was luring them out of their comfort zones, promising an endless supply of pretty young things, and once she got them there, she had them. A classic honey trap. Then all it would take would be straightforward blackmail, extortion or a ransom deal of some kind. She'd get her money and they'd run without telling a soul. If they survived, that is."

"Unlike Grenville and Peter Fleming."

"Because they got too close to who she really was, which is exactly why I think we're on the right track," said Reigns. "Don't worry. We'll get to the bottom of this, so you're as well informed as I can possibly manage."

Morgan remained silent, deep in thought.

"Well, Alex Morgan, I hate to love you and leave you, but I should probably go," she said. "And you should really get some rest. You look like you could sleep right there. I just wanted to catch you before you left. We didn't have much of a chance this morning and after the flight home and everything, well …"

Morgan sensed she had something on her mind. He decided to leave her with her thoughts. He didn't know if he was ready for the complication of her but he didn't want her to go either.

"I hope you're going to finish your drink first. You can't leave me here all on my own."

"OK, but then I'm going," she replied, and they fell into an awkward silence for a few moments. She squeezed his leg and smiled back at him as she sipped the sauvignon blanc. Morgan was torn. He couldn't allow himself to be so distracted by her and yet he wanted to be completely distracted by her. Despite himself he needed to know how she felt.

"What's on your mind, Beth?" he began. "You've been bursting to say something ever since you arrived. So, come on then."

Reigns placed her glass down on the table and turned so that she was facing him directly, hands in her lap, her face delicate and vulnerable in the soft lighting of the bar.

Morgan wasn't sure if he was ready to hear whatever it was she was about to say. Somehow, he knew what was coming and suddenly felt resentful of her.

"There's no other way for me to say this, Alex," she said. "So I'm just going to put it out there. I don't think you should go on this one. You're burned out, you've just lost your closest friend and you've not had a break in a long time. When I walked in here, you were barely awake. You need time to grieve and decompress. You're not ready for another mission. Not back to back. Not by a long shot."

"What ... we spend one night in the sack together and you think you know me?" he said coldly. "Well, you don't. Jesus! You've been in the firm five minutes and suddenly you're an expert. I don't need to be told what I should or shouldn't do, and I sure as hell don't need to be mothered, not by you and not by anyone else. Did you share this opinion of yours with Davenport?"

"Of course not! Why would you think that?" Reigns' entire demeanor had hardened defensively. She gathered up her handbag and cell phone and stood. "I knew I shouldn't have said anything."

Morgan stayed seated, seething with rage and frustration. He looked up and she was standing over him, her eyes wet with tears but her face and body telling the opposite story. She wasn't taking any of his shit.

"You know, last night might just have been a night in the sack for us both. I get that. But like it or not, we have some kind of connection. I don't know why because clearly you're a complete asshole ... we just do. So, take it from me: if you're determined to go after these people then make sure you're ready, because we're all relying on you. Don't fuck it up."

Chapter Thirty-Three

BELIZE, CENTRAL AMERICA

"Your phone call this morning," the man began in Polish, "was it satisfactory?"

"Very," she replied. "They're impressed with the operation and can see the fit it would be with their own businesses. I believe they'll proceed."

"Are you sure you're ready to be controlled, Dee?"

"Nobody will ever control me again, Dariusz," she answered. "They're offering ridiculous money, more than I ever envisaged, including an ongoing percentage once the deal is done. As it stands, I could take their money and walk away from all this. But if they want me to stay and run things then it will cost them more and it will be on my terms. Don't worry, I'll look after you. Or maybe *you* could run it for them."

She sipped coffee, black, from a gilt-rimmed antique cup and paused a moment to enjoy the light breeze that washed over the terrace, bringing with it the smell of the ocean. She breathed in deeply through her nostrils and closed her eyes for just a moment as the breeze gently whispered through her hair. Past the palms and across the high perimeter wall she could see a pair of double-crested cormorants swooping out above the sea, quarreling with each other as they searched for food. She decided that a swim after lunch would go a long way toward easing the burden of her responsibilities.

"Do they want to see you again?" he asked. "These investors."

"Once more," she replied. "In a few days, to discuss the details. And, of course, they want to understand more about the arrangement with the Chinese. As far as I know they aren't aware of what happened in Hong Kong, which is why we have to resolve things quickly before it becomes more of a problem. We have to secure Wu Ming's end of it – and the money of his Triad backers – as soon as possible."

"How have you explained it to them so far?"

"Simple. Wu Ming is old and tired. He wants the cash without the work. So, he is hungry for his operation to join mine. Handing over control of his network and labor-supply chain to me ensures him a healthy slice of my global income without any effort or ongoing liability. And adding his operation to mine gives me almost twenty-five percent of the industry globally. The investors know that. And as they run most of the rest, they see their opportunity. In fact, they were about to explore a deal with the Chinese themselves, when they learned from our partners in the Middle East that there was already a negotiation in play. So they're happy to leave me to close the deal with Wu, and then it's just a matter of how badly they want it all."

"That's good, very good," he replied. "But I think you have something else on your mind, too?"

"I'm concerned, Dariusz," she replied. "The police infiltration in Hong Kong has unsettled me. I feel like my personal security is fucked."

He dismissed this out of hand. "What are you concerned about? Hong Kong was nothing. The cops were chasing the chinks, not us."

"How do we know that?" she said, her voice slightly raised. "How do we know that they weren't after me?"

"You're being paranoid, Dee. Look where you are. Nobody else knows you're here. You have nothing to worry about."

"Nothing to worry about?" She placed her cup down carefully, ensuring that it sat perfectly within the circular recess of the saucer. Then she stood, towering over him. "There was an armed raid by the Hong Kong Police Force on a factory I was supposed to be visiting, and there was a fucking police undercover agent working in the same factory. I think I'm entitled to be paranoid! Why do you think I've been taking precautions all these years?"

"But you weren't even there – it was Ştefania in your place. Your precautions worked. They always do."

"You don't get it, do you? The police obviously thought it was me. The only reason Ştefania was there instead was because *I* decided to send her. Not you. I've had a feeling for a while that things haven't been quite right." She took a deep breath and calmed herself. "I can't afford for this to be happening right now. I'm feeling exposed."

"Like I said, you're paranoid."

"How could they have known unless someone is informing on me?"

"Do you suspect someone? Do you suspect me?" His tone was sharp and suddenly aggressive. The conversation was beginning to turn sour.

"I promoted you. You should remember that," she

remarked. "Try to stay on track. Someone is informing and I need to know who. We're about to seal this deal with the Chinese. It's beyond important and I don't want anything to fuck it up."

"That won't happen."

"I want to know every detail."

"But we went through all this already, last night," he said. "What more do you want to know?"

"I want to hear it all again," she snapped. I need to know if I'm missing something. So start talking."

"Dee, we got everyone out before the cops even knew we'd been there. Wu lost a few of his guys. Who fucking cares?"

"But what about ours? I thought you said we had two killed as well?"

"They were the two assholes I hired in Hong Kong – Czech crooks on R and R. They looked enough like us and wanted some extra cash to buy more girls. I told them they'd be guarding someone; nothing special, easy money. But they ended up dead in a gunfight. R and R!" He laughed. "I didn't even have to pay them."

"None of ours got killed?"

"None. When the trouble started upstairs in the factory, I sent the Czechs to see what was going on. They didn't have a fucking clue. Meanwhile, we got that little bitch Ştefania out."

"Wu won't be happy that his people were killed, but he's not to know that the Czechs weren't actually mine. We can use that; convince him we lost people too. We need to arrange to meet him again. Soon."

"I brought two of the boys back with me, the others are coming in from Guadalajara. They'll be back later tonight.

They can help Godek take care of your little protégées and the others can take a few days off."

"The returning crew are not to touch the girls anymore," she said. "Godek knows that, right?"

"Of course. I've told them already myself. Besides, there's plenty of fresh meat to choose from in town, or they can go up to San Pedro. Backpackers everywhere there. The boys won't bother with your two."

"Where's Godek? I haven't seen him this morning."

"I've sent him up to Belize City to collect Marcos and have a break. He'll be back tomorrow."

"OK." She paused. "Do you have any new ones to show me?"

Dariusz picked up his iPad from the table, tapped in a couple of commands and handed it over.

"Marcos has his eyes on those two. They're Norwegian, working in a bar up in Cancun and they're homesick. Apparently one of them has a sick relative or some shit." Dariusz watched her scrolling through the images on the iPad. "They're both around nineteen or twenty, and fucking hot. They've been traveling for almost a year, are running short of funds and trying to save enough to get back home."

She looked up at him. He returned her smile.

"They're perfect," she said. "We can give them to Wu. The personal service. A goodwill gesture."

"Exactly. He loves the blondes."

"He'd pay good money just to fuck girls like these two. If he gets to keep them for a while, I'm sure he'll be happy to reconvene our meeting. Only this time it will really be with me and it will be here."

"You want to bring Wu here?"

She nodded but kept looking at the girls on the screen.

"OK," he replied. "If you want those girls for Wu, then Marcos will get them for you."

"I want them. How will Marcos play it?" she asked.

"He told me he's already spun them a line about being a talent scout for a movie being shot down here – the next *Mission: Impossible* or some shit like that – to get them excited. He'll tell them he needs beautiful, tanned blondes for a big scene, promise them walk-on parts because he reckons they're perfect, and once they're done with the movie he'll get them a ticket straight back to Norway."

"Tell him to go ahead, only change is that the movie's being filmed in Hong Kong. They'll be a lot more cooperative and excited if they think they're already on their way back home. Once he gets them there, Wu can have them. We have to keep the business with the Chinese moving, especially now that we're being considered for expansion. You got any more?"

"Just some possible new partners who each have a strong supply chain of laborers, one in the Philippines, one in Vietnam, and another one in Guatemala. But I have to check their figures some more. I can take you through that later."

"OK. So, how is Ştefania?"

"Who cares?" he said.

"Just tell me."

"What can I say? She freaked when the shooting started but we got her out quickly. She didn't see anything."

"It wouldn't be the first time we'd lost one" She paused, thinking. "What was her name – the one who got stabbed when the deal went wrong in Cambodia?"

"Abelina," he answered immediately. "The Swede. Now she was a great fuck. She loved it."

"Yeah, that's right. She was sweet. Shame. At least she didn't die in front of anyone."

"That would have been hard to explain," said Dariusz. "As far as anyone knows, you made a miraculous recovery."

"What if it was her – Ştefania? Informing on me to the police. Have you thought of that?"

He remained silent for a while, contemplating this. "I hate that little bitch," he said. "I should have had one of the boys slit her throat before we got on the plane to leave Hong Kong. I was close, believe me. She talks too much … in the airport, on the plane; ordering the boys around like she's actually in charge. She's dangerous."

"She's reckless, but we can deal with that. All it means is that we retire her earlier than usual. Is there any chance she could have been alone somewhere long enough to contact the police? Borrowed a cell phone from a stranger? Left a note somewhere, or even an email?"

"There's no way," he replied emphatically. "I've never trusted her. One of us is with her at all times. She's never alone. I won't even let her take a piss on her own."

"OK. Where is she now? Did you get her back in one piece?"

"Yes," Dariusz replied. "She's here, in her room. I haven't allowed her access out here yet. Not until I saw you."

"Good. Does she suspect anything?"

"Nothing. The bitch was excited about coming back because she believes you're actually going to release her." He laughed. "She's even fallen for all that shit you tell them about getting a big payout and starting their lives over."

"The system works. Anyway, now we have a replacement," she replied. "Jovana will be ready soon, but not soon enough. I'll have to make the trip to meet with the investors myself. So, in the meantime, we stick to the plan. Give Ştefania her reward week. Then arrange for her to meet Marcos, and he'll take care of everything from there. But she must not meet the new girl."

"Don't worry. Ştefania's in a room at the opposite end of the house, nowhere near Jovana. Besides, Jovana's just getting started with all the treatments and shit you give them. They won't run into each other."

"They'd better not. Jovana is special. I don't want anything unexpected messing her up before I need her."

Chapter Thirty-Four

THE REMBRANDT HOTEL, LONDON

"*I need you?*" Elizabeth Reigns was standing in the hall outside room 333, Morgan's room, brandishing her cell phone, Morgan's text message still on the screen. He was leaning against the open door, looking sheepish and deflated.

"You speak to me like I'm trash, wait until I'm almost home and then text me 'I need you.' What the fuck, Morgan? Have you been drinking?"

"No, of course I haven't. I left the bar when you stormed out."

She glowered at him.

"OK, that didn't come out right, either. When you walked out. I left the bar when you walked out, and I came back up here. Are you going to come in?"

"I haven't decided yet. I came back just to make sure you hadn't done anything stupid. You look like you're OK to me."

Reigns stood her ground, arms crossed, sizing him up.

Morgan could almost hear her foot tapping. It wasn't but it might as well have been.

"OK, listen, you were right."

"About what?"

"About me being a complete asshole. I'm sorry I spoke to you like that. It was fucked up and wrong and I'm sorry. I'm just not thinking straight."

Now she was looking into his eyes. The cell phone had disappeared and her arms were uncrossed. She was softening but still not happy.

"Please come in, Beth," said Morgan. "I promise I'll behave."

"If I see that look of 'asshole' come over you once, Morgan, just once, I'm outta here."

Reigns walked in, kicked off her shoes, dropped her bag and phone on the floor and wandered over to the window. Morgan closed the door, followed her back into the room and sat on the end of the bed. She pushed the curtains aside and looked out across Thurloe Place to the Victoria and Albert Museum.

"It's even more beautiful at night," she said. "Have you ever been in there?"

"Not for a long time."

"Some girl drag you through? I can't imagine you going in on your own."

"Something like that," he said. "I take a bit of encouraging when it comes to museums and opera."

"How did I guess?" She smiled and Morgan caught her reflection in the window. He sat studying the silhouette of her lithe body against the blaze of streetlights. Spectacular, he thought. She returned his gaze through the reflection for just a second, pulled the curtains closed again and sat down on the sofa, tucking her feet up underneath her, just as she'd done the night before.

"I wasn't sure if you'd come back," he said.

"I almost didn't," she replied. "Seriously, I'm pissed about what you said to me, but I couldn't just leave you over here, moping."

"I'm glad you did. I would have understood if you hadn't, though."

"I meant what I said, Morgan," she replied. "So, I hope you're not expecting me to be all 'Oh, poor baby, I didn't mean it,' because I won't be. I meant it and you needed to hear it."

Morgan just nodded, walked across the room and put the kettle on.

"Jesus! Are you making tea? It's, like, ten pm. What is it with you and tea?"

"It helps me think," he said. "And just making it takes my mind of other stuff. Besides, it's better than getting pissed."

"I'd already decided before I got here that if you opened that door and were drunk, I was going to turn right around and head home."

"Fair enough. So, would you like one?"

"Sure. Chamomile if you have it. Then you can tell me what's going on."

"You're over near the Festival Hall, aren't you?" Morgan found the chamomile and as the kettle finally boiled, dropped the bag into a cup and poured steaming water over it.

"Yeah, the White House Apartments," she replied. "It's close to everything, which is great. And you? I think Mila mentioned you had a place in the country somewhere?"

"Yeah," he replied. "In a town called Farnham, in Hampshire. I love it down there. You should visit sometime. Do you want me to leave the bag in or out?"

"Oh, in. I prefer it in," she said, and flicked him a look he definitely didn't expect to see tonight. He smiled in response. "Maybe I will visit sometime, when I'm invited properly."

"There you go," he said, handing over the tea. He returned to collect his and headed back to the end of the bed.

"No, you're not sitting over there. Come sit with me. I won't bite." She patted the cushion beside her. Morgan obeyed.

They were close again. Close like they'd been downstairs in the lounge bar but private now, like they'd been in her cabin aboard the Gulfstream.

They both sipped their tea in silence, watching each other, thinking, assessing, exchanging glances, and then eventually placed their cups on the floor.

"So, come on then, Alex Morgan. Enough stalling. What's going on with you?"

Morgan took a deep breath and exhaled slowly.

"I've been thinking a lot about what you said downstairs," he began. "All of it was true; too true. You hit a raw nerve and I reacted badly. I've kept myself going these past few months because I knew that the boss needed me. We're busier than we've ever been and he's had us all in the field. But I decided before I went to Africa that I was going to take a break as soon as I was finished there. I needed it. I could tell I was close to burning out, you know? Then, no sooner had I wrapped up in Malawi than the call came in to meet Dave and stand by to extract you." Morgan stopped for a while and rubbed his face. He didn't want to sound like he was whining but he couldn't stop the words from pouring out. Reigns put her hand on his shoulder. "Where I come from, we never, ever let down a colleague who's in trouble. That's a no-brainer. So, I diverted to Hong Kong, thinking, OK once this one is done, I'll take a break. And then—"

He stopped again. He could feel his hands beginning to shake and his face becoming taut. He began pressing his thumbs hard into the flesh of his palms, kneading until it hurt. Reigns reached across and took hold of them. To Morgan, his own hands suddenly felt like bricks in the soft cradle of her delicate fingers. Instantly, he relaxed. Somehow, she had a way of making everything seem OK.

"I know I'm burned out, Beth. It's fucking obvious. I know it. You know it. Fuck, the boss probably knows it, too. And, if things were different, there's no way I'd be getting onboard any flight that wasn't taking me straight to a beach somewhere with nothing but grass huts, hammocks strung between palm trees, and no fucking phone reception, but that all changed today. It changed when that fucker walked into Dave's hospital room and killed the poor bastard in his bed." Morgan stopped. He wiped his sleeve across his eyes. "I can't stop now, Beth. I can't. I don't have any choice in this. I owe it to Dave. He'd do the same for me. So I'm going after these fuckers like a shark after blood and when I'm done, and only then, I'll rest. Not before."

Elizabeth Reigns released Morgan's hands and stood up. She lifted his face to look at her, holding his gaze, her face full of warmth, understanding and hunger. As Morgan sat, transfixed by her raw power, she unbuttoned her blouse and dropped it to the floor. Then she took his hands and brought them up to the zip at the back of her suit pants. Morgan eased the zip down slowly until the pants loosened around her waist and slipped easily from her body into a crumpled mess around her ankles.

She stepped out of them and led him over to the bed.

Chapter Thirty-Five

BELIZE, CENTRAL AMERICA

Alex Morgan arrived in Belize on a day when the heat haze across the 9700 feet of runway at Philip S. W. Goldson International Airport obliterated everything beyond the cyclone fencing of the perimeter. Meanwhile, in the distance, he could see dark clouds rolling in from the sea to the east and noticed that the palm trees dotted around the airport's boundary were being whipped by heavy gusts. He had arrived at the tail end of the Caribbean's hurricane season and hoped that Mother Nature was simply reminding everyone that there was still a bit of puff left in the low-pressure systems sitting off the coast but that would be it.

Morgan had flown in on Avianca TACA flight 410 from San Salvador, via Guatemala City. He'd planned the stopovers en route to Belize to bolster his cover as a private security consultant specializing in infrastructure vulnerability assessments and personal security, undertaking aftercare meetings with multinational clients operating in Central America. To enhance the cover further he'd met with two former colleagues, one in Guatemala City and the other in San Salvador, both of whom he'd known for years through the airborne and special forces community and both of whom were actually conducting those tasks for major international security firms, Control Risks and NYA International respectively. The stopovers had added a couple of days to his travel arrangements but they were necessary in terms both of ensuring that, if anybody were to check on his movements prior to arriving in Belize, his story would hold up – at least to a cursory examination – and secondly, to re-establish contact with some trusted allies operating in the area whom he could call on if things became 'hectic'.

The extra day also allowed Elizabeth Reigns more time to confirm certain information that Morgan would be relying on in the field, specifically the identity of the Night Witch and her connection to the crew travelling on the Belizean passports. Of course, once he was on the Night Witch's turf, there was every likelihood that his contact with Intrepid HQ would be necessarily cut off. So, in lieu of formal confirmation, he'd be relying on the old-fashioned, direct enquiry approach to close in on her, beginning with the bar manager at the Paradise Palms Resort.

Morgan eventually cleared customs, traveling on an Australian passport under the name Daniel Culliford, and made his way through the terminal to the Tropic Air lounge. He was booked on Flight 551, departing at 15.20 and arriving at Placencia at 15.55. He removed the jacket of his lightweight beige suit and dropped it on the seat beside him as he waited for the boarding call. With the suit he wore a fitted, navy blue military-cut shirt and brown leather shoes and belt. It was appropriate for his cover, formal enough to meet clients in the tropics yet casual enough to cope with the humidity. He checked his watch, the trusted old TAG Heuer that he'd worn for years, wondering whether it was worth getting a drink before they took off. It was 14.50. They'd be boarding soon, he thought. Best wait until he reached Placencia.

Fifteen minutes later, he was settling into his seat aboard a Cessna Grand Caravan 208B. Despite all of the usual preflight activity and scurrying around outside by ground crew, he once again fell into a mood of quiet contemplation. A long-haul flight from the UK to the US, followed by a few days of short flights around Central America, along with a couple of nights sharing stories with comrades, had given him a lot of time to think and, most importantly, to finally accept that his friend Dave Sutherland was dead. But even though he had accepted it, Sutherland's premonition of death had got under Morgan's skin. How many times had he himself questioned his own likelihood of surviving a particular situation, or even getting through it without serious injury? To date, he'd beaten the odds, but how long could that last? As he looked beyond Sutherland's shadow on the slow march toward his own fortieth birthday, his bouts of facing those same questions about mortality were becoming more and more frequent, while the answers became less encouraging. *Fuck me, what is wrong with you?* Morgan thought, annoyed by his own malaise. *Snap out of it, for fuck's sake, or you'll definitely get yourself killed.*

The captain came aboard and welcomed his half-dozen passengers, apologizing for the slight delay, as they were awaiting the arrival of two more passengers. No sooner had he spoken than Morgan's attention was drawn to two men strolling nonchalantly across the tarmac. One was young, late twenties, tall, good-looking but surly about it, with dark hair. He was dressed in the latest jeans, a casual shirt and shoes; one of those young guys who spent a lot of time on his appearance and was constantly on the search for his next conquest. The second man was the complete opposite and Morgan was surprised to see the two of them together. He was a monster: about Morgan's height, fight-smashed face, buzz-cut hair, and built like a tank – thanks to the 'roids and plenty of time in prison, probably. The ape's heavily muscled body was covered in tattoos and he'd somehow managed to push it all into a tight short-sleeved shirt and cargo shorts.

"Ah, and here they are now," said the captain nervously when he spotted them. "Mr Kawowskee?"

"Ki-kov-skee," the big man grunted and with little regard for courtesy clambered awkwardly aboard, shoving past the captain and only just managing to maneuver his body down the narrow aisle between the seats.

"Welcome aboard," the captain replied. "And you must be Mister Velasco?"

The cool kid just nodded and followed silently in the wake of his traveling companion. *What a pair*, thought Morgan. Not a combination one would expect. They weren't gay – well, the big guy definitely wasn't – they didn't appear to be related, and there wasn't a principal/bodyguard vibe going on between them, in fact the big guy appeared to be in charge. All of which suggested that they were required to be together for a reason, rather than by choice.

Ki-kov-skee. Kajkowski? Morgan was sure that he'd seen that name on the list of Belizean passports Reigns had shown them back at HQ. Could this guy be one of the crew – one of the Night Witch's bodyguards? Morgan caught the man's eye briefly but deliberately as he squeezed past. On the surface, Morgan gave him no more than a desultory glance but in reality he took a detailed mental snapshot, instantly storing every line, angle, marking, contour and imperfection. He wanted a clear, up-close picture of the face so he'd remember it when the time came. That said, it would be a hard mug to forget in a hurry. Upon a Slavic canvas, the nose was smashed flat against the face, the ears were cauliflowered and the eyes just slits above shattered cheekbones. Morgan also managed to catch a tattoo on the man's left jowl, three interlocking triangles – a badge favored by white supremacists.

Ever since leaving England, Morgan had fought a nagging doubt about whether or not they'd made the right call in following the trail to Belize. Now, those doubts had gone. He was sure they were right after all. He could feel it in his gut. With a welcome sense of purpose and resolve, he returned his attention to the airstrip and watched with faux interest as the withdrawing ground crew readied themselves to release their bird into the air. No matter what lay ahead of him in the seaside resort of Placencia, he knew it was about to become an underworld battleground, with two opposing forces facing off for war, Morgan on one side, the Night Witch and her army of Aryan brothers on the other.

Only time could tell who would be left standing.

Chapter Thirty-Six

PLACENCIA, BELIZE, CENTRAL AMERICA

"Oh, my dear," said a gentle voice as a small woman came scurrying into the room. "I wasn't expecting you for another fifteen minutes. I'm so sorry. Come in and sit down. I'll get you a nice cup of herbal tea."

Jovana stood rigid in the foyer area of what could only be described as an exclusive beauty salon. Behind her was a sumptuous sofa. Opposite, a huge mirror surrounded by evenly spaced lightbulbs sat above a broad white benchtop that was stocked with every kind of hair and make-up accessory: hairdryers, curling wands, rollers and hairsprays. Make-up was arranged within a tiered glass display, organized by label: Dior, Chanel, Estee Lauder; nothing but the best. Two comfortable-looking chairs faced the mirror. To the left was a massage table and behind it, shelves packed to the gunnels with an array of oils, scents and beauty products. Diana Krall's *The Look of Love* album was playing softly in the background. On every available inch of wall space there were photographs of women, all young, all pretty, and all made up to look exactly the same. In the opposite corner of the room, between the mirror and the massage table, was a door through which she could hear water running.

Jovana was alone with the Asian woman, petite and very beautiful, dressed in a knee-length white dress with a mandarin collar and short sleeves. Her hair was jet black and pulled back in a compact bun just above her collar. Her skin was fair and her complexion absolutely flawless, radiating health and vitality. She wore only the merest hint of make-up, highlighting her eyes and adding a subtle strawberry hue to the outline of her lips. Her fingernails were short and impeccably manicured and her tiny feet were sheathed in fine leather sandals, strapped above the ankles.

"My dear," she said, holding out her hand, "please, come and sit down."

Jovana couldn't speak, suddenly realizing what she was looking at. Instead she shook her head.

"You don't want to sit?"

Jovana simply shook her head again, clutching self-consciously at her body, clothed in nothing but a gown, the only thing she could find in the room just off the salon where they'd put her two days ago. Right now, she didn't want to sit down. She didn't want to feel the pain again.

"Very well, dear," the lady said. "Then follow me through here. I have your bath almost ready. Once you're nice and warm and relaxed, I'll take you straight to your new room, where you can sleep some more and then we can begin your special treatment whenever you're ready. You're with me now, my dear. Everything will be all right."

In that moment, with those few reassuring words hanging in the air, Jovana handed herself over completely to the care of this woman. She had no strength to resist. And anything was better than where she had come from.

Chapter Thirty-Seven

DOMINGO'S BAR, THE PARADISE PALMS RESORT, PLACENCIA, BELIZE

"Can I get you another drink, sir?" the young barman asked. The nametag on his shirt read 'Oliver'.

"That'd be great," said Morgan. "Another Red Stripe."

"You were in last night, weren't you?" Oliver asked, getting Morgan's beer from the fridge behind him. "I was just going off shift when you came in for dinner."

"Yeah, that's right. I arrived yesterday. Taking a few days off."

Oliver wiped down the bar and placed the beer in front of Morgan on a new coaster. Morgan took a long drink while Oliver engaged him in amiable small talk about the weather, work and women; clearly a well-practiced patter he'd established over countless similar encounters across the bar. Morgan didn't mind. It gave him a chance to get more of a feel for the place. Last night's attempt at gathering any kind of information was a wash out. The bar had been dead quiet with only a few hotel patrons having dinner, young couples mostly. He'd stayed until about 11pm before deciding to cut his losses and, after a much-needed sleep in, had spent the day recovering by the pool. The hours spent swimming and reading, with the occasional retreat to his room to sleep, gave Morgan time to unwind, consider his mission in a more objective light and, importantly, recharge. He couldn't help but be reminded of the time he'd spent poolside with Arena Halls in Barcelona, which inevitably led him to think about time spent more recently with Charlotte-Rose Fleming.

Somehow, despite his feeling ready to commit to the right woman and settle down once and for all, the erratic trajectory of Morgan's life and the pressures of his profession had quashed any naïve dreams he'd had about achieving a normal relationship.

He recalled how he and Arena had miraculously escaped the bloody civil war in Malfajiri intact, afterward taking refuge in Spain. Their time together had been brief but intense – the war in Malfajiri and her abduction at the hands of Victor Lundt in Sydney weighing heavily in the mix of things that eventually tore her from him. Arena was "the one," or so Morgan had thought at the time, and he had felt her loss on an almost daily basis ever since. But the chances of a couple, even a couple with a bond as strong as theirs had been, surviving that scale of trauma and being able to maintain a healthy long-term relationship were slim at best. At least, that's what he told himself over and over; it helped him keep her inevitable departure from his life in perspective.

"I can't stay here any more, Alex," she'd said on that Monday morning at Heathrow. *"I thought I could but I can't. I need time for me. I need to put all this behind me."* And that had been that. They'd hugged. She'd smiled through tears and walked off to her flight, and Morgan had driven, utterly depressed, all the way back to Farnham, settled himself in

at the Wheatsheaf and spent the next two days getting as drunk as was humanly possible. And like it or not, despite the time that had passed since then, he still missed her and often wondered where she'd ended up and if she was happy. He hoped she was.

Charly Fleming had been a completely different story. Their relationship was forged during an equally traumatic time, but their connection had been deep infatuation and fondness rather than real love. Morgan had adored Charly and he knew she adored him, but their lives were too different and a future together inconceivable. She was a world-famous classical pianist and he was an Intrepid agent. The months they'd spent fighting against the odds to maintain a relationship, with her life in the spotlight and Morgan's in the shadows, eventually came to an end when they'd realized, almost simultaneously, that it was over. There'd been sadness, but they knew it was right to end things when they did. They were still in contact, which he was surprisingly happy about – Morgan wasn't usually the type to maintain contact with ex-girlfriends – and whenever their schedules allowed, they tried to catch up for dinner or at least a drink, always in strictest privacy.

Thinking of Charly inevitably brought Morgan's musings back full circle to the death of her father, Lieutenant Colonel Peter Fleming, decorated and much-respected veteran of the Special Air Service and close personal friend of General Davenport. In all likelihood, Colonel Fleming had died on the orders of the Night Witch and Morgan felt an overwhelming responsibility to avenge not only Dave Sutherland's death, but also Fleming's. He owed it to Davenport and, of course, to Charly.

Then his thoughts turned to Elizabeth Reigns. Damn!

Reigns was a shock to the system. A very welcome

shock, but Morgan was still conflicted. She was exquisite, confident, strong, independent and incredibly hot. There were no two ways about that. Thinking of her naked was the equivalent of hours of therapy. In such a short space of time, Beth had become a huge part of his life and he knew, no matter which way the wind might blow in the future, she was going to be important to him. It was her faith and confidence in him that had given him the impetus and courage he needed to deploy. It was her blessing on his bid to avenge Sutherland's murder that had made everything OK. *"Come back to me, Alex Morgan,"* she'd said as he'd left the room at The Rembrandt that morning. *"I will,"* he'd replied from the door. And he'd meant it. The thought of getting back to Beth at the end of this mission was what was keeping him going. That much he did know.

"So tell me, Oliver," said Morgan. "Why's this place called Domingo's? Why isn't it just called the Ocean View Bar, or something like that?"

"You know, some people think it's the boss's name," Oliver replied. "After all, he built the place before the hotel was even here. He got bought out a few years back but he did such great business that the hotel people cut him a solid deal to keep him working for them. This place has changed a lot since he first set it up and the owners of the resort can make life pretty shitty for him at times. It's still very much his place, but it's not his name."

"You seem to know a lot about it, mate," Morgan replied. "How come?"

"I'm his son. I've grown up in this bar," said Oliver proudly. "And one day I'll buy it back from the new owner. Papa's name is Javier. He's retired now but he's getting me ready to take over. Well, that's what he keeps telling me.

Maybe he's just stringing me along to keep me working here!"

They laughed.

"So, Domingo's?" Morgan asked.

"Sorry." Oliver laughed again. "Sure, well, years ago, around the time my dad first came here, it was pretty wild, you know? The village was small and there were only a few bars, mostly catering for sailors and fishermen, and the mangrove swamps hadn't been reclaimed by the developers like they have now. So, back then, the wildlife lived a lot closer. You know what I mean? Like, the mangroves were all around here."

"What do you get down here?" Morgan asked. "Alligators, right?"

"No, sir," Oliver replied. "A lot of people think we have 'gators but we don't. We have crocodiles, and back then there was one big motherfucker, twenty-five feet long and, get this, two thousand fucking pounds! And his name was Domingo."

"Jesus," said Morgan. "That is a big croc. Why Domingo?"

"Well, the English say that Domingo means, like, 'the Lord' or some shit. And the Spanish say it means 'born on Sunday.' Well, according to my dad, the first time that croc showed up in Placencia was a Sunday and he took a kid, the son of one of the fishermen. So, the locals, they were pretty religious people back then, superstitious, you know? They thought that God Himself had come down as this monster fucking croc and taken the son of a fisherman because he wasn't happy with them. So, somehow, Domingo kinda stuck."

"Bloody hell," said Morgan. "Great story. The old croc obviously left an impression."

"Some say he's still around here," said Oliver. His mood had changed, almost like recounting the story had spooked him. "He almost took my dad once."

"Seriously?"

"No shit. He's lucky still to have his left arm and he's walked with a limp ever since."

"Fuck," said Morgan. "What happened?"

"You can ask him yourself. He may be in tonight," Oliver said. "He occasionally drops in on busy nights. He likes to meet the guests, make sure everyone's happy. I'll introduce you if he does."

"That'd be great," Morgan replied. *Finally*.

Talking to Oliver and seeing the obvious admiration for his father in the young man's eyes, Morgan got a sense that Javier Vasquez was an old-school, family-oriented businessman. That could prove to be helpful in terms of what he might be prepared to share, inadvertently, with Morgan if he didn't have any loyalties to the criminal fraternity, because according to Rodgers' recollections, Vasquez had been more than willing to share his observations on the Night Witch all those years ago. Wishful thinking, perhaps, but it would be interesting to see what the man was like today.

The place was starting to get busy and Oliver was called away to serve other customers, so Morgan took the opportunity to leave the bar. He found a dining table in the angle formed by two solid brick uprights that supported the roof. It gave him a sweeping view of the entire place as well as of the ocean. Palms were swaying in every direction and the ocean breeze gently swept through Domingo's, rustling the eaves of the cabana roof, drawing the vacationers from their towels by the pool and on the beach, up to the open-air bar. Under better circumstances, he'd be happy to take a genuine vacation in a place like this. The weather was perfect, the food and service excellent. Above all, the place was as yet not over-commercialized.

Morgan began to peruse the menu and was contemplating ordering a steak when a strikingly beautiful girl walked into the bar. She was tall, catwalk tall, with an even tan, wearing a loose-fitting sheer dress over a yellow bikini. Her peroxide-blonde hair was cut short, but not styled — she'd obviously just been to the beach — and her eyes were like bright blue glass. She walked to a table that gave her a view back down to the beach, not far from Morgan's. Oliver appeared within seconds from behind the bar and placed a beer on the table in front of her. He withdrew without a word. The girl took a lazy sip and put the bottle back on the table.

Morgan watched her, subtly glancing her way without appearing to stare at her, which most of the other men in the bar were doing. His mind was full of images and descriptions he recalled from the briefing in COBRA. Elizabeth Reigns had described the Night Witch as, tall, white, Eastern European features, athletic physique, with very short, almost white-blonde, hair. She'd also mentioned a prominent birthmark down the right-hand side of the Witch's face. Morgan tried to get a clearer view without being caught out. The woman definitely met all of the key physical criteria, there was no doubt about it, but was the face just ten feet away from him the same as that on the passport photo he'd seen back in London? Or, more importantly, the one on criminal records released by the Ukraine Ministry of Internal Affairs? This girl had tattoos, words of some significance apparently, that snaked around each ankle beneath the straps of her sandals. They were subtle and unobtrusive. And he noticed a similar one that ran down the inside of her left forearm. But he could not see any form of birthmark down the right side of her face.

She had just come from the sea. Her towel-dried hair and the way in which the sheer dress clung to her body told him that she'd been swimming, not just sun-bathing. It was highly unlikely that make-up would still be able to mask an imperfection of that magnitude – or was it? How the hell would he know anyway?

One thing was for sure: this girl was beautiful but troubled. She didn't have any of the animation or unabashed confidence of a young, good-looking girl on vacation in the Caribbean. There was a distance there, a reserve, almost as if she felt she couldn't have fun even if she'd wanted to. She was, on the surface, a dead ringer for the Night Witch, but with none of the poison-laced charisma that had been described by witnesses. This girl was vulnerable, cautious, someone on the payroll who did exactly as she was told. This was the girl on the passport, Ștefania Yovenko, of that he was certain. But she was no killer and she was definitely not the head of a brutal human trafficking cartel. Morgan's thoughts turned to the staged car accident in Poland and the discovery that the girl who'd died in the crash, although bearing a close resemblance to her, was not Darja Voloshyn.

Reigns' doppelgänger theory was starting to look more likely by the minute.

Chapter Thirty-Eight

PLACENCIA, BELIZE, CENTRAL AMERICA

"You busy?" Dariusz asked.

"I was just about to take a bath," she replied. "Why, what is it?"

"I have news from Hong Kong. You're not going to like it."

"What?"

"I think I'd better come in for this."

As she stood to one side, Dariusz entered the room, a huge, extravagantly furnished boudoir with 270-degree views of Placencia and out across the ocean. She was dressed in nothing but a bathrobe. Her hair was tousled and her tanned skin shone against the soft white fabric. He wanted to compliment her but knew it wouldn't be welcome. He didn't need another excuse to send her into one of her tirades – what he was about to tell her was going to be enough. Truth be told, he was tired of her erratic behavior. She had a medical condition, like a multiple personality thing. If he'd known earlier, there was no way he would have hung around as long as he had. She took medication for it, he didn't know what, and some kind of psychotherapy treatment with a shrink up in LA. What he did know was that if she didn't keep up the meds then she was a howling, fucking crazy bitch to be around and he was sick of it. He was already making his moves to leave. He just needed a little longer. He had to get her through this deal with the Chinese.

Dariusz walked in, crossed the room and took a seat on the sofa, bracing for an explosion. She followed him through but didn't sit. Instead she stood in front of her bed with hands on hips staring at him, waiting for him to deliver the bad news.

"We've only just heard about this but the information is already days old," he began tentatively. "With all the travel and our teams coming in and out, this has somehow slipped through the net."

"What the fuck is it, Dariusz?"

"Wu ordered a hit on the HKPD guy, the inspector who was running their undercover operation in his factory, and whoever the other cop was who got shot the same day."

"So, we'll get him on the phone and I'll tell him to call it off," she said, walking toward her cell.

"It's too late," Dariusz replied. "It's already happened."

"What? You can't be fucking serious?"

"It's confirmed. The story even had coverage on CNN. I've got it right here." He waved his cell phone and, picking up the remote from the coffee table, turned on the TV. A few moments later the digital screen came to life with the bulletin covering the shooting at the Queen Elizabeth Hospital in Kowloon.

"CNN! How the fuck did this end up on CNN?" she whispered, sinking onto the bed, her eyes glued to the screen.

"Wu hired some hospital maintenance guy to carry out the hit. He found the HKPD cop visiting the other one in ICU – shot them both. But the ICU was being guarded by a US Marine."

"A US Marine. Why?"

"Because the second cop wasn't HKPD, Dee. He was an American."

"No. No. No! This can't be happening. How can an American be operating in Hong Kong? Is he Interpol? FBI? Fuck, is he CIA?"

"I think it's most probable that he's Interpol. The FBI don't get into gunfights in other countries and the CIA wouldn't be doing a street op with foreign cops. My money is on Interpol."

"So now Interpol are after me. Is that what you're fucking saying, Dariusz?"

"No, that's not what I'm saying. I think Interpol are after Wu Ming. They just happened to hit him on a day when you were there – or should I say, Ştefania was? They would have had no idea about you, Dee."

But her hands were in her hair now, tearing at it right down at the roots. Her jaw was clenched tight and he could hear her teeth grinding. She'd drawn her legs up underneath her and was rocking slowly, almost imperceptibly. Controlling the temper. He could see the effort it was taking her. In the past there would have been lots of screaming and shouting, things would be getting thrown around and somebody would be getting hurt, badly. He remained silent. The therapy was definitely helping.

"How could he move without checking with me first?" she said to herself. "I as good as own him already. This is my operation now. He could have blown everything! If the investors hear about this—"

"They won't, Dee," he offered, knowing it was a mistake, regretting it instantly.

"It's been all over CNN for three days! Look! You said so your-fucking-self!" She was on her feet now, stalking the room as though looking for something to smash. "What is wrong with you? That Chinese prick has enraged the authorities – the Hong Kong Police, Interpol … Who knows who else? I can feel them all over me already. It's only a matter of time before they find me here."

She came to a sudden halt at the balcony and stood looking out to sea with her hands along the balustrade, drawing in deep breaths and releasing the air slowly. It was as though the view calmed her. He wondered if she had selected it as a therapy trigger for that very purpose.

"We have to contain the fallout as best we can," he said. "So you can keep the discussions with the investors moving. We can't be sidetracked by this."

"From now on everyone comes to me. No one represents me anymore. I do it myself, on my terms and on my turf. I want Wu Ming to get his fat Chinese ass on a plane and he can come to see me here in Placencia."

"Whatever you want, Dee. I'll make it happen. What about your meeting with the investors?"

"I have to go back to Los Angeles for that in a couple of days; it's already fixed. That will be the last trip I take for a while. So arrange my flights."

"Don't you think it would be best to stay put? I mean, if you're feeling exposed, don't you think it would be best to minimize your travel and get them to come to you?"

"It doesn't work that way, Dariusz. People go to them, and this will be the last time I have to. Once this deal is done and I have my money, I'm out."

Chapter Thirty-Nine

DOMINGO'S BAR, THE PARADISE PALMS RESORT, PLACENCIA, BELIZE

An hour or so later, Morgan had finished his meal and moved back to the bar, quietly watching the comings and goings, and all the usual interactions you'd expect among a bunch of young guys and girls enjoying the freedom of a beachside vacation paradise. The place was almost packed and the volume of the music was getting steadily louder, in readiness for the late-night crowd. He'd been able to maintain his vigil over the girl, Ştefania, who was still sitting just a few tables away. But now she wasn't alone.

Halfway through her meal she'd been joined by a cocky, good-looking guy, late twenties, with dark hair and dressed in the latest gear. It was the same guy Morgan had seen board the plane with muscle-head. This guy's name was Velasco, Morgan recalled. And the other guy was Kajkowski. Ki-kov-skee. Morgan was absolutely certain that Kajkowski too was a member of the group traveling on the ill-gotten Belizean passports, confirming his view that they were right to focus on Central America. Kajkowski was absent, and Morgan had the chance to observe Velasco and the girl, but the vibe between them left him thoroughly bewildered.

It was clear from their intelligence that Ştefania Yovenko and Kajkowski were part of the crew that had fled Hong Kong together and, therefore, knew each other. And Morgan had personally seen Kajkowski and this kid Velasco traveling together from Belize City. Yet, watching Velasco approaching Ştefania earlier on was not what he would have expected of two people who were in any way familiar with each other or at least part of the same crew. There seemed to be no preexisting connection at all – it looked like a straightforward pick-up. He'd watched the entire process evolve before his eyes, almost from the moment that Velasco had entered the bar. He had all of the cocksure arrogance you'd expect from a guy who thought he was good enough to make a move on a beautiful girl like Ştefania and succeed.

At first, despite enjoying the attention, Ştefania had obviously been reticent even to be seen speaking to Velasco. Her body language gave her away. She was constantly looking around, for who or what Morgan couldn't say, nervously chatting and laughing, while squirming uncomfortably in her chair. Velasco was undeterred. He had the gift of the gab and kept her smiling and laughing while plying her with drinks. Harmless enough, considering their age and the environment; the same scene was being played out at half-a-dozen other tables in the place, but this was the only table that had Morgan's interest and his instinct smelled a rat.

And there it is.

It took Velasco less than a split second. With the deft work of a skilled magician, he had his hand up and back in a flash. The girl didn't have a hope of noticing that a pill had been dropped in her vodka and tonic.

Morgan immediately stood and walked across to their table, approaching from behind Velasco. Ştefania looked up at him, surprised but smiling, a little tipsy, clearly enjoying herself. She was reaching for her drink. Velasco was oblivious to his presence.

"Hello," she said.

"Hello," replied Morgan. "I apologize for the intrusion, but I wouldn't drink that if I were you. It's not what you ordered."

"I'm sorry?" Ştefania said. Her expression told him she had no idea what he could mean and she immediately turned to Velasco, who was now glaring up at Morgan.

"This is none of your business, man," he said in a Spanish accent. "You should fuck off."

"I'm happy to do that," said Morgan calmly. "Once you've finished her drink."

"What is happening?" asked Ştefania, looking from Morgan to Velasco. "Marcos, who is this guy? What is he talking about?"

"This prat has just spiked your drink," Morgan told her. "Now, unless you think I'm interfering with your evening, I suggest you get as far away from this asshole as you can while he and I have a chat."

Ştefania stood up immediately, gathering her bag from under the table. Morgan's reading of her reticence and nervousness was spot on. The last thing she wanted was a scene. Without another word, she stepped away and disappeared into the crowd. He took her place, picked up the spiked drink and offered it to Velasco.

"OK, Marcos," Morgan began. "You obviously had the

balls to make a move on that girl tonight, but have you got the balls to drink what you just slipped her?"

"Fuck you. I'm out of here," Velasco replied. But then the arrogance returned. "No, wait. Here's my friend. Why don't you make him drink it, asshole?"

Morgan looked up to see Kajkowski forcing his way through the crowd like a juggernaut bursting against its rivets, dragging a terrified-looking Ştefania along with him. His smashed face seemed ready to burst as he fought to contain his default setting: carnage.

Morgan remained calm.

"This guy's trying to force me to drink that," Velasco declared.

"Shut the fuck up," Kajkowski growled. "And get the fuck out of here. Take her with you."

The muscle-head thrust Ştefania toward the pretty boy.

"She stays," said Morgan from his chair. "She's not going anywhere with him."

The crowded bar was beginning to clear around them as people watched the exchange. The music hadn't caught up though.

"Who the fuck are you?" replied Kajkowski. His chest was heaving, fists clenching. He had put on his war face, breathing heavily through his flattened nose like a bull preparing to stampede. This was going to get primal rapidly, if Morgan gave the bull its chance. He needed to act first. Difficult from a chair, but not impossible.

Morgan stood suddenly, feigning an attack, and then instantly dropped back down into a crouch, catching Kajkowski completely off guard and prompting the man to react without thought. As expected, Kajkowski's reaction was clumsy, the Hulk-SMASH approach. His swinging fist cleared the table, sending debris flying in all directions.

Morgan, who'd dropped beneath the arc of the punch, grabbed a chair and swung it like a blade at the back of Kajkowski's knees.

The guy was too heavy and cumbersome to respond quickly enough and he delayed for that second too long. Morgan dropped the chair where it fell, exploded upward, and struck Kajkowski directly under the chin with both palms. The man's head snapped back and his body began to overbalance. His feet, struggling to find clear space, became tangled among the chair's legs and he fell heavily. His head smashed against a table behind him, causing him to crumple and collapse on to his side. Morgan instantly retrieved a bit of broken chair and was readying himself to strike again at the other man when there was silence. The music had stopped and the crowd had parted, many of them spilling out of the bar and out on to the beach.

Morgan spun back to the groaning Kajkowski only to find a woman standing between them, identical in almost every way to Ştefania Yovenko. Only this one was older, dressed more conservatively and had a look in her eyes that could freeze an ocean.

Morgan could just make out the faintest hint of a birthmark around her right eye.

Chapter Forty

"So, who are you?" she asked. Her tone was businesslike, no-nonsense with a hint of an eastern European accent.

"Just a guy trying to unwind," Morgan replied. "And who are you? You seem to have a lot of influence around here."

"Dahlia Vardøger," she replied. "I own the hotel. You can call me Dee."

"Daniel Culliford," Morgan replied. So now she was Dahlia Vardøger, not Darja Voloshyn. A new name, although still using the same initials. Hopeless cover. Dahlia, he recalled, was Voloshyn's grandmother's name. He wasn't sure about Vardøger. It could just be a random name she'd picked out but somehow he doubted that. He leaned across the coffee table and shook her hand. "You can call me Daniel."

Morgan and the woman were now alone in a private sitting room just off the foyer of the resort's reception area. Her entourage, including Kajkowski, Ştefania, Velasco and a couple of other steroid abusers, had been left to cool their heels out in the foyer. The woman was wearing a short summer dress with sandals, a couple of gold bracelets and just enough make-up to hide, not quite successfully, the birthmark. Her hair was a shock of white-blonde, cut almost to the scalp at the sides and back, with the longer hair on top styled up. Her features, while symmetrical and attractive, were hard, and despite her obvious physical allure, there was an ugliness to her that Morgan couldn't get past. He suspected she was younger than she looked; a thirty-something who looked more like a forty-something. One thing was for sure: Vardøger was Voloshyn, and Voloshyn was the Night Witch. He knew that from the moment he looked into her eyes.

"I've never seen anyone get the upper hand over my Godek before," she said, indicating Kajkowski in the next room. "I'm intrigued. Where did you learn to take care of yourself like that – are you a policeman?"

"God, no," Morgan replied. "Army. Paratroops."

"Wow. A paratrooper," she said. "That's like Special Forces, isn't it? Are you still in?"

"Not for a while now. I work for myself."

"Have you been to Afghanistan?"

"Yes."

"And Iraq?"

"Yes."

"Have you ever killed anybody?"

"Yes."

"You're impressing me more and more."

"Why would you be impressed by that?" he asked, genuinely curious.

"What do you do now?" she continued, ignoring his question.

"I feel like I'm being interrogated," he said. "I would

have thought you'd be relieved that I averted a disaster for you. It wouldn't look very good for your hotel if that girl had had a seizure and died. It's been known to happen when assholes like that kid slip a girl a Mickey. Quite often, in fact."

"You seem to know about those things. Why is that?"

"Because I'm paid to look out for other people's interests; anticipate things before they happen."

"What does that mean exactly?" Voloshyn's expression became intent.

"I'm a security consultant. I assess risks and vulnerabilities and advise businesses and certain individuals on how to reduce their exposure."

"Really?" she said. "That's very interesting. And what are you doing here in Placencia, Mister Security Consultant? Is there somebody in trouble here in paradise? Seems very unlikely. Apart from yourself, perhaps."

"And why would I be in trouble?" said Morgan. He could play this game all day.

"Well, you haven't walked out of here yet. After what you did to Godek, I think he would love to have another crack at you."

"Are you suggesting that I'm not allowed to leave until you say so? What if I call the police?"

"They won't come to your aid here unless I say they can."

"Well then, I'm afraid that's going to be embarrassing for you, Dee. Because when I'm ready to walk out of here, I will, and your attack dog and his litter of Aryan love children over there won't be able to do a damn thing to stop me. So I suggest you cut to the chase and let me know what it is you really want to talk to me about, otherwise I'll say good night."

"OK," she said, bristling but clearly not wanting the conversation to reach a dead end. "You mentioned you were here to unwind. Is that all there is to it?"

"Yeah," he replied. "I just finished some jobs in Guatemala and El Salvador and thought I'd treat myself to a few days off the grid by the pool before I head home to Australia. A friend mentioned this place, it sounded perfect, and so here I am."

"Are you for hire?"

"Depends on the job."

"What if I told you that my life was in danger?"

"What if I told you that I'm not surprised?"

"What the hell does that mean?"

"It is what it is. You're a young, attractive European woman, obviously very wealthy, who runs a fancy resort in a tropical paradise. In this part of the world, that's enough right there to make you a prime target for every unsavory character within a thousand miles. But your biggest risk exposure is standing over there." Morgan gestured over his shoulder toward Godek Kajkowski and the others, all shuffling their feet in the foyer. "You've surrounded yourself with rock apes. It's a classic mistake. Sure, if you're doing the trendy nightclub circuit or dodging the paparazzi, they're perfect. They all love the gym, and judging by the tattoos and self-inflicted scars on them, they've all done time somewhere, so they'll put up a good fight at close range. But by then it's too late. If someone is really after you and all that stands between you and them is those guys, then you're fucked. They wouldn't have the first clue how to look after you against proper opposition."

Morgan watched her jaw muscles. To his surprise, her eyes began to water slightly. She stood up. Morgan stood with her.

"I'll send a car for you in the morning at ten. It will bring you to my home, where I'd like to continue this conversation in more detail. In the meantime, I want you to consider my hotel at your disposal. Nobody will bother you, you have my word. Your bill will be taken care of, of course."

"What about that young girl?" Morgan asked, looking over at Ștefania.

"She won't come to any harm. You have my word on that, too. If you visit my home tomorrow then you can see for yourself that she is safe. Agreed?"

"Agreed."

Chapter Forty-One

Jovana was waking with the birds each morning and her sleep was less troubled now, so a 5.30am swim had become her routine, if a week qualified as an established routine. She still could not believe her situation had changed so dramatically in such a short space of time. And now her hair was so short. Shorter than it had ever been.

Her new accommodation was totally private, in a wing off the main house along a quiet corridor that eventually connected to the spa and beauty area. It was like a five-star hotel suite appointed in cream and gold, with plush carpet, oil paintings, a large sofa and armchairs, a dinner-cum-writing table, a huge digital TV screen, a separate bedroom with a king-sized bed, an en-suite bathroom complete with a huge spa bath, and a walk-in wardrobe of designer suits, dresses, casual clothes, and accessories. The room was large and full of natural light from the ornate French doors set in the one exterior wall, which opened on to a small private courtyard planted with tropical palms and ferns. This was enclosed on the other three sides by a high brick wall. There was a day bed to one side and a small table with two cane chairs in the center by a fountain.

The tiny woman she had met on what Jovana was told to refer to as "Day One" was named Jessie. No one ever mentioned the days before "Day One." Did they even know about them? Jessie was responsible for Jovana in every way and she had two assistants who helped her: Abbie and Mikkie. Jessie, Abbie and Mikkie were almost identical. All of them were pretty, petite, and Asian. Jovana guessed correctly that they were Thai. They were all gentle and caring and looked after her in a way she had never known before. Jessie, a trained nurse, took care of Jovana's health needs, including her exercise regime, nutrition, and her schedule throughout the day. Abbie ran Jovana's beauty and spa treatments. And Mikkie looked after Jovana's room and clothes, and made sure that all her meals were delivered to her at the correct time and that they were being eaten.

Jovana took all of her meals, which she was allowed to select from a set menu, in her room. They were brought to her promptly at 7am, midday and 7pm every day. The food was the best she'd ever tasted although it was always very healthy and served in modest portions. Sometimes she craved a burger and fries with a chocolate shake but those things were discouraged and definitely weren't on the menu.

She decided not to think about anything too much any more and instead focus only on today. After a long swim in the pool followed by some time lying on a sunlounger listening to the waves crashing against the beach nearby, she'd return to her room for a light breakfast of fruit, yoghurt and juice. When this had been cleared, she'd take a few minutes to enjoy a herbal tea before venturing down the corridor to begin her treatments. This morning it would be an organic body scrub, hot oil wrap, full body massage and a facial. The entire process would take exactly four hours. Then she would return to her room for lunch, and after that the afternoon and evening exercise routine would commence.

Jovana shut the door to her room with a gentle click. She walked along the corridor and past the spa, then strolled out through the gardens to the pool. She enjoyed these short walks and her swim first thing in the morning; it was the only time of the day when she was allowed to be alone outside. She wasn't permitted to leave the compound and go to the beach, despite being able to hear the ocean a few hundred feet away over the wall – yet strangely she had no thought of trying to escape or even venturing near the gates that she'd seen in the huge wall that wrapped around the property. It just didn't occur to her.

The woman, the one who had saved her and then the next moment subjected her to utter degradation, was nowhere to be seen and no one seemed to want to talk about her. When Jovana had asked Jessie, Abbie or Mikkie about her, they would all give an ambiguous response, like, "You'll have to ask her" or "She'll tell you when she's ready." No name was used. No title. Just *she* or *her*.

Jovana soon reached the pool, dropped her towel upon the tiles and jumped in. She swam back and forth, luxuriating in the warmth of the water as it caressed her skin, then stretched out on a sunlounger. She drifted off to sleep for a few minutes and was startled then instantly calmed by the sensation of long fingers moving gently through her wet hair, combing it back against the cushion, nails lightly grazing her scalp. She breathed deeply and opened her eyes.

"How are you feeling, my darling?"

Jovana found herself gazing up into the eyes of the woman who, despite her absence, had become everything to her: savior, guardian, benefactor and jailer. Her face was fine featured with high cheekbones. She, like Jovana, had razorcut white-blonde hair. She was naked but for a black string bikini, tall, well-muscled and evenly tanned, and more strikingly beautiful than Jovana remembered, although surprisingly she was wearing make-up to swim. Her body was strong and powerful yet still feminine. Jovana felt a sudden surge of anxiety at the closeness of their bodies.

"I'm better," she answered, eyes still locked on the other woman's. "Better than before."

"It takes time and time is what you have," the woman answered, caressing Jovana's face. "Your youth. Your beauty. Your whole life still ahead of you."

Jovana wondered if she could believe that. What had her life been so far but endless misery? Of course, that had changed in the last few days, but how long could it last? How long would she be allowed to live the way she was now?

"I know what you're thinking," the woman said. "You're wondering if this is all just a dream. Right?"

Jovana remained quiet, gazing into the beautiful blue water of the pool.

"My darling?"

"I don't know what to call you," she said honestly. "No one has told me."

"You can call me Dee," she said warmly. "Just you."

"Dee," said Jovana, and smiled. "Is this a dream?"

"No, my darling. It's real and you'll never have to go back to your old life again if you don't want to. I'll take care of you now."

"But why? Why am I here?"

"Because, when I first saw you, I knew that you were a girl just like I was once, a long time ago. And when I looked into your eyes I knew immediately where you had come from and what your life had been like. You deserve better; much better. All I want to do is take care of you. You're a very special girl, Jovana. Destiny has brought you to me. I'll give you everything you've ever wanted. All I ask in return, when you're ready and I've trained you, is for you to represent me from time to time in certain places, at business meetings and things like that. That's all. You'll see the world. You'll be safer than you've ever been. You'll be looked after, day and night, and you'll never want for anything ever again. You see, I used to be just like you once, a young girl with no one to look after her. I know what it feels like."

"What happened?" Jovana asked. "How did you end up here?"

"There's plenty of time for you to hear about that," Dee answered. "Right now, the most important thing is that you rest and get well, and there is no better place in the world to do that than right here, with me."

Dee smiled at her. Reaching down, she took Jovana by the hand. The girl responded obediently, naturally. She stood up until her face was just inches away from that of this cruel, mysterious, beautiful woman to whom she owed both devotion and fear. Dee led her to the edge of the pool and then released her hand. Jovana watched as Dee undressed, undoing the straps at her back and on her hips, allowing the threads of the bikini to drop to the ground before stepping into the pool. She swam languidly out into the middle and then turned to face Jovana, still standing mesmerized at the edge.

Without a word, Jovana undid the ties on her own

bikini, dropped into the crystal blue water and swam over to her.

Chapter Forty-Two

Alex Morgan looked out north-west, across the mangroves, palms and buttonwood of Placencia lagoon and beyond to the distant Cockscomb Range. High above the Maya Mountains a mass of rain clouds were galloping like a field of wild mustangs around the flanks of Victoria Peak, racing unfettered across the hinterland toward the border with Guatemala. What a relief. With the heavy blanket of cloud being pulled away to the west, the sunshine was finally making a welcome return to the coast.

Morgan was in the rear passenger seat of a Mercedes-Benz GL550 SUV with one of the steroid abusers driving. They were heading north toward Riversdale along the red dirt road that ran from Placencia Village and eventually connected with the southern highway. Familiarizing himself with a local map in the hotel, Morgan had discovered that the Placencia region was essentially a long peninsula, about twelve miles from end to end, that hugged the southern Belizean coastline. It seemed they were currently heading for the mainland.

The road was little more than a winding red-dirt line within an almost endless tunnel of mangroves. At this end of the peninsula, the mangroves began at the roadside and grew well above twenty feet. In contrast to those bordering the lagoon on the other side of the road, the seaside mangroves had the appearance of a massive fortress wall, too high to scale and utterly impregnable. The coast was to their right, and the occasional breach through the mangrove wall revealed small private roads built over white sand leading to a scattering of established residences and new developments of luxury condominiums, all with beach frontages no doubt, facing directly on to the Caribbean Sea. Sporadic "For Sale" signs told him that many of the developments had been a gamble on the burgeoning popularity of the area. Developers had been capitalizing on the damage caused by a hurricane back in 2001 and were hungry to make Placencia the new goto destination of Belize. From what Morgan had seen of the place so far, they had the right idea but were a long way from achieving it.

The steroid abuser hadn't said a word since arriving to collect him from the Paradise Palms Resort. Morgan had watched the car pull in, immediately recognized the driver as one of Godek Kajkowski's crew from the night before, and jumped in. As soon as he was settled, the driver sped off without a word. That didn't bother Morgan. He preferred the silence. It gave him time to think.

So far, all he knew was that Voloshyn had invited him to her home under the pretence of engaging his expertise. *What if I told you that my life was in danger?* It sounded legit enough considering her line of work. Her security was shit, that much was obvious. Otherwise the intelligence data available on her via the Interpol database wouldn't have got Intrepid this far. All the information was already there, it just required someone to connect the dots; follow it from the page to the person, as General Davenport would say. The fact that Voloshyn had allowed her protection to be handled by the likes of Kajkowski confirmed, in Morgan's view, her background. Night Witch or not, she was from the street, where the biggest, strongest, ugliest bastards were the resident experts on security. Their philosophy was if there was a problem, hit it, and, in fairness, it worked – up to a point. It worked in the underworld where violence was respected. And it worked in clubs and bars, places like Domingo's, where fear and intimidation cowed impressionable young people who were only really interested in having a good time. But it didn't work for long if you were trying to keep the world's law-enforcement agencies, with all the global resources available to them, off your trail.

Of course, the invitation to Voloshyn's home could just be a blatant ruse, designed to get Morgan out of the hotel – *please bring all of your belongings* – and as far away from public view as possible, before killing him for interfering in whatever it was they had in mind for the girl, Ştefania. No matter what the reason, he had to follow his instinct and see the operation through. It wasn't enough just to ID the Night Witch: he had to learn as much about her operation as possible, including whatever she was up to with the Chinese. Then all he had to do was dismantle it and bring her in. Simple.

Jesus! What a job.

A cell phone rang in the front. Morgan watched the driver lift it to his ear. There was no chitchat; the guy was listening to orders. Morgan caught himself being checked out via the rear-view mirror. Great. The call was about him. It took less than twenty seconds. The guy grunted a barely coherent "OK" and tossed the cell back into the center console.

They arrived at a break in the mangrove wall on the eastern side leading to the sea. The Mercedes-Benz turned off the main road and on to a private, barricaded, single-track road. It was built within what could only be described as a tunnel through the mangroves and it curved in a series of tight bends before reaching a heavy metal gate built into a wall. Morgan noticed that the vegetation had been cleared back from the wall for about ten feet or so. A boundary patrol route no doubt. Two men with the distinctive features of their Mayan ancestry stood guard. Both were armed with M16s and Browning 9mms. As the Mercedes pulled to a stop, the guards stood fast and the gate opened automatically.

The SUV passed through the gate and the driveway took a sharp right-hand turn to the south, approaching a stunning five-story Spanish-style villa, surrounded by snow-white sand and framed by the columns of magnificent palms, all swaying in the wind. Morgan was instantly taken by the opulence of the place. It had been built on a north–south axis, the eastern side of the house configured toward the sea. Surmounted by an aged terracotta-tiled roof, the villa's stucco was not quite white and not quite beige, with stone features the color of a weak latte. All the windows and glass doors were set within sweeping arches, and generous verandahs wound around the entire structure. There were ten-foot-high walls separating the garden in front of the property from a compound at the back that appeared to be enclosed within further walls surmounted by three strands of barbed wire.

The car looped around a bizarre fountain featuring stone figures of a tethered Ulysses attended by a siren at each of the four compass points and pulled up alongside some wide concrete stairs leading up to the front entrance: a pair of magnificent antique studded doors. It looked like a dream home in paradise, but Morgan knew the ugly reality. This was no dream home.

The driver got out and Morgan won a private bet with himself when the guy walked around the front of the car, bounded up the stairs and disappeared inside, leaving him to get the door himself. Morgan knew he wouldn't be receiving any special treatment from Kajkowski's crew. He'd sensed latent hostility from the guy throughout their short drive and gathered that there was some kind of tribal retribution in the offing; all they were waiting for was the safety catch to be released. Made sense, considering what he'd done to Kajkowski at Domingo's last night. For a guy like him there'd be no getting past that kind of public humiliation in front of his men and Morgan would have to remain prepared for a sudden, unfettered reprisal. At this stage at least they were still obeying Voloshyn's orders. But it was only a matter of time. As he stepped out of the air-conditioned comfort of the Mercedes and into the oppressive cloak of humidity, he couldn't help but wonder what he was about to walk into.

"There's been a slight change of plan," Voloshyn announced. "But I'm sure you're trained to expect the unexpected, right?"

Morgan was standing in the entrance foyer of the house, looking up at a grand central staircase. The Night Witch was leaning Scarlett O'Hara style against the balustrade at the very top of the stairs. She was dressed immaculately in a white jacket and matching short skirt, complemented by a thick gold chain around her neck, gold bracelets and rings, and finished off with a pair of gold sandals with straps that sat high above her ankles. A huge painting, *The Departure of the Witches* by Luis Ricardo Falero, dominated the wall behind her, capturing the eye from the moment one entered. He doubted it was a reproduction.

"OK," he replied. "Care to enlighten me?"

"I like to challenge the people who work for me, to see how they react to my sudden changes of heart."

Kajkowski and the driver both entered silently, edging into the foyer a little to Morgan's right. They stood there quietly, deliberately out of his sight line. Morgan could hear Kajkowski's labored breathing through his smashed nose.

"I see. Well, for a start, who said anything about me working for you? I only agreed to continue our discussion about your security and to enjoy your hospitality." Morgan began to ascend the stairs. He figured he'd at least try to gain the advantage of higher ground in the event that the two bodyguards decided to take him on. He also needed to demonstrate that he wasn't in the least bit intimidated by this obvious attempt to unsettle him. "So I think you're jumping the gun a little if you're expecting me to roll over and fetch or howl along to the radio like the rest of your crew."

Behind him, Kajkowski took a deep breath, causing a strained whistling sound as the air struggled to make it past his smashed septum. *Here it comes*, Morgan thought. He wondered if they were armed and if there were more of them somewhere close but still out of sight. If there were, then this probably wasn't going to go well for him, but he liked his chances better by being higher and close enough to use the Night Witch as a shield if necessary.

"That's not very nice," she said. "You're not a very nice person, though, are you?"

"I'm nice when people are nice to me. I just don't like being dicked around. So, unless you have some legitimate business to discuss, you can send one of these guys to do whatever it is that they don't do around here and get the other one to drive me back to town. The ball's in your court."

Morgan was now just three steps below where she was standing, close enough to reach her in a bound if he needed to. Kajkowski and his shadow were shuffling nervously at the base of the stairs, crying out to be let off the leash.

"I like you," she said. "You don't take any shit. It's very sexy."

Morgan said nothing. His expression remained impassive.

"It's quite simple," she said. "I don't want you to stay here anymore."

"If you didn't want me to stay," Morgan replied, trying to gauge her tone and mood, "then why did you invite me all the way out here?"

Voloshyn began walking down the stairs toward him. She maintained eye contact all the way. This was a game, he decided, nothing more. A cheap power play designed to unnerve him. She was obviously very used to getting her way and to other people falling into line, but it wouldn't work on him. Finally she reached him, standing just a step away, and ran a spindly finger across the line of his jaw.

"My plans have changed. I have to fly to Los Angeles and I want you to come with me."

Chapter Forty-Three

BOUCHON BISTRO, BEVERLY HILLS, CALIFORNIA

They were sitting out on the terrace of the Bouchon Bistro overlooking the Beverly Canon Gardens. Alex Morgan had never been to Beverly Hills, he'd never had the need. His first impressions, particularly given the contrast between his current surroundings – a stone's throw from Rodeo Drive – and almost everything else between LAX and here, was that it was all a little too perfect. The houses, the lawns, the palm trees, the cars, and especially the people, were a thousand miles removed from the life he knew. That said, and despite the circumstances, he wasn't averse to soaking up the affluent atmosphere, although he couldn't get over the nagging sense of shame he felt for every moment he spent pretending to be nice to Voloshyn. The devastation she left in her wake every day as a result of her business endeavors, the ruined lives, the broken families, the heartbreak, the suicides, the penury, the imprisonment and the bondage of innocent people simply trying to get by, none of this collateral damage seemed to register with the woman. It was nothing more than the consequences of the slave trade, and not something she concerned herself with.

He couldn't accept that any human being could be so indifferent to the suffering they caused others without there being some kind of medical reason for it. From what he'd seen of her so far – the erratic shifts in her moods and attitudes; the highly vulnerable, unsure and confused Dee, paranoid about her personal safety, pitted against the aggressively assertive, violent contradiction of her alter ego, the Night Witch – Morgan was leaning toward dissociative identity disorder. In fact, he'd put money on it.

He took another glance across the gardens, trying to quell his revulsion, distracting himself by studying the Spanish Colonial style of the Montage Hotel where they were staying. Morgan, Voloshyn and her business adviser, a man introduced only as Dariusz – but who Morgan recognized from the Belizean passport photos he'd seen back in London – had flown to Los Angeles via Houston and arrived in LA late the previous evening. There'd been little conversation en route, not even during check-in, and what he had gleaned so far was the result of snippets of overheard conversation between Voloshyn and Dariusz. On arrival at the Montage a grand deluxe suite had been retained for her and a standard guest room each for Morgan and the business adviser, who was at that moment back in his room, neck deep in their financials, preparing for a meeting with an investor group apparently eager to take over Voloshyn's business.

Morgan wasn't hungry. He'd eaten an early lunch in his room before meeting her in the lobby and knew he wouldn't need anything else until dinner. Besides, he wanted to maintain the pretence of being serious about her personal security, which after all was what she was paying him to do.

Leaving her to order the *soupe à l'oignon* followed by the *salade maraîchère au chèvre chaud* while he sat quietly sipping black coffee, monitoring their immediate area, obviously made her feel like she was safe – confirming her complete lack of understanding of what security really was. While the entire charade made Morgan feel sick to his stomach, it was an absolute grand slam in terms of General Davenport's ultimate objective of bringing down the global trafficking cartels. Morgan had been forced to maintain a communications white-out while he was working under cover as Voloshyn's security consultant, but knew the team at headquarters would be tracking his passport and so would at least be aware of his location.

Morgan was glad that Voloshyn had followed his guidance and left her pet dog Kajkowski at home. Apparently he was usually never more than two paces from her whenever she traveled abroad – or left the house for that matter – so it was a huge turnaround to convince her that he wasn't necessary on this trip. The only fly in the ointment at this point was Dariusz. He was openly suspicious of Morgan, even hostile, but he wasn't a gunslinger and therefore unlikely to be a problem. Morgan gave him as little attention as possible, focusing on her instead and the pantomime of his security responsibilities. That he had finally managed to get her alone while she ate her lunch was nothing short of a miracle.

"So, Mr Security," she said, "what are your thoughts so far?"

"What about?"

"All this," she began. "Beverly Hills. This trip. Do you think I'm safe?"

"It's very hard to say," he began. "So far, you're utilizing me pretty much the same way that you employ your bulldog

Kajkowski. Apart from handling any threats within the immediate vicinity, I'm not a great deal of use to you like this."

"How the fuck *am* I supposed to utilize you then?" she demanded. "You tell me. I've had to take care of my own security for a long time and I've gotten pretty good at it. What makes you so fucking special?"

"If your security is as stitched up as you're trying to convince yourself it is, then why do you need me at all? You asked me along, remember?"

Voloshyn remained quiet for a moment as a few Hollywood-looking types shuffled to the next table. They were a group of men in their thirties and forties, all animated and laughing. Morgan picked up on conversation about a new book franchise they'd just acquired. The guy who appeared to be the center of all the excitement was Californian cool, most probably a producer: leather jacket, black T-shirt, sunglasses and jeans.

"I've had a strategy," Voloshyn began, once things had settled down over at the Hollywood table. "But it seems to be unraveling."

"I'm listening," said Morgan.

"Have you ever seen that movie *The Thomas Crown Affair*, with Pierce Brosnan?"

"Sure."

"Do you remember the end, in the art gallery, how he tricked the cops by paying a whole bunch of people to dress exactly the same as him in overcoats and bowler hats? There were so many of them that the cops couldn't work out which one was him."

"I remember."

"That movie gave me the idea – the whole bowler hat and overcoat concept was inspired by a painting called *The*

Son of Man, a self-portrait by René Magritte. It's featured in the movie. I own the original now; it's in my house. I thought, why couldn't I employ girls who look and dress exactly like me to go to meetings in my place? No one need know if it was really me or not. It worked for a while. We lost a couple, but at least it wasn't me, right? But now I think the system's run its course. We've had one close call too many."

"What do you mean by 'lost a couple?' Did some girls resign?"

"You could say that," Voloshyn replied. "They were killed. But the people who killed them were actually after me. Does that shock you?"

"No. I've seen enough of the world to know a lot about death. But did these girls know what they were getting themselves into when you hired them?"

"Of course! They got to live the high life, with all the clothes and travel and whatever else they wanted. Better than the lives they had before, that's for sure. They knew enough to understand it was dangerous. What's the matter – are you squeamish?"

Morgan managed to contain his anger and ignore her question. He was sure the girls didn't have a clue what they'd been getting themselves into. How many had there been and, most importantly, how many were left?

"Listen, you need to bring me up to speed on what it is we're really doing here," he said. "Apart from a vague reference to your life being in some sort of danger, and getting the better of my professional curiosity by coaxing me here with a free ticket to LA and a room in a flash Beverly Hills hotel, you've yet to explain the actual source of your problem, or the business you're in, for that matter. If you want me to look after you properly, you're going to have to give me some details. It's impossible to know what I'm dealing with unless you do."

"You know, before we left Belize, I had you checked out," she said. "Your story stacked up. Army officer. Captain. East Timor, Afghanistan and Iraq. Injured. Honorable discharge. Now a private consultant. I wasn't surprised, but I needed to be sure."

"I'm glad you did that," said Morgan, knowing his cover was solid. It was based exactly upon the CV of one of his oldest friends. Morgan and the real Daniel Culliford were the same age, not dissimilar physically, and had known each other since day one in the army. When Morgan was establishing his mission profile, he'd contacted his friend to give him the heads up and get the all clear to borrow his identity. Dan was more than happy, knowing only that Morgan was now involved in some kind of secret work. In return, he received an all-expenses-paid vacation so he could lay low for a while.

"I thought you were exactly what I needed," she continued. "Someone from the other side of the world who has no idea who I am or what I do, and an expert in security who doesn't ask questions."

"You're right on everything except the 'doesn't ask questions' bit. I need to know," Morgan said, pressing home his point. "Protecting you from an ex-husband, the paparazzi or an angry debt collector is vastly different from protecting you against, say, the mob. So, which is it?"

Voloshyn squirmed a little in her seat, not accustomed to being spoken to on an equal footing, but Morgan could see she was taking the bait. He needed to know all about her operation, though of course not for her protection.

"OK, but you must respect my privacy. There's only so far I'm prepared to go in terms of talking about my business, because I really don't know you at all and I'm taking a huge fucking gamble already in bringing you on board … but I'm desperate."

"I'll be a lot more use to you if I understand what we're dealing with."

"I run a multi-million-dollar business specializing in … let's just say, manpower," she said. "I'm currently in the middle of a major business transformation where one of the biggest global players in my field wants to take me over. Just prior to their making their intentions known, I was in the middle of my own takeover of a similar business operating in Asia, specifically Hong Kong. Just as we were about to close that deal, something happened that put it back by weeks. Now my soon-to-be new business partners want the Asian deal sorted before they'll progress to the next level. I've assured them it will be and this trip is all about me reassuring them that it is back on track, while giving them the full financials on my business as it is right now as well as where it will be when I've closed the deal with the Hong Kong group."

"So where are these threats to your life coming from?" Morgan asked. "It sounds to me like this is all pretty straightforward. But who wants you dead?"

"Interpol. The Triads. My new partners. Hell, my own people, for all I know."

"Fuck me," said Morgan. "What are you into?"

"Like I said, I need you to respect my privacy. For now, at least. Until I know I can trust you. I've already gone out on a limb telling you all this. I really shouldn't have. Does it shock you?"

"It's a bit late to ask me that now, even if I did want to bail," he replied, trying to sound agitated. "If you've seriously got Interpol *and* the Triads after you then there's probably someone with eyes on us right now! Why the fuck are you accepting meetings like this, out in the open and away from your base? It's crazy."

"I had no choice, alright?" she snapped. His tone had had the desired effect. "You're freaking me out. Are you serious about them watching me right now?"

"Hey, you're the one telling me who's after you. Do you actually know all this for sure?"

"Of course I don't know for sure. What I do know is that Interpol had an undercover operative on the inside, working in a factory in Hong Kong that I was expected to visit. All hell broke loose. I lost a couple of people and the Chinese lost a few more. They'll be pissed about it and probably suspect my organization of being the source of the leak."

"How do you know there's a leak?"

"How the fuck did they manage to get someone on the inside if there wasn't?"

Morgan didn't answer for a moment. He needed to give her the impression he was considering this like it was all new to him, which, of course, it wasn't. He took the chance to check their immediate surroundings to make sure that their conversation hadn't attracted any attention from the other tables. Fortunately, the Hollywood crew were so into their own celebrations that their volume was covering just about everything else. Good.

"So, you don't even know if it's one of your own people, right?"

She nodded.

"Which is why you've opted to confide in the first seemingly competent outsider that you came across. Yes?"

Another nod.

"OK, Dee, here's what I think you should do." He

leaned across the table, encouraging her to incline her head closer to his. "I heard you and your man Dariusz saying something in the cab about getting the Chinese to come to you. Is that right? Because if so, that's the best idea I've heard so far. If you're serious about your security and you really believe you're under scrutiny, by the authorities or these Triad guys, then your best chance is to stay on home turf until it's sorted out. As soon as you've finished your business here we get on a plane back to Belize."

Morgan noticed a slight tremor in her hands. That was good. He wanted her to be a little rattled. Feeding her paranoia was definitely the way to go.

"OK," she said quietly. "So you're saying we shouldn't even stay here another night?"

"We may have no choice," he answered truthfully. Connections out of the US to Belize weren't exactly regular. They'd just have to try their luck. "I suggest you leave that to me. I'll check out our flight options while you're having your meeting. If we have to stay another night then we'll just have to take some precautions. But the sooner we're on a plane and back there, the better. Meanwhile, I'd get your boy working on the Chinese and tell them to come to you. At least then you'll know how serious they are about closing the deal."

The cell phone on the table buzzed.

"It's Dariusz," she said. "They're ready for me."

Chapter Forty-Four

PLACENCIA, BELIZE, CENTRAL AMERICA

Ştefania woke with the birds, just as she had ever since she'd begun her new life in this place. It wasn't hard to fall back into the routine whenever she returned from her trips away. She decided she'd take a swim before breakfast. It was a little earlier than usual for her but it couldn't hurt and, besides, there seemed to be no one else around.

Her dreams of the past few nights had been full of freedom. She could almost smell Sevastopol in the summer, and the evening breeze drifting into her mother's living room from the Black Sea. She was on the home straight now and felt relieved beyond words, although something about that scene at Domingo's two nights ago didn't make sense to her. So what if that guy Marcos had tried to slip her something? He was cute and everybody did it, and at least it made it easier to forget when they did. She couldn't understand why he seemed to know Godek, though, and still had no idea what had happened to him afterward. He didn't come back to the house with them, Dee would never allow that. The last she saw of him was when he'd disappeared back into

Domingo's from the hotel foyer. The only good thing about it all was that last night she'd heard Dee, Dariusz and that cute new guy who'd interfered in the bar, whoever he was, leaving for the airport. After that, Godek and the others were drinking and making noise for a while before it all went quiet again. They'd probably all gone to Domingo's and, judging by the lack of uproar in the middle of the night – which would mean they'd returned home – she was sure they'd gone up to San Pedro. That meant they wouldn't get a boat back until later this morning.

For the first time in a long time, Ştefania felt completely unsupervised. There'd been no knocks on her door during the night from any of the guys wanting sex, no check calls to make sure she was accounted for, and no chaperone shadowing her every move. She felt free. Soon she'd be done with it all and the Witch would finally let her go, with enough money to start a new life.

Dressed in just a bikini, a towel thrown over her shoulder, Ştefania strolled from her room in the main house along the tiled path that led to the pool. For a moment she thought she could hear someone in the water but knew that was impossible – no one else was ever up at this time, not even the Witch. She kept walking, a little more cautiously now, wrapping her towel around her waist and listening. There it was again. She slowed her pace and carefully approached the pool.

Even though she was due to leave in just a couple of days, there were strict rules about being outside the house and especially about using the pool. She reached the bed of ferns and palms that separated the house from the poolside and stopped dead in her tracks. There was another girl, someone she didn't know, pulling herself up and out of the water. Ştefania stood frozen, watching her. Was it the

Witch? It couldn't be. She'd left last night. But the girl in the pool looked exactly like her in every way. Ştefania's hand came up to her own face, trying to comprehend why there was another girl at the house who could have passed for her own sister or for Dee.

"Hello," she said timidly, walking out from behind the ferns. "Who are you?"

The girl seemed startled by the unexpected voice. She grabbed for her towel and wrapped it around her.

Ştefania walked across to her, each of them sizing the other up, mesmerized by their similarities – height, weight, body shape, hair, even the length of their legs and arms, but above all their blue eyes – everything was as close to identical as possible without an actual biological connection.

"Who are you?" whispered Ştefania, shocked. They were much closer now, just a few feet apart.

"Jovana," the other girl answered, equally breathlessly. "Who are you?"

"Ştefania," she answered.

It was as if the two of them were in a trance, standing so close they could study each other in intimate detail.

"What are you doing here?" Jovana asked. "I mean, where did you come from?"

"I've lived here for months," Ştefania answered honestly. "But I've been away."

"You live here?" Jovana asked. "But I've never seen you."

"How long have you been here?"

"Only a week or so. I've seen your face in the make-up room. Your picture is on the wall, with all the others."

"With all the others?" Ştefania asked. "Other girls?"

"Yes," Jovana replied. "I thought those were pictures of models they were using to make me look like … her."

"Like Dee," said Ştefania. She wouldn't dare say 'the Witch' out loud.

Jovana nodded. "And ... like you, I suppose."

"This is too random," said Ştefania. She sat down on one of the sunloungers and Jovana did the same. The whole situation was starting to make sense. Ştefania was moving out and Jovana was being moved in to replace her. She started thinking closely about her encounter with Marcos. He knew Godek. She'd seen them talking like friends ... "We really shouldn't be seen together," she realized suddenly.

"But why? No one's ever told me anything like that. Why can't we talk?"

"Because every minute of your day is planned for you – what time you get up, what time you can swim, eat, shower, piss – am I right?"

Jovana remained silent.

"That's because she doesn't want you to see anybody you shouldn't."

There was a clamor of activity coming from the house. Male voices. They'd returned from their night off.

"Fuck! They're back already," said Ştefania, frightened. "They can't find us together. Come on!"

She grabbed Jovana by the hand and the two of them ran back to the house, avoiding the main path as they did. Ştefania led the way through the palms and ferns, the branches whipping at their arms and faces as they ran. Soon they were through and clear. There were just ten feet of open space between the end of the garden and the tiled path back to their rooms in the guest wing. The two of them stood still for a second, watching and listening. There was nothing. The men were all over on the other side of the house, on the floor above. No one had come outside on to the balcony.

"OK," whispered Ştefania, still holding Jovana's hand. "They're all inside. It sounds like they've brought some girls back with them. Quickly!"

With that, they broke cover and ran for the door.

Standing just far enough back from the balcony so he couldn't be seen from below, Godek Kajkowski watched the girls. His right arm was outstretched and in his hand was an iPhone. The phone gave a series of digital clicks, capturing the scene perfectly. He dropped the phone back into his pocket and headed downstairs.

Chapter Forty-Five

Jovana was in her room. She was on the bed, clutching her legs protectively against her body. Her eyes were closed tight and she was rocking back and forth.

She was thinking about the girl, Ștefania, and what she had said about Dee. Why did they look so alike and why had Dee chosen her, Jovana, when she already had another girl who was identical to her, almost her twin? And what did Ștefania mean about every minute and every day being planned? It had seemed that way at first but Jovana thought that was just because it was all so new. Was she being taken care of or was she being used – again? Why did it always have to be so hard? Why did this have to happen to her? All she wanted was her freedom, her life back. Why did people always think they could own her?

She'd heard a commotion outside in the corridor. A lot of noise, the voices of men, cajoling, howling and whistling. "Ștefania!" they were calling. "Ștefania, where are you? You've been a bad girl again." It was the younger guys. Two or three of them, she thought. *Assholes*.

Tentatively, Jovana got off the bed, went to the door of her room and pressed her ear against it, listening, terrified. What did they want with Ştefania? Had they been seen together? She stayed pressed against the door as the voices passed by and continued further along the corridor, still calling out, taunting.

She reached for the handle and grabbed it, but froze immediately.

A loud series of bangs – one, two, three – in quick succession startled her and she jumped away from the door. It happened again – *bang, bang, bang!* The sound of a heavy fist pounding on a door down the corridor.

"Ştefania! Open the door!"

She heard the voice and knew it immediately, deep, cruel and older than the others. The leader of the pack; the animal with no compassion – Godek. He had given Jovana the worst of the treatment she'd received on the night they'd brought her back, fucking her as if she was nothing more than a lifeless sex toy.

"Ştefania!" Godek demanded again. And then, when there was no response from the room, she heard him bark at one of the other men, "Open it!"

What followed terrified Jovana. As the men burst into the room, she heard Ştefania screaming, pleading with them to leave her alone, but that wasn't going to happen. Jovana fell to the floor and curled into a fetal position by the door, shaking and crying, covering her ears, trying to block out the unimaginable trauma of hearing the girl, one just like her, being attacked by the men. Her attempts to block it out proved futile until Ştefania's exhausted screams became nothing more than muted cries.

Sometime later – Jovana didn't know how long – she was wrenched from a fear-induced semiconsciousness by a deafening thump on her door. It sounded like a kick. Instantly she was awake. She scurried over to the bed to huddle there before the door opened. She waited in panicked silence, clutching a pillow, shaking uncontrollably. But the door didn't open. All she could hear was the sound of an utterly defeated Ştefania protesting in vain as she was dragged from her room and along the corridor. Jovana tried to call out, to offer her comfort or even hope, but fear froze the words in her mouth. Outside, the volume of the girl's cries diminished as they took her away.

A key rattled in Jovana's door. She recoiled, stumbled into her en suite bathroom, slammed the door shut and locked it, pressing herself as far back into the room as she could, looking for something to defend herself with – realizing that there was absolutely nothing that she could use as a weapon.

An unnerving silence ensued. It lasted for about thirty seconds and then a voice, very close to the door, jolted her.

"You're lucky you're not getting the same treatment as your friend right now, little princess," whispered Godek. "But the Witch has other plans for you."

"Leave me alone," she screamed. "Go away!"

"Don't worry, I will," he sneered. "But when I come back, you might not be so lucky."

Chapter Forty-Six

"So, the investors want to send some of their people along to attend your meeting with the Chinese. What's the problem with that?" Morgan asked, purposely rattling Voloshyn's cage. They were in the Mercedes SUV returning from Placencia Airport. You could cut the air with a chainsaw. The Witch was in the back with Dariusz and Morgan was up front with the driver. Voloshyn had her eyes glued to her iPhone, tapping furiously. She looked disturbed, like she'd received bad news, and Morgan wanted to push her buttons. "Sounds like they're protecting their end of the deal. Makes sense."

"Why the fuck does it make sense?" she demanded, annoyed, dropping the iPhone back into her lap.

"Well, from what you've told me, they're investing some serious money in your operation and the uncertainty around this Hong Kong angle seems important to them. Fair enough, too. After the trouble you had there – you said so yourself, something about putting the deal back by weeks? Well, if you ask me, it makes sense that they'd want one of their own people on the ground here."

"I don't care what they want. I don't like being fucking supervised," she snapped. "And nobody fucking asked you! You're on the payroll to make sure nothing goes wrong, not to give me fucking business advice. So start thinking about that."

Morgan remained silent for the rest of the drive. He was pleased with her reaction, albeit with reservations. She was definitely on edge, as he'd seen from the moment she had emerged from the meeting with the investors back in LA. He had been relegated to nothing more than a guard dog, sitting obediently outside the hotel suite. Occasionally Dariusz would come out to see if he was still there, behaving.

Morgan had decided to play the bodyguard role to the hilt. If they wanted him to be a hired gun, then that's what he'd be. At least now he was on the inside and close enough to see exactly what was going on around her. When the meeting eventually finished, he had escorted her back to her suite – after making a show of clearing it – and withdrawn to his own room until they checked out that morning.

When Morgan had first climbed into the Mercedes for the trip from the airport, he'd known nothing at all about the outcome of the meeting. Now, by listening to their muted conversation, grabbing the few strands he could decipher, picking his moment and choosing the correct strategy, his direct questions had unsettled her. In the space of just a few minutes, he'd confirmed that Wu Ming was coming to the villa in two days' time to close the deal, and that the "investors," whoever they were, were sending down a representative. For Morgan, this was a potential goldmine of intelligence and, more than anything, an unprecedented opportunity to rattle Voloshyn's cage to maximum effect.

"Rather than enduring any more of your silent treatment," he began, after a few moments, "I'd actually prefer to enjoy the rest of my day. You can drop me back at the hotel. If you decide you'd actually like to utilize my expertise then one of your boys can collect me in the morning. If not, I'm going to squeeze some quality downtime out of the next few hours and wish you all the best with your meeting. I'll fly out tomorrow."

Morgan didn't receive a response but noted an exchange of looks between the driver and Voloshyn via the rear-view mirror. Then, as they approached the Paradise Palms Resort, the driver suddenly spun the wheel hard left off the main road and the Mercedes came to a stop in front of the hotel's reception foyer. Morgan stepped out calmly and just managed to extract his bags from the back of the SUV before the driver planted his foot again and they all sped away.

"Cheers," he said to the back of the vanishing car.

"Welcome back, sir. May I help you with your bags?"

It was one of the hotel staff Morgan had met when he'd first arrived in Placencia. He was smiling broadly and holding the doors open.

"Thank you very much," Morgan replied as he wandered through. "But I can manage."

"Good afternoon, Mr Culliford," came an equally pleasant greeting from a young woman who appeared to have been waiting for him personally at the reception desk. Her nametag said "Emily." She turned and withdrew an old Lockwood key on a tag from a board behind her. They hadn't quite advanced to smartcard technology here yet. "We've kept your room for you."

Morgan considered the futility of requesting another room within a hotel owned by his adversary and filled to the gunnels with staff on her payroll. He accepted the proffered key without protest. If the Night Witch wanted someone to access his room they would do it. Changing rooms wouldn't make the slightest bit of difference. Besides, he had nothing on him or in his luggage that could compromise him. He wasn't even carrying a gun – or any other weapons, for that matter – which made him feel naked. Even the cell phone he was using was a standard, commercially available iPhone. That said, before he'd left LA he'd managed to get a call through to his friend Bill in Guatemala. He, like Morgan, was ex-Parachute Regiment and they knew each other well enough to call in favors. If things were going to heat up as much as Morgan expected they would, then he was going to need some tools. He checked his watch and looked around the foyer, hoping Bill remembered that today was the day he needed them. Nothing and no one. *Shit.*

Morgan made his way back through the hotel, up to the third and top floor, and meandered to his room. Despite the east-facing, ocean-view aspect, and the fact that it was being advertised as a four-star luxury destination favored by international guests, the hotel was three star at best. Morgan didn't care. Anything that didn't involve him sleeping on the ground under a square of porous plastic was five star in his eyes. He was just glad to have some time away from Voloshyn and her crew. Over the past couple of days, he had found his necessary association with them, particularly her, nauseating. He knew it was a gamble, leaving her with an ultimatum as he had, but he felt she'd take the bait. She was panicked, stressed and vulnerable. She knew it and she also knew she was surrounded by morons at a time when she could least afford to be. Above all, with the pressure of the visit by Wu Ming and her investors' watchdog looming ever larger on the horizon, she was desperate. She needed Morgan more than she realized.

When he entered his room, he dropped his bag on the spot made for it, sat on the bed to pull off his R. M. Williams boots, and then dialed reception.

"Hello, sir. This is Emily, how may I help you?"

"Hello, Emily. I wonder if you would book me a flight to Belize City, leaving late tomorrow morning?"

"I'm afraid the earliest flight out tomorrow isn't until two pm, sir."

"That's absolutely fine," he replied. "Go ahead and make the arrangements for me and I'll pay the airline once you let me know."

"Very well, sir. I'll call you back shortly."

"Thanks," he replied, and hung up.

That would take no time at all to get back to Voloshyn. At least she'd know he was serious about leaving. Now he had time to think and knew he needed to focus on how to approach his duties over the next few days. He would be expected to pull out all the stops ahead of an important meeting with her commercial partners involving a deal worth multi-millions, in fact billions, of dollars. He'd nettled her enough. When she sent her driver to collect him in the morning, and she would, he needed to show her that he knew what he was doing, and to do that he needed to have a look around her villa without her knowledge.

He walked over to the writing desk and found a map of Placencia among the piles of tourist guff. He laid it out on the bed and refreshed his memory of the key landmarks along the coast between the Paradise Palms and Voloshyn's villa, about six miles due north. If he took a cab even partway, word would get around within seconds of his leaving the hotel. Scratch that. Alternatively, it'd take him a bit over an hour and a half to walk it or about forty-five minutes to run. That was an idea. He loved to run. It was a rare bonus when an opportunity to strap on the trainers occurred while deployed on a mission.

Back home in Surrey, running was his morning ritual, usually about five miles. Twice a week, time permitting, he'd stretch it out to a fifteen-mile circuit – from his house on the outskirts of Farnham, through the town, up the hill past Farnham Castle toward Odiham, then Fleet, then back via Church Crookham and home. It would usually take him around two hours, give or take. Running kept him honed physically and grounded mentally. The inherent stress of his profession and living in the constant shadow of his own mortality obliged him to take care of himself. If he let the ritual slip when he was at home it would be too easy to fall into old habits from his army days.

Morgan loved a drink to shut down, always had, and never more so than when he could enjoy a few with his closest friends, but with a nagging tendency toward melancholy – which he blamed on his Welsh genes – he wasn't about to allow complacency to get the better of him. So, he decided, after all the traveling and sitting around he'd done so far on this mission, a run would do him a lot of good right now.

Then there was a knock at the door.

Morgan sprang across the room noiselessly and waited a moment. There was a pause of a few seconds followed by a second tap and then a business card was pushed under the door. Morgan reached across and picked it up.

AJ ARMSTRONG

PRINCIPAL CONSULTANT
IRONSIDE SECURITY

There was an email address and a series of numbers – cells, landlines and faxes – all listed by country and all prefixed with the international codes for Mexico, Guatemala and Belize respectively. Morgan flipped the card. A handwritten note on the back read: *Bill says hello*.

Standing next to the wall for cover, Morgan reached across and opened the door.

"All right, boss?" came a jovial greeting, accompanied by an equally jovial face. The man was about Morgan's height, somewhere in his late twenties or early thirties, a rugby player type. He was stocky with dark hair shaved almost down to the scalp, cauliflower ears and a flattened nose. He was dressed in the obligatory soldier's 'day-off' rig: cargo shorts, sports sandals and T-shirt. Looping a finger through the collar of the T-shirt he dragged it down just enough to reveal the cap badge of the Parachute Regiment with the Roman numeral II beneath it, tattooed across the left side of his chest. Morgan smiled warmly, holding up three fingers in response to indicate he had served with 3PARA.

"Right to come in, am I?" asked the new arrival.

"Of course, mate," Morgan replied, relaxing and shaking the man's hand. He held a cautionary finger to his lips, indicating that he expected the room was bugged. He got an "acknowledged" nod back from the other man as he stepped into the room. "Come in. Great to see you again."

"So how are you, boss?" the man asked. The two men had never met before. "It's been a while."

"I'm good, AJ," replied Morgan warmly. "Jesus, I haven't seen you in ages."

"Yeah, it's been fucken forever. Kabul, I s'pose, when you was with the Aussies, yeah?"

AJ crossed his eyes and made a wanking gesture with his hand, taking the piss. He knew the score. While he spoke, he slipped a daypack from his shoulder and extracted a heavy but compact parcel from within it. It was an olive drab waterproof dry-sack fastened tight across the top. He handed it to Morgan and made a pistol signal with his finger and thumb, followed by a slitting motion across his own throat. Morgan nodded gratefully and gave him the thumbs up.

"Hope you don't mind me droppin' in unannounced and all that but, you know, I was sure I saw you down the bar a couple of nights ago only I was with a client then, know what I mean? So, here's me, I had time up me sleeve today an' I thought I'd see if you were still here, like. And, fuck me, no sooner had I walked into the foyer than there you were disappearing into the fucken lift. I've knocked on almost every door on this fucken floor."

The two men laughed.

"I tell you what, mate," Morgan replied. "Why don't we go down to the bar and have a drink? You got time?"

"I've got time for one, boss," AJ replied professionally. Morgan walked into the bathroom as AJ continued to talk about his faux plans for the day, and deftly stashed the dry-sack in the cistern of the toilet. "But then I'll have to fuck off, you know, because I have to fly back to Belize City on the five o'clock. Still, it'll give us time for a quick catch-up and you can tell me what you've been up to all these years."

"Sounds like a plan," Morgan replied, stepping back into his boots. He walked past AJ, grabbed his room key from the writing desk and the two of them walked out. "At least we'll have enough time to swap a few stories."

Out in the corridor they spoke openly. AJ Armstrong was a former corporal with 2PARA. He had served in Iraq and Afghanistan with Morgan's old friend Bill, who had been AJ's former company sergeant major. Now AJ did occasional contract work for him, operating mainly out of Mexico. It was obvious that he held Bill in the highest regard and his willingness to get on a plane from Mexico City the previous night and fly to Belize, just to source and personally deliver an obviously illegal firearm and knife, was testament to the inherent loyalty written into the DNA of the regiment.

Morgan and Armstrong maintained the pretence of being a couple of old army friends catching up over a beer in the bar. They kept it short and sweet. As soon as they'd finished their beer, Armstrong stood up to leave. They shook hands and he said to Morgan, "I don't know what it is you're doing down here, boss, but if you get in the shit and you need a hand, give me a fucken shout, all right? I mean it. I'm fed up with corporate assholes who keep gettin' themselves kidnapped, you know what I mean? My details are on the card or just leave a message for me with George Hemsworth down the road at the Drop Zone Bar. It's his place. He's ex-Reg. 2PARA and Pathfinders, back in the day. Good man. He'll get a message to me. And if you need a good old-fashioned hard case, then go no further than George. They don't make 'em like him anymore." And with that, AJ turned and headed out to get a cab.

Morgan returned unhurriedly to his room. So, he had allies. That was good to know. The paratrooper network was alive and well, even all the way down here. Back in his room he changed into his swimming gear, checked to see that AJ's package hadn't been disturbed, and then went back downstairs to spend some time by the pool. At least he could still pretend to be on vacation. That'd give Voloshyn's spies something to report on, and the chance of a swim would do him good. After that he'd shower, dress, grab some early carbs from the buffet, go back to his room and prepare his gear, take a rest until it started getting dark – and then he would see what he would see.

Chapter Forty-Seven

Three hours later the remnants of the sun had withdrawn behind the Maya Mountains and it was finally dark. Morgan checked the luminous face of his TAG Heuer. He had made the run between the Paradise Palms and Voloshyn's villa in good time. When he'd left the hotel he'd taken a deliberate right-hand turn out on to the coast road, to all intents and purposes making his way south to the village of Placencia. He took off at a relaxed pace, keen to convey to Voloshyn's spies that he was doing nothing more than enjoying an evening run before turning in. Quite a normal thing to do, considering his background and cover as a security consultant; of course, he'd be the type to run at night.

The only thing that might have appeared strange to the more than casual observer was his clothing: long track pants, albeit ultra-lightweight and a long-sleeved shirt, also ultra-lightweight. He was, after all, in the Caribbean and the onset of thunderstorm season was giving the humidity reading a solid nudge, although the occasional unexpected downpour did take the steam out of the air a bit. The one concession to looking like a seasoned runner was the Camelbak Classic two-liter hydration pack he always carried with him on deployments, just in case. On this occasion it was also concealing the US Marine Ka-Bar fighting knife that AJ Armstrong had scored for him.

Morgan left at dusk, when he could still be clearly seen. After taking a roundabout detour toward the village, he had successfully backtracked behind the Paradise Palms. With his body now propelling him very definitely due north, Morgan rolled down his sleeves and disappeared into the dark embrace of nightfall.

The detour had added two miles to the run so he'd been at it for almost an hour. He'd kept his pace steady all the way, careful not to overstride and risk twisting or even breaking an ankle in the darkness. The further north he ran, the closer the mangroves grew against the roadway. Still he kept running, his eyes adjusting to the scarcity of light. All that mattered was that there was enough for him to see where he was going. A thin ribbon of white sand along the beach side of the road helped.

The air was warm as he breathed in and perspiration dripped from his face. This time he wasn't running for the pleasure of it; this time he was running toward an adversary. Toward danger? Possibly. If he was caught snooping it would be pretty hard to explain, but he'd come up with something plausible. "I wanted to see how serious you were about your security." That was an option. Or, "If you left it up to these goons to show me what measures you have in place, they'd only show me the stuff that won't make them look bad." That was more like it. Difficult for Voloshyn to argue with that. Anyway, who knew how this would all turn out?

Whatever happened, Morgan knew this would be Intrepid's one-in-a-million shot at bringing down not only the Night Witch and Wu Ming, but possibly even a much bigger global trafficking cartel. He owed it to Sutherland.

He counted off the clearings in the mangrove forest that were driveways to the beachside villas. He'd made note of them all on his previous trips back and forth along the road over the past few days. He was familiar with the turnoff to the Voloshyn villa and as he counted off driveway number seven, he reached the large, fallen buttonwood tree he'd selected as his marker. At this point he slowed to a walk and then stepped off the road, across the strip of white sand and into the pitch darkness of the mangrove swamp.

The cacophony of the bugs' nightly overture was just getting warmed up and the stench of anaerobic decomposition, heightened by the heat and humidity of the day, was an onslaught not yet soothed by the cool night air. The smells reminded him of the open monsoon drains he'd encountered in places like Malaysia and Thailand: rancid. The mangroves in the area had obviously been altered due to the development that accompanied the construction of the luxury villas along the coastline. Where tracts of land had been cleared to make way for homes surrounded by pristine white beach sand, the refuse had been discarded in the no man's land between the more extravagant properties, Voloshyn's being the jewel among them. The result was lots of secondary growth and the going would be slow until he managed to get beyond it. With every pace Morgan felt his feet sinking deeper into inches of sludge and prop roots. He would be ankle deep in no time if he strayed too far into it.

Sure enough, within seconds he was swallowing back an impulse to gag when both feet sank deep into the muck and a sudden burst of hydrogen sulfide gas bubbled up as he struggled to release them. *Rotten fucking eggs*, he thought, stifling a cough. *Jesus!*

Morgan pressed on, moving mostly by feel and instinct through the darkness. He could make out the lights of Voloshyn's villa in the far distance, about a hundred and fifty feet away. Not wanting to veer further into the swamp, he decided to keep the road as close to his left as he could. It provided an obvious break between the inland and coastal mangroves. Staying near it would also keep him from wandering too far toward the water. Luxury villa or not, the location had been chosen well, fortified by the thick wall of coastal flora and fauna that surrounded it to the south, west and north. In this part of the world, coastal mangroves attracted all sorts of wildlife, not the least of which were crocodiles, and Morgan wasn't keen for any unwanted attention.

Once he'd pushed far enough in from the road, he crouched down and listened. He needed a moment to allow his body the chance to settle after the run. Who was he kidding? Any chance to stop for a few minutes felt like a vacation. He really needed one – as soon as this job was done. His general fatigue had exacerbated the impact of the run. In less than a minute bugs were crawling all over the exposed skin of his hands, neck and face – mangrove spiders, crickets, scorpions – whatever they were, they were nipping and tugging at his flesh and hair, while thousands of mosquitoes buzzed deafeningly in his ears. Annoyed, he slapped them away, wiping away the carcass of something big, God only knew what, from the back of his neck. It was winged but too big to be a mosquito. *Fuck this*.

He slowly, deliberately, focused on his breathing, bringing his body back from the exertion of the past hour so that he could finally begin the task at hand. He had to reconnoiter Voloshyn's villa, identify any vulnerabilities within her security arrangements and, if possible, attempt to find options for extracting her covertly when the time came to make the arrest.

He took a drink from the Camelbak and then checked the holster he was wearing under his shirt. In addition to the Ka-Bar, AJ had scored him an M9 Beretta with a DeGroat suppressor and an elasticized holster rig. During the run Morgan had worn the rig beneath his shirt, higher than usual across his torso to reduce bounce while he was moving. Now that he was in situ, he adjusted it, dropping it back down to his right hip. He had a spare magazine and the suppressor on the rig, and an additional spare mag in a pocket on the Camelbak.

He had pushed through the mangroves for almost half an hour since leaving the road to begin his surveillance of the area and approaches to the Night Witch's villa by the sea. But he had reached a dead end, stuck within the thick undergrowth of the swamp, in the right angle formed between a long wire-mesh fence to his right and a high, whitewashed brick wall directly ahead. He was cornered, frustrated and dog tired. The wire-mesh fence was constructed around what appeared to be a small cabin with a single door standing in the very heart of the mangroves. The fence ran completely around the cabin and then formed a tunnel at its northern end, enclosing a path that led all the way to the whitewashed wall, which disappeared in either direction across the rear of Voloshyn's villa. No doubt the continuation of the perimeter wall Morgan had seen at the front of the property when he'd first been taken there. At the foot of the wall the mangroves had been cleared to provide a path around the perimeter, but also allowing just enough moonlight to give him a clear view of his predicament.

He definitely hadn't been expecting to see the cabin. He could see that the pathway's fenced tunnel ended abruptly at a large gate within the wall. This was shut. Now, the idea of having the wire-mesh fence around the cabin made sense: it was to keep out unwanted visitors from the mangroves. But why have a caged cabin all the way out here in the first place? The thoughts that streamed through his naturally suspicious mind weren't encouraging.

Morgan froze, listening, shutting out the excruciating distraction of bugs crawling all over him. His entire body was coiled. Eyes closed. Mouth open. breathing steady. His whole world became nothing but a single sound among the raucous chaos of the mangroves. He focused on it with concentration and discipline.

Splosh. Splosh. Drag. There it was again. A slow, muffled sound through the mangroves, getting closer. What was it? How close was it? *Splosh. Splosh. Drag.* It was impossible to tell.

Morgan remained locked in place, his fears about the cabin on hold as the mysterious sounds continued around him. Even the screeching of the competing bug species seemed to be hushed as the thing moved. It sounded long and cumbersome, and was passing by somewhere close, though it was impossible to define just how close. All he had to go on were the sounds. And those sounds left him in no doubt that this was a large crocodile.

Morgan slowly reached for the Beretta M9 and peeled it silently from the elasticized confines of the holster. With equal caution he slid the suppressor out too and carefully fitted it to the gun. If he had to fire, the last thing he wanted was to announce his presence to Voloshyn and her goons.

With the Beretta prepared and ready to fire, he repeated the eyes-closed-mouth-open routine again, heightening his ability to hear what he could not see. But there was nothing more to be heard – the croc had stopped moving. Had it stopped and locked its attention on Morgan? Had it sensed danger now, predator against predator? The almost impenetrable wall of mangroves that surrounded him made any kind of unfettered movement by the crocodile against him challenging at least. Of course, that applied equally to Morgan. The pitch darkness, stifling proximity of the mangroves and legions of crawling, buzzing insects, were a claustrophobically small space that was shrinking around him by the second, leaving him with no way out.

Morgan racked his brain, searching for anything he'd stored away years ago when he'd undertaken survival training in northern Australia where salt- and freshwater crocodiles were prevalent. Soon there was another sound. More splashing and dragging. Only this time, it was to his left and a little further away. And then more ahead of him. *Fuck!* So not just one. This was a pack. What did he know about crocodiles? How did they hunt?

Oliver the barman had told him that in this part of the world they were American crocodiles. They hunted primarily in the first few hours after nightfall and the average male grew to around fifteen feet in length and weighed about eight hundred pounds. Among the largest crocs in the world, they were also an endangered species. Not tonight, they're not, he thought. And what was it that Oliver had said about the croc that got his father – twenty-five-feet long and two thousand pounds? Domingo. *Jesus!*

Then something changed. There was another sound. The hairs on the back of his neck bristled. He strained to catch it through the background noise, trying even harder to pick his way through the ephemera of swamp noise. To Morgan it was a new sound, but was it new to the crocs? He realized they were quiet, too. Also listening. Also waiting, nostrils quivering above the waterline to discern the exact location of the source of the noise. And there it was again. It was human. Someone else was out here.

Morgan rose to his feet, hoping that some extra height might help. Now he could hear clearly. It wasn't a cry or a yell, it was the faintest whimper, somewhere close within the mangroves. The final prayer of someone desperate, exhausted and alone, who had lost all hope and accepted that there was no escape from their fate: "Help. Help me, please." The crocs weren't after Morgan at all. They were already on the hunt and now they were spoiled for choice. The voice he could hear was that of a young woman, and she wasn't local. Her accent was different. European? Whoever she was, she was terrified, alone in the darkness, being stalked by a pack of nature's most evolved killing machines. And if Morgan could hear her, the crocs could, too.

He had to do something.

Morgan was on his feet and moving, carefully at first, clawing his way free from the mangrove cell that had briefly imprisoned him. Crocodiles or no, he had to find the girl before they did. Ankle deep in muck, the Beretta clasped tightly in his right hand and reaching through the branches and vines with his left, Morgan set off as fast as he could. He'd accepted that there were probably even more crocs out here than he'd heard already, but he had a gun and if he was going down he'd go down fighting. He had to find her. He was torn between his desire to call out to her, to let her know she wasn't alone, and his instinct not to inadvertently incite her into a flurry of hopeful cries and movements that would only draw the crocodiles straight to her. Coldly, objectively, he erred on the side of caution and remained silent, tracking her against the odds, against a pack of prehistoric reptiles that were somewhere nearby, using hunting methods honed over millions of years. Man against beasts. One trying to save a life, the others fueled by blood lust, hell-bent on killing.

A confused pause seemed to fall over the swamp, as if the beasts had worked out that there was now competition; a race for the prize. And then it was on, Morgan and the crocodiles – moving, pausing, listening; moving, pausing, listening. The girl was crying now, her desperation carrying across the overwhelming humidity of the blackened, eerie hunting ground. Morgan felt rather than knew he was getting closer. Her sobs and pleas seemed just within reach. But where? Where was she? To find her he had moved away from the cabin, away from the dead end that had stalled his progress, deeper into the swamp, toward the edge of the sea. The water was around his knees now and he realized that the girl must be up to her waist in it, blinded by the darkness, clinging to the roots of the mangroves with nowhere else to go. But the crocs had her scent, there was no doubt of it. Morgan could sense them, preparing to make their move. Cold, calculating, knowing the prize was just a snap away. Morgan heard the splashes as the animals submerged in succession, like a fleet of submarines. They were ready to close in and he knew he didn't have a hope of getting to her in time. *Fuck! FUCK!* He had no choice but to call to her.

"Crawl into the roots!" he bellowed into the darkness. "As hard as you can! Now!"

For a split second, a total, terrifying silence fell upon the mangroves. Then, from behind him, back near the cabin, voices, men's voices, began to shout.

"Fuck, there's someone else out there!"

"Get a light on him!"

"Who the fuck is that?"

There was no mistaking the last voice. Godek Kajkowski, Voloshyn's enforcer. Beams of brilliant white light suddenly exploded from the vicinity of the cabin like air-raid searchlights and streamed through the latticework of trees and vines, seeking Morgan. With the illumination saturating him, he found himself exposed, caught in a rare patch of wide-open space.

"Help me!" the girl cried from somewhere nearby, followed by a scream. "Help! Help!"

"There!" Kajkowski yelled. "Straight ahead."

A hail of gunfire instantly followed. The short automatic bursts were from at least two 9mm sub-machine guns, most likely HK MP5s. The crack and ping of ammunition slicing and ricocheting through the heavy foliage of the vegetation sent Morgan flat on his face into the water. A lot of yelling ensued as the crew, safely ensconced behind the wire-mesh fence, barked directions at each other, laughing and goading, as they brought more firepower to bear upon the place where they'd spotted Morgan. To them it was a turkey shoot, nothing more.

But Morgan was already gone, scrambling clear of the deadly fire lane marked by the lights. He burst through vine after vine and branch after branch, the vegetation tearing at his face, eyes and hands, stumbling and falling all the way. Then he tripped badly and collapsed hard upon a fallen buttonwood tree, cracking his head against the stump. The impact dazed him for a second but then he was moving again, as quickly as he could manage in the darkness. Parallel to the beams of high-powered torchlight and endless bursts of wasted ammunition, he backtracked around to the cabin. He had no choice. He had to deal with the guns first – he was no use to the girl dead.

Throughout it all, her screams were unrelenting. She was hysterical. How had the life of a young woman come to this? Morgan knew. He was looking at them right now. Three silhouettes. The source of her misery. To them this was sport. Just fun. They'd released the girl, probably on the promise of escape, knowing her chances of survival in the crocodile-infested mangroves, in pitch darkness, unprepared and unarmed, were less than zero.

"Did you get him?" Kajkowski yelled.

"I think so," came the excited reply. One of the young steroid abusers, no doubt, eager to impress his mentor. "I saw him go down over there."

"Poor Ștefania," Kajkowski called out, taunting the girl. "You're on your own again."

"Domingo will take care of you!" yelled one of the others, laughing.

Morgan was close now, close enough to hear them clearly. Close enough to hear everything. Ștefania. Ștefania Yovenko. The girl from that night at Domingo's Bar. The girl who'd been the Night Witch's understudy in Hong Kong and who had been one of the positive IDs that had led Intrepid to the illegally obtained Belizean passports. Ștefania Yovenko. "*She won't come to any harm. You have my word on that.*" Voloshyn's words stung his ears. So this was the Night Witch's idea of the girl not coming to any harm.

As well as being close enough to hear everything, Morgan was also close enough to make his shots count. The

M9 was up, extended in a classic double-handed grip. There was just enough light for him to line up the gun, his gaze sighting along the top of the slide and through the suppressor to the very center of the torches and all the brave talk. Ready, he closed his eyes to avoid night blindness from muzzle and chamber flash, took a breath, stabilized the weapon and began firing.

The festival at the cabin instantly lost its spark.

The silent cough of the suppressed M9 dropped both of the apprentices soundlessly. Only Kajkowski was spared, shielded by the other two. He was still taunting the girl, not even aware that his associates were dead. But he soon quietened down when he realized his boys weren't joining in.

Kajkowski was no idiot though. He quickly doused the lights from the torches. Morgan fired again, blindly, where he'd last caught sight of the enforcer. Then Kajkowski recovered. He'd found an MP5 and began firing manically into the swamp straight at Morgan, hurling abuse with every burst.

Morgan didn't have time for any more of this. He knew Kajkowski would drop the defiance soon enough and run while he still could. He was a sitting duck wedged between the back of the cabin and the fence and he didn't have an audience any more. He didn't have to maintain the bravado in the eyes of the stupid young assholes – dead young assholes – who had, up until just a few minutes ago, probably worshipped the bastard.

Morgan was back on the move, avoiding the erratic gunfire, trying to retrace the general direction he'd been traveling before the gunfight, to find the girl. But her cries had fallen silent and he was struggling to lock in on her last known direction.

"Ştefania?" he called. "Ştefania?"
He was too late.
She was gone.

Chapter Forty-Eight

Morgan tore through the mangroves like a man possessed. At first fear had taken hold of him, fear that he would not hold it together long enough to survive. Almost dropping the Beretta, he'd fought back the shakes that had followed him from England and come for him in the darkness. But then he'd wrestled his fatigue into a corner and thought of Beth's face on the pillow of his king-sized bed back at the Rembrandt. *Come back to me.* It was all he needed. The fear evaporated and was replaced instantly by anger; this, and an all-consuming sense of frustration and failure, drove him west to the road. He, Alex Morgan, had failed Ştefania. Christ knows what had become of her. He had lost her in the blackness of the swamp and now she was gone, taken in the most terrifying of ways, by an animal. It was primal, Darwinian natural selection; the strongest had prevailed and the weakest had perished. His thoughts were an unforgivingly relentless stream of what crocodiles did with their prey.

She would have struggled and fought as only a human

being fighting for their life could, until the crocodiles pulled her under and drowned her in the most horrific of final moments. Right now Ştefania's body was being stored beneath the reeds and mangroves, beneath the sludge and the muck, stashed in some prehistoric meat locker to be tenderized by the warm water and parasites until the crocs were ready – *No! Fuck, no!* The branches and squadrons of insects struck at his face as he pushed his way from the stench, trauma and death of the mangroves, trying desperately not to think about Ştefania's fate.

Finally, he tripped and fell on to the edge of the road. He was clear.

Morgan stood up and gratefully filled his starving lungs with air again and again, until light-headedness threatened to topple him. He removed the suppressor from the M9 mechanically and carefully returned both to the holster beneath his shirt. Free from the swamp, his interest turned to the commotion happening back at Voloshyn's villa. There was yelling and engines revving, and perimeter lights filled the night sky. The engines told Morgan he had only minutes before Kajkowski and the rest of his dogs would be scouring every inch of road along the edge of the swamp, hunting for him. There'd be none among them who would risk actually entering the mangroves, not even Kajkowski, knowing what was in there and what they used it for. No, they wouldn't risk their own necks. They'd stand at the edge of the road, point their guns into the mangroves and clear by fire. Morgan had to get away from the area and back to the hotel before they put two and two together and worked out it'd been him out here. *Fuck.* They probably suspected it was him anyway.

He spat a mouthful of insect carcasses and dirt on to the road, took a long drink of water from the Camelbak, stamped as much mud from his shoes as he could and, using the Ka-Bar, slashed his saturated track pants into shorts to get rid of the shit and muck clinging to them, weighing him down. He threw the rags into the swamp on the far side of the road and started running, as fast as his tired legs would carry him, relishing the feel of the cool air against his skin.

"Help me! Help me! Help me!" Ştefania's pitiful cries played over and over in his head.

He was way beyond feeling any kind of impartiality toward this mission now. It was more than just a mission; more than just a personal need to avenge the death of his friend. He had seen at first hand what these people were capable of, their disregard for the value of another human life, and now that he had seen it, there was no objective distance any more. Morgan knew what had to be done. Fuck international justice. These fuckers didn't deserve a cell. What happens in the field stays in the field.

Now it was war.

Chapter Forty-Nine

The following morning, Morgan slept until eight and then showered, dressed and took breakfast in the hotel restaurant. He began with scrambled eggs and bacon with toast, the obligatory long black coffee with two sugars, and finished off with some yoghurt and a concoction of local fruit.

Despite his general exhaustion, his return to the hotel after the hell of the mangroves went smoothly, considering, and without interference. Running steadily, pure adrenalin had powered him all the way back to the Paradise Palms within an hour. There had been no traffic along the road but he'd heard a lot of shooting back in the direction of the swamp about ten minutes after he'd set off. Just as he'd suspected – even armed to the teeth, the gutless bastards still wouldn't venture into the mangrove themselves. But then his subconscious, practiced and objective, reminded him of the one pulling the strings and the reason why he was there in the first place. Darja Voloshyn: the cold, heartless, money-grubbing, androgynous bitch who made her fortune by trafficking in lives, and paid her attack dogs to kill anyone who didn't toe the line. Her line. At one point, she was nothing more than a theory and a silhouette on Interpol wanted posters. Now, there was a face and a name. The Night Witch was no longer just a theory.

When he'd eventually reached the outskirts of the resort, he'd made his way to a discreet side gate normally used by the staff. Here he'd paused for a few moments, catching his breath in the shadows, then peeled the mud-encrusted trainers from his feet and tossed them, along with the socks, deep into the bushes nearby. Next, he removed the Camelbak and then the holster containing the Beretta and placed them both on the ground. He drank the last of the water and stashed the holster alongside the Ka-Bar inside the Camelbak. Finally he removed his shirt, wrapped it tightly around the water pack and, standing in nothing but the track pants he'd slashed into shorts, had quietly pushed the gate open and entered the hotel grounds.

He was in a quiet corner of the complex that, to the right, led into the hotel basement but, to the left, directly to the hotel pool. The place was almost in darkness but for a few perimeter lights. Keeping as much as possible to the shadows, Morgan had strolled casually up to the pool, grabbing a couple of guests' towels already laid out on sunloungers for the morning along the way. Moments later he was submerged in the euphoric tranquility of the beautifully warm, crystal-clear water.

Forgetting the time and everything else, he'd swum around lazily, without a care. This was better than any therapy. He allowed his head to clear itself of what he'd just experienced. He needed his mind to be sharp if he was to proceed with his objective. There was no room for feelings getting in the way of a mission, and he'd given General

Davenport his word, his personal guarantee, that he was up to this task.

Finally he submerged and swam the length of the pool twice, the water streaming across every inch of his body, every stroke cleansing him of the baggage he was carrying. Finishing back in the shallow end, he pulled himself up onto the edge of the pool, got comfortable, closed his eyes, and breathed slowly in and out, in and out, until his shuddering body calmed. Then he turned his face to the sky and opened his eyes to look at the moon and stars. Wherever he'd been in the world, no matter what he'd been facing, this simple private custom had been like a mental tethering point for him. It grounded him when he felt troubled or conflicted. It was, after all, the same moon from which he had sought counsel throughout his life, even as a boy. And, to date at least, it hadn't let him down.

One of the hotel's nightwatchmen had appeared in Morgan's peripheral vision. "You OK, sir?" he'd asked. "It's very late to be swimming." And he'd pointed to a sign on the wall that read NO SWIMMING AFTER 11 PM.

"Bloody hell, I didn't see that," Morgan had replied, in friendly fashion. "Sorry. I couldn't sleep. Just needed to relax a bit and thought a swim might help."

"OK. OK, sir. Try not to be too much longer though, otherwise they'll kick me in my ass!"

The two of them had laughed in a shared sense of defiance; the foreigner breaking the hotel rules and the local man letting him.

"I wouldn't want you to get into any trouble on my account, mate," Morgan had told him. "I'll come out now and get my head down. The swim was all I needed."

Back in his room – after strategically and very carefully rearranging some furniture to give him early warning of any potential intruders – he'd fallen into bed and had slept undisturbed until his phone alarm woke him at eight. The late-night swim had been what he'd needed. Now he was rested and fed and ready.

Signing the breakfast docket for his room, Morgan was approached at his table by the young doorman who'd greeted him yesterday. The guy seemed a little agitated, like he was under pressure.

"Hello, mate," Morgan said. "You looking for me?"

"Yes, sir," he replied, clearly relieved that he was about to be rid of this particular task. "There is a car, that Mercedes, waiting for you in front of the hotel. The man told me to tell you to ..." There was a pause. The young man was clearly uncomfortable about the message he was required to pass on.

"It's OK. Spit it out. Whatever it is."

"The man told me to tell you to bring your bags and ... and ..."

"Yes?"

"To hurry the fuck up!"

Morgan laughed out loud and clapped the young man on the back. "Well, doesn't he sound like a nice bastard?" said Morgan jovially, tipping the guy. "Could you arrange to have my bags brought down from my room, please? And have them put in the back of that miserable prick's car."

"OK, boss," the doorman replied, smiling broadly. "I'll take care of it myself."

"Thanks. I'll pull up a pew in the foyer and have a read of the paper while you get it sorted."

"My guests arrive tomorrow."

"What's that got to do with me?" Morgan asked.

"That's up to you," Voloshyn replied. "Do you want the security job or not?"

"Possibly, but if I accept, we do it my way. These idiots need to know that. I don't have any interest in Neanderthal pissing competitions."

Kajkowski was standing within earshot, and Morgan heard the sharp intake of air whistling through his smashed septum as the jibe hit its mark.

"Agreed," she answered, a little reticently.

"That's my only stipulation. Let me take over and everything will go smoothly."

"You can guarantee that?"

"If you let me do my job, yes."

After a moment or two too long, she said: "I don't trust you, you should know that. There's something a little too arrogant and cocksure about you."

"If this is a problem for you I can fly out today, it makes no difference to me. I'm already booked on the afternoon flight. You're the one who sent the car to collect me. I'm here because I'm interested enough to get involved. If you're having second thoughts, I'll leave and you can have your gorillas look after the meeting for you."

They were sitting at a dining table set up beside the pool. The morning breeze was coming in over the perimeter wall, the smell of the ocean and the cry of the seagulls reminding Morgan that he was with one of the most deplorable creatures he'd ever known, in one of the most isolated and idyllic locations in the Caribbean. The irony wasn't lost on him.

Voloshyn stood up and walked in silence to the edge of the pool. She was wearing a black string bikini under a short, sheer, leopard-print cover-up. She looked tired, as if she hadn't slept all night, which didn't surprise him. He was expecting her to drop straight into the pool; she looked like she wanted to, but she didn't. Instead she stared off vacantly into the trees, caught up in her own thoughts. He waited patiently, casually following her gaze across the rear area of the house, beyond the pool. It was the first time he'd been out here. Of course, last night he'd been on the other side of the wall.

He noticed a break in the trees on the far side of the pool, suggesting a path, most likely leading down to the big gate he'd seen that led out into the fenced tunnel and the cabin. He was wondering what had become of the two men he'd shot when Voloshyn began speaking again.

"I think the authorities are here, in Placencia. We had some trouble last night. Did you hear about it?" She turned and cast a suspicious, accusatory gaze at him. "Any chatter at the Palms?"

"I haven't heard a thing," he answered honestly. "What sort of trouble?"

"Somebody was watching my house. We don't know how many of them there were, but they were out in the swamp. At night, in that swamp! Why the fuck would anybody want to be out there – day or night – unless they were after me, right?"

"It's a big swamp," he said. "How close were they?"

"Close enough."

"Some cops will go to extraordinary lengths if they're after someone. But how do you know they were there – what happened?"

"Godek and some of the boys were out." She paused for a moment. "Checking the perimeter. They do that sometimes."

"OK," he replied. *They weren't checking the perimeter, you bitch, and you know it.* "And?"

"They heard something out there. When they flashed their torches around toward the noise, they were shot at."

"Could it have been locals, stumbling around in there? It's pretty easy to discharge a weapon if you get spooked, especially at night."

"Two of my boys were killed!" she snapped. "These people weren't fucking locals. They were trained."

She swiped away tears with her sleeve.

My God, he realized, *she's not sad that two of her bodyguards were killed. No, she's panicked, scared for her own miserable skin. And the murder of the girl hasn't even rated a mention.*

"Jesus," Morgan said out loud. "So, did you get raided? It's highly unlikely that police would be undertaking a surveillance operation and then shoot people without following up."

"What are you saying?" she asked, anxiously. She was facing him again now.

"Did you get *raided*? Have the cops been here since the shooting?"

"No!"

"Then I seriously doubt they were cops."

Her stunned silence prompted him to continue.

"Cops would have followed up. They would either have launched a raid the moment the shooting started or they would have been 'round here in numbers at first light."

"So who the fuck *was* out there then?"

"Well, consider the possibilities: A curious local who has a crush on you? A wayward fisherman camping out?"

"Now you're just being an asshole, which you're very good at, by the way."

"Or," he continued, undeterred, "it's someone looking

out for your visitors. Like a forward recon team, making sure that their boss is going to be safe here."

"Are you serious?"

"Of course. The first time we met, you as good as told me you had the local cops in your pocket. The only ones who seem to worry you are the big guns: FBI, Interpol, whoever. Now I can tell you for sure that those guys wouldn't be sitting on their hands if they'd been involved in a firefight last night. This place would be crawling with them by now. No, my money is on your potential business partners."

"But why? I mean, putting me under surveillance ... What the fuck?"

"Maybe this isn't all as straightforward as you originally thought." Morgan was relishing the unease he was causing her – it was written all over her face. "Maybe they're not happy about that trouble in Hong Kong you mentioned. Have you confirmed that their main guy is actually coming or are you not really sure?"

"What do you mean? Of course he's fucking coming." Her face was contorted with annoyance and uncertainty. "You're really freaking me out."

"I'm paid to examine every possibility, the unexpected, the anomalies in a plan. If you're trying to finalize this multimillion-dollar deal—"

"Multi-billion," she blurted, biting a nail. "This deal is worth billions!"

"Right, billions," he replied, unmoved. "Well, you need to be prepared for your partners to be as paranoid as you are. Who knows? Maybe this Triad guy has a twin, too. Just like you."

Voloshyn dropped back into the seat across the table from him. He needed her to be on edge. She operated effectively, almost mechanically, when she was in total control of her environment. Morgan's strategy was to take control away, including, most importantly, of the environment. Right now she was completely unsure what she was getting herself into. She wasn't in control and this was uncharted territory for her.

"What time are you expecting these guys tomorrow?" Morgan asked.

"About midday. They're coming in on a private charter."

"OK, so we have exactly one day to prepare and, while we're at it, to check and see if any new arrivals have been noticed in town."

"OK," she said. "Tell me what you need."

Chapter Fifty

Morgan spent the rest of the day making a show of his detailed analysis of the property and the Night Witch's extant security arrangements, which were negligible. He had decided to be collaborative, at least on the surface, in order to appear professional and, above all, committed to the task she was paying him for. His objective was to cast his eye over as much of the property as he possibly could to find its vulnerable points so that when the time came, he could exploit them. In the meantime, if an opportunity presented itself, he would attempt to weaken the current security footprint without creating any noticeable gaps.

From a genuine security perspective, all that was needed were a few very rudimentary strategies that were important enough but would appear to the inexperienced eye to be much more significant than they really were. He began with the obvious stuff like CCTV and the main access points. For a start, most of the cameras he could see were pointing directly into overgrown trees. That was pretty common. It told Morgan that no one was actively managing the surveillance gear. Good to know. It meant it was highly unlikely that his image had been captured anywhere last night, although he couldn't guarantee that.

He got Voloshyn's gardener and his apprentice, a local man and a young boy, probably his son, to start cutting back the trees to, he told them, allow the cameras to get a much clearer view of all the approaches to the house and around the perimeter fence. Next, he headed for the gates. The first was the main gate, the north one. The second was the south gate at the back, the one he'd seen the night before that led into the property from the cabin and the fencing tunnel. He couldn't let on that he knew about that one, so he expertly allowed himself, under the ever-watchful eye of Godek Kajkowski, to discover it in the presence of one of the local guards. Morgan eventually realized that there was another gate, located in the eastern wall, that led directly out onto Voloshyn's private beach. As they came upon it, it appeared to be unlocked, secured by only a simple slide bolt with no evidence of a padlock or chain anywhere. Interesting.

His first step in weakening what security Voloshyn had was to reduce the number of Kajkowski's men onsite at any one time. He ascertained that, with the loss of the two he'd killed last night, they were now down to just four: Kajkowski plus three. Dariusz didn't qualify, although he definitely was around and loitering, mostly by the pool or else poring over the accounts on his ever-present laptop. Perhaps Dariusz could be of use.

Morgan set off to find the Night Witch. She'd withdrawn to her own quarters, no doubt shaken by the events of the previous evening.

"I need to float something by you," he said. "You got a minute?"

Voloshyn was sitting at her desk in the office that

adjoined her private suite on the villa's top floor with its million-dollar views of the ocean.

"Sure, come in."

"Of the two guests you have coming tomorrow," he began, walking into the room but remaining a respectful distance from her desk, "which is the most important?"

"Well, whoever the investors send to represent them, obviously. I expect they'll send accountants. Probably a couple of the men we met with in LA. They're across all the financial details. The meeting with the Chinese is purely for their benefit. I have to impress them and show that I can bring the Chinese into the deal."

Morgan could see that the performing seal role didn't sit well with her. "OK, that's what I thought. So, as a subtle but necessary show of respect, acknowledging their importance, I would recommend that you send your man Dariusz to meet them at whichever airport they'll depart from, and that he travels with them all the way back here."

"Why would I do that?"

"Traveling to Belize isn't straightforward. There are transfers, layovers, a dozen little hoops to jump through just to get down here. Dariusz could be your eyes and ears. When there's down time, he could be reinforcing your position and gauging where they really stand on the whole Chinese end of the deal. And at the same time you'll be impressing them by showing that you appreciate the significance of them sending their emissary so much that you sent your own right-hand man to accompany him. Consider it commercial diplomacy."

"What's this got to do with you?" she asked. "It doesn't concern my security."

"I'm afraid you're wrong. An integral part of what I do is protecting reputations. Achieving that comes with all sorts of challenges. You want this to run smoothly, and sending Dariusz to escort them down here will instantly put you on the front foot. It means that your influence begins from their point of departure, not just when they get here. You're in control all the way."

Voloshyn spent a few moments searching the ocean for guidance. Then she said: "I'll think about it. But how will Dariusz get up there in time? He would have to be in LA by first thing tomorrow morning in order to meet them and travel back here. It's not possible, even if I agreed to it."

"There's a flight leaving Placencia this afternoon at two pm. I was booked on it. If he hurries, he'll make it. Then he'll be able to connect at Belize City for LAX this evening and get in late tonight. Meanwhile you can liaise with the investors and let them know what you're doing. Dariusz is a big boy, I'm sure he'll be able to sort it out."

"OK, is that it?"

"Yes."

"I'll let you know then."

Morgan walked back downstairs in search of Kajkowski. He needed to lose another one and a simple solution came to mind. He found the big Pole at the dining table by the pool, apparently conspiring with Dariusz. The two of them fell silent as he approached.

"What the fuck do you want?" Kajkowski said.

"I want you to send one of your boys to sit at the airport as our forward recon man between now and tomorrow, before all this shit starts to happen."

"Forward recon? What the fuck for?"

"So he can report back to us about any unusual new arrivals coming into Placencia ahead of the main players. I doubt that a Triad boss is going to travel anywhere outside his own patch without an advance party, and we know they only really trust their own. So he should keep an eye out for any Chinese-looking types. They'll be nondescript, gray men; good at blending into the background. Not gym junkies like you and your circus troupe. Your guy only needs to call it in if he sees anything, and then follow them to see where they're staying. I'm sure even your men could manage that."

Kajkowski stepped slowly around the table and approached Morgan, shaping up for a confrontation. He had obviously used this particular approach against easily intimidated ne'er-do-wells from the underworld, who most likely instantly responded with retreat mode. His movements and openly aggressive, puffed-chest demeanor were like a pantomime; all slow motion, pause-for-effect stuff that Hollywood was to blame for. With great showmanship, Kajkowski's powerfully muscled arm reached around to the flashy silver Magnum he wore in a leather holster under his arm, but before he'd even managed to close his fingers around the grips, Morgan had the Beretta drawn from the elasticized holster beneath his loose polo shirt and aimed directly at the other man's gut. Kajkowski stopped dead in his tracks.

"Jesus," said Morgan casually. "Two or three more minutes of that routine and I reckon you would have had me."

"I'll fucking kill you!" the other man snarled, but didn't risk drawing the gun. Instead he spat on the ground at Morgan's feet.

"Godek!" Dariusz barked. "Not now."

"I'm happy to sort this out," said Morgan, eyes fixed on Kajkowski. "The sooner, the better, so I can get on with my job."

"You know, Mister Big Time Security Expert, you might

have her believing your bullshit," Dariusz began, "but Godek and I think it was you out there in the swamp last night."

"Great minds think alike, I suppose. I don't give a shit. Think what you like. Now, are you going to let your dog off his leash so we can settle this once and for all, or are we going to send a man out to the airport so we can start protecting your boss and get this deal done? If I understand correctly, you stand to make quite a bit of money out of this yourself, am I right? Two of your guys being killed outside the wall last night as well as a gunfight here in the grounds today, the day before this deal is supposed to be done, won't exactly fill your investors with confidence, will it?"

"They'll never know, you fuck!" said Kajkowski.

"They will," said Morgan. "How do you know I'm not working for them right now?"

A stunned silence ensued until a cell phone on the table buzzed and broke the deadlock.

"Get one of your guys out to the airport now and forget about this creep," Dariusz said, picking up the phone and dismissing Kajkowski. "There'll be plenty of time to deal with him later."

The big man dropped his hand from where it had been hovering near his gun and kicked a chair hard enough to send it flying, narrowly missing Morgan. He didn't budge and the Beretta remained locked on its target.

"When this is over and she doesn't want you around anymore," Kajkowski yelled, full of frustration, "I'm going to slit your fucking throat!" He stormed off.

Calmly, Morgan holstered the Beretta and turned his attention back to Dariusz.

"He doesn't sound very happy." The cell phone, which

had stopped buzzing during Kajkowski's tantrum, had started up again. "You really should take that call."

"What's it to you?" said Dariusz.

"Nothing. But once she gets through telling you where you're going, if you pack really quickly, you might just make the flight in time."

Chapter Fifty-One

The departure of Dariusz came with an unexpected bonus. Such was the level of anxiety and paranoia circulating among Voloshyn, Dariusz and even Kajkowski – following Morgan's carefully timed suggestions about the property being under surveillance by Triad forward recon teams, and that he himself may or may not be working for the investors – that Dariusz flatly refused to leave the villa unless he was accompanied by a bodyguard. Now desperate to regain some control, Voloshyn reluctantly acquiesced, leaving herself down to just Kajkowski, one of his men, and a slack handful of local guards to cover her own protection and security for the villa. And, of course, she still had Morgan. His deliberate attempt to destabilize her security had had the desired effect.

Earlier in the afternoon, when Kajkowski had personally driven Dariusz to the airport along with the bodyguard who'd been selected to accompany him, Morgan managed to convince the last of Kajkowski's men to show him the security control room which, in theory, should have been the villa's nerve center. It wasn't. Instead, Morgan found a hang-out space for the crew. The room stank of booze and cigarette smoke, and the walls were covered with explicit images of naked women. Some were clearly favorites torn from the pages of the literally hundreds of porn mags that littered the space, but many others appeared to be computer printouts of images snapped from cell phones. These included the all-too-familiar mugs of Kajkowski and his men in graphic selfies snapped during sessions of group sex with a variety of young women. All featured half-a-dozen men, always including Kajkowski, and only ever one girl. The pictures adorned the walls like trophies. In every case, the young girl seemed to be completely out of it, drugged out of her mind, no doubt, and passed around like little more than a sex doll for a pack of depraved assholes. Gang rape, not group sex. What Morgan was looking at was nonconsensual. It had to be.

Across the range of the photos, he counted at least a dozen different girls. All of them looked to be white Europeans, tall, attractive, and no more than seventeen or eighteen years old. He thought one of them was possibly Ştefania and wondered how many of the others had met a similar fate.

Hiding his revulsion and ignoring the obscenely juvenile boasts of Kajkowski's man, Morgan turned to the rest of the room. He eventually discovered a computer tucked away in a small alcove at the back, together with multiple flat screens, a filthy keyboard, a joystick and a variety of games consoles. The monitor was on standby. He could see the flickering of an external modem, indicating that it was connected to the internet. Through a disjointed few seconds of gesticulating and broken English he soon ascertained from Kajkowski's man that this was also the CCTV operating system but it was never used for that, just games and porn. Excellent. An idea began to form.

At 5pm Morgan looked at his watch. He was outside again now, checking around the perimeter of the property. He could see that the gardener and his boy, chainsaws in hand, were still working away, clearing the final few obstructions to the CCTV fields of view. They'd made good time considering the extent of the work he'd ordered, and would be done within the hour. Then they'd have to clean away all the debris they had created before nightfall – the place had to be immaculate by first thing in the morning.

Their progress and the absence of the others gave Morgan an opportunity to return to the security control room again, this time unaccompanied. If anyone asked, he would say that he was checking on how much the view of each camera had been improved by the hacking and slashing of overgrown vegetation. His actual intentions were a little more complicated: if he could get it working properly, the CCTV system could be of real value.

Carefully, Morgan eased open the rickety flywire door, flicked on the single-bulb light and stepped inside. He was making his way across to the computer when something on the photo trophy wall caught his eye. Was that what he thought it was? He stepped between the maze of dilapidated lounge chairs, empty beer cans, spilled ashtrays and stacks of porn magazines, to one of the trophy photos. Four guys, a girl, and just visible in the shadows of the background – barely captured by the cell-phone's flash – a tuft of peroxide-blonde hair and a face of pure evil, laughing in ecstasy. She was surrounded by her attack dogs, sitting in a big chair, watching as they pack raped just another girl. Darja Voloshyn. The Night Witch liked to watch.

Who the fuck were these people?

Morgan shook his head and moved on to the computer, intent only on his mission now; he couldn't allow any more emotional baggage to cloud his judgment. He didn't have time to acknowledge how much his mind and body ached for respite. He didn't have time to consider just how many girls had fallen victim to this pack of sub-human scum or how long these people had been free to operate worldwide, unfettered. He didn't have time, because in less than twenty-four hours, two of the world's biggest players in the slavery trade were going to be here, under the same roof and within striking distance of Intrepid. He was ready to activate the extraction plan.

He sat down at the computer, moved the mouse and listened to the whine as the machine came back to life, slowly. It wasn't top of the range, that was for sure. After minimizing a dozen screens featuring first-person shooter online games and sex sites, he eventually reached the desktop and identified the CCTV operating system icon. It was an old model, about ten years old. No surprises there. As he maneuvered his way within the various fields of the operating system, he soon found the activity log and confirmed just how neglected the system had been. According to the log, the last recorded use of the CCTV system was almost six months ago. Complacency wins once again.

Now that he had the cameras going, he ran a general visual sweep across the entire property, all the while formulating a number of potential plans for how he might extract Voloshyn when the time came. Morgan opened a new tab, found the website he was looking for, established a guest user account – designed as a try-before-you-buy option – and then diverted the entire battery of CCTV cameras, twelve in total, to his new personal surveillance monitoring site. He picked up his iPhone and activated an app that linked him to the monitoring site he'd just created and was instantly able to both monitor and control the cameras from his phone. He hid the monitoring site, cleared the immediate past history, and expanded the pages he'd minimized, returning the computer to the state he had found it in.

Finally, again via his iPhone, he sent an email warning order – a heads-up – to his new contact, AJ Armstrong, and then emailed a link for the monitoring site along with a cryptic pre-arranged message direct to a faux-business email address that had been set up to support his cover as a private security consultant. In reality, the email address would divert straight through to the Intrepid operations duty officer, who would immediately report any activity to the chief of staff, at that moment Mila Haddad, and ultimately General Davenport. His message read: *Four Three: 2 8 3 6 4 3 7. Twenty Four.* He hit send and dropped the phone back into his pocket. Now they would know what he was up to, what he needed and when.

Just at that moment he heard a familiar voice rasp: "What the fuck are you doing in here?"

Chapter Fifty-Two

"What's this all about?" snapped Voloshyn, annoyed by the sudden interruption. "What are you all doing up here?"

"I caught this piece of shit sticking his nose where it shouldn't be. He was in our muster room downstairs, and fucking about with the security equipment. He has no business being there."

"Is what Godek says true?" she asked. "Were you in their room?"

"Yes," Morgan replied, unperturbed by the inquisition. "Apart from the 'no business being there' bit."

"Fuck you," Kajkowski growled behind him. "I think this fuck is a spy or a cop! You should let me kill him right now!"

Morgan had allowed himself to be frogmarched by Kajkowski and his apprentice all the way up to Voloshyn's private quarters. They'd spilled into the space to find her sitting at a dining table out on the balcony, the remains of her evening meal being cleared away by one of the servants. For some reason, Morgan got the impression the table had been set for two, his subconscious must have picked up something, and he noticed that her eyes kept darting to the slatted sliding doors that separated this area from her bedroom.

Morgan reasoned that allowing Kajkowski to make yet another commotion in front of the Night Witch would only reinforce his own standing as an objective professional who was constantly being diverted from his responsibilities by an interfering fool.

"Explain yourself," she ordered.

"Of course." He walked over to a huge digital screen that sat on an ornate wooden cabinet on the far side of the room, collected a remote control and switched on the screen. Then he selected the channel he was after, dropped the remote casually onto a nearby sofa and turned to the Night Witch.

"May I borrow your iPhone?"

"What? What for?" she asked. "No, you can't have my phone."

"I assure you it is completely necessary if I'm to demonstrate to you once and for all that this man's obsession with derailing my work is doing nothing but putting your life at risk. If you ask me, he and your friend Dariusz are just waiting patiently until this deal is done before they conduct a hostile takeover of your business. And then they'll kill you, along with whoever it is you've got hiding in there." His gaze flicked to her bedroom and his hand reached out for her phone.

Voloshyn stared at him, clearly uncertain again of how to take him or what to believe. Her eyes moved across to Kajkowski but instantly turned away. She picked up her phone from the table beside her and tossed it across to Morgan.

"Thank you," he said as he caught it. "Now if you'll just bear with me for a moment while I download an app …"

He stood in the center of the room, halfway between Voloshyn and Kajkowski, and tapped away on the screen of her phone.

"This is fucking bullshit," said Kajkowski. "This fucking guy has been ordering everybody around all fucking morning. You made Dariusz fly all the way to America just to turn around and fly back. And I've had one of the boys sitting on his ass at the airport all day, waiting for the chinks to turn up and, so far, nothing. This guy's full of shit and he's making fools of all of us – of you!"

"No, I think you're doing a good enough job of that yourself," said Morgan, still focused on the phone. "I haven't heard you offer one legitimate suggestion yet."

"Shut up, both of you," said Voloshyn. "I'm sick of this shit. Godek, not another word from you until I say so! And you – you have exactly one minute to stop fucking around with my phone and make your point or I will let him kill you."

At that moment the digital screen flickered and an image came to life. After a few seconds of adjustment, the image intensified and became clearer.

"What is that?" Voloshyn asked, suddenly interested.

"That is the inside path along your western perimeter wall. This morning you wouldn't have seen any more than ten feet from the camera due to the amount of overgrown vegetation obscuring the view. In fact, this morning, you wouldn't even have seen that far because that camera and most of the others were not actually switched on. God knows how long they'd been like that." Morgan turned an accusatory look squarely on Kajkowski and then continued. "The shot is taken from the camera that's up on the back corner of your house, over on this side." He pointed in the general direction. "With the vegetation cleared you can now see almost to the back corner of the property, but not quite. So now we'll check in on what the camera there can see."

Morgan tapped a new set of commands into the phone and the image altered. He noted Voloshyn's demeanor had changed completely, from unimpressed to totally engaged. Her paranoia over her personal safety had skyrocketed ahead of the arrival of the Chinese and the representative from the investors, and Morgan's simple but effective display had obviously captured her attention. The screen was now displaying the reverse image of the first, the view from the opposing corner facing the house. The two cameras had been sited well and between them provided an expansive and detailed view of the entire west side of the property.

"When your man found me downstairs, I wasn't snooping around their muster room. I was activating and checking every security camera so I could be sure that the measures I'd taken to clear the fucking jungle that had been allowed to grow wild had been effective. In addition, I set up this program so that we can run and check the cameras from our phones." He waved hers and then handed it back to her. "I've downloaded the same program to my phone so I can check all of them from wherever I am. That's what you're paying me to do.

"I told you the only way I'd accept this job was if we did it my way, with no interference from Gorbachev over there, or anyone else. If he had half a clue about security he would never have put up with the outdated system you have in this place. Now, if you can spare a few more minutes, I'd be happy to show you how to run all of the cameras from your phone and either watch them on it or else here on the big screen. Up to you."

Voloshyn was sold. "Of course," she replied. "Godek, get out. I'll deal with you tomorrow."

Morgan watched as Kajkowski and his buddy stormed from the room. Morgan didn't relish having such a hostile enemy working against him while he was trying to establish and maintain his cover, but the memory of their first encounter and the man's constant interference had made conflict between them unavoidable. A showdown was inevitable at some point and, as he watched Kajkowski disappear down the darkened stairwell, Morgan knew that it could only end in the death of one or both of them. There'd be no in between with Godek Kajkowski.

Morgan spent about ten minutes more with Voloshyn, taking her through the basics of maneuvering her way around the CCTV system via her phone, but she was clearly distracted by what he'd suggested about Dariusz and Kajkowski. Sowing the seeds of uncertainty and distrust among Voloshyn and her closest associates was definitely the way to go. Her paranoia and precarious mental state would do the rest. When the scared-out-of-her-mind Darja Voloshyn withdrew, it would take only half a second for the reappearance of the Night Witch persona, the one everyone hated and feared, even her closest associates.

And when the time came to take her down, any hesitation or reluctance among her so-called protectors to go above and beyond for her could mean the difference between life and death for Morgan. There was no honor or loyalty among thieves.

Eventually Voloshyn was done with the novelty of controlling and viewing the CCTV, so she dismissed him. He headed to his room, which was beneath hers. On the way he stopped off in the kitchen and grabbed some fresh fruit, vegetables and bottled water to sustain himself. He heard raised voices down in the bowels of the house somewhere. It sounded like Kajkowski, venting again. No doubt there'd be booze involved. Hopefully the man would be smart enough to keep his anger contained, at least until after tomorrow's meeting. But Morgan knew how volatile and unpredictable Kajkowski was and the last thing he could afford to do was assume that there wouldn't be trouble ahead of time.

Back in his room, Morgan finished off his scrounged meal of fresh produce and washed it down with a bottle of water. He quietly wedged a wooden chair under the door handle, checked that the windows were latched, stripped off and took a shower with the Beretta resting on the soap shelf. Then he towelled himself dry, checked that the door and windows were still secure, dressed in a pair of shorts and a T-shirt – just in case – adjusted the ceiling fan to a lower speed so that the noise wouldn't impede his hearing, and stretched out on top of the bed.

Morgan's body seemed to submerge into the mattress. His limbs felt like lead and his head slumped readily into the soft caress of the pillow. He did not want to fall into a heavy sleep but he feared that his exhausted body would soon betray him. Mechanically, he reached underneath his pillow and closed his fingers around the butt of the Beretta. OK, he was settled. The room was as secure as it could be. If anyone tried to break in he'd hear them for sure.

Moments or hours later, he couldn't be sure, there was a quiet *tap-tap-tap* on the door. Morgan was instantly awake. He lifted himself up and moved cautiously across to the door. The gun was in his right hand.

Standing clear of the door, he said "Who is it?"

"I'm sorry, sir," came a very quiet, very timid, local voice. "I need your help." A pause. "I'm frightened."

Morgan thought it was the voice of the housekeeper, a small woman of Mayan ancestry he'd seen and spoken to a handful of times. Reluctantly, he moved the chair aside and opened the door. He was right. The housekeeper was standing in the dimly lit corridor, shaking and cowering. Apology and fear were written all over her face.

No sooner had he read all of the warning signs than he realized his fatal mistake. He'd been conned.

The door burst wide open, a Taser appeared from nowhere, and Morgan bore the full brunt of fifty thousand volts directly above his heart.

Chapter Fifty-Three

Water was pouring down his face. It was incessant, barreling down in endless torrents, threatening to drown him. The noise was overpowering. His body was rigid with trauma, heavy and unresponsive. He couldn't make sense of it. There was pain everywhere and an unnerving sensation of small creatures crawling all over his skin. He tried to move, to scrape them away, but his arms wouldn't budge. He tried again and again to get them moving but all he got in return was searing pain burning his wrists through to the bone. Exasperated and fighting off an illogically panicked reaction to the bugs, he tried to pull himself up but both shoulders failed him, feeling as though they were about to dislocate.

The pain made Alex Morgan emerge from the stupor that had brought him here.

The water and noise were caused by a tropical downpour thundering through the scant canopy of the mangroves. But why was this so sparse? He remembered it as being thick, almost impenetrable, even to heavy rain. Then he remembered his room, the housekeeper, fear, a

Taser, electrocution, convulsing on the floor, a blow to the head and darkness. Morgan's body shuddered at the memory of it all and reports of pain of every kind raced in. His face, ribs, back, arms and legs had all been battered, kicked, most likely. Everything ached like hell. His head was pounding. He became particularly aware of a throbbing pain emanating from his right thigh – the flesh there felt as though it was split wide open. What the fuck was that? When he attempted to look down, he realized that the area around his eyes was swollen and pulsing with pain, too.

Unable to move his arms, he shook his entire body, forcing it to respond, and the barely audible rattle of the cyclone-mesh fence he was lashed to brought his situation home to him. He was tied by the wrists, arms strung high above his head, to the fence around the cabin; the isolated place he had seen the night before in the center of the mangroves. But he was on the outside, exposed and incapacitated in the no man's land of the deadly swamp, facing all its vicious dangers.

He moved his legs and felt the sludge of the swamp lapping around his calves. His memory instantly turned to the crocodiles that had taken Ștefania. They had hunted and closed in on her as a pack, then dragged her down to a slow, terrifying, lonely death. The same end that Kajkowski had now chosen for Morgan, only this time the victim had been presented like a sacrificial lamb, tenderized and skewered, with absolutely no chance of escape.

But Alex Morgan was not yet willing to surrender his life.

He fought to recover his senses and reinstate his instinct for self-preservation. He tried to yank his legs clear of the mud and felt the swamp instantly pulling against him, unwilling to give him up so easily. He fought back, pulling, slipping and losing ground and energy in a bizarre tug-of-war with the living swamp. It took him minutes finally to pull his feet free.

With some control regained, albeit minimal, his confidence surged. Still hanging by his arms, he shuffled his mud-encrusted feet back out of the sludge until they were directly beneath him again. They were not quite ready to take his weight but he pushed them regardless. Tentatively, his body slid up against the fence and the unbearable pressure on his arms was instantly relieved. Now his elbows were bent, his shoulders returned fully to their sockets and his hands were close enough to his head to allow him to get to work on the rope bindings with his teeth.

Morgan turned his head away from the rain and gratefully took a series of deep breaths. He couldn't think about the crocs. If they were closing in on him he couldn't hear them, so he wouldn't know anyway. If they attacked he'd just have to deal with it. He shut down a relentless stream of thoughts and images of what that death would feel like, and tried to focus his rapidly expiring energy on his immediate objective – escape.

Morgan craned his neck awkwardly as far around to the right as he could possibly manage without actually breaking it. Painfully he bit down hard, got a solid purchase on the rope with his teeth, and began the impossible task of easing apart the knotted, rain-soaked, swollen strands.

A face suddenly appeared through the honeycomb of the wire fence, close by, just inches away through the mesh. Morgan recoiled, ready to fend off another attack, but the rope grappled him back against the fence. A torch illuminated the face for a moment, rain strobing against its light as it bounced around. Morgan saw a tuft of white-blonde hair and blue eyes wide with fear, level with his own. A hand appeared, clutching a knife. It sawed through the rope on the other side of the fence. The blue eyes held his then looked away at something or someone else. He couldn't tell who his rescuer was. Voloshyn? It couldn't be. The hand with the knife and the hand with the torch were now working in unison. For a second Morgan was blinded but he clamped his eyes shut, feeling the desperate energy of the stranger, the girl with the knife, as the fence shook under her assault, and slowly but surely the ropes around his wrists began to give way. The moment he felt the strands fall apart he pulled himself free.

"Here!" the girl cried above the rain, and he saw she was now standing at an open gate in the fence just a few feet from where he had been tethered. "Quickly!"

Morgan raced for the gate but stumbled, his legs barely able to support him, and fell headlong into the putrid muck of the mangroves. All he could think of was crocodiles. He clawed desperately for the fence, fighting for a lifeline in the darkness, something, anything, to grab on to. The girl shone the torch at him but then let out a scream.

Morgan knew he would never forget what he saw. The beam of light fell upon two crocodiles that had somehow broken through the thick wall of mangroves and were less than five feet from him and moving in fast. In the briefest glimpse by the wavering light of the torch he saw two sets of eyes, trained on him, targeting him from the surface of the water. The eyes of one of them were about as far apart as the headlights on a school bus. *Fuck! FUCK!*

"No!" the girl screamed. "Come on!"

Morgan's arm shot out of the swamp, stretched to its limit. He found a solid purchase against the roots of the mangroves, kicked with everything he had left and launched himself up. Mercifully his fingers closed around the latticework of the fence and he dragged himself free from the swamp with one heave. Then he was back on his knees, then his feet, and tumbling through the gate just as the girl slammed it shut behind him.

Morgan collapsed in a heap at her feet, sucking in deep breaths before he managed to get up on his hands and knees.

"Who are you?" he said.

"Jovana," she replied. "You have to get me out of here!"

Chapter Fifty-Four

Jovana helped Morgan into the cabin and laid him down on the bare concrete. She gently cradled his head in her hands before easing it down to the floor. He let out a deep, exhausted, grateful sigh. She examined him by torchlight. He was naked but for a pair of shorts. His face was swollen and the skin of his cheeks and lips was split. There was a deep cut in his right thigh, which looked like it had been slashed by a knife, and his legs were covered in leeches. The rain had been washing the blood away, but now that they were undercover it began to run freely again.

She took off the soaking wet sweater she was wearing and then peeled off the T-shirt underneath. The shirt was marginally less wet than the sweater so she used it to dab the blood from his face before wrapping the shirt firmly around the gash on his leg.

"You're pretty good at this," he said. His voice was rasping and shallow.

"I've had a lot of practice," she replied, thinking of her friends, other girls she'd nursed and cared for when Drago had finished abusing them. "You're not one of them, are you?"

"One of Kajkowski's crew? No," he said. "I definitely am not. Speaking of which, we have to get out of here."

He sat up, gingerly, and picked up the torch and turned it on himself. There were at least twenty leeches, each the size of a large finger, sucking greedily on his legs. He asked her for the knife and then began the painful process of cutting and lifting the parasites from his sodden flesh.

"Where did you get this?" he asked. "It's mine, isn't it?"

"Yes," she said. "I found it in your room. I snuck away from her and was coming to find you, to ask you to help me get away. I was on the stairs coming down when I heard Godek and the others burst into your room. I was too scared to make a sound. I waited on the stairs. Did they use electricity?"

"Yeah, they did."

"That's what they use on the girls they bring back here; the ones who won't cooperate. They took you down the other stairs and when they were gone – I don't know why – I raced into your room. I found your knife in your bag and then I followed them. I saw them dragging you out here. They were drunk out of their minds, laughing and kicking you all the way past the pool. You started to come 'round just before they reached the gate and that's when they began to beat you. It was horrible to watch but I didn't know what else to do. I just hid among the trees, clutching the knife. Hoping they wouldn't find me."

Morgan held his ribs, as if recalling the beating. Jovana ran her palm over his hair and face.

"Godek likes to hurt people – likes to kill. He enjoys being cruel," she said. "You must be very strong. He didn't kill you."

"I suppose that's something," Morgan replied, still cutting away leeches. "How the hell did you end up out here?"

"Once they'd finished beating you, they were falling over everywhere, they were so drunk. I knew they would bring you here. It's what they do when they want to do bad things to someone."

"Do you know anyone named Ştefania Yovenko?"

"Ştefania! Yes. How do you know her? Did she get away?"

"I'm afraid not," he replied. "I believe they brought her out here last night."

Jovana sighed. She was used to loss.

"They took her away days ago, from her room. Godek did it. I heard him. Heard her screaming," the girl said absently. "They probably kept her out here and used her until they were ready to kill her."

"Did you know her well?"

"No. We only met once. I think she was one of the Witch's robots, too. No, not robot. What is that English word? Clone. Yes, a clone – like me. She tried to warn me. Warned me about the Witch, about what they would do to me if I didn't perform, you know. I told her I already knew what they could do."

"You're a very brave girl, Jovana," said Morgan. "But why are you helping me? You don't know me at all. I could be just like them."

"You are nothing like them. I know men, believe me. I heard the Witch talking about you with Dariusz and Godek. They didn't want you here, but she did. She is frightened for her safety. She doesn't care about anyone else. They argued about you. I listened. You're an outsider, some kind of security person. When I saw you upstairs tonight, showing her the cameras, I knew you were not one of them."

"You're the one who was in her room?"

"Yes," she replied. "She doesn't like anyone from the outside to see me. I'm supposed to hide all the time until she thinks I'm ready. But you should know, she plans to kill you once this whole thing with the Chinese is settled. She doesn't trust Dariusz or Godek any more, so she used you to protect herself from them. You've been useful to her so far but when the meeting is all done, the Chinese will kill you for her. She told me."

"How clever," he mused. "That poor-little-me act ... I did wonder."

"No, she's crazy. She can be sweet and tender and caring sometimes. But when the other one appears, the Witch, that's when she is dangerous."

"Are you two ... lovers?"

"At first I thought it wasn't so bad. She was gentle with me. Nothing like the men I have known; they were animals. I thought she really cared about me. She told me she was once a girl just like me, knew what I had been through because she'd been through the same. I believed her. It felt nice to be cared for, to be loved. I've never had that before. But then I realized there were two sides to her, possibly more. What she wants, she takes. When she is the Witch, she abuses me just like the men did. She is disgusting. I have to go along with it. I know what happens if I don't." Jovana's eyes followed the beam of the torch to the metal-framed bed in the center of the cabin and she shuddered, holding herself tightly. "You have to get me out of here. Do you understand? *You have to.* I can't stay here anymore. I have to get away from her."

She began to cry, quietly at first and then so uncontrollably that she fell into Morgan's arms. She had never cried so hard in her life. Finally she felt safe. Somehow she knew that this man would save her.

After a few minutes, he lifted her up so that they were both sitting again, facing each other.

"Jovana," he began, "I will get you out of here, you have my word. But I need you to be brave for just a few more hours. Can you do that?"

She nodded, sniffing and wiping her face on the sleeve of her sweater.

"OK," he said. "Now, I need you to tell me exactly where Godek and his friend went after they'd tied me up for the crocs."

"That's easy. They did what they do most nights. They went back to their rooms to get more drink then they sat around under the verandah near the pool, drinking and talking shit, and then they fell asleep on the loungers. Why? What will you do next?"

"I have an idea, but first we need to get you back to your room."

Chapter Fifty-Five

Thirty minutes later, Alex Morgan was running again – more like shuffling – back along the thin line of the coast road, parallel to the mangroves, just as he had done the night before. This time his body was failing him. The deep gash in his leg had slowed him down significantly and the workover they'd given his ribs and back was making every breath a painful experience. Despite all that, he was alive and he was moving – not so fast as last night, but he wasn't being drowned then shoved into a crocodile's meat locker and tenderized either. Thank God for small mercies, that was what his mad Catholic mom would have said. He laughed. She always berated him whenever he called her a mad Catholic. What would she be doing right now? Probably making a cup of tea and sitting down to a quiet evening in front of the TV. Like a normal person. Normal. Morgan had no idea what that was like.

Exhaustion and pain were streaming a bizarre collection of disparate thoughts and ramblings through his mind. He had to stay clear-headed, just for one more day, if he was going to bring them all down.

With Jovana's help he'd managed to get back inside the compound. They'd skirted the pool via the gardens, with Jovana leading, until they reached the rear verandah. The rain had abated; more drizzle than downpour.

"Look," she'd said, and grabbed his arm. "Up there. Can you see? There they are, all three of them."

Sure enough, Morgan had seen Kajkowski and two of his minions passed out on sunloungers up on the verandah. They wouldn't present any problems unless Morgan walked right up and woke them personally, so he'd known he had some time. Jovana had led him back to her room, opened the door and ushered him inside.

"Come in quickly and I will help you with your wounds."

"Are you sure she won't notice that you're gone?"

The girl shook her head. "Every night she takes a sleeping pill when she's done with me, and when she's asleep I leave and come back here. She doesn't care. Now, sit down over there while I get the medical box."

Morgan had agreed on the basis that if he didn't deal with it now, the wound on his leg would get much worse. Jovana had found a first aid kit, cleaned the wound with antiseptic and then bandaged it firmly. He'd taken the rest of the antiseptic and a couple of bandages, and then, reassuring her that he'd be back within twenty-four hours, he'd quickly returned to his own room. There he'd collected some key items like his trainers, trackpants, shirt, a credit card and some cash and, after a frantic search, his trusty old TAG Heuer. The band must have broken during the scuffle when they were Tasering him and thankfully the watch had dropped out of sight. He'd also found his phone on the floor, cleared some data from it and then stamped on it to break the screen. The Beretta had been taken, no doubt by Kajkowski. So, whatever was left, the general stuff like his toiletries and other clothes, he'd thrown all over the room then set to work overturning a chair and bedside table. When he'd finished, he'd headed off.

Out on the road and running in total darkness with only the light rain for company, Morgan maintained a steady shuffle. He had a plan and needed some backup. He knew where he could get it. It took him the best part of two hours to make his way back into the village. It was 3am and he was almost on his last legs. There was no one else around. All the bars had cleared out and the heavy rain earlier had sent the last of the diehard drinkers packing.

Morgan meandered his way through the back streets that led to a couple of the main beachside bars he'd seen on the tourist brochures. The ability to note and file away trivial information that could potentially be useful was a fundamental skill of any secret agent; often their life depended on it. In this case, Morgan needed an ally who could help him mobilize the forces he needed to take down the Night Witch and, if possible, Wu Ming and the representatives of the secret investment cartel. It would all depend on careful timing and whether Voloshyn fell heavily enough for his deception plan.

Finally he arrived at the Drop Zone Bar. The lights out front were off and all the shutters had been pulled down and padlocked. But it was the lights in the apartment upstairs that he was most interested in. He took hold of the old wooden railing and began to climb the stairs. Every second step brought a fresh stabbing pain in his thigh. He knew that the wound had opened again and the dressing would definitely need to be changed. If he'd recalled the information he'd been given correctly, then the guy who owned this bar would know exactly what to do.

After struggling all the way up, Morgan banged hard on the door. Inside, a dog, a big one from the sound of it, barked from deep down in its broad chest. A guard dog – a good sign. Fitted the profile of the owner that Morgan had in mind.

"Heel, boy!" He heard the short, sharp command through the window beside the door. The silence that instantly followed told him the dog was used to obeying its master.

"Who is it?" a deep voice called out.

"George Hemsworth?" Morgan answered, his breathing labored. "You don't know me, George, but AJ Armstrong sent me. Told me if I was in trouble I should come straight to you."

There was a slight delay but then the door opened and Morgan found himself face to face with an older man, about six foot tall and built like a rugby fullback. Morgan put his age at about fifty, give or take. The dog, a German Shepherd, appeared by his master's side, eyes fixed on Morgan and a growl brewing in the back of its throat.

"You better come in then," said George. He helped Morgan drop into a chair set by a heavy wooden kitchen table. Then he fetched some water and handed it to Morgan, who downed it all. "AJ told me to expect you. What's your name, son, and what's this all about?"

"Morgan. Alex Morgan," he replied. They shook hands. "Ex-3PARA. I'm told you're an ex-member of the regiment, too. 2PARA and Pathfinders, wasn't it?" From his pockets Morgan produced the bandages and antiseptic he'd taken from Voloshyn's villa and laid them out on the table. He leaned heavily on its top, exhausted.

"You're never an ex-member of the Parachute Regiment, son. You're either a serving member or a former serving member. But you never leave the regiment, because the regiment never leaves you. You'd do well to remember that."

"You're right," he replied. "Forgive me."

"Forgive me? Oh, Jesus! You're an officer. I'll have to fumigate."

"Yep." Morgan laughed. "Major. You?"

"I worked for a living, son," said Hemsworth. "Color Sergeant and, yes, I was with 2PARA and the Pathfinders."

"Well, I'm bloody glad to meet you, Color Sergeant Hemsworth. I just hope you can help me."

"How about I start by sorting out whatever's wrong with you while you tell me what the fuck's going on and what you need, and we'll take it from there."

Hemsworth made sure the door was locked again. At a click of his fingers, the dog lay down on the mat in front of it. Then, with a wry smile, Hemsworth grabbed a bottle of Captain Morgan Old Jamaica Rum from a shelf and poured them each a glass.

"Get that into you," he said. "Looks like you need it."

"Thanks. Why are you up at this hour?"

"You think an old man like me should be tucked away in bed or something, do you? I only shut the fucking bar at two. It takes me some time to wind down. I was just about to turn in as you bashed on my fucking door."

"Right. Sorry. Listen, George, are we alone here?"

"Yeah," he replied. "The missus is back in England visiting her sister."

"Good. I work for Interpol and I'm investigating a global human trafficking cartel, which is being run from right here in Placencia."

"Jesus!" Hemsworth exclaimed. "Is it that Russian bitch who lives up on the north road?"

"Yes. What makes you say that?"

"I've had a feeling she was into something bad, but I didn't know what. She's been buying the place out from under everybody. She's become quite the influence around here. The wife and I don't like it. We're talking about moving once I can get enough money together. Human trafficking? Fuck me. Bitch! What do you need?"

"There are some out-of-towners arriving here later today. They're all major players in the same line as her and I plan to arrest them, along with the Russian. Now, I don't want to get you any more involved than I already have but I'm kind of desperate and I need some reliable backup. It could be dangerous. You up for it?"

"Whatever you need, if I can do it, I will."

"AJ said I could rely on you."

Morgan and Hemsworth spent the next thirty minutes working their way methodically through Morgan's plan. Every problem he raised, Hemsworth met with a solution. Eventually, they reached an agreed and, most importantly, achievable strategy.

"So, all I need now is a phone, a computer and, if it's OK, a spot to get my head down for a few hours."

"I've got a spare cell phone I keep up my sleeve, just in case. I'll charge it up and have it ready for you by the morning," said Hemsworth. "You can doss down there in the spare room. We're about the same size so I'll get you some clothes. Meanwhile, you can use this to make your calls and I'll get you the laptop once I've sorted out that leg and whatever else is wrong with you."

Without another word and with the faultless economy of effort particular to former warriors, Hemsworth grabbed a telephone handset from a wall-mounted cradle and brought it over. Morgan immediately got to work on his calls back to London as Hemsworth gathered a collection of medical supplies from a cabinet beside the fridge, sat down opposite him and prepared to clean and dress the wound on Morgan's thigh while casting an appraising eye over the Intrepid agent's face, checking the rest of the damage.

Chapter Fifty-Six

Jovana took her early-morning swim just as she usually would, being sure to maintain her routine to the letter. This morning the water tingled against her skin with every stroke and kick. She felt as though she could swim forever, imagining herself not in the pool but in the ocean, swimming away. Swimming home.

Home ... Jovana didn't even have one to go to or any idea, apart from some of her earliest childhood memories, of what a safe, loving home could be like. When she imagined one, her only reference points were the Hollywood romantic fantasies she'd devoured whenever Drago had left her. The Witch didn't allow her to watch anything unless she chose it, and then it was nothing but horror, murder or deviant porn.

Jovana allowed her imagination to carry her away to her dream future. Today was the day she truly believed she might begin her journey toward it.

As she dried herself off by the pool then wrapped the towel around her body, she took in a deep breath, thinking that this would be the last day she would spend in this horrible place in the heart of paradise. She walked unhurriedly back to her room, noticing that the men were no longer sleeping on the sunloungers. They'd probably crawled back to their rooms when the sun broke through last night's rain clouds and shone directly on their faces. Today there would be confrontation and violence, but she was used to that; so used to it, in fact, that she was almost resigned to it. All she had to do was keep out of the way until he came for her. As she knew he would. Without knowing him at all, she trusted him more than any man she had ever known. She could see it in his eyes. That's why, when he'd said that she needed to stay here until he came back for her, she'd agreed without fuss. He would come back for her. She just had to be patient and wait.

When she returned to her room, Jovana showered for longer than usual, washing her hair and daydreaming. She had no idea what the day would hold for her but she didn't care. There was nothing she hadn't been through already. She needed to be strong and ready for when he came for her.

Her bathroom door burst open. Standing there, holding the door open, eyes blazing with anger, was the Night Witch.

Chapter Fifty-Seven

Morgan rolled out of the bed in Hemsworth's guest room and slowly got to his feet. His face felt like it was about to burst, his ribs – front and back – ached when he breathed, and there was an occasional stabbing pain whenever he stupidly attempted a deep breath or, worse still, a yawn. The slash on his leg was in much better shape than he'd thought it would be. It was throbbing like hell but George had done a great job of patching him up and Morgan was dosed with just enough painkillers to take the edge off without completely wiping him out. He couldn't afford a B-grade game today.

There was a tap on the door, Color Sergeant Hemsworth called out, "Coffee," and Morgan replied gratefully, "Be right there."

At the kitchen table, the two ex-soldiers sat together quietly; the older man offering unstinting support to the younger, who was still in the game. Morgan was tapping away on Hemsworth's laptop, checking in on the emails he'd sent from his ghost account in the middle of the night and verifying that the various components of the hastily hatched plan were now in motion. Feeling relieved, he sat back in his seat and downed the rest of the scrambled eggs and bacon Hemsworth had served up, and finished off his second cup of freshly brewed black coffee with two heaped spoons of sugar.

"So, we all set, son?"

"We are, George," Morgan replied. "Very much so, thanks to you. I'm sure you know how invaluable it is to have someone you can rely on in your corner, especially in my current circumstances. I'm very grateful. I'll make sure you're well compensated for everything you've done and are going to do. You can count on it."

"You know, son, when I was just a young paratrooper, a Tom, I was with 2PARA at Goose Green. I copped a seven-six-two in the gut from an Argie FN and was stuck out in no man's land in the middle of the battle, thinking, *I'm going to die out here tonight*. May twenty-eighth, 1982 it was. I was just eighteen. All I could see was the black sky above me and tracer rounds going straight over my head. The noise was like nothing you can ever imagine. I was losing blood, holding my guts in my fucking hands like this, and the longer I lay there, the colder and colder I got. I was crying like a baby, blubbering, if you must know. And then, out of nowhere, the Company Sar' Major, Geordie Pickering, appeared. 'What's up with you, Hemsworth?' he says. 'Gut shot, sir,' I says back to him. 'That wasn't very fucking clever, now was it? Right, let's get you out of here then,' he says. So, he did a rough field patch-up on me, scooped me up in his arms and carried me over two hundred yards, under fire, straight to the medics. I found out later that he'd been running back and forth between the platoons throughout the entire fucking battle, throwing the boys boxes of ammo, collecting casualties and taking them back to the Company Aid Post. Non-stop. The whole time, he was in the thick of it. Above ground, directly in the enemy's line of fire, while the rest of us were shitting ourselves, burying ourselves like ticks in among the rocks and frozen fucking ground."

Hemsworth stood, lifted his T-shirt and showed Morgan the latticework of scars that criss-crossed his abdomen. Battlefield surgery. "I wouldn't be here now if not for Geordie Pickering. And you know what? When they offered him the Military Medal, he turned it down. He told 'em, 'I'm a Paratrooper. I don't need a medal for doing my fucking job.' They should have given him the Victoria Cross. Bravest man I've ever known. So, don't you worry about compensating me, my boy. Let's take these fuckers down, and if we come out of it with our heads still on our shoulders, then that'll be more than enough compensation for me."

Morgan stood and shook Hemsworth's hand across the table.

"But, for fuck's sake," Hemsworth added, "don't tell the missus I was involved, or else she'll kill me."

Chapter Fifty-Eight

"Do you know anything about this?"

"No! Of course not. How could I?"

"You didn't hear anything?"

"No," Jovana replied. "When I left you I went straight to my room. What happened here?"

She was standing in the corridor outside the room that had been Morgan's. It was trashed. Furniture, sheets and the few belongings he had left behind were strewn in every direction. It certainly wasn't like this when she had come in and found his knife. She genuinely didn't know how it had happened.

In the center of it, the Night Witch stood glowering between the mess and Jovana, her face flushed red and her fists clenching and releasing. Jovana was preparing for one of the Witch's tirades, half expecting to see everything in the room – the bed, chairs, table and clothes – all suddenly lift from the floor, swirl up and spin around the Witch in a violent cyclone before flying out of the window. The idea that it could happen was distressing enough, but when the shuffling of feet behind her broke into her thoughts, Jovana stepped back. It was Godek Kajkowski. This time he was not looking quite as intimidating as he normally did. He reeked of alcohol, which was not in itself unusual, but he looked as though he had consumed far more than even he had expected to. And today was not the day for it. His expression and demeanor declared guilt. He had confessed without breathing a word.

"No," the Witch began, her eyes now locked on to a new target. "Don't tell me you're responsible for this? Where is he?"

Kajkowski didn't answer. He massaged his temples and rubbed his eyes. Suffering. When he opened them again, the Witch was standing just inches away. Jovana didn't even see her move.

"Where is he?" she screamed. "Tell me!"

"We strung him up for Domingo!" Godek yelled back. "Out in the swamp."

The Night Witch slapped Kajkowski as hard as she could across the face. He felt it, Jovana could tell, but he didn't move. He just stood there, full of guilt and violence. If he snapped he could kill them both easily.

"You did this to me today, of all days? Do you even comprehend how much money is at stake?" His lack of response answered her. "Of course you do. I'm beginning to think that Mr Security was right about you and Dariusz. You're waiting until the deal is done, waiting to see that the funds have been transferred, waiting for them all to leave – and then you'll kill me."

Before Kajkowski could respond, the Night Witch turned and marched to the stairs, Jovana following. Kajkowski obediently trailed them.

"Come and show me where you put him," the Witch said. "And let's see if there's anything left."

Jovana didn't know how far she would be allowed to go; she'd not been allowed past the pool since she'd been brought here. She decided not to say anything, hoping that the bitch would be distracted enough to forget about her.

The Witch led them along the path that ran from the house, past the pool and through the gardens to the metal gate that led to the cabin and beyond to the mangroves. Her skin began to crawl as she approached the gate and she didn't know if it was from fear of the swamp or recalling the trauma of what they had done to her in that shed. Godek must have seen the change in her because as he moved forward to open the gate for the Witch, he gave Jovana a cruel smile. She looked away from him and clutched her arms protectively around her body.

"What about her?" Kajkowski asked.

"She can come," the Witch replied. "She can see what you have done, too."

The three of them moved through the gate – the Witch, Kajkowski and Jovana – then along the path through the swamp bounded by the cyclone-mesh fence. Jovana clutched herself a little tighter as they got close to the cabin. What if she and the man had left signs that they had been there? Could there be anything she'd left behind that would betray her? She went rigid as the Witch pushed the door open and turned on the light.

Jovana stayed outside, directing her gaze out into the swamp. Then she saw some strands of rope, the ends torn and frayed, dangling from the wire mesh where he had been hanging. Below that, outside the fence, there was one long strand that disappeared into the reeds and mud. She didn't remember there being anything left in the fence. She was sure that when she'd cut the rope, the man had pulled himself free from the fence and all the rope fell away, apart from the strands that remained bound around his wrists. It had been so dark, she could easily be mistaken. But had he returned here after he'd left her? Had he laid out these ropes and trashed the bedroom to incriminate Godek? She smiled to herself as she connected the dots.

"Look!" she cried. "There ... on the fence."

The Night Witch emerged immediately, Kajkowski standing sheepishly behind her.

"Up there." Jovana pointed. "And there, too."

The Night Witch took a deep breath and then released it slowly. When she turned to Godek, Jovana was strangely fearful for him. The Witch had a way of making people feel that way.

"So, perhaps you'd like to inspect your handiwork," the Witch began. "What do you think has become of him?"

Kajkowski pulled the rope clear of the mesh. It was about eighteen inches long, still damp from the rain although it was slowly steaming dry in the early-morning heat. There was a faint pinkish tinge to it that suggested blood watered down by rain. The ends were ragged and looked to have been torn apart.

"Well?"

It was obvious that Kajkowski was proud of his savagery and sick of pretending to be a naughty schoolboy. His attitude hardened.

"Well, what I think is that I took care of a problem for you ... something you would have told me to do sooner or later anyway. Before or after your meeting, it makes no difference. The crocs tore that motherfucker from the fence and dragged him back in the swamp where he belongs. By now he's either eaten or rotting in their meat stash. He got what he deserved. Now, let me get on with my fucking job, which is to make sure none of those chinks are coming here to kill you!"

Chapter Fifty-Nine

Alex Morgan stepped out of the hire car, surveying the area around him. A clear blue sky above and a warm breeze wafting in from the sea gave him a sense of well-being. He felt buoyed by his alliance with George Hemsworth and AJ Armstrong, both of whom were crucial to his plan. This was quite literally to be a sea, air and land take down, a fitting tribute to his friend and former US Navy SEAL, Commander David Sutherland. It made Morgan feel as though Sutherland were still by his side. That very thought gave Morgan the strength and resolve to do what had to be done to take down the Night Witch and whoever else he was going up against. The fight had returned to him. He was absolutely clear on what he had to do and why. He would avenge Sutherland's murder and then return to Elizabeth Reigns. Nothing was going to get in the way of him achieving those two things.

Morgan was parked on the edge of the mangroves in a secluded spot about a mile from the villa, where he couldn't be seen from the road. The first phase of the plan was all about timing. Surprise was a key principle of war and Morgan needed to capitalize on it as much as possible, leaving the Night Witch little or no time to react or adjust. About twenty minutes earlier, AJ Armstrong, who Morgan had installed at the airport, had confirmed that Dariusz and a couple of Americans had arrived. They were picked up by one of Kajkowski's crew in a Mercedes sedan and were heading for the villa.

Morgan opened the CCTV app he'd set up on the smartphone George had given him and checked the current status of the cameras at the villa. As expected, they hadn't been used since his demonstration to Voloshyn last night. He took the opportunity to carry out a last-minute scan then shut the system down completely. Every camera was now offline and he knew Kajkowski didn't have the first clue how to bring them back up. He jumped back into the car, reversed out on to the road and headed straight for the villa, speed-dialing a number.

"It's me," he said.

"I know it's you. I gave you the phone, you pillock!"

Morgan laughed. "All right, George. AJ's confirmed that the Chinese crew is on the way to the house. You all set?"

"All set," Hemsworth replied. "And ready for anything."

"Good man. Ninety minutes, OK?"

"Roger that. Nine-zero minutes."

"See you soon."

Seconds later Morgan pulled up to the front gate of the Night Witch's villa and one of the local guards walked straight up to him, an M16 slung over the guy's shoulder. When he reached the driver's window and recognized Morgan he looked like he'd seen a ghost.

"She's expecting me," Morgan said bluntly. The guard just stood there, shocked, not knowing what to do or say.

"You want me to call her? She's not going to be very happy with you. Her guests are about five minutes behind me."

After a few more seconds, the guard finally fell for the bluff and pushed the heavy metal gates back. Morgan drove casually through, circled the fountain and parked up near the house.

He knocked on the front door. The housekeeper who'd been used to lure him out of his room last night appeared. For a moment Morgan was sure she was about to faint but she managed to hold her ground.

"Your mistress may be a little surprised to see me," he began calmly. "So how about I just go upstairs without too much fuss and let her know I'm here myself? That sound OK?"

Morgan couldn't swear to it, but he was sure that he saw the hint of a twinkle in the old girl's eyes as she stood aside to let him in. She pointed to the mezzanine landing. Morgan began the steady climb up the staircase, holding on to the rail and pulling himself up to spare his damaged leg too much effort. The last thing he needed was for that to start giving him problems now. He knew that once things really got going then the adrenalin would kick in and get him over the line.

Kajkowski rushed onto the landing, immediately followed by Voloshyn. Both of them could barely mask their disbelief.

"What the fuck?" Kajkowski exclaimed.

"We thought you were dead," Voloshyn said. "When they rang from the gate to say you'd arrived …"

"Good afternoon," Morgan replied. "Well, I'm very pleased to report that I'm not dead yet. I hope I haven't disturbed your lunch?"

"But what are you doing here? How did you …?"

"Are you kidding me? The amount of money you offered me to do this job, I couldn't allow a little issue like your man there trying to have me eaten alive to get in the way, now, could I?"

"We don't have time for this!" Kajkowski yelled. "This fuck should be dead!" He made a ham-fisted attempt to draw the Magnum from under his jacket and lunge at Morgan at the same time, once again relying on his bulk to intimidate. But it worked against him. When the perfect opportunity presented itself Morgan reacted seamlessly.

He dropped into a low crouch, braced against the heavy ornamental balustrade, and coiled his body like a spring. As the Pole barreled down the stairs with the Magnum in one hand and the other reaching out, Morgan sprang upward, using the man's own momentum to advantage. It was a gift. He grabbed Kajkowski's gun hand around the wrist, pivoted so that his back would take the load and then, with a twist and flick, heaved Kajkowski up and over the balustrade, sending him tumbling ten feet down onto the ceramic-tiled floor.

He landed with a thud and a loud crack. While Voloshyn watched, Morgan dropped straight back down the stairs to check the damage. The Pole was dazed and blood was spilling from a deep gash on the back of his head. Morgan saw his own Beretta jutting from the gangster's belt and retrieved it.

"I think you and I are through talking now, Gorbachev. I'm here to speak to your boss. Just rest there quietly for a while and try not to make too much mess."

Somewhere upstairs, probably the dining room where Morgan knew Voloshyn was planning to have the meeting, a phone was ringing.

"That'll be your guard at the front gate telling you that

the Chinese have driven in," said Morgan. "I expect they're pulling up right now, just the other side of that door."

Voloshyn stood frozen with indecision.

"So, am I working or not?" he pressed her. "We don't have long."

There was a knock on the door.

"Very well," she replied. "Get him out of sight and answer that!"

Chapter Sixty

In the dining room, the table had been set for a meeting rather than a meal, although hors d'oeuvres were laid out on silver trays and there was plenty of expensive champagne chilling in buckets of ice. Flowers Voloshyn had obviously had flown in from somewhere adorned key visual points in the room. Morgan knew that the events manager and some staff from the Paradise Palms had been drafted in to do the setup and serve the drinks. They'd done a good job.

The tone in the room was superficially effusive, masking the underlying tension and distrust. The gunslingers, Voloshyn's and Wu Ming's, had all been relegated to the sidelines, the Triad pair in one corner and the Night Witch's two diagonally opposite in another. They all looked far too twitchy as they eyed each other off, and Morgan got the distinct impression that one false move from either camp would result in a bloodbath. Kajkowski was still out of action but would surface again at some point, since he wasn't dead.

Morgan assessed the new arrivals: two Americans representing Voloshyn's mysterious investors and, of course, the principal guest and reason for the meeting, Wu Ming.

He turned first to the Americans. They were what he expected: studious-looking accountant types. One mid-forties, thinning hair, slight paunch and a presence that said he was the main player – the one entrusted to make the final recommendation to his masters, whoever they were. The other guy was the apprentice. Late-twenties, eager yet serious. He'd be carrying the bags. Dariusz had been attending to them, particularly the older man, and the three were slowly breaking away from their huddle to join Voloshyn and commence the introductions to Wu Ming. It might have been paranoia, but Morgan was sure they'd all cast a glance in his direction. Had they been discussing him? Fuck it. Time would tell.

He directed his own attention toward Wu Ming, who definitely fit the description that both Reigns and Inspector Lam had provided. Solidly built, packed tightly in the shoulders, bald. Yet there was something about him that didn't quite fit Morgan's expectation of a major Triad kingpin. Morgan had faced off against a lot of dangerous bastards in his time, killers, war criminals, and gangsters, and they all had one unmistakable element that could be seen in their eyes and felt in their presence: menace. And, try as he might, Morgan just didn't feel the same vibe from this guy.

Meanwhile Voloshyn was charming everybody, which Morgan found excruciating to watch. He couldn't stomach the notion that anyone could enjoy these luxurious surroundings and lavish hospitality while smiling and chatting nonchalantly about the billions to be made from buying and selling human lives. But human beings weren't considered people by this group. Individual lives were worth nothing to them, they were only numbers on a ledger.

Morgan watched Dariusz and the older American close in on Voloshyn's chat with Wu Ming. He wasn't surprised to see the young apprentice mucking about with a cell phone, probably reporting to their boss, whoever that was – Morgan would love to know. Voloshyn left the introductions to Dariusz and the feigned cordiality was even more gruesome to Morgan than watching her charming the bastards. Finally, the group broke up and each found a seat around the ornate circular table. Morgan checked his watch. Forty-five minutes to go.

On the other side of the world, Violet Ashcroft-James was in the midst of an exquisite meal in the private dining room at The Wolseley, surrounded by some of her oldest and dearest friends from Oxford, when her cell phone buzzed. She excused herself from the table. Every other phone in the group was switched off – it was considered *the* rule of their annual dinner. However, most of those at the table knew who Violet was these days and so a blind eye was turned. Of course, they weren't to know what was a work call and what was private.

Ashcroft-James withdrew to a quiet corner of the dining room that allowed her a view through the arched windows onto the main restaurant below. She had received a text message with an attached photo file. The message accompanying the photo read: *FYI, unidentified security consultant here. Extent of his involvement unknown. Sending this image to our security team for urgent ID.*

Ashcroft-James tapped on the image, which appeared to

have been taken surreptitiously across a crowded room via phone. It was not ideal quality but expanding it to focus on the face of the target gave a much clearer result. When she saw the face, her heart almost stopped. She knew it well. She had met him a number of times, personally and professionally. And now she was about to guarantee that he would be dead within the hour. So, Nobby had been interested all this time. She tapped her directions into the phone and hit *Send*.

The conversation at the table was much more formal than the pre-meeting chitchat. Voloshyn opened proceedings much like the chairperson of a board would, with lots of syrupy sweet compliments being dished out in Wu Ming's direction. Morgan felt like drawing the Beretta and the Magnum and letting rip right at that moment but self-control prevailed. He needed at least one, ideally all, of them in one piece, and he couldn't achieve that on his own. He had to stick to the plan. He checked his watch. Thirty minutes.

Following her introduction, Voloshyn handed over to Dariusz, who proceeded to talk numbers, which were laid out on a laptop in front of him. His equivalent on Wu Ming's side, Chang, produced a similarly expensive device and continued nodding and acknowledging as the briefing continued. Wu remained absolutely silent. Morgan began to get the impression that his assistant was in fact the brains of the outfit. He still wasn't sure what to make of Wu Ming. Something was bugging him and he remembered that, amid everything that had happened yesterday, Kajkowski's guy at the airport had reported no sightings of a Triad team arriving ahead of Wu. Interesting. Morgan checked his watch. Fifteen minutes.

After an excruciating financial soliloquy from Dariusz, throughout which he didn't make eye contact with any other person, followed by an equally painful Q and A exchange between him and Wu's assistant, the lead representative from the investors piped up with some apparently palatable assurances that received lots of nods and positive-sounding grunts from the Chinese. Finally it looked as though the first hour was coming to a close. Not before time.

"So, I believe it would be fair to say that we are very close now to an agreement?" An acknowledgment from the Chinese confirmed Voloshyn was correct. "Great. May I suggest, Mr Wu, that we break here for an hour while Dariusz and your man draft the final paperwork for us and we'll reconvene at two to finalize everything?"

They all stood and there was much handshaking going on when Voloshyn quietened everyone down. "Now, Mr Wu, there has been a room prepared for you down the hall. I'm sure you must be weary after your journey. So, in honor of our partnership to date, I have arranged a very special gift for you, an appetizer. I think you'll enjoy her very much and, if she pleases you, then please feel free to keep her, with my personal compliments."

The door from the mezzanine landing opened and Godek Kajkowski appeared with a terrified-looking Jovana on his arm. Her eyes flashed across the room to Morgan, instinctively looking for acknowledgment. He didn't give it. The last thing he could allow to happen right now was for anyone to get the idea that Jovana had colluded with him. Her appearance wasn't anticipated but it could be helpful.

Across the room, a cell phone buzzed. The apprentice's.

He looked like he was reading a text message and then, with an expression of utter disbelief, he gazed directly at Morgan and handed the phone across to the older man.

"That man works for Interpol!" snarled his senior, pointing at Morgan. "What the fuck is this?"

"What?" cried Voloshyn. "That's impossible!"

"I knew it!" Kajkowski said. He pushed Jovana out of the way and headed straight for Morgan, hands outstretched and eyes full of death.

The first explosion stopped everyone in their tracks.

The second one sent them all diving to the floor.

Chapter Sixty-One

Nobody was prepared to move for fear of there being a third explosion. Morgan played along but used the first moments of confusion to seize the advantage. He ran to Jovana and lifted her to her feet, turning her to the door she'd just entered through.

"Is this your doing?" she asked, clearly in shock.

"Yes," he replied. "Now, get out of here. Get to the beach and find my friends AJ or George. Tell them who you are. They'll take care—"

The gunfight erupted around them.

A dozen rounds splintered the woodwork of the doorframe they were standing in front of, showering them both in debris. Jovana screamed. Morgan dragged her to the floor and pushed her out the door on her hands and knees.

"Go!" he yelled. Then he had the Beretta and the Magnum out. He was also kitted out with a Glock 17 from Hemsworth's stash, and plenty of spare mags for it. He'd empty the other two first and then discard them.

The shots were coming from what remained of

Kajkowski's crew. Kajkowski was nowhere to be seen. He was probably trying to find a gun because Morgan had taken his or else was saving his own skin. Morgan returned fire with the Beretta but he couldn't get any clear shots. No matter what happened, Morgan couldn't let Voloshyn get away. If she did, she'd vanish off the face of the Earth. She'd change her name and appearance, recruit another team of clones to mask her movements, and she'd be gone. Everything that had happened up to this point would have been for nothing. He had to get to her before she managed to escape from the villa.

There was no chance that she'd be getting involved in the gunfight. Which meant she had to be making for the kitchen, which was just off the dining room, and, apart from the mezzanine level entrance, provided the only other access to the outside from this floor.

He had to follow her.

But right now, he was exposed. He crawled across to a point beside a long antique cabinet that ran almost the entire length of the room and took cover behind it. Taking stock of the shooters, he saw one of the Poles stick his head up from behind a settee. Morgan used the heavy-caliber Magnum and emptied three rounds arbitrarily into the settee. He saw the man's body slump to the floor. Good. He felt no compunction about killing these men – they were bottom-of-the-barrel scum, willing to drug, abuse and murder young women. Then there was some swearing in what sounded like Polish – the dead guy's offsider had just seen his mate. He loosed off half-a-dozen rounds to cover himself and made for the kitchen exit. Very brave. A sudden burst of fire from where the Triad bodyguards had been standing hit the guy squarely in the back as he tried to escape. Karma.

Morgan fired into the Chinese corner and received a hail of rounds back in response. But they were all haphazard, fired without aiming, and peppered the cabinet and the walls above his head without getting anywhere near him.

He laid low and their guns fell silent. He paused for a moment longer, listening for their mag changes, and as soon as he heard the first unmistakable clicks of magazines being ejected, he was on his feet with the Beretta in his left hand and the Magnum in his right. He caught sight of a tuft of black hair behind the far end of the same cabinet as was shielding him. He fired the last three rounds of the Magnum directly at the target and saw what was left of the guy fall forward in a bloody, mangled heap.

Morgan dropped the empty Magnum and transferred the Beretta to his right hand just as the second of the Triad bodyguards disappeared through the kitchen door. Morgan was on the move, straight after him. There was no one left in the dining room now but three dead bodies. He hoped that Jovana had made it safely to the beach, but right now all he could think about was finding Voloshyn.

He checked the Beretta. Four rounds left. He thumbed them out of the magazine, dropped them into his pocket and tossed the gun. If things got really desperate he might need those four rounds later. Hopefully they wouldn't get that bad.

Now armed with the Glock, Morgan stepped into the kitchen, his eyeline naturally traveling along the gun's top slide, through the forward sight and beyond, searching for targets.

He tracked carefully through the kitchen, which was huge by normal standards, and, thankfully, empty. The staff had all fled, leaving behind half-prepared trays of food and things still warming in the ovens. He moved quickly through the room, checking every corner, but then decided that it was clear. The Triad gunman wasn't waiting around to kill Morgan, he was only interested in saving his own skin and getting back to his boss. Checking the lie of the land outside from a window beside the door, it looked as though the coast was clear on this side of the house.

Morgan rushed through the doorway as quickly as he could and kept going, straight down the stairs. He was heading for the driveway. Escape by car was Voloshyn's best option.

As he rounded the corner of the building he was met with a spray of gunfire from an automatic. Morgan instantly hit the ground, disappearing into a thick carpet of ferns. It was Dariusz, firing from the center of the driveway, taking cover behind the fountain. Morgan fired back in the general direction until he could crawl forward into a better position. When he reached the limit of the ferns he was on the edge of the pebbled driveway. Expensive engines were revving, screaming under the whip of panicked feet. Two of the remaining Chinese, Wu Ming and his bean counter, were clambering into the Mercedes SUV while their bodyguard, fresh from the kitchen, had been relegated to driving. Dariusz had left the fountain and was clumsily trying to fold himself into the front passenger seat of a Mercedes sedan. Voloshyn was at the wheel with the two Americans in the back.

"Get in, Dariusz!" she was yelling. "Come on! Come on!"

The car was already moving, barely giving him a chance, and Dariusz was hopping on one leg, not able to gain a solid foothold. Morgan stood up amid the ferns. The Glock was leveled. The target was acquired.

"Dariusz!" he bellowed.

The man looked back and stumbled. Morgan fired two rounds a millisecond apart. Both of them struck Dariusz in the side of his chest. Morgan was already sprinting past the fountain, making for the car. The passenger door was still open. Nobody inside was shooting at him. He leaped over Dariusz's limp body and hit the front seat with a thud, shouldering Voloshyn. Yelling erupted. Morgan's gun fell to the floor. He fumbled, grappling for it. She began hitting him uselessly with one hand while she stamped on the gas. The car tore away from the house. The accountants were leaning over the seat backs, bashing Morgan as best they could given the confined space and their complete lack of skill.

Morgan took the beating and grabbed the wheel, forcing Voloshyn to change direction. He leaned over her, completely blocking her control of the wheel. He grabbed it with both hands and yanked down on it hard. He knew where he was taking her. It had been decided earlier that morning around George Hemsworth's breakfast table. The explosion had served a greater purpose than simply providing a diversion.

Voloshyn hadn't yet pulled her foot from the gas pedal – it was still rammed down hard as she fought him. She was screaming at him, clawing at his face and eyes with her long fingers and manicured nails. Morgan was squinting, contorting his face to fend off the onslaught as her nails tore at the flesh around his eyes. He needed to see and she needed to back off.

He propped himself up on her lap with one elbow, felt rather than knew that the position was right, and then threw his head back twice, *bang, bang*, as hard as he could within the tight space that separated them. The attack relented immediately. The car slowed too but he pushed his hand down on the pedal and shoved it to the floor. He saw two huge gaping holes in the property's perimeter wall on the coast side, the result of the explosions. *Good job, George.* With one hand on the wheel and one down on the gas pedal, Morgan bounced the Mercedes over the top of paths, gardens and outdoor furniture, straight for the first hole. All he could see beyond was white sand and clear blue ocean. Perfect.

Morgan became aware that only one of the accountants was still laying into him. The other, the older one, was now scrabbling for something over Morgan's legs. What the fuck was he doing? The gun! The bastard had spotted the Glock and was going for it.

Morgan kicked madly, back and forth like a piston across the other seat and into the passenger door, determined to take out whatever body part the idiot had a mind to put in his way. It worked: one kick got an arm and the follow-up collected the side of the guy's face as he withdrew to the safety of the back seat. The car ploughed through the final stretch of fern garden that ran as far as the perimeter wall and smashed over the rubble left by the explosion. Only the front wheels made it before the car stalled with a final shriek, but Morgan had achieved his objective.

Chapter Sixty-Two

Morgan punctured the steering-wheel airbag with his knife, got the driver's door open, crawled awkwardly over Voloshyn, under the side-curtain airbag, and tumbled out onto the debris.

At the moment of impact he'd buried his face in Voloshyn's crotch to avoid copping the full impact of the airbag in the face. As it was the lower part of the bag still smashed him in the back of the head. It felt like a punch from a prize-fighter, but fortunately the Witch bore the brunt of it.

Morgan staggered to his feet and fell against the car, feeling like he couldn't take another day of the punishment he'd suffered throughout this mission. His body had endured too much over the past few years. The line had been crossed. He knew that, but he couldn't give in. Not yet. Not now.

He braced himself against the car, struggling to breathe and to concentrate, thanks to the airbag-induced concussion and general exhaustion. He moved slowly along the side of the car, pushing aside the airbag curtains and surveying the interior. Voloshyn was right in front of him, still at the wheel, semiconscious from the impact. In the back the two accountants were locked in a tangle of arms and legs. They were not yet stirring, still out cold. It seemed they'd smashed heads during the crash. From the look of them, bloodied faces and all, they'd be out for a while.

With her bloody nose and sweat-streaked make-up leaving parallel trails of red and black lines down her white face, Voloshyn looked every bit the Witch. And without her small army of steroid-abusing Polish gangsters to drag her out of the shit, she was finally exposed and vulnerable. She showed none of the power or menace for which she was so renowned. She had eluded international authorities for years by remaining a ghost in the shadows, sending all those young girls, her clones, out into harm's way to save her own neck. How many of them had she betrayed?

Mental flashes of Dave Sutherland suddenly gripped Morgan: the firefight at the back of the factory in Hong Kong when they'd extracted Beth and Inspector Lam; the battle through the alleys and streets as they'd dashed for the Land Rover, running for their lives, firing all the way; Sutherland closing the rear doors to keep everyone else covered; Sutherland hit, blood everywhere; trying to patch his friend and colleague up as the car sped through Kowloon. As the memory of his last moments with Sutherland hit him – propping him against the wall, covered in blood and bandages, utterly helpless – tears welled in Morgan's eyes. They fixed like twin 40mm Bofors upon the motionless form of the Night Witch, slumped at the wheel of the crashed car.

Morgan brought both fists down hard upon the roof of the Mercedes. His revulsion was palpable. Every instinct told him to finish her off right now. Who would ever know? He looked around. There was no one in sight. Hemsworth and Armstrong hadn't arrived yet but they soon would. Every moment, every aspect, every excruciating minor detail of the operation to find and capture Voloshyn was now streaming unfettered through his mind; her betrayal of thousands of human lives – men and women, children, entire families – all serving life sentences to work in her brothels and factories while she traveled the world first class and lived in luxury off the back of their forced labor. Every year thousands of innocent, desperate people were lost into the black hole of the multi-billion-dollar industry that was human trafficking. And all so that people like Darja fucking Voloshyn, the Night Witch, could profit from it. It was time for her to die. Morgan wiped the tears from his eyes and reached for the Glock. *Fuck!* Where was it? Then he remembered.

He made his way around the front of the vehicle. He stumbled over the bricks and rubble, fell down, got up, fell down again, frustrated and angered by his own physical failure. He reached the passenger side of the car and, after a few arduous attempts, managed to prize the jammed door open. There was the gun. He reached in and grabbed it. Then, with the familiarity of one more used to handling heavy lumber than human beings, he took hold of Voloshyn's wrist and pulled her from the driver's seat, across the center console and the passenger seat and out of the car. As she fell heavily upon the bricks and rubble she let out a scream, but Morgan was unmoved. He pulled her through the debris until he reached a secluded patch of sand, shielded from view by a small copse of palm trees and ferns. He dropped her and stood back.

"On your knees, Voloshyn," he said. "This is as far as you go."

"What are you doing?" she cried. "You can't!"

"Knees!" he ordered. "Now! And look me in the eyes, because I want you to see in mine the lives of every poor bastard and child you've ever profited from. Today, they're all getting payback."

"You can't just kill me!" she snarled. "Godek was right – you're a cop. I should have known. That's why you kept coming back, putting up with his shit. So, cop, you know that if you kill me, your life is fucked!"

Morgan raised the Glock and took a pace forward so that the end of the barrel was just inches away from her forehead. His anger barely contained, he kept his eyes on hers, channeling her attention. He wanted her to see, hear, and smell every second of her last moments as they unfolded in painful slow motion.

The sound of an outboard motor getting louder and louder caused Morgan to turn and look down the beach. He saw a twenty-five-foot aluminum fishing boat approaching fast across the surf from the south, with one man standing at the controls and another at the bow.

Morgan turned back to Voloshyn, his hand curling even tighter around the grip of the gun, arm outstretched. She was looking up at him, an unnerving arrogance in her face. She held his gaze with confidence, like she'd already won ahead of the toss.

"I'm guessing they're your friends," she said. "Wouldn't look good to be seen murdering a defenseless woman in cold blood, would it? So I reckon you'd better get it over with before it's too late."

Morgan's resolve faltered. Could he kill her now, in clear view of Hemsworth and Armstrong? Surely they'd understand? Do the same in his shoes? Yes, they would. Without question. Perfect alignment of eyes, weapon and target. Finger on the trigger and squeeze ...

A broken piece of brick hit Morgan on the forehead, just above his left eye. He pulled the trigger but the round bit uselessly into the powder-white sand and the Glock fell. Before he had time to recover it, the Night Witch was all over him. She launched herself like a banshee from the sand, talons out, teeth bared and eyes blazing. She punched and kicked wildly, clawing his eyes. Morgan fended off her attacks, wave after wave, blocking with shins and forearms, blood gushing from the deep wound above his eye. The two of them fell to the ground, locked in battle. Voloshyn screamed and screamed. Morgan had never experienced such an inhuman encounter. Her unrestrained violence had the detachment of a wildcat killing to survive. Morgan's only hope was his resolve to avenge his friend's death and his commitment to deliver the Night Witch to justice.

With Voloshyn's crazed eyes just inches from his face, Morgan brought his hands up and under her chin, drove his thumbs deep into the sides of her wide open mouth and locked his fingers over her ears and around the back of her neck. He clamped down hard. She gagged, and as the shock of the move checked her attack, Morgan brought the bridge of her nose down repeatedly, as hard as he had ever managed the move in his life, against his forehead. He felt her nasal bone shatter under the third impact and her body wilted on top of his. Morgan brought his knees up and lifted her over him with a flick. She landed on her back in the sand. In a second he was up, blood streaming down his face, and sitting on top of her. With her face clasped between his thumb and fingers once more, Morgan squeezed hard, just short of breaking her jaw.

"Now you listen to me, you fucking bitch," he began. "If I had five more minutes, you'd be fucking bait. The only reason you're still alive is because of those two guys out there, coming in on the boat. I know they'd have my back if I killed you, but I would never put them in that position. Consider yourself lucky."

With the gun back in his hand, he grabbed her by the collar of her jacket, hoisted her to her feet, marched her across the sand and slammed her back against the car.

"You alright, son? You don't look so good," said a familiar voice.

"Couldn't be better, George," Morgan lied. He was exhausted beyond words and took a moment to regain his bearings. "Where's AJ?"

"Tying off the boat, he'll be along any minute. How's the leg?"

"It's holding up. Good job on the wall, by the way."

"Thanks," Hemsworth replied. "The second breach is about fifty feet back that way."

"You never did tell me how you got hold of all that PE and det-cord," said Morgan.

"Don't ask me questions I can't answer," said Hemsworth.

"Fair enough. You got the gear?"

"Right here in the echelon bag."

"Great," he replied. "You mind taking care of this one?"

"Gladly," replied George. "This is her, right, the Russian?"

"Yeah, it is. Watch her, mate. Don't give her an inch."

Morgan went to the back of the car and began herding the two bean counters out and down to the beach.

With Voloshyn on her face in the sand and one of his knees in the small of her back, Hemsworth extracted a large coil of rope from the echelon bag and began the process of binding her wrists and ankles with a single strand so that they were joined down the front of her legs, with just enough give built into the knots and binding around her ankles to enable her to shuffle. Then he took a roll of duct tape and taped her mouth shut. With a permanent marker he wrote "Voloshyn" on her forehead and right hand. Finally, he dragged a sandbag over her head and secured it loosely around her neck.

"Here you go, AJ. She's all yours."

AJ Armstrong had walked up from Voloshyn's private jetty where he'd secured the boat and was now standing beside Morgan.

"Watch her, AJ. She's the catch of the day," he said. "Take her down and secure her onboard while George and I sort out these two. We'll bring them down to you when we've got them ready."

"No worries, boss. Sweet as a nut," said Armstrong, ignoring the deep, bloody gouges on Morgan's face. Without another word, AJ led a stumbling, moaning Voloshyn to the boat.

"Fuck! Jovana," said Morgan. "Where is she?"

"She didn't come," said Hemsworth. "I kept an eye out for her further down the beach but no-show."

"Poor kid's probably scared out of her brain, hiding somewhere. Jesus! OK, let's get these two sorted and I'll go back and find her."

Hemsworth set to work urgently on each of the accountants while Morgan covered them with the Glock. Both men tried desperately to plead their innocence, offering inordinate sums of money to buy their way out of trouble, but Morgan and Hemsworth remained absolutely silent. Just before he sandbagged them, Hemsworth labeled them "Bean Counter #1" and "Bean Counter #2" with the permanent marker. Then Morgan and Hemsworth marched the two prisoners across the beautiful white sand and along the jetty and handed them both over to Armstrong.

"Right, boys," said Morgan. "You know the plan. Stay on the heading I gave you for twelve miles until you're out in international waters and an inflatable from the Royal Fleet Auxiliary ship RFA *Wave Knight* will be waiting for you there. Hand these three over to them and then come back and wait for me here. If I'm not back by seventeen hundred hours, then get yourselves out of here and call that number I gave you."

"So what about those Triad guys?" asked AJ. "Have we missed 'em?"

"Don't worry about them. We'll have them intercepted at one of the airports. I have a feeling they weren't the main players anyway. Time will tell."

With that Morgan turned and ran back along the jetty toward the villa. Voloshyn was quite literally in the bag, along with the two accountants from the investment cartel. Dariusz was dead, as were two of the Night Witch's bodyguards, and the Triad gangsters would be picked up at a frontier somewhere. Morgan's instinct was telling him that Wu Ming had played Voloshyn at her own game by sending a doppelgänger to represent him, because there was no way a Triad crime lord with the reputation of Wu Ming would travel halfway around the world for anyone, let alone with just two bodyguards and one accountant to accompany him. Kajkowski had flown the coop, probably out through the front gate in one of the other cars. With luck he'd be picked up too.

Now all that was left was for Morgan to keep his word – he had to find Jovana and get her out of this mess.

A scream from the center of the mangroves told him exactly where he was headed next.

Chapter Sixty-Three

Alex Morgan sprinted down the beach and ran through the second hole Hemsworth had blown in the wall. He found himself in the lush tropical gardens at the rear of Voloshyn's villa and oriented himself immediately toward the gate that led to the mangrove swamp. He heard Jovana scream again, this time more clearly. It was a desperate cry for help.

He ran as fast as he could, legs burning from the effort, found the gate, tore it open and raced down the funnel of wire-mesh fence and path all the way to the cabin. He was closing fast. He raced around a long bend and, when he saw her, realized instantly that she had not fled here to hide. She was lashed, just as he had been, to the outside of the fence, arms above her head and feet dangling into the sludge and muck that lapped around the edge of the fenceline. Another human sacrifice. Morgan had the gun up and was scanning frantically for the perpetrator. It could only be Kajkowski. Only he would be vindictive and sick enough to do this in the midst of everything that had gone down today.

Morgan slowed his pace and moved cautiously toward

the cabin. He didn't call out to Jovana, try to reassure or console her. He had no concept of how he was still functioning. His subconscious appeared to be in control now, his mind and body on autopilot and he was going with it. He shut down any consideration of exhaustion or pain or any further moral conflict. He didn't have the reserve capacity to entertain those things.

Jovana was crying out. It was loud, desperate and building in intensity. He kept moving, slowly, staying as much as possible in the cover of the palms and ferns that had grown through the fence. The Glock was firmly clasped in both hands, the line of the sights moving in practiced unison with his eyes. He took the final fifteen feet even more slowly, left shoulder leading, eyes following the line of his right arm and along the top of the gun. The girl was terrified but, from what he could see, not in any immediate danger. That was good. She was being used as bait. Nothing more than a distraction. Kajkowski had decided on a hostage to buy him some time while he worked out how he'd escape, and perhaps squeeze in a thrill kill for good measure.

So, now to find him.

Morgan reacted instinctively to a movement on his left side. It was the merest flash, the sudden appearance of a silhouette where there hadn't previously been one. Something that didn't belong in the mangroves. Something that broke the previously straight line of the corner of the cabin. A man's head and shoulders. And a gun.

The Glock erupted with three well-placed rounds. They hit within inches of the target but bit uselessly into the rendered cement exterior of the cabin. The attack was answered with half-a-dozen shots in his general direction. Morgan moved fast. He threw himself forward and landed heavily on the path, crawling behind some overgrown ferns. But his cover was only from view, there was nothing to protect him from the bullets here. His opponent had the advantage – the cabin provided cover from fire, plenty of actual protection. Morgan kept his eyes locked on the cabin, his peripheral vision scanning constantly. The silhouette appeared again, this time on the opposite side of the cabin with Jovana helplessly strung up behind it – Kajkowski. If Morgan fired and missed he would almost certainly kill her.

He aimed and deliberately fired two rounds in quick succession into the wall near where Kajkowski had fired from. Both rounds buried themselves in the brickwork. The move let the other guy know that Morgan was aware of where he was and that he wasn't afraid to engage, no matter how close he was to the girl. In the seconds it took Kajkowski to realize that, Morgan seized his chance to get up and move. He sprinted straight for the open door of the cabin and bounded inside, his movements masked by the noise from the mangroves and Jovana's terrified cries.

Not long, darlin'. Just a little bit longer.

Kajkowski was moving back around the cabin to where he'd originally fired from, Morgan could hear him. His shoes were scraping across the rough strip of concrete that edged the foundation slab. Step by step, Morgan could almost trace the man's exact location on the other side of the wall. He waited patiently. Kajkowski reached the corner again. He would be preparing now, remembering where he'd last seen Morgan. The gun would be up, pointing at the sky just like in the movies. Morgan heard a quick shuffle of shoes, a pause – two, three – and Kajkowski fired again. Three rounds first, followed by two more. Morgan didn't react. He remained inside the cabin but moved slowly, quietly, into a position far back in the room from where he could clearly engage anything that traversed the doorway. He brought his breathing under control and raised the Glock into a steady, perfectly aligned firing position. And waited.

Kajkowski was waiting too; waiting for a response from Morgan's Glock that wasn't going to happen. Morgan could feel exactly what the guy was going through right now, wondering if he'd killed or at least badly wounded Morgan. A guy like Kajkowski would probably prefer to wound, then he'd be able to enjoy some quality torture time with his victim. Well, not today.

Two more shots echoed across the mangroves. Morgan braced for action. He was listening intently now for the scrape of Kajkowski's shoes or a stumble, anything, because now the bastard would have to find the body to make sure Morgan was dead. But all he could hear was Jovana sobbing, scared beyond words, thinking that her only chance for rescue had just been killed.

His eyes were locked on the doorway. It was just like a training shoot: *"Target will appear for three seconds. You must engage within the three seconds. Impact areas are head and center of the chest only. Hits outside those areas will not count."*

OK then. Let's see that target.

A gun barrel appeared at the right-hand edge of the doorframe, followed by hands and arms. Then they stopped moving. They were not coming into the cabin. Kajkowski was looking for Morgan's body. Keep moving, Morgan willed him. For a time the gun, the hands and the arms stayed put, but then they moved again and the arms became a shoulder, a flank, a head and back, all now framed in the doorway. *"Target will appear for three seconds. You must engage ..."*

"Gorbachev!" Morgan yelled.

Kajkowski spun around, positioning his body perfectly, front on, gun pointing at the sky. *Target appears. Engage.*

Morgan fired — three rounds to the chest, directly into the heart. Kajkowski was frozen, mouth agape, shock and disbelief plastered across his tattooed face. The last output of his still-functioning brain managed to drop his gaze to inspect the small cluster of red bullet holes in his chest. The head and gaze lifted back to Morgan once more and then the body fell backward against the wire-mesh fence, bounced off it and tumbled face first through the doorway into the cabin.

Morgan walked over, kicked the gun out of Kajkowski's twitching right hand and fired two finishing shots into the back of his head.

Then human impulse returned to him.

He raced out to Jovana. She'd been through enough for one so young and it was up to him now to change all that for her. He holstered the Glock and with infinite care cut her free from the bindings and eased her down. Her body had been through all it could take and now she needed help, care and protection. Once he had her down, he lifted her in his arms and carried her along the path and out of the mangroves. Away from the villa, away from Placencia and away from the cruel life that until now had been all she'd known. She lay against his chest with her arms wrapped around his neck like a small child being carried off to bed. Her eyes were closed and her breathing labored. Soon she'd be getting all the attention she needed.

Morgan retraced his steps through the gardens and found once more the second breach that Hemsworth had blown out of the perimeter wall. In moments they were on the beach and the sound of the waves and the smell of the ocean acted on Jovana like smelling salts, reviving her instantly. She lifted her head from Morgan's chest. Looking out to sea, she said, "Please let me swim. Just for a few moments."

Morgan gazed across the beautiful azure waters of the Caribbean Sea as the surf swelled around his ankles and the spray drenched his face. He knew that she was right. It was the only thing they really needed to do.

Next in the Black Ops Intrepid Series

vinci-books.com/helldiver

When INTREPID falls, only Morgan can pick up the pieces.

Alex Morgan faces his most perilous mission yet as he plunges into the shadowy depths of Europe's criminal underworld. Tasked with toppling an oligarch and extracting a spy, Morgan soon discovers that his target may be closer than he thinks.

Turn the page for a free preview…

Helldiver: Chapter One

SUPERYACHT GEMINI, DUE SOUTH OF OAHU, HAWAIIAN ISLANDS

2015

Alex Morgan cast an appraising eye out over the pristine tranquility of the Pacific Ocean and wondered, not for the first time, how in any version of his life he could possibly have ended up here. In every direction he could see out to the far horizon without even a cloud in sight and only the slightest breath of wind. A seamless transition in cyan between sea and sky conjured the idea of being cocooned within the very center of paradise. He guessed it was a genuine feeling of serenity that he was experiencing. How long it would last he couldn't say, but for now it felt right and he was running with it. He pushed a hand through his thick mop of brown hair, realizing he was way past due for a haircut, and then began stroking the beard he'd been growing for the past couple of months. A very rare thing indeed, he thought; he hadn't had one since the desert. Standing only in a pair of swimmers and sporting a pair of well-worn Ray-Ban tortoise shell Wayfarers, Morgan breathed in deeply, sipped more black coffee and allowed himself the opportunity to thoroughly enjoy the stillness of this particular moment.

His shift wasn't for another hour, but the idea of staying in his lower-deck crew-quarters cabin didn't appeal, despite a standing order direct from the owner that the hired help were supposed to be invisible at all times unless they were doing something they were being paid for. Yeah, right. Morgan wasn't really one to abide by rules imposed by assholes and at this stage, based on the arrogance alone, Zolner definitely qualified. He was going to enjoy his coffee in peace and outside.

Despite his nautical ancestry apparently dating as far back as Sir Henry Morgan, Alex Morgan had never had much interest in boats – or the sea, for that matter. He considered himself more of a landlubber at heart, although he was dive qualified and had turned out to be quite good at it under the expert tutelage of his late friend, former US Navy SEAL Dave Sutherland. In a strange, roundabout sort of way, he decided he could blame Dave for his current situation. After all, if not for the diving experience he'd gained with Sutherland, he never would have got this job. Good old Dave. Bastard. It had been Sutherland who'd really got him interested, dragging him around the world on numerous dive quests when they'd been on breaks between missions for Intrepid. There'd been a lot of water under the bridge since his last mission. Dismantling the human trafficking empire established by Darja Voloshyn, aka the Night Witch, had come at a hefty price, most significant of which was Dave's murder in Hong Kong. Morgan himself had even come close to death in Belize not long after. Over most of the past year he had been through the hell of both personal and professional reconstruction as he dealt with the fallout.

It all seemed like a lifetime ago, someone else's lifetime rather than his own.

Shutting down any deeper introspection, Morgan tossed the last mouthful of coffee over the side and, turning his back on the sea, gazed up at the stacked, multiple decks of the *Gemini* that disappeared beyond view into the blue sky above him.

The Superyacht *Gemini* was in every way a super yacht. Almost 300 feet long and 3000 tons, it had a master suite with 360-degree views and luxury that would rival the Royal Suite at the Ritz. Below that were a dozen staterooms, crew rooms, bars, dining areas, three tenders for ship-to-shore transfers, wave runners, a dive deck – everything. With a top speed of 18 knots, cruising at 15 knots, she'd been built by Derecktor in the US and was in a category reserved for the most prestigious private yachts in the world. Even with the fleeting exposure to the A-list standards of luxury he'd enjoyed with Charly Fleming, Morgan had never experienced anything on this scale. The past month he'd been aboard, he'd seen extremes of indulgence he'd never thought possible, or even thought morally defensible. But within the circles frequented by his employer extravagance was the norm, in fact it was expected. Meanwhile the minions, like Morgan, were required to remain below decks and only emerge as and when required. Of course, in fairness, it was slightly different for the security detail.

"Hey, new guy. You're eager." It was Norland, former US Army, who was also security detail 2IC. Morgan liked him.

"Me, eager? Nah. Just getting ready to take over in—" Morgan checked his trusted Tag Heuer "—thirty minutes. You must be ready for a kip. I can take over early if you like."

Helldiver: Chapter One

"Thanks, bro, but no thanks. You know what the bossman is like – if you're paid for twelve hours, you do twelve hours. Whether he's around or not."

"I keep hearing that. Where is he now?"

Norland pointed off the stern. There was a shotline tethered to the *Gemini* that disappeared below the surface and out of sight, reaching all the way down to the bottom, close to the wreck.

"Early dive. He wants to take some more footage of that fucking plane."

"The Helldiver, right?"

Norland nodded. "You've probably guessed, he's got a real thing about them. Tracks wrecks all over the world; doesn't care what condition they're in either. If there's a Helldiver to be found, he'll be there. That's why we've spent weeks out here trying to find this one and why we spent a shitload of time in and out of Indonesian waters last year, just because he heard a rumor there was a Helldiver wreck down there. He didn't find it the first time around but he found it on the return trip. He's obsessed with the fucking things; something to do with his first wreck dive when he was a young guy."

"What happened?"

"Nothing. Apparently he just liked that 'Helldiver' was kinda like his name, you know, the H-D, Hedeon. Now he uses the name 'Helldiver' as a sort of personal brand. Kinda like Madonna!" They laughed. "Anyways, when you've got as much money as he does, you can do whatever the fuck you want."

Morgan turned back to the water. "What time did he go out?"

"About forty-five minutes ago, give or take."

Morgan checked his watch. He knew their employer,

Helldiver: Chapter One

Hedeon Zolner, was renowned for being a damn good diver. He also knew that the Helldiver wreck Zolner was so curious about was submerged under fifty feet of water, hence their current position. With the tanks they were using, and an average consumption rate of around five gallons per hour, at fifty feet he would have around fifty minutes of dive time. "He's right on the limits of his air already. He should be coming up. Anyone go out with him?"

"Shit, no. He hates that, bro. Only dives alone when he's searching for those wrecks. He doesn't like the distraction of us 'incompetent assholes,' or so he says."

"Well, incompetent or not, we can't do much for him from up here while he's down there. Anything could happen to him and we wouldn't have a clue. He should be up by now."

A panicked call stopped everything.

"Help! Somebody, quickly. Sharks! Oh my God. Hedeon is still out there!"

Morgan's eyes locked onto the source of the commotion, the very top deck of the *Gemini*, the owner's deck. He could see Zolner's wife, Kristina, an auburn-haired, brown-eyed, over-indulged heiress, draping herself over the balustrade, waving her arms around to summon the attention of the minions. He followed her gesticulating and line of sight out to the suddenly energized waters above the Helldiver. He could see a definite surge of surface activity along with the fin or two that had drawn her concern.

"Fuck me," said Morgan. "Grab a rifle."

Norland disappeared as Morgan sprinted back to the dive room to grab his gear – Tusa face mask, Mares X-Stream fins and HUB Avantgarde integrated buoyancy compensator, weight, and regulator system. In no time he was back at the platform pulling on his dive booties.

As Norland returned with the rifle – a .308 Browning BAR Mark II Safari – Morgan kitted up, managing a quick look in the general direction of the sharks. He estimated that there was probably half-a-dozen of them in the immediate vicinity. It was impossible to tell how big or what type they were but their sudden appearance just off the *Gemini*'s stern and clear interest in whatever was going on beneath the surface suggested a top-end predator. In these waters that meant they were most likely tiger sharks. He hoped not.

"Deal with those if you can, without hitting us," he yelled at Norland, pointing toward the sharks. "I'll get Zolner." Without another word he pulled on his fins, slipped the mask down over his eyes, clamped the regulator mouthpiece between his teeth and dropped into the water.

The explosion of bubbles evaporated as the cool water grabbed him, dragging him down into the uncertainty of the deep blue-green water. He cleared his ears, then twisted around and kicked off, reaching for the shotline. Finding it was a godsend and keeping himself as close to it as possible, Morgan made the line the center of his universe and swam like hell straight for the ocean floor, his speed in check only to avoid over-pressure in his ears balanced by the need to constantly valsalva during the descent.

The threat of the sharks and his reservations over how Zolner might react to his sudden intrusion on the wreck dive dominated his thoughts, but he had to shut all that out and just find his boss. Whatever was happening down there he'd deal with it as it hit him. For all Morgan knew, Zolner was probably fine and already ascending the line, but his gut suggested otherwise and he tended to trust it.

Hedeon Zolner, billionaire, was the son of a former Russian General, Igor Zolnerowich. As a boy, the young Zolnerowich rose through the ranks of the Komsomol, the

Young Communist League, later getting noticed when he began exploring business opportunities during the economic reform era of Gorbachev's glasnost and perestroika in the late 1980s. In the nineties he benefitted extraordinarily under the mass privatization of state assets strategy introduced by Yeltsin. Critics claimed the influence of his father, a respected military figure much in favor with the political elite, saw him ideally situated during the initial privatization process, which, under the second wave known as the loans-for-shares scheme, resulted in the accumulation of vast resources and wealth by a select few who became known as the oligarchs. Consulting Wikipedia, Morgan discovered that he had shortened his name to Zolner in the late nineties when his business interests and public profile began to spill out of Russia and across Europe to England and the United States, an overtly deliberate attempt to distance himself from the association with his father's name and influence. By 2005 he had very cleverly adopted the unofficial moniker Helldiver almost exclusively. And in a world where major news stories lasted only as long as a Facebook feed, most people were oblivious to the travails of the Russian economy of the 1990s, and many didn't know that Helldiver, the eccentric businessman who occasionally appeared in the news, was even Russian. Nor did they care. Why would they?

Morgan kicked hard, the X-Stream fins powering him fast along the length of the shotline. Marine life fled in every direction while he selfishly barreled through their water. As he neared the ocean floor he pushed off the line and followed a short course due west through the coral toward the wreck. Butterfly fish, yellow tang, octopus, manta ray, moray eels; they were everywhere, but every one of them made way for the intruder. He kept checking for the sharks but couldn't make out any in his immediate area. Before he could allow himself the naïveté of feeling lucky, he caught sight of two large bodies passing closely, their size and a flash of their distinctive stripes confirming the species as their tails disappeared into the murk about five yards away. Their sudden proximity was unsettling. Morgan preferred it when he could see them; watching the speed with which they'd vanished into the darkness and not knowing where they'd vanished to or how quickly they could reappear put Morgan instantly on edge. But he couldn't be distracted by it. He had to find Zolner. He had to keep his head down and power on.

As the new guy on the security team, Morgan hadn't even been allowed within arms' reach of Helldiver, not once. Morgan was very definitely aware that he was on trial only and considered backup, an additional pair of hands just in case. As a result, he'd not been allowed to do any diving with Zolner, and as Norland had said, as far as diving the wreck was concerned, not even the most trusted members of the security team were allowed that privilege.

It didn't take long before he saw the wreck. He immediately gained speed, pulling his way even faster through the water. First he saw three misshapen blades of the propeller, and then the barely recognizable engine housing. The wings were basically invisible with just the hint of their span discernible. The tail section was completely gone. All that remained was broken, rusted and barnacled metal amid forests of the spectacular, multicolored coral that had reclaimed the shell of the long dead beast, submerged for seventy years.

And there in the midst of it all, grappling desperately with something within the cockpit, was a panic-stricken Hedeon Zolner. He was a big guy, around six-four, heavy

Helldiver: Chapter One

set, and despite the fact that he was only fifty-one, his hair was completely white. Down among the depths, the shock of white hair was like a beacon. A stream of blood was billowing from beneath him in thick plumes like black smoke, while circling high above, like vultures readying to swoop on a carcass, were the tiger sharks. There was three of them, all at least twelve feet long, one of them verging on fifteen, most likely a female. Morgan knew there'd be more nearby. Not good. He decided it was time to activate his Freedom7 SharkShield. Switching it on, he powered the last few feet straight for the wreck.

Zolner saw him approaching and began pointing wildly inside the cockpit. It took Morgan less than half a second to see that the man had caught his right foot and most of his calf within the collapsed, rusted and barnacled controls of the ancient Helldiver. Blood was erupting from a deep gash in his calf and all of his frantic clawing to free himself was getting him nowhere – if anything, it was making things worse. Morgan could also see that Zolner's diving rig was jammed among the wreckage of the rotting bomber and, worst of all, the gauges on his tank indicated that his air was as good as spent. Zolner had been so consumed by his struggle to get free that he hadn't noticed the sharks or how bad his air situation was, and just as Morgan was about to read the gauges, Zolner's air ran out. Everything was suddenly, painfully slow, everything except the sharks. And as Zolner looked up to Morgan for help, he finally noticed them.

Trying to communicate calmly and logically with a person who had just realized that they were being circled by half-a-dozen predatory sharks and that he had just run out of air was impossible, multiplying the complexity of their predicament exponentially. Zolner's blood was leaving his body in steady streams directly into the electroreceptor path of the shiver of tiger sharks now homing in on his location. Struggling to breathe, Zolner gave up on trying to free his leg and instead began grabbing for Morgan's regulator. Morgan fought to remain composed, deftly brushing aside Zolner's attempts while grabbing the second mouthpiece of the octopus regulator he'd dived with, forcing it into Zolner's mouth. Zolner took hold of it and began to steady his breathing while looking to Morgan for direction.

Then the first of the tiger sharks made an approach, circling within five feet of them. The second and third sharks followed suit. The speed of their movement caused a surge in the water that buffeted the men as the pack began their approach for attack. Zolner's eyes were wide with fear and he began to panic, striking irrationally at Morgan. All Morgan could do was take the beating against his rig while reaching for the six-inch titanium dive knife from the sheath attached to his right calf. The three sharks disappeared again, circling their prey and gathering more speed before the fast return and final attack. Morgan raised a threatening arm to quell Zolner's terror and then turned in the direction he expected the sharks to approach from. Sure enough, in seconds they reappeared, growing in size and menace as their heads and open jaws sped toward the Helldiver. Morgan braced, placing himself between the predators and the helplessly trapped Zolner. The knife was a paltry deterrent but it was his last line of defense. It was in his hand and poised, ready to strike at an eye or snout, wherever he could reach first to inflict an injury. Behind him Zolner was rigid with fear, his hands holding on tightly to Morgan's left arm. The tigers were within just a few feet, in dive formation, gaining speed, getting bigger and bigger. Morgan's breathing was steady but strained, the adrenalin threatening to tear him apart. They closed in fast. Morgan's eyes locked onto those of the leader: the biggest of the pack. His hand curled even more tightly around the knife and his body coiled, ready to counter-attack. And just as he prepared to strike, all three of them suddenly turned away; one, two, three, each in succession had closed in for the kill only to pull away abruptly at the final moment. As the first three withdrew, two more – lower in the pecking order than the others but just as hungry from the scent of blood in the water – made their move, spiraling down from directly above the wreck. By now Zolner was still attempting to free himself. Morgan redirected his counter-attack stance, readying to strike upward into the flesh beneath the lower jaws of the sharks but again, they balked and pulled away.

In that moment Morgan knew that the SharkShield was doing what it was supposed to do. The length of thick antennae cable trailing behind him was creating an electronic field that caused a reaction in the electroreceptors located in the snout of each shark. Once the sharks came within range of the electronic field they were instantly affected by it and withdrew. Sutherland had introduced Morgan to it ages ago but until today, his only point of reference had been the theory. He was fucking glad it worked in practice.

He returned his attention to a thoroughly bewildered Zolner and set to work on getting him free. He began with Zolner's rig, which was caught on strands of rusted metal that had once been the aft headrest for the tail gunner. With the rig clear, Zolner had more freedom to move and, eventually, to wriggle his calf and foot free with some help from Morgan pulling back the offending wreckage that had caused the restriction. A much relieved Zolner finally pulled clear. Morgan cut some strips from Zolner's wetsuit and quickly bound the gash. It would be enough to get him back to the surface and aboard the *Gemini*, but it'd need proper attention soon.

Holding Zolner close, tiger sharks still circling and the SharkShield cable trailing behind, Morgan kicked off, taking them both toward the surface and the clear blue sky.

Grab your copy...
vinci-books.com/helldiver

About the Author

Chris Allen is an author, senior executive, leadership mentor, public speaker, veteran and father. He is a member of the Australian Crime Writers Association (ACWA).

The formative years of Chris's career began in the Australian Army, initially as a soldier before being selected for commissioning as an officer. His service included airborne forces, military intelligence, attachments to the New Zealand Army, the British Parachute Regiment and deployments to Africa, South East Asia and Central America. After almost fifteen years of military service, Chris was medically retired at the rank of Major.

Chris's post-military career continued to reflect his commitment to service. He led security and logistics operations for CARE International in East Timor during the 1999 emergency. Later, in the wake of the September 11 attacks of 2001, he oversaw the upgrade of Counter Terrorism First Response (CTFR) measures at Sydney Airport. And in 2003 when protestors painted 'No War' on the sails of the Sydney Opera House, he was headhunted to take over the protection of the iconic landmark. In 2008 he was appointed Sheriff of New South Wales, one of Australia's most historic law enforcement appointments.

In more recent years, Chris has continued his career as a senior executive, broadening his experience across a diverse range of roles within Commonwealth and state government departments, and the not-for-profit sector.

Today, Chris lives on the New South Wales south coast with his sons, Morgan and Rhett.

Acknowledgments

I'd like to acknowledge one of my favorite actors of all time who sadly passed away while I was writing Avenger.

Lewis Collins was best known for his portrayal of the hard-hitting CI5 agent Bodie in the British TV series The Professionals and later starred as Captain Peter Skellern in the SAS movie Who Dares Wins. He was also a member of the Parachute Regiment's Territorial Battalion, 10 PARA, having completed selection during his time on The Professionals.

At one time Lewis was considered the natural successor to Roger Moore in the role of James Bond and while his no-nonsense screen test foreshadowed Daniel Craig's Bond, unfortunately he was considered too hard for 1980s audiences.

Lewis Collins' performances as Bodie and Skellern left a lasting impression on me. He was a major influence on the development of my protagonist and, in my mind's eye, he will always be the prototype Alex Morgan.

Lewis Collins 27 May 1946–27 November 2013. RIP